THE STREAKER MURDERS

A NOVEL BY PHILIP DORIAN

Dorrance & Company • *Philadelphia*

1 / *Saturday, June 1, at 7:15 P.M.*

"*The Mushroom in the Meadow!* There it is, the new convention center of Wauconda Falls." Curt Conners leaped out of the squad car and looked up at the huge concrete hemisphere. A smile crinkled his freckled face, and the June sunset caught the carrot red of his hair. "How about that, Mike?" he called over his shoulder. "Isn't it beautiful?"

Officer Mulvany slammed the car door. "Beautiful—hell. Call a toadstool beautiful, Red? That's what it looks like—a stinkin' old toadstool."

"Whadda ya mean, Mike? You sound like my old grandma. You know what she says? 'I ain't never going into that place. Think I want it to come crashing down on my head? Never heard of a roof without posts to hold it up.' "

Officer Mulvany merely grunted his disgust.

Officer Conners shook his head. "Trouble with you, Mike, you're way behind the times. For Christ's sake, this is the hundredth anniversary. Little old Wauconda Falls is getting up to date. Why, that could be in Chicago or St. Louis or Denver."

"Well, listen at you," Mike jeered. "You sound like something out of Harold Anderton's chamber of commerce. Sorry, I got bad news for you. There's a big centennial pageant here tonight, see. Half the town's gonna be sitting in that homely hunk of concrete and glass, all crowded together, see. And guess who are the lucky ones who get to keep law and order? Like who, Red?"

Curt Conners' smile faded. "Oh, yeah. Just look at the mob of people already pouring in. Could mean trouble. Lucky, you say? So lucky I can hardly stand it."

"Well, listen at him now," Mike sneered. "Where'd all that

chamber of commerce crap go to now?"

"You know how I hate crowd control, Mike. Better check the squad car again for security. Can't tell what hoods will be hanging around."

"Come on, Red, quit your griping. It's going to be easy tonight." The two policemen were walking around to the "stem of the mushroom," a long low annex that housed the dressing rooms, scene shops, and smaller meeting halls.

"This toadstool may be ugly as hell, but it's built for easy crowd control." Mike gestured with a wide sweep of his arm. "Lots of space, lots of exits, fireproof."

"Now who's talking like Anderton's press releases!" said Curt.

"Better still, we only got the lieutenant governor to protect. Nobody takes potshots at a lieutenant governor. I was damned glad when the top man had to cancel and send number two in his place."

Mike pointed to the horde crossing the parking lot toward the main entrance. "We won't even have to worry about some rowdy kids trying to start something up in the balcony. Jeez, they must have about every kid in school or college *in* this show. Mostly parents in the stands, none of the beer-drinking, bets-on-the-side louts ready to kill the referee and toss pop bottles."

"Hope you're right," said Curt. "Give me regular patrol any day. I hate crowd control. Now if a nice little murder or robbery came along so I could try some detective work, that would be my dish. Not much chance in little old Wauconda Falls on a family night like this."

Both cops nodded to the doorman. "Evening, O'Malley. All under control?"

"Yep, nobody's got in but what had a pass made out." O'Malley frowned. "Got an awful lot of actors tonight. They been comin' in pretty fast."

"Spotted any troublemakers?" asked Conners. O'Malley shook his head.

"No, Red, this isn't gonna be so bad tonight."

"Hope you're right, but I got a feeling."

Mulvany and Conners walked down a short passageway that led to the main hallway. As Mike opened the inner door a wave of sound beat on their ears.

"My God, sounds like a boiler factory," shouted Mike, bending close to Curt's ear. "Let's look over the rooms at the far end first, then work back toward the main arena." Curt nodded, and they turned to walk down the long hallway off which doors opened.

"Heads up! Look out there!" yelled a voice, and the two cops flattened themselves against a wall as heavy spotlights on dollies were pushed past them by stagehands in coveralls. "Sorry, officers," called one of the stagehands. "Didn't see you comin' through the door. Almost got you."

"O.K. this time, but watch it," called Mike sharply. "Lot of people here, 'specially little kids. Hard to see 'em, so keep your eyes open." The stagehand waved a salute in reply.

When Mike pushed the first door open, a crowd of half-naked little boys in loincloths was revealed, applying brown body base and lurid war paint as adults adjusted the feathered headdresses. War whoops resounded from all corners of the room. "Beats me how such little guys can make so much noise," yelled Mike. Curt shook his head.

The next door opened into a room where girls in leotards were bending and pirouetting as a brassy-voiced director called out the routine. Next they checked a smaller room with men and women in various pioneer costumes joking and laughing. Over at one side a knot of children were dressed for the country schoolroom scene.

At the far end of the hallway was a huge room. Here singers in choir robes were milling about while orchestra players were blowing, scraping, and pounding. "Guess they know what they're supposed to do," said Mike, "but it sounds like a crazy house to me."

"See why I don't like crowd control?" laughed Curt. "Let's get out of here and try the other direction." He pulled the double doors shut behind them.

After they passed the room with the Indian boys they came upon a group of white-wigged, knee-breeched, and wide-skirted colonial dancers. Then came buckskin-clad explorers and two Catholic priests going over their lines. The policemen glimpsed a troop of Civil War soldiers lining up for inspection, then a bunch of Charleston dancers swinging hands and feet in rhythm.

"Sure got everything here tonight, haven't they!" said Mike as he paused before a door labeled MEN'S LOCKER ROOM. "Better take a look in here—just in case." He pushed open the door and dodged around a metal screen into a large room lined with lockers. "All clear here," said Mike, moving on past the shower stalls and into the toilet room. A couple of youths looked over their shoulders un-

3

easily, as if embarrassed at being observed by a policeman. Mike opened several swinging doors. "Nobody hiding in here," he said. Then he walked over to where two men, made up as if ready for the stage, were smoking and talking. "Sorry, no smoking in here. You'll have to go down to that side entrance and step outside if you want to smoke."

"Sorry, officer," said the men politely and left. The young men busied themselves with their zippers and hurried out.

"Hmmm, like I said, Curt, things are easy tonight," said Mike. "First time in a long time I've seen a men's room without a couple of characters hanging around ready to make trouble."

As the two officers returned to the main hallway, they heard a girlish scream and an adolescent yell, "Hey, look, it's Sonny Hitchcock!" Bodies came popping out of doors, heads turned to stare, and there was a rush down the hall.

"Uh-oh, I think we're needed," shouted Mike Mulvany, and he pulled Conners along to the entrance where a tall, handsome man and his companion were being surrounded by a shouting crowd. "It's that television star, and they're about to mob him."

The two policemen pushed through the squealing, shoving horde. "Take it easy, folks. Cut it out, you guys. Lay off, gals," they shouted as they worked their way up to the celebrity.

"I'm all right, officers, these are my good friends," boomed out the voice so familiar to Sunday-night television fans. "Hi, gang," the celebrity called, showing his dazzling teeth in a wide smile. "Glad to see you all. Look, kids," he said, waving his hands high in the air, "let's make a deal. We've got a show to get on the road right now. How about you and me meeting right here after it's all over. I want to see all of you, shake your hands. Right here, all of you, afterward—O.K.?"

"O.K., Sonny," they called good-naturedly, and they fell back a bit to let him through.

"Get my things, Dennis, will you?" Sonny called to his companion. Smiling, waving, shaking a few hands, the glamorous Sonny Hitchcock moved along the hallway to a door labeled GREEN ROOM. As he pushed it open, he turned back to the two policemen.

"Thanks, officers. I'll be all right now." He flashed another smile. "They're a swell bunch of kids, but you never know—so thanks." He turned to face a harried-looking man standing in the doorway.

"Mr. Hitchcock, are you all right? Sorry about that little—er—

4

fracas. Hope you're not too shaken up." He extended a hand. "I'm Harold Anderton, master of ceremonies tonight."

"Sorry? Don't be, not at all." Wayne (Sonny) Hitchcock's voice was bluff and hearty. "It's when people *stop* pushing and shoving to see me that I've got to worry."

Mr. Anderton shook his head. "I must have forgotten to tell you about the special entrance on the other side of the building for you visiting artists. We didn't expect you to come in with all the local teen-agers."

"Special entrance? Dennis, did you hear anything about a special entrance?" The companion nodded without speaking. "Oh, yes," said Sonny Hitchcock. "I must have gotten mixed up."

He turned. "I won't be needing you for a while, Dennis. You better go see to those details." Dennis nodded and headed for the main part of the building.

"The hell he forgot," muttered Curt. "Our little local celebrity wanted that to happen. Can't blame him, though. He didn't get to be the star of *Battleground* every Sunday night by being a shrinking violet." He looked over at Mike Mulvany. "Like I told you, Mike, this job isn't going to be easy. Thing could have gotten rough down there, with those kids."

Mulvany shrugged. "But they didn't." He turned to look after the disappearing Dennis. "Besides, he had a bodyguard. Come on, let's take a look at our territory before the crowd gets too big and the rest of our very important people get here. Glad to see it's only a few steps from this Green Room to the entrance to the arena."

He pushed open the big double doors and moved along a runway leading to the main floor.

"Space!" gasped Curt Conners. "Jeez—Chri—look at all that space!"

Before them stretched a vast expanse of floor, its hard-polished wood gleaming in the reflected lights. "Big enough for two basketball games, side by side, with enough room left over for a wrestling match," marveled Curt Conners.

Completely encircling the arena floor, rows of seats rose in a gentle slope like the outside rim of a saucer, ending in brick walls. At regular intervals this curved border of seats was slashed by openings, wide runways that gave easy access to the outside lobby or to the annex and dressing rooms. Looking higher, the men saw a balcony, a more steeply sloping shelf, also encircling the entire area and extending far up to meet the steel girders that supported the vaulted roof of "The Mushroom."

"How about that, Red?" exclaimed Mulvany. "They weren't kidding when they said this would seat five thousand people. Almost half the people in this town under one roof." He turned slowly, scanning the rows of seats, then nodded. "You know, give us just four men, one on each corner of this playing floor, and they could keep a sharp eye on every cotton-picking person in this place. Just let one of our pretty boys try to start something! With all these runways and aisles, one of us can get to him in ten seconds. Like I told you, this layout makes things a hell of a lot easier."

Mulvany turned to greet a uniformed man who was approaching. "Evening, Henderson. I see you're casing the place like we are." He nodded toward his partner. "Do you know Curt Conners, otherwise known as Rusty or Redhead or just Red?" He turned to Red. "This is Fire Marshal Henderson, Red, commonly known as Smoky."

"Everybody knows the cop with the red hair," said Henderson. "How are you, Conners?"

"Evening, Henderson. How about this layout? What do you think of the Mushroom in the Meadow?"

Mulvany added, "Better give this redhead a pep talk, Henderson. He's real antsy about crowd control; thinks there may be trouble tonight."

"All of us get twitchy, Conners," said the fire marshal. "You never can tell what some fools will do if they panic. But you notice that every seat in the place isn't more than ten feet from an aisle, and every aisle leads to an exit. Bet we could clear this building in less than five minutes if we ever get a bomb scare or a tornado warning."

"You really think so?" asked Conners. "Sounds good to me."

Mike Mulvany added, "Yeah, after all those years in the high school gym. It was built to hold two thousand; we'd have three thousand—gad, what a miracle we never had a riot. I remember a night when three thousand packed in for a basketball tournament, and those hoods from over Greenville way started a fight with a couple of our local toughies. Took our whole force to get to 'em so we could break it up. God, what a mess with all that screaming and pushing, only two exits—and them blocked by fools stretching and crowding to see what's going on."

"Well, not tonight, men," said Smoky Henderson. "This is one time you can stand back and enjoy the show. Oh, by the way, just *what* are you two supposed to be doing tonight?"

"We're bodyguards to the special guests, the VIP's," said Mike. "Got some big shots in from Capital City. We got to see that no crackpot takes a shot at any of them. Plus his honor the mayor, of course, and the local committee. Those are the special seats over there on the other side of the main floor." He turned to Conners. "And maybe we better get on with our looking things over. Be seeing you, Henderson."

"Likewise. Glad to have met you, Conners," said the fire marshal. "Hope you enjoy the show."

"Thanks, I'll try. Hope you don't get any bomb scares. You sure won't be getting tornado warnings on this June night."

Mulvany and Conners walked casually across the east end of the arena floor. Although there was still a half hour before the pageant was due to start, a crowd was already assembling and the bleacher seats were filling up rapidly.

"Looks like family groups, you notice," said Mike. "All the moms and dads and grandparents getting here early so they're sure to see their kids perform. Can't see anybody that looks like he needs watching. More than likely it'll be the smallfry wanting to go potty in the middle of an act that'll give us the trouble."

The two policemen had crossed to the opposite side of the arena floor by now. Along the edge there was a roped-off section segregating two rows of chairs, widely spaced. "This must be our spot," said Mike. "Front row for the real biggies, back row for the local VIP's, and plenty of space between us and the front row of bleachers."

Conners nodded. He was scanning the people already seated in the section behind the reserved chairs. Out of the corner of his mouth he said softly, "Harmless looking bunch, wouldn't you say?"

Mulvany smiled. "Like I said, family night. Now, if you stand behind the last chair on that end, you can keep your eyes on the audience and our special section at the same time. And if I do likewise at this end, we got it made. O.K., Red?"

"O.K., Mike. Just a routine job—no riots, no murders, no excitement."

2 / *Saturday at 7:40 P.M.*

The voice over the loudspeaker boomed out. "It is now twenty minutes before opening. Will members of the choirs and the orchestra please take their places on the south bleachers and the south playing floor?"

"Better get back to see where our special guests are," said Mulvany.

As they crossed to the dressing rooms, they heard a voice still announcing, "In ten minutes the Indians in the opening scene should be in the west runway ready for their entrance. All other actors remain in your assigned quarters until you are called."

Dodging past a stage set mounted on wheels ready to be moved into the arena, the two officers approached the Green Room door. They pushed it open and entered to find that a sizable group of handsomely dressed notables had already assembled.

"There's our glamorous Mr. Hitchcock," muttered Curt, "well-surrounded by admirers. Our local people, I'm guessing." He nudged Mulvany. "Over there on the other side of the room—that's got to be our lieutenant governor."

It was easy to recognize Lieutenant Governor Alcott from the campaign posters that were displayed all over town, advertising the coming election. Hamilton Alcott stood over six feet tall, with a roach of iron-gray hair and the prominent square chin that cartoonists were fond of exaggerating as his identifying features. Next to him stood a gorgeous creature, the notoriously beautiful Rosemary Alcott. Curt stared at her appreciatively, noting the flowing platinum-blond hair, the full, pouty lips, and the luminous melting eyes.

"Wow, some dish," Curt heard Mike Mulvany murmur in his ear. "Wish I was a bachelor like you, so I could get married to *that*."

"She'd marry *you*?" Curt jeered. "Have you noticed she looks just like that sex kitten—you know, the one that just died? Tell me, Mike, how is it she's completely covered—well in front, anyway—yet you can tell everything she's got?"

"Beats me," answered Mike. "I've seen my wife put on all those extra helps, but somehow it never comes out like that."

"Well, put your eyeballs back in place and tell me who's the guy giving them the big sales pitch. Poor old Mayor McGinty can't get a word in, nohow."

"That's Redmond, president of the community college. He's playing politics, buttering up Alcott and making passes with his eyes at Mrs. Alcott." Mike's lip curled. "Want to watch a real pro at work, Red? Watch Redmond. He didn't get our little college out of that beat-up old building by sitting home reading his schoolbooks. Notice how he operates. And while you're looking," Mike added, "Cast an eye on Mrs. Redmond, the dame in the gold dress." He nudged Curt. "See her playing up to those three women from Capital City? They say Redmond wants that new fine arts building awful bad, and they're from the State Arts Council. Can you guess what she's talking about?"

"How the devil do YOU know all this?" asked Conners. "You been listening at keyholes?"

"No, just keeping my eyes and ears open like a good cop should."

Harold Anderton's voice was heard. "If you please, ladies and gentlemen." He smiled unctuously, and the room got quiet. The crowd around Sonny Hitchcock turned reluctantly. The mayor maneuvered up next to the lieutenant governor and gently urged him away from Dr. Redmond.

Harold Anderton cleared his throat officiously. "As president of the Wauconda Falls Chamber of Commerce, I want to welcome you on this auspicious occasion and to say how happy we all are that you have favored us with your presence." He paused to smile ingratiatingly. "We'll be making our entrance in a few minutes. Will you please line up in the order in which you will be introduced?"

He paused to consult his notes. "Immediately after Mrs. Anderton and me, Your Honor, Mayor McGinty and Mrs. McGinty, please."

"Say," whispered Curt, nudging Mike. "Who's the extra woman with the mayor? Has his honor got two wives?"

"No, that's the woman that's with her all the time. You're not supposed to talk about it, but Mrs. McGinty is lame, so she has this cousin of hers to lean on wherever she goes."

The master of ceremonies was continuing. "Next Lieutenant Governor Alcott and Mrs. Alcott, please." Mr. Anderton bowed pompously. "Then Dr. and Mrs. Redmond, then the three distinguished members of the State Arts Council, Miss Sears, Mrs.

Warren, and Mrs. Yates. All of you will sit in the front row of chairs when you get to the reserved section, please."

"In the second row," he continued, "will be Mrs. Quinlan, our able coordinator of the entire festival presentation, and Dr. Quinlan."

Esther Quinlan interrupted. "My husband isn't here yet. He's been at the hospital on a case; must have been delayed."

Harold Anderton frowned with annoyance, then beamed. "Good luck. He's on the end of the row. We'll see that one of the ushers slips him in whenever he arrives." He went on with his directions. "Mr. Kubitz, of the Businessmen's Association, and Mrs. Kubitz next; then Mr. Ryan, of the Labor Council, and Mrs. Ryan." He paused to consult his notes. "Oh, yes, Mr. Dawson, who wrote the original script for our pageant tonight, and Mrs. Dawson; then Mr. Katzen, who arranged the music so gloriously, and Mrs. Katzen; Mr. Goodman, who coached the actors, next, please. Then our promotion man, Mr. Balkan, with Mrs. Balkan; and our festival treasurer without whom we could not function, Mrs. Cohen." He smiled and gestured. "Over this way, please. Mr. Hitchcock, you will be announced separately, but please be at the arena entrance."

As the distinguished people took their places, the lieutenant governor could be seen talking to Mr. Anderton very determinedly. Mr. Anderton was looking disturbed, shaking his head, pointing to his notes. Hamilton Alcott spoke more earnestly; Mr. Anderton objected more feebly, then paused and shrugged his shoulders. Calmly the lieutenant governor moved to the head of the line with his beautiful wife gracefully touching a hand to his arm.

"Well, how about that? Did you see what happened?" whispered Mike Mulvany. "Guess who's demanding top billing—and getting it." He snickered. "Will you look at old Mayor McGinty and Redmond. Can't tell who's madder!"

He was interrupted by the voice over the loudspeaker. "Three minutes to starting time. Will the master of ceremonies and our distinguished guests of honor please move to the entrance aisle?"

"Guess that's our cue, too," said Curt Conners. "We better split up so we don't look like part of the procession. You go around to the left of the main floor, Mike, and I'll circle around to the right. See you over on the other side."

The house lights were dimming as the two policemen moved to their places. A ruffle of drums sounded, a fanfare of trumpets blared. Spotlights played on the entrance runway, the orchestra struck up a stately march.

The crowd quieted down, then burst into applause as the lieutenant governor appeared. There was an overlay of whistles and wolf calls as the spotlight caught the glamorous Mrs. Alcott. Slowly the procession moved across the expanse of floor and filed into the reserved section. Mr. Anderton bustled to the microphone placed before his chair and intoned, "Ladies and gentlemen, our national anthem."

The pageant, reviewing the hundred years of Wauconda Falls history and inaugurating the new Convention Center, had begun.

The guard at the door, O'Malley, sidled into the main hallway to catch the opening ceremonies, so there was nobody to notice as one car near the entrance backed out of its parking place and another moved in. Nobody saw a figure step out, nor heard the whispered order, "About 9:30, remember. Pull out into the roadway and have the motor running."

Like a shadow, the figure moved into the building and into the room just vacated by the little Indians.

"Hey, where are you going?" called O'Malley, just returning to his post.

A pair of naked shoulders and a head half concealed by a huge Indian headdress reemerged. "I been to the—you know," came an intense, sibilant whisper as a finger pointed toward the men's locker room.

"Well, get along with you." O'Malley took a few steps toward the figure. "Program's already started. You're supposed to be in your place."

The figure waved a final farewell and melted away.

3 / *Saturday at 9:30 P.M.*

"It's been a long day," said Officer Garrison. "God, my feet are hurtin'." He took a last puff and tossed his cigarette. "Workin' overtime is for the birds."

"Except for the money. The extra dough will sure as hell come in handy with my wife expectin' number three next week." Officer Kottke flicked his cigarette to light next to his partner's smouldering butt. Then he strolled over to press a shoe on both of them. "You gotta admit, Ted, this new convention center makes our job a damn sight easier, compared to the old high school gym. Plenty of room to work in. Couldn't have got all these people in any other place in town."

"How far along are we?" asked Garrison. "Hope they're nearly done."

"Let's see." Kottke pulled a program from his pocket. "Story of Wauconda Falls in twenty scenes. Can't be much longer." He opened the double doors leading from the outer lobby to the big arena. A blast of sound assailed his ears. He closed the doors quickly.

"Yep, that's the rock-and-roll number, all right. Number eighteen, only one more to go before the finale." He opened the doors again and motioned Garrison to join him.

"God, look at those high school kids throwin' themselves around. Wild!"

"Just ten years ago you and me was doin' likewise," said Garrison. He closed the door again. "Don't think I could make it out now."

"And me and my wife couldn't either, especially the shape she's in. We couldn't either one—"

He stopped in mid-sentence. From inside the arena came a roar mixed with shrieks and whistles. The voice of the announcer boomed out, but this time his words were blurred by the roar of the crowd.

Officer Kottke dashed to the doors, flung one open in time to hear, "Let the streaker beware. His end is in sight."

Louder and higher-pitched shrieks came from the crowd with the noise of stamping feet and clapping hands.

Ted Garrison's voice shouted in Otto Kottke's ear. "Did he say *streaker*?"

In the runway that cut between the sloping tiers of bleacher seats, four ushers were gesticulating wildly and laughing raucously.

"Did you see him?" An adolescent voice cracked into a squeal of excitement. "Came right through those dancers and stood there, naked, bare naked."

"Yeah, just like the statue, only no fig leaf," a deeper voice guffawed.

12

"Did ya see him shake hands with that big shot?" shouted a third.

"Sat on her lap, you mean!" The first voice broke again.

"Lap, hell—he *kissed* her."

Their chatter was obliterated by the sudden blare of music as the orchestra, which had faded into silence, caught the director's signal. The dancers recovered from their confusion, caught the beat, and resumed their frenetic gyrations.

"Well, whadda ya know," said Otto Kottke into Ted Garrison's ear. "Looks like we missed something."

"Sure as hell did." Garrison tapped the nearest usher on the shoulder. "What happened, kid?"

The usher gave a start when he made out the uniform of the policeman in the dim light. "It was a streaker, officer. He came out of that runway over there by the chorus, did a spread eagle and bow when he got to the spotlight. Then he raced over to shake hands with the lieutenant governor—"

"Kissed his wife, you mean."

"Aw, cut it out, Hal. He didn't either."

"Guess I know what I saw. He leaned right over and kissed her."

Officer Garrison interrupted. "Then what? What became of him?"

A babble of voice broke out. Ted Garrison held up his hand. "Hey, one at a time, guys. You, Hal—if that's your name."

"He turned and streaked across to that exit over by the announcer. Cut right through the dancers and was gone."

"Didn't anybody try to stop him?" asked Otto Kottke.

Another babble of voices, another "Quiet, kids. Hal's doing the talking."

"There wasn't time. It all happened so fast. You know, all of a sudden there he is. You stretch your neck to see, and can't believe he's really got the nerve to show his—" He stopped and looked at the policeman. "Well, you know . . . his. . . . Well, everybody's laughing, and the girls are shrieking, and the crowd is cheering when he sits on the lady's lap—"

"Kissed her, you mean."

"It's all in fun, officer. Why spoil it—even if I *could* run that fast."

"You sure it was a man?" asked Ted Garrison. "Are you real sure?"

"You gotta be kidding." There was a poke in the ribs from one of the other ushers, and a coarse laugh. "When that spotlight was on him, with his legs spread wide and his hands up high, you could see everything he had—"

"And he had plenty to show." The poke was returned.

"What's the matter, Pete? You jealous?"

"Jealous? Me? You mean *you*. You're the one that's jealous with your little undersized—"

"Hold it!" said Officer Garrison. "Here comes Mulvany."

Out of the dimness of the arena floor another policeman appeared. He motioned the four ushers out into the lobby and turned to the two cops. "It's Kottke and Garrison, right? Come with me."

Out into the brightly lit lobby Officer Mulvany gathered the policemen and ushers into a close circle.

"Now listen. Something very serious has just happened." Mulvany's voice was intense. "Kottke, I want you to call headquarters. We'll need an ambulance. Tell them to hurry. It may be a heart attack or maybe a stroke, so ask whoever's on switchboard to alert the hospital emergency room."

Kottke nodded and turned to go.

"Wait. Tell them to try to get here before this show lets out and there's a traffic tie-up. Better tell them to come to gate three. We'll keep it blocked off. And one more thing, tell them to send a photographer and to try to locate Barney Ross."

"Got you, Mulvany," said Kottke and started off. He stopped suddenly and turned back. "A photographer for a heart attack? Barney Ross for a stroke?"

"Get going, Kottke." Mile Mulvany shook his fist violently. "Can't you figure it out without my yelling it at you?"

"Oh." Kottke started and whispered, "Got you, Mulvany. Oh, my God," and he was gone.

Mulvany turned to the tallest usher. "Where's your boss?"

"You mean Mr. Sheppard? He was over by gate four a minute ago. Want me to get him?"

"Sure do. On the double. Tell him it's an emergency."

"Garrison," continued Mulvany, "we'll need at least four men to cordon off the VIP section to keep the crowd away. Schmidt and Janssen should be at the other end of the lobby. Get them and bring them here right now. Oh, and see if that Henderson guy is handy—the one in charge of riot control."

14

Officer Garrison wheeled and took off, just as the tall usher was bringing an older man up.

"This is Mr. Sheppard, Officer."

"Glad to see you, Mr. Sheppard. I'm Officer Mulvany. We've got an emergency and we need your cooperation."

"Sure thing, Officer. What can I do?"

"Can you put at least one usher at each exit door and at each stairway—better have two at the center stairs and main exit. They're to keep the crowd moving right out of the building as fast as possible."

"I think we can do that all right," said Sheppard.

"Hi, Henderson," said Mike. "Can you give Sheppard here some help?" Henderson nodded. "Can you block off gate three? There'll be an ambulance there in a few minutes, and we don't want any gawkers to get in the way."

"I'll try, Officer," said Sheppard, motioning to the four ushers. "Come on, fellows. I think we'll work it this way." His voice was drowned out by a fanfare of trumpets and a ruffle of drums from inside the arena, followed by a burst of applause from the crowd.

Mulvany nodded his approval as he saw the four ushers scattering in four directions while Sheppard motioned to an assistant and talked excitedly into his ear. Henderson headed toward gate three.

Officer Garrison was coming up with two more policemen. Mulvany pulled them in close. "Men, we've got an emergency—" He stopped as he noticed Officer Kottke approaching. "All O.K., Kottke?"

"Yes, ambulance on the way; hospital alerted. Should be about five minutes. They're trying to find Detective Ross."

"Good, very good." Mulvany nodded. "Now here's what you four have to do." He spoke earnestly and fast. The others nodded.

On the main floor the pageant was moving into its grand finale. The Wauconda Falls marching band was blaring a military march. Soldiers, sailors, marines, with flags flying, moved to the center of the arena floor and formed a tableau. Baton twirlers strutted, the combined choruses broke into song, and the audience rose to its feet, clapping and stamping.

In all the patriotic fervor, nobody noticed Mulvany as he slipped into the runway, past the row of chairs of the important guests to where a figure lay stretched out on the bare floor as another figure,

15

stethoscope in hand and plugs in ears, was bending over the recumbent body. Nor did anybody notice the half-fainting woman who was being supported by two companions nor the two men hovering anxiously opposite.

As Mulvany drew near, the examiner rose, shook his head, and crossed to pat the shoulders of the older man nearby. He whispered something into his ear. The older man recoiled, then bowed his head.

Catching sight of Mulvany's uniform in the dim light, the doctor put his mouth close to Mike's ear and yelled, "She's already dead."

He pointed to the corpse stretched out on the floor. "Killed almost instantly by this," and he turned a small pocket flashlight on to reveal the handle of a knife protruding from just below the breastbone.

"Oh, my God, Doc. Stabbed to death?" Mulvany bent closer to look. "Who did it, Doc? The streaker?"

"Who else? He came right at her, bent over her, then turned and streaked across the floor before anybody could realize what was happening."

"Who is she, Doc?"

"The mayor's wife, Maude McGinty."

4 / *Saturday at 9:30 P.M.*

Officer Curt Conners was enjoying the evening after all. For once Mulvany and Henderson had been right. In the new convention center, crowd control was a snap.

He was nervous all through the opening ceremonies. The master of ceremonies, Harold Anderton, had his floor mike right there in front of the lieutenant governor's chair. With the house lights dimmed down and the spotlights hitting him full in the face, he was a sitting duck for anybody who wanted to take a shot. Not that anybody would want to shoot Harold Anderton, nor, for that matter, Mayor Joe McGinty. Even so, when His Honor was cracking his Irish jokes, Curt kept his eyes moving over the crowd, especially the people sitting close to the chairs reserved for the honored guests.

It was all very well to say nobody would try to take a shot at a lieutenant governor, but you never can tell. It was only a few days ago that Governor Shackleford announced that he couldn't come and that he would be sending Lieutenant Governor Alcott instead, so the word might not have gotten around that it was just number two man tonight. Then there were always some cranks running loose.

He need not have worried. Even when the Alcotts stood exposed in the blinding light, there wasn't a suspicious move. Lots of whistles and woo-woos when Rosemary Alcott was introduced, of course; a polite smattering of applause when Hamilton Alcott finished his short, conventional speech of congratulations.

The rest of the guests of honor modestly said nothing. They merely stood and bowed as their names were called and the spotlight zeroed in on them. Then the lights swung to the opposite side of the floor where, on a raised platform, stood the narrator for the pageant. When Sonny Hitchcock, star of the popular Sunday night television series *Battleground* was introduced, pandemonium broke loose for a three-minute ovation. Sonny was obviously enjoying the heady experience as he waved, gestured, and even tossed a few kisses.

After the national anthem, the orchestra swung into the overture, and the massed chorus that filled the entire south bleacher stood up for the rousing opening number. The lights gradually dimmed. Sonny Hitchcock began to read the opening narrative over the booming loudspeaker. Officer Curt Conners took one last look at the audience and relaxed.

The show was well written and well rehearsed. The children were cute, which pleased their elders. The adults tried hard, and their friends smiled and applauded. The chorus sang lustily; the orchestra played with spirit, mostly tunes the audience already knew well. And there was the showman Sunny Hitchcock who knew how to make the most of his lines, ad libbed freely, and played each scene to the limit.

Curt Conners let himself watch the show as the story of Wauconda Falls from early Indian days and the coming of the first white man progressed up to the present day. He found himself laughing at Sonny's jokes, humming some of the tunes, tapping his foot along with the dance scenes.

Occasionally Curt would recall his responsibilities, scan the two rows of chairs reserved for the very important people, then turn to sweep the bleacher seats with his gaze. Several times he walked unobtrusively over to where Mike Mulvany stood at the other end of the section and whispered, "Everything O.K., Mike?" and got a reassuring, "All O.K." Then he would let the drama absorb his attention again.

Until IT happened. The show was well along. The stage band broke into a violent rock-and-roll beat, a group of teen-age dancers rushed onto the floor and began some violent gyrations. Out of the entrance runway a shadowy figure appeared. Dodging between the dancers, the shadow made for the center of the arena floor. In the full glare of the spotlights it posed, feet wide, hands upraised, naked.

The crowd sat in stunned silence for a brief moment, then a vast AAAHHH gushed forth, followed by whistles, shrieks, and the yell "STREAKER, STREAKER." The figure executed a deep bow, rushed across the floor toward the row of honored guests, bent over one of the figures in the front row, then turned, and streaked back through the broken line of dancers to disappear in the exit runway.

The music stopped in mid-beat. The dancers paused in confusion. The audience broke into a cacophony of shrieking, cheering, clapping, and stamping.

It was Sonny Hitchcock who recovered first. Over the loudspeaker came his voice with a clever joke, and the audience broke up into gales of laughter and waves of applause.

"And now, Mr. Orchestra Director," came the voice of Sonny Hitchcock, "if you please . . ." The director raised his stick, the band resumed its violent sounds, the dancers caught the beat, and the show went on.

For a split second, Curt Conners had frozen. Then he wheeled and circled around the far end of the reserved seats. By the time he had made it to the open floor, the streaker was bending over somebody in the front row. Curt sprinted toward him, but too late. The streaker had turned and dodged through the lines of dancers toward the exit.

Not wanting to add to the hysteria by running across the floor in the glare of the lights, Curt reversed and made for the far end of the arena floor, intending to head off the fleeing figure. Too late he realized his mistake. The marching band, which had been lined up for the finale, had broken ranks, and Curt was blocked by groups of uniformed players pushing and stretching necks to see what was going on.

"Hey, lookit, here comes a cop," called one player.

"Git him, copper. He went that-a-way."

"Hey, what'll you do if you catch him?"

"Aw, have a heart, cop. He was just having fun."

"You'll never catch him. He streaks too fast for you."

"Come on, you guys, open up there. Let the cop through."

Good-naturedly they made a path for him. With a quick "Thanks, kids; wish me luck," Curt dodged between sousaphones, bass drums, and trombones. Keeping to the darker shadows at the end of the floor, he made for the runway on the far side.

He caught sight of a jumper-clad stagehand. "Did you recognize him?" Curt called.

"Hell, no. Couldn't see his face. He was going awful fast. And it seemed like he was wearing a mask." He laughed. "Besides, I wasn't paying much attention to his face; something more interesting further down. I couldn't really believe anybody would—"

"A mask? Did you say a mask?"

"Yeah, one of those things that fits over the eyes and nose. And another thing. Most of him was real brown like an Indian, but down by—you know—his hips—he was *white*."

"Thanks. Don't go very far away till I talk to you some more."

Curt had caught sight of another figure down the hallway, a second stagehand just coming out of the men's locker room, zipping up his coveralls.

"Did you see him?" Curt called.

"Who? See who?"

"The streaker that just came down this way."

"Streaker, did you say? Oh, for Christ's sake. I just take a couple minutes to go to the can and I miss a good show." The stagehand jerked his cap down over his eyes and grunted. "Naw, I ain't seen nobody. I was in there. Hey, was he a real streaker—you know—in the raw?"

"That's right," said Curt and rushed on. He turned into the side hallway, leading to the parking area exit.

"Hey, O'Malley," he shouted to the guard just coming in from the parking lot. "Did you see him?"

"See who?"

"The streaker. Did he come out this door?"

"Streaker? Oh, my God, so that's what it was."

"You mean you saw him?"

"Not really. I was down at the far end of the lot. Some joker had driven in and was blocking that exit door down there. So I went down to clear him out. I was just on my way back when I saw somebody dash out the door and pile into the first car. By the time I got here, they'd pulled out and driven away. Couldn't have been more than a couple of minutes ago. Did you say streaker? No clothes?"

"Couldn't you tell?"

"Hell, no. He came out so fast I couldn't see much of anything. No clothes on, eh? Yes, could have been."

"What kind of car? Could you see that?"

"Well, you know, that was a funny thing. When I came on duty there was a beat up old Dodge in the first stall. I figured somebody had to get here real early—one of the crew maybe—to get such a good place. But awhile later I noticed the old jalopy was gone and one of them rented cars was there instead. Didn't think much of it, but the space's empty now, it must have been that rented job."

"A rented car, huh, with a driver waiting for him?"

O'Malley nodded. "Shouldn't be hard to find out who rented a car for tonight. Want me to find out?"

"Do that, will you, O'Malley? I'll be back later." Curt Conners turned back into the building. The stagehand beckoned to him.

"Did see something earlier. There was this Indian hanging around. Not one of the kids. They mostly put on their clothes and went out to see the rest of the show. This was an older guy, sort of hanging around by himself."

"Indian, you say? Can you describe him?"

"Not really. He had lots of war paint on; a headband with a feather sticking up; one of those pieces of cloth coming up between his legs and hanging down over his . . . You know what they call it?"

"Loincloth, you mean?"

"Yeah, loincloth held up with a kind of belt made out of beads." The stagehand grinned. "I remember wondering, what if the belt broke? Say, maybe that's what happened. Maybe that loincloth fell off and he didn't know it."

"Hardly think so," Curt said patiently. "Now could you tell me about his size? Tall, short, fat, skinny?"

"Medium height, I'd say, like five feet nine or five feet ten. Not real skinny, not fat. Funny, now that I think of it—I never got a real good look frontwise. He came out of the dressing room down there and when he saw me, he sort of dodged back in. It happened again, so I thought maybe he was bashful about being seen with not much on, and all the war paint and all." The stagehand gave another tug to his cap. "Do you suppose maybe he was hanging round, watching till all was clear? Then he took off that little patch of—what-do-you-call-it—loincloth and rushed out to put on his act?"

"Very possible," said Curt. "Can you tell me more about him?"

"Well, his hair was real black, and he had a sort of feather stuck in it."

"Could it have been a wig instead of his own hair?"

"Coulda been. Not many fellows have braids hanging over their shoulders."

Just then there was a burst of music from the arena. "Oh, oh. Gotta go. Gotta go. Sorry I can't talk anymore," said the stagehand and he made for the runway leading into the arena.

Officer Conners looked after him thoughtfully, then he went the other way. He stopped at a door opposite the side hall. Cautiously he opened it. A pile of war bonnets across the room showed him he had the right place. There was nobody there, so he stepped in, looked around, picked up a few articles, and shook his head.

As he turned to go, he paused, stooped down to pick up a length of brown material with a beaded belt attached, and a circle of brown cloth with a long plastic red feather. To nobody in particular, he said aloud, "Could be." He looked at the head band, especially the feather, for a long time. "But if it is, I don't see—unless—" Carefully he rolled up the cloth and the circlet and put them in his pocket.

5 / *Saturday at 9:40 P.M.*

By the time Curt Conners returned to the main arena, the finale was in full swing. Since the entire cast of a thousand actors and dancers was in formation on the floor, he had no trouble circling around the far end without being seen.

It wasn't until he was almost at the section reserved for honored guests that he noticed that something was wrong. While the rest of the audience was stamping and clapping noisily in time to the martial music, Curt's special charges were sitting immobile.

A figure loomed out of the dimness. "Is that you, Red?" a voice said into his ear.

"Yes—Why it's you, Barney—Barney Ross," Curt shouted over the din of crowd and band and chorus. "But what—why—" He lowered his voice to a half shout and cupped his hand to Barney's ear. "What the hell are you doing here?"

"Don't know—yet. Got a call to get on down here. Saw you coming from over there. Thought maybe they'd sent for you, too."

"No, I was coming from—" Curt paused and grabbed Barney's arm. "Look over there."

"Yeah, I see. Come on, Red."

Moving cautiously in the shadows cast by the brilliant lights on the main floor, Detective Ross and Officer Conners moved around the two rows of guests to where a figure lay motionless on the hard floor.

"You Dr. Quinlan?" asked Barney, leaning close to the man with the stethoscope. "I'm Detective Ross." His badge gleamed briefly as it caught the light. "Officer Conners there." He gestured toward the supine body. "Is he—"

"She, Detective. Yes, she's dead."

"She, did you say? Who is she?"

"Maude McGinty, the mayor's wife."

"Mayor's wife! Whew!" Barney put his head very close to Dr. Quinlan's ear. "How did she die, Doc?"

A flashlight beam glowed, picked out the knife handle protruding from the chest.

Quickly Barney stooped to look more closely. Not touching anything, he peered into the darkness. "May I have the flashlight, Doctor?" he asked. Curt moved in close to Barney, and the two followed the beam of light as Barney moved it about. Curt whispered into Barney's ear, "Notice the handle of the knife, and the angle it makes with the body." The flashlight beam lingered a moment, then Barney stood up. "Thanks, Doc," he said, and he returned the flashlight.

As Curt rose, he stepped toward the chairs. "Where was she sitting?" he asked.

"In the middle seat of the front row," answered Dr. Quinlan. He nodded toward three empty chairs.

"And who was on each side of her?" asked Barney.

"Her husband was on one side," Dr. Quinlan indicated the mayor standing a short distance away. "And on the other side sat her cousin, Mrs. Cline." He nodded toward the half-fainting woman supported by a companion. "I asked my wife, Esther, to be with her. Mrs. Cline's taking it badly, you can see."

A tremendous crescendo of sound drowned out their voices, then there was sudden silence. Waves of applause began to swell from the audience. The actors, singers, dancers, and bandmen held their poses as the clapping and cheering continued. Over the tumult, the voice of the narrator, Sonny Hitchcock, was heard booming through the loudspeaker.

"Let's let the people who prepared this wonderful pageant know how much we appreciate all their hard work. First Mr. Dawson, who wrote the original script."

The spotlight swept over the reserved seat section, and Mr. Dawson rose and bowed.

"Quick, Red, Dr. Quinlan," shouted Barney, pulling them into positions so they half shielded the body from full view.

"And Mr. Katzen, who arranged the music," continued the announcer, "And Mr. Goodman, who coached the actors."

"Quick, Esther," called Dr. Quinlan. "You'll be next." Swiftly the doctor's wife left Elsie Cline and moved closer to the chairs—just in time to bow as the loudspeaker boomed, "And Mrs. Quinlan, our coordinator for the entire festival presentation."

The three men stood stiffly, hiding the body until the spotlight swept to the other side of the arena. "Now applause for our band director . . . our orchestra director . . . and our chorus director." Barney Ross relaxed, and the other two followed suit.

"And now, my good friends," the voice of Sonny Hitchcock continued, "I bid you good night from the bottom of my heart. This is your narrator, Wayne Hitchcock."

A wild scream rent the air. "Sonny . . . oh, Sonny . . ." and a surge of humanity moved toward Wayne Hitchcock. Out of the stand, from the runways and lobbies people streamed across the arena floor, dodging between the actors and players who hadn't made it to the exits in time to avoid them.

"Thank God," said Barney Ross. "That makes our job much easier." He turned to shake his head at the hysterical fans, then he surveyed the guests of honor. Most of them were standing up, some

23

intending to leave, some moving toward the corpse.

"They're all confused. It all came so fast they haven't quite caught on," said Doctor Quinlan. "Most of them are probably aware it's serious."

Barney Ross raised his voice. "I'm sorry to tell you, ladies and gentlemen, that we will have to ask you to remain in your seats awhile. As you can see, there has been an accident. Until the body has been—er—removed, will you please remain here?"

A chorus of voices broke out. "What happened? Was it a heart attack, Doctor? Who is it? Looks like Maude McGinty. Mayor's wife? Do you suppose she fell without her cane? Looks like it might be a stroke! Maybe she's just fainted."

"I'll bet it was the streaker!" came one voice, loud and clear. "The Streaker?"

"Sure, the streaker. Oh, my God, d'ya suppose he scared her to death?"

Harold Anderton bustled up to Detective Ross. After a short, intense bit of talking, while there were still murmurs of "Streaker, streaker" through the others, Anderton raised his hand.

"You can see, my friends, what has happened. It looks like the streaker was more than an entertainer. Maude McGinty is dead." There was a sudden hush. Several men moved closer to the mayor.

Mr. Anderton cleared his voice and continued. "We want to cause as little disturbance as possible among the general public. We notice that there are people waiting to speak to some of you," he glanced ostentatiously at the lieutenant governor, "and are being restrained by our good ushers from coming near. Perhaps you would like to move toward them and give them their chance to speak with you. We ask only that you keep them clear of this area and that you then return to your places here."

As if relieved at having something positive to do, the group dissolved. Hamilton Alcott was quickly surrounded by a group of handshakers and autograph seekers. Women gushed at Mrs. Alcott. The various directors were shaking hands and murmuring thanks for compliments.

As the space cleared for this activity, several men who had been lurking nearby moved in. Then ensued the popping of flashbulbs, producing of tape measures, drawing of diagrams, and the dusting for prints. When that business was ended, several men approached, bearing a stretcher. Deftly they lifted the body of Maude McGinty.

Before they could exit, Mrs. Cohen, pageant treasurer who had moved over to comfort Elsie Cline, approached Detective Ross. "Excuse me. Her cousin says there's a necklace, an amethyst necklace. It's very special. Could she have it to give to the mayor, before something could happen to it?"

Barney Ross looked up thoughtfully. As if on cue, Curt Conners moved over to the stretcher, bent and lightly touched the red-purple stones. He looked at Barney and shrugged. "See no reason," he signaled. Barney nodded.

Judith Cohen moved to Elsie Cline. In a very short time she was tapping Barney's shoulder again. "She says, could *you* do it? She can't bring herself to touch—to touch—well, you know."

Curt, on signal, found the necklace, and gently moved his fingers till he felt the clasp. He fumbled a moment, then worked the release. Gently he lifted the gleaming beads and brought them carefully to Elsie Cline. She shrank back as he moved to put the amethysts in her hands. Curt picked up her purse as if to put the beads into it. Quickly Elsie snatched the purse and shook her head, clasping the purse to her bosom.

"Want me to take it for you?" asked Mrs. Cohen.

Silently Elsie moved her head up and down. She extended her handkerchief and Mrs. Cohen carefully wrapped the stones in it.

The stretcher bearers departed with the body. Barney Ross moved over to Joe McGinty. "We have a car here, your honor," he said.

The mayor stared at him. "What? Car? Where?" he stammered.

Barney raised his voice. "Officer Crandall will drive you and Mrs. Cline. We'll see that your own car is brought to your house later."

At the mention of her name, Elsie Cline said, "Must I go to the—to the—"

"I think Mayor McGinty should not be alone. There will be questions to answer and decisions to make. I think you would be a great comfort to him."

She nodded. "Oh, yes. Joe will need me." She took the mayor's arm, and slowly the two followed Officer Crandall.

The auditorium was nearly cleared of people by now, except for the vociferous group still milling around Wayne Hitchcock. The important guests of honor were moving uncertainly back to their seats.

Barney Ross raised his voice. "Ladies and gentlemen, I am Detective Ross. That is Officer Conners. As you may have begun to

suspect, we think Mrs. McGinty did not die a natural death."
Again the murmur of voices spread through the group. "Not
natural? Not a heart attack? You mean somebody...? But who?
Why? Who would do this to Maude?" Then the voice of Hamilton
Alcott, loud and clear, said, "You mean she was *murdered?*"
The rest fell silent.

"You mean she was killed right here before our very eyes?" the
lieutenant governor continued. "In front of all these people? And
before all of us while we were sitting here?"

"That's what it looks like," said Barney.

"Surely," broke in Harold Anderton, "you don't think any one of
our honored guests could have done such a thing?" He smiled
apologetically as he looked from one person to the other. Then his
face lit up. "The streaker. Why, of course. You mean it was the
streaker?"

"At this point, I am not naming anybody nor accusing any
person," said Barney calmly. "You were here. I wasn't. So I'm sure
you can tell me some things I want to know, and some things you
may think it desirable for me to know."

"May I ask you to sit down?" continued Barney. "I'd like to know
who was sitting where. I hope you are sitting in the same place you
occupied throughout the evening."

There were a few minutes of delay as people rearranged themselves, murmuring among themselves.

"Now, if you will be patient, let me make a chart," said Barney
with notebook in hand.

"Front row we have the Honorable Hamilton Alcott and Mrs.
Alcott; Mr. and Mrs. Anderton, then three chairs empty now but
occupied by Mayor and Mrs. McGinty and Mrs. Cline. Then come
Dr. and Mrs. Redmond, Mrs. Sears, Mrs. Warren and Mrs. Yates."

"*Miss* Sears, if you please," said a crisp voice.

"Oh, sorry." Barney Ross looked up to smile politely at the lady
from the State Arts Council. Then he continued. "Now in the second
row are Dr. and Mrs. Quinlan. Then our representative from the
merchants, Mr. Kubitz, and Mrs. Kubitz. From the Labor Council
Mr. and Mrs. Ryan." He smiled ingratiatingly.

"Now our pageant staff: Mr. and Mrs. Dawson, Mr. and Mrs.
Katzen, Mr. Goodman, Mr. and Mrs. Balkan, and Mrs. Cohen."

Bleachers

	Dr. Quinlan
Lt. Gov. Alcott	Mrs. Quinlan
Mrs. Alcott	Mr. Kubitz
Mr. Anderton	Mrs. Kubitz
Mrs. Anderton	Mr. Ryan
Mrs. Cline	Mrs. Ryan
Mrs. McGinty	Mr. Dawson
Mayor McGinty	Mrs. Dawson
Dr. Redmond	Mr. Katzen
Mrs. Redmond	Mrs. Katzen
Miss Sears	Mr. Goodman
Mrs. Warren	Mr. Balkan
Mrs. Yates	Mrs. Balkan
	Mrs. Cohen
Front row	Back row

As Barney Ross was writing, Curt Conners was moving about, seemingly without purpose. Quite by chance, as Barney finished, Curt was standing behind the Dawsons in the back row. Something about his position or expression must have drawn Barney's attention, for the two stood looking at each other steadily for a few seconds. Then Barney cleared his throat for silence.

"Let's start with you, Mr. and Mrs. Dawson. You wrote the script, I believe, Mrs. Dawson."

The Dawsons looked up with startled expressions. "Us?" they said.

"You were sitting almost directly behind the—er—behind the mayor and his wife. Mr. Dawson, did you notice anything unusual during the early part of the evening?"

"Unusual? What do you mean?" Mr. Dawson peered through thick glasses.

"I mean, did you see anything occur between Mrs. McGinty and her husband, or did she do anything out of the ordinary that you noticed?"

"No," said Mr. Dawson thoughtfully. "I'm afraid I was very

much engrossed in the progress of the pageant. I was watching how my story continuity went and what the audience reactions were."

"Quite understandable. Now, did you notice anything when the streaker appeared on the scene?"

"I'm afraid we were all startled at first with the shock of seeing a man quite without clothes. Then maybe we panicked when we saw him running toward us. It all happened so fast, you know."

There was a chorus of agreement from the others. Mr. Dawson's high-pitched voice rose even higher.

"Then when he approached the place where Mrs. McGinty was sitting, I remember grabbing my wife and pulling her head down onto my chest—I suppose I was protecting her from a possible attack, or maybe I just didn't want her to see . . . to see this naked fellow." The murmurings of the others were louder now. "And then, when he had gone, I'm afraid I was mostly angry. What right did he have to come spoil my show with his crude exhibition? What a revolting, disgusting interruption to what was an inspiring evening."

"I see. Thank you, Mr. Dawson," said Barney Ross. "Mr. and Mrs. Ryan, you were behind the McGintys, too, I notice. Did you see anything unusual?"

"Can't say I did." Mr. Ryan's voice was coarse and heavy to match his bulky body. "I remember I was real disgusted. We were enjoying the show real good when out comes this naked Indian. I thought it was a helluva—I mean a lousy—thing to have him bust in on an act like that, 'specially in a family show. And when he came over to kiss the lady, I got just plain mad. We'd never allow things like that down at the labor temple."

Mrs. Ryan's husky contralto joined in. "I thought it was part of the act too. I was too mad to see anything but that guy making a show of himself."

"You said 'Indian,' " said Barney. "What made you think he was an Indian?"

"He had one of them feathers in his hair," said Ryan.

"And long black braids and real dark skin," added his wife.

"I'd have grabbed him and knocked him down, only it all happened so fast. He was a streaker, all right, streaking real fast."

Harold Anderton interrupted. "Excuse me, Officer Ross. Couldn't we move to a more comfortable place? They're beginning to turn off the lights. I'd suggest the Green Room."

Barney glanced at Curt Conners, who gave a slight nod toward the side where several outsiders were waiting by Officer Mulvany. "A good idea, Mr. Anderton. Would you be good enough to lead the way? I'll be along in a few minutes."

With obvious relief, the group rose and slowly moved across the arena floor to the opposite exit. Except for some stagehands and hangers-on, the rest of the building was empty now.

"Hi, Barney," called a voice, and one of the men lingering nearby dashed up.

Barney gave a grimace of annoyance, then with an effort to sound casual he said, "What? Oh, it's you, Hickson."

"Yes, it's me. Looks like a story's ready to break. The mayor's wife hauled out on a stretcher, the rest of these VIP's kept for quizzing by our Detective Barney Ross. How about filling me in on the facts?"

"Not quite yet, Hickson. There's a story all right, but you'll have to wait a few minutes. I've got some details to get straight first."

"Oh, come on. Have a heart. I've got a deadline to meet."

"Oh, sure, you always do. But ten minutes. I'll give you plenty to write about then. You know ten minutes won't hurt you. I promise the wait will be worth it."

The reporter wheeled. "Come on, give me a start anyway. Mayor's wife laid out on a stretcher. Detective Ross on the job. More than a heart attack, wouldn't you say?"

"TEN MINUTES, Hickson. And no trying to talk to those people either. And no listening at the keyhole. Don't be surprised if we have to take a little trip across town too."

Muttering, the reporter stepped back.

"Damn nuisance," said Ross. "Keep an eye on him, will you, Kottke?" he asked one of the policemen still standing nearby.

"Barney, got another minute? Mulvany here's got somebody you better talk to," said Curt softly.

"Oh, hello Mike," called Barney to yet another policeman. "You on duty here tonight?"

"Yes, I've been right here all the time" said Mike Mulvany. "I'd like you to meet Harry Manson, Barney. Harry, this is Detective Ross. Harry says he's the chauffeur for the lieutenant governor."

"That's right." Harry Manson's voice was hushed. "I think I may be able to help you a little bit in this business."

Barney studied Harry a moment, curiously. Not an impressive-looking fellow, not the kind you'd ever notice in a crowd. Unless you looked at his shoulders, he thought. "Did you say 'chauffeur'?"

"That's right. I drove the lieutenant governor and his wife up from Capital City. I happened to be sitting over there nearby, and I noticed a few things you may be interested in."

Barney and Harry exchanged glances. "I see," he said. "You've met Officer Mulvany, now I'd like to have you meet Officer Conners. You'll have no trouble remembering him with that red hair."

Harry Manson nodded impassively. "Glad to meet you."

"Would you like to come with us? We've got some business with these people. We can talk as we move along." He looked over his shoulder to see that the reporter wasn't following. "You say you have something to tell us?"

In the Green Room, the "distinguished guests" had broken up into little groups, talking excitedly in low voices. As Detective Ross entered with Curt Conners and Harry Manson, he heard the resonant voice of Wayne Hitchcock.

"You mean she's *dead*? What was it, a heart attack?"

The buzz of voices stopped abruptly. All eyes turned to the television star and then to the detective.

"Good evening, Mr. Hitchcock," Barney said calmly. "I see you have heard about it. Perhaps you'll be willing to join us for a few minutes? Maybe you can tell us something about the circumstances."

"Me? Why, I don't see how I can help much. I was on the other side of the arena all evening, you know. And I'm afraid I don't know the lady." He shrugged. "But, of course, I'll stay if you think I can be of some help. Just let me tell Dennis a few things before I send him on his way."

"Dennis?" asked Barney.

"Excuse me." Sonny Hitchcock pointed to his companion. "This is Dennis Peters, my man Friday. I couldn't get along without him."

Unobtrusively Curt Conners moved across the room. After Wayne Hitchcock had finished a few whispered instructions, Curt said, "Excuse me, Dennis, haven't I seen you someplace before?"

Dennis looked startled. "I don't think so, Officer. Unless—oh, sure! Weren't you one of the policemen who came to rescue us when those teen-age fans gave us the rush before the program started? I was there then, you know."

"Oh, yes," said Curt Conners. "But I was thinking of some other time. Where were you after the pageant started?" asked Curt.

"Why, I—I went over to sit in the audience. I do that lots of times to check on things. You know, like is the loudspeaker working all right or is the spotlight focused on Sonny—I mean Mr. Hitchcock—things like that. Now, if you'll excuse me, I've got some orders to carry out." Dennis turned and headed for the exit.

Curt Conners looked thoughtfully at him until he had disappeared. He heard Barney Ross saying, "It's late. Instead of questioning each of you, perhaps I can save time by asking some general questions. Did any of you get a good look at the streaker? I mean, a good enough look so you can describe him."

It was Pheobe Sears who spoke up shrilly. "He had blue eyes." There was a slight titter in the room. "Yes, blue eyes," she said firmly. "I remember thinking how he couldn't be a *real* Indian with blue eyes. They should have been brown. But in the spotlight they showed very plainly a light blue."

"And he was young," added one of her companions, Mrs. Warren. "He had a very slim waist." There was more than a titter. "Well, you know how older men get a—a—well, a paunch."

"And he wasn't very tall," said the third woman in the Art Council group, Mrs. Yates. "He didn't have to bend down very far, I remember."

"Bend down, Mrs. Yates?" asked Barney.

"Yes, when he bent down to kiss the mayor's wife."

"Did he kiss her?" asked Barney. There was an awkward silence. "In fact, did the streaker touch Mrs. McGinty at all?" He looked around. "Some of you who were close, in the front row."

It was Dr. Redmond who spoke. "Now that you mention it, Officer, I don't believe he really did. He just bent down as if—well, as if he was going to kiss her, but he really didn't."

"Where were your eyes, Redmond?" It was the sharp voice of Phoebe Sears. "Touch her? He sat all over her. Landed in her lap."

"And did he touch her?" asked Barney.

"He certainly did." Miss Sears' voice was strident now. "I noticed especially. First he put his hand out, as if he were steadying himself. You know, when you're running fast and try to stop all of a sudden, you reach out in front of you to grab something. Well, that's what he did."

"That's right," said Mrs. Warren. "He reached out. I saw it too."

"Yes," said Mrs. Yates. "As he was coming toward us, he put his hand up to his head like—well, like he was afraid his wig was coming off."

"His wig?" asked Barney.

"Yes, his wig. Then he reached out as if he couldn't stop himself fast enough."

"I told you he wasn't a real Indian." Phoebe Sears was triumphant. "Those long braids just had to be a wig, with those bright blue eyes."

"And did you see the streaker actually touch Mrs. McGinty?" Barney asked.

"Why, yes. He put an arm around her neck, and it looked like he kissed her," Phoebe Sears proclaimed, and Carolyn Warren echoed, "Yes, kissed her."

"Which arm was it, Miss Sears?"

"Which arm? What a question!" Phoebe's voice was sarcastic. "Why, it was his right arm, of course."

"Yes," echoed Mrs. Warren. "I'm sure, because I had a front view of him all the time."

"Carolyn!" Marjorie Yates sounded shocked. "A front view? And you looked?"

Carolyn Warren's face turned pink.

"And where was his left arm?" asked Barney.

"Why, up against Maude's chest. Where else could it go?" said Phoebe Sears.

There followed an awkward silence, as if people were trying to think of something to add. It was the unctuous voice of Harold Anderton that broke the quiet.

"It is getting late, Detective Ross. These people have been here a long time, and they are all busy people with demanding schedules. Do you think you could let them go?"

Detective Ross glanced toward Curt Conners, who gave the slightest nod. Barney assumed a hopeful look. "Does anybody have anything more to add?" Nobody spoke. "In that case, I thank you for your time. I appreciate it very much."

Barney looked at the lieutenant governor, then at the three ladies from the State Arts Council. "Are any of you leaving Wauconda Falls tonight?"

"We plan to take the one o'clock plane tomorrow afternoon," said Phoebe Sears.

"Yes, the one o'clock plane," said Mrs. Warren.

"And we will be driving back to Capital City," said Hamilton Alcott. "We won't be leaving until late tomorrow morning." He looked at his chauffeur. "About eleven o'clock."

"And I'm planning to stay here for a few days," said Wayne Hitchcock. "Visit old friends and that sort of thing. I'm not scheduled for a run-through back in Hollywood until Wednesday."

"In that case, there is no need to detain you any longer. If something should come up, I can get in touch with you out-of-town people before you leave. The rest of you will, of course, be right here in Wauconda Falls. May I tell you again how sorry I am we have had to trouble you and how grateful I am for your patience and understanding."

"Oh, yes, there is one thing I should mention, Officer." It was the voice of the lieutenant governor. "There was a change in the seating arrangement at the last minute this evening. If Mrs. Alcott and I had been in the announced order, we would have been seated where the mayor and his wife were, and the Streaker would have—well, it might have been my wife instead of Mrs. McGinty."

6 / *Saturday at 7:00 P.M.*

"Joe McGinty, not even close to dressed yet? What in heaven's name have you been doing this last half hour?"

"I'm looking for my shoes, if you have to know. I wish you'd tell me, Maude, how the hell that cleaning woman manages to hide them so well."

"Nobody's hid them. Haven't you got eyes in your head? I can see them from here, right by your dresser. You must have stumbled over them half a dozen times by now."

"Oh, those white jobs? If you think I'm going to wear those la-di-da white shoes, Maude, think again." Mayor McGinty crossed to the door and yelled, "Oh, Elsie. Elsie."

"Think again, should I? Well, I have thought again. You're not going to wear those old black shoes of yours. This is one of the biggest nights in Wauconda Falls' history, and you're his honor the mayor, and you've got to walk that floor with the spotlight on you—and me." Maude McGinty tapped her cane impatiently. "It's June, you're wearing that sharp-looking white jacket and it's just got to be white shoes."

The mayor interrupted his wife. "Oh, there you are, Elsie. Do you know where my wife has hidden my black shoes?"

"Why, yes, Joe," said the worried-looking woman in the doorway. "I believe they're—"

"No, you don't, Elsie," cut in Maude sharply. "You don't believe you know anything about them." She turned to her husband. "It's no use, Joe. The black shoes are out. You're wearing the white ones."

Joe looked at Elsie, who promptly lowered her eyes. He looked at his wife, who was staring at him fixedly. He returned the stare awhile, then he shrugged. "Aw, what the hell. It doesn't really matter." He reached for the white shoes.

"Elsie," said Maude crisply, "you were going to get my new amethyst necklace for me. Bring it here. Joe hasn't seen it yet."

"Yes, Maude," said Elsie Cline and disappeared.

"Amethyst? Did you say amethyst?" asked Joe. "Aren't they kind of—well—expensive?"

"Oh, a little, I suppose. But it's *my* money, remember. Now that I've decided to let my hair go gray, I'm going into the purple shades." She drew herself up and half turned. "You haven't noticed my new dress, by the way. How do you like it?"

"Very nice."

"Something new, in honor of our big night. It really all started with the amethysts. I saw them down in Carter's window, and just like that the idea came to me. I had a little talk with Carrie. She's a real treasure of a dressmaker, you know. She helped me find that material. It's really a hard shade to get." Maude preened. "There won't be many like it, you can bet. Carrie whipped it up, and you'll have to admit that it does something for me. Oh, you'll be proud of me, Joe, when we make our entrance tonight."

The mayor looked up from tying his shoelaces and grunted.

Maude moved haltingly over to the mirror and turned from side to side. She looked at Joe from beneath lowered lids and said softly, "It's floor-length, Joe, so it won't show that—Well, if you give me your arm on one side and if Elsie is on the other and we don't walk too fast, maybe I won't have to use this." Maude gave an impatient jerk to her cane.

Joe stood up, looked at his wife, half annoyed, half worried. "Now, Maude, why do you keep worrying about your—your—"

"About my limp? Go on, say it. Why pretend? Don't you think I know what people have been saying about me all these years? Poor old Maude . . . such a shame . . . our mayor's wife. Well, tonight, for once, I'm not going to be leaning on this—this—*thing*." She waved the cane in the air.

"Oh, there you are, Elsie," Joe said with a sigh of relief. "I'd like to see these beautiful jewels my wife here is squandering her money on."

As Maude turned to take the box, her waving cane struck Elsie's outstretched hand. The box flew across the room and landed at Joe's feet.

"Oh, Elsie, you clumsy fool!" exclaimed Maude. "I don't see how you can always be so—so ungraceful. If you've hurt that necklace the least bit, I'll—"

"Now, Maude," Joe interrupted, "that wasn't Elsie's fault. You did it." He stooped to retrieve the box and handed it to his wife.

Maude opened the box. "Well, that's lucky. No harm done." She held the necklace up to her throat. "Isn't it lovely? Fasten it for me, Elsie. Careful!"

"Sorry, Maude," Elsie's voice was apologetic. "If you'll just hold still."

"There, now. Don't you agree it goes with this dress handsomely, Joe?" Maude admired herself in the mirrow.

"Yes, I guess so. But you haven't told me how much it cost. Wasn't it pretty expensive?"

"Oh, never you mind how much it cost. I've told you it's my money, not yours." Maude drew herself up before the mirror. "The important thing is that I'll make a good appearance tonight. Oh, Joe, you'll be so proud of me as we make our entrance. You, the mayor of Wauconda Falls, and I, his wife, leading the procession."

The mayor looked at Elsie helplessly. When she avoided his gaze and turned away slightly, he shrugged his shoulders and sighed.

"Oh, and speaking of entrances," Maude continued, "come here. Joe, give me your arm. Now, Elsie on the other side of me." Maude threw down her cane and took a firm grip on Joe and Elsie. "Now slowly. No, no, Elsie, give me more support. Hold me up. There, that's better."

The trio walked the length of the room. "See, what did I tell you?" Maude exulted. "I don't need that cane. Nobody will be able to tell that I'm different from anybody else, or that there's anything wrong with my leg. Oh, Joe, it's going to work."

"Why, sure, Maude," Joe said almost too heartily. "You were walking just fine."

"With you in your white coat on one side and Elsie in that light green on the other, you'll set off this light purple shade just perfectly." Maude's voice grew shrill with excitement. "My old green turned out to be quite a success on you after all, didn't it, Elsie? You're so much larger than I, I was afraid it wouldn't— Well, thanks to Carrie's clever needle, nobody would ever suspect—and it's such a soft, modest shade, it suits you very well. You may as well keep it. I won't be wanting to wear it again, ever."

Joe spoke. "Look at the clock, Maude. Don't you think we'd better—"

"Oh, heavens, yes. Elsie, get my white coat and gloves. And my formal bag is in the top left-hand drawer."

Elsie nodded and left.

"Joe," said Maude thoughtfully, "I've been trying to plan when to make my formal announcement. I'd love to do it tonight, but I don't see how it would fit in. Do you think it could?"

"What are you talking about, Maude? What announcement is that?"

"My endowment of the recital hall. You remember, I was telling you about it yesterday. You just don't listen to me, do you? Well, Harold Anderton was saying they've run out of money, so they can't complete that darling little auditorium on the far west side of the convention center. Well, I looked at the place. Oh, Joe, it's a perfect little jewel of an auditorium, with a small stage and tiered seats. It would be *so* right for the music club recitals and the fortnightly lectures and—oh, a hundred events each year."

Joe looked apprehensive. "So what's that got to do with you and your announcement?"

"I told you. Well, I think I did. They've run out of money. I could just see that darling little auditorium in my mind—soft-cushioned seats, deep red, with carpeting to match. I think paneled walls and a special ceiling with a fancy chandelier and the stage hung in ivory, with a concert grand piano and—"

"Wait a minute, Maude. That sounds like a lot of money. You aren't thinking of—"

"Oh, not as much as you might think." Maude smiled complacently. "Harold Anderton said that for three hundred thousand dollars it would look quite handsome."

"Three hundred thousand dollars! Did I hear you right?" Joe's usually ruddy cheeks went pale. "Why, you must be crazy. You haven't got that kind of money!"

"Oh, but I have. I've gone over my portfolio very carefully. For three hundred thousand dollars I can endow the Ezra Medille Recital Hall, dedicated to his memory by his daughter Maude Medille McGinty."

Joe's voice dwindled to a husky whisper. "But, Maude, if you give it away, you won't have anything left for yourself."

"Why won't I?" There was a strange smile on Maude's face. "Why, I'm married to Joseph McGinty, Mayor of Wauconda Falls and prosperous businessman, who is perfectly able to support his wife in the style suitable to his important station in life."

"Maude, you can't do this. You must have gone out of your mind."

"Now, you listen to me, Joe. When you married me, you were poor—just a struggling fellow trying to get started. My father was well-to-do and he was smart. You used my dowry to expand your business. My father put you wise to that land deal and loaned you the money to buy and subdivide. He used his influence to make you a director of the First National Bank. He advised you to be a silent partner in the Belouski Construction Company and then helped you get the contracts for the hospital and the library. And lots more. Well, thanks to my father, you're in good shape, Joe. You might even say you're rich."

Maude gave a hard dry laugh. "You know you didn't marry me; you married my father's money and influence. Not that I'm complaining. A girl with a—handicap—doesn't get many offers. I was glad to get a fine, handsome husband. Really, it's turned out to be a good investment. You're the mayor and maybe you'll be our next senator."

"Good God, Maude, what makes you talk like this?"

"Why shouldn't I talk like this? I'm talking about my father's money, the money he inherited from *his* father. He schemed and worked and scrimped to make it grow into a nice little sum of money. Then he died before he could enjoy it." Her lip curled. "He wasn't like his sister, my Aunt Ethel, and her husband, Uncle Bradford. Together they spent money like water. They lived in that big house. They had a maid and a yardman when my mother was having to do with a part-time hired girl. It was my cousin Elsie that had the pretty dresses, got the fancy piano lessons and dancing and elocution. Naturally she had the boys hanging around her like flies. Oh, they lived it up till Uncle Bradford's fancy dealing caught up with him and he put a bullet in his brain." Maude's laugh was scornful. "Aunt Ethel had to come down to running a boarding-house. None of that spending and showing off for my father."

Maude's hard, shrill chatter stopped for a moment, and her expression softened. "Don't you see, Joe? My father skimped and saved, never got much honor. We've had the use of his money. Now it's time to give it back to him. We haven't given him any grandchildren to inherit it all. So what's going to become of the money he worked so hard to get? Go to *your* nephews?"

"How about your cousin Elsie?"

"Oh, her! She had her chances. Her mother gave her everything she wanted. She was the stuck-up cousin! I was the plain one, the lame one. She was the beauty in her fancy clothes. She played the piano so beautifully. She could have had her pick of the best boys in town. She had to be the silly fool. She ran off with that dance band drummer. Nobody knows what became of *him*, but she was back in a couple of years, helping her mother run the boardinghouse and giving a few piano lessons for pin money."

"My God, Maude, that's your own flesh and blood you're talking about."

"I was her flesh and blood once, when she was lording it over me. And I've done all right by her, haven't I? I took her in, she's got a nice home, a room of her own, plenty to eat, good clothes to wear. She can go anyplace we go. I give her plenty of chances to play her piano and go to her clubs."

"You mean you're going to give away all of your money? Just like that?"

"No, not quite all." She smiled maliciously. "There'll be plenty left for you to bury me in proper style." Her voice grew cold and businesslike. "I'm seeing the lawyer first thing next week. You can be sure my father's hard-earned money will go where it deserves to go—to endow the Ezra Medille Recital Hall, with his portrait hanging in the lobby for everybody to see and remember him by."

"I believe you really mean it, don't you, Maude," said the mayor. "How long you been thinking about this without telling me?"

"I've been thinking about it for a long time now. My mind's made up; that's the way I want it, and nothing's going to stop me."

"I have to wonder if that's really wise, Maude. You never know what might happen . . . to me, for example. Then where'd you be?"

"Don't try to persuade me, Joe. That's the way I want it done, and I mean it."

They stood there silently, looking at each other for a while. Then Joe McGinty lowered his eyes. "Well, if that's the way you want it, Maude. I just hope you won't regret it." He turned away.

"Elsie!" called Maude. "Where are you with my bag and gloves?"

"Here they are, Maude. Sorry to keep you waiting," said Elsie, entering hurriedly. "I heard you two talking, so I went back to get your throat lozenges. They're here in your bag, and here are your gloves and your white coat."

Maude drew herself up before the mirror as she adjusted the coat. "Well, aren't you two ready yet? Give me your arm, Joe. Elsie, I think I'll use the cane until we get there, so you'd better take my bag." She smiled complacently. "Did you hear, Elsie, that the mayor has ordered us a motorcycle escort?"

7 / Saturday at 7:00 P.M.

"Will you help me out, Ham, dear?" Rosemary Alcott called to her husband. "There's a zipper—not a very big one—I just can't reach."

Lieutenant Governor Alcott looked up from the notes he was studying. "Of course. What's your problem? A zipper you say? Where in that lovely dress of yours is there a zipper?"

"Sorry to be a bother, but since we couldn't bring Tilda along to maid me, you'll just have to help out. It's hidden down there someplace just where I can't find it. This dress is supposed to look like nothing's holding it up, so it's hidden where it doesn't show."

"Well, here I am, kneeling before you," he said with mock gallantry. "I mean behind you, but I can't seem to find it. If you'll stop wiggling and hold still, . . . there, I think I've got it." Very gently he exerted pressure, and miraculously what back there was to the dress closed. He struggled to his feet.

"Yep, there it is, and you're right. There's nothing showing unless you know where to look. You're sure it will stay up? Don't see how it does."

"That's because you're a man. Don't you see it's stretched tight up here in front, so it can't possibly slip over—well, look."

"That I will, with pleasure, and touch, too. You sure know all the tricks, Roz." He slid his arms around her waist. "And I'm grateful. You're such a beautiful creature, which is a great help on the campaign trail."

Rosemary pulled back. "Is that what I am to you? A help?" A faint frown appeared between her carefully lined eyebrows. "I'm glad if I'm giving satisfaction. I wouldn't like to think I'm falling down on my job. I want to think I am—well—earning my keep."

"Don't worry, you are. One of the luckiest days of my life was when I persuaded you to team up with me. You're one of my strongest selling points, Roz. I quote from that writing of Penny Perry, society columnist: 'That *darling* beautiful Rosemary Alcott! Such a charming hostess! Wears clothes so stunningly! Entertains so effortlessly!' Yes m'dear, you're the delight of the capital news hens—always good for a scintillating item when they need to fill their columns."

He walked back to his chair and picked up his notes. "That was quite a new angle in Penny Peery's blurb last Sunday. 'Former concert pianist gives up career to become wife of rising young politician.' "

The lines in Rosemary's forehead deepened into a definite frown. "That wasn't my idea. I just happened to mention I used to be a pretty good pianist with thoughts of playing professionally. Well, one thing led to another, and gushy Penny came up with that one."

Hamilton looked up at her sardonically. "Didn't tell her you were playing in a nightclub, did you, Roz? Not that that's a disgrace these days, but a concert pianist—well, wasn't that cheating a little?"

"Don't think I couldn't play a little Beethoven or Chopin if I had to." Rosemary pouted. "I was the pride of my piano teacher when I was fourteen."

"Don't worry, Roz, you probably won't have to prove it. Right now you're the wife of Lieutenant Governor Alcott." He changed his voice into a singsong, as if reading from a paper. "They're so devoted, so much in love, the perfect couple. The lieutenant governor so tall, ruggedly handsome." Here he rose for an exaggerated pose. "His wife so softly feminine, so beautiful." He bowed toward his wife.

Rosemary shrugged her shoulder pettishly and turned away. Hamilton shook his head in admiration. "You are a wonder, Roz. You honey up to old Colonel Packer, and his wife just smiles and calls you 'darling.' You lead Judge Randolph on till he almost makes a fool of himself, yet Mrs. Randolph gives a tea with you as guest of honor. When all the young buds should be jealous when they see how their husbands look at you with a gleam in their eyes, they flock around you, hang on your every word. Keep it up, Roz, and you'll be queening it as the governor's lady one of these days."

"The governor's lady. Is that what you're aiming for, Ham?"

"Why not? Ten years ago I was a green young lawyer just out of college back in little old Millville. We've come a long way in ten years, thanks a lot to you, along with a couple of lucky breaks." Hamilton lowered his voice. "The governor's about at the end of the line. He's made some stupid blunders lately. I give him one more term at the most and the opposition will be on him so hard our people won't dare run him again. They'll be looking for a younger man, one with charisma—and a beautiful wife to grace the governor's mansion."

"But what if I don't want to grace the governor's mansion? Maybe I'd prefer to live back in your little hometown of Millville. Maybe I'd like a loving husband all to myself in a nice little house instead of a public figure who's dashing off here, there, everywhere. You're always having to go to some conference or to make some speech, or you're out politicking and shaking hands. Oh, Ham, maybe I don't *want* to be the gracious hostess to a bunch of people on the make— office seekers, climbers, shifty-eyed politicians."

Hamilton Alcott looked at his wife coolly. "Sorry, m'dear. That's the way I want it, and that's the proposition I made to you 'way back—well, you know when. Either a divorce or a business partnership with you the model wife and hostess and me the upstanding young lawyer and future leader of the people."

He struck a pose in front of the mirror a moment, then turned to speak even more softly. "And each of us free to go our own way, as long as we are discreet."

"Discreet?" Rosemary's voice took on a sharp edge. "There's nothing for *me* to be discreet about. I'm your wife, Ham, and have been ever since I married you."

"And how about before? What about Ben DiVacco?"

"Ben? Oh, yes, always back to Ben. Can't you understand he was an escape? I married him to get away from home. My mother had just died, and my father was becoming a drunken sot. I was hardly eighteen and I couldn't cope. Ben was smooth talking, sharp looking, and he was going to give me a dreamworld." Rosemary laughed. "A nightmare, he should have said. In a week I knew I'd made a big mistake. Thank God he got caught in that bank holdup and went to prison." She shivered slightly. "Well, I needed money. I had a way with the piano, and I was lucky enough to get a job playing at Torini's Casino. It was a living."

"I'm sure it was," said Hamilton in a mocking tone.

"I seem to remember you taking pleasure in watching me make that living. You gave me quite a rush."

"Not many were as green as I was, a smalltown boy not dry behind the ears. I thought the only way to lay claim to a beautiful doll was to marry her, and you never got around to telling me about Ben till after I found out for myself."

"I didn't tell you about Ben because—well, I was a little bit ashamed, for no good reason, and then I didn't think you'd ever have to know. I was afraid if you did, you might change your mind about me—and I wanted you."

"I'm sure you did," Hamilton responded sardonically.

"Yes, can't you believe that? I wanted you just because you were—well, *you*. I supposed you were going to take me back to that little town where we would live quietly and maybe raise a family." She tossed her head. "Big ideas, politics, moving to Capital City— these I never dreamed about. I looked forward to not having to please the customers and play up to the boss."

"You didn't seem to mind the attentions of Torini, and you never held back when that slick salesman was around."

"When a gal works in a nightclub, she has to smile at the boss and kid along with the customers. Torini's hugs and pats were like a father's, nothing more. And Hank was just a show-off who liked to joke. I had to play along with his corny stuff because it was good business."

"Good business, eh? O.K., Roz, if you say so." He moved over to look directly at his wife. "Well, we'll just keep on with this strictly business line. You keep on smiling at the customers and kidding them along. Only, you're working for a different boss now, and the customers are in a different league."

The two stood staring at each other for several seconds. Then Hamilton Alcott's expression softened. "I'm sorry if I've hurt your feelings. I don't know how we got into this big scene. Poor timing on my part." He patted her cheek gently. "Maybe you'd better go back and fix your makeup. It's gotten a little runny with all this emotion." His voice became crisper. "This is new territory for me, Roz, and I've got a lot of people to win over. I'm counting on you to give us lots of help tonight."

Rosemary Alcott continued to look at Hamilton a while longer, then she turned slowly and moved away. At the door she stopped and looked back uncertainly. "I didn't know if I should tell, but since you mentioned Ben, I guess I have to."

"Tell me? About Ben?"

"Ben got out of prison last week. He was paroled for good behavior and put on probation."

"Your first husband is out? Are you sure? How do you know?"

"I got a newspaper clipping in an envelope. The desk clerk handed it to me. No name, no message, only the newspaper article that Ben is out on probation."

"You got it *here*? How could that be? Nobody up here at this end of the state knows about you or me."

"Ben knows. I think I saw him today."

"You what? You saw him *here* in Wauconda Falls?"

"I'm not sure. It was in the lobby. You were shaking hands with all those people on the committee. I saw this fellow coming out of a phone booth. He had on dark glasses and was wearing a hat, so I couldn't see his face very well. But he was the right height, and somehow the way he looked at me, it wasn't just like he'd look at somebody passing by or like he wanted to whistle at me. It was more steady-like, more unfriendly. Then he was gone in the crowd."

"Ben here. H'mmm." Hamilton shook his head. "I hardly think so, but if he is, I'll find him." He smiled at her gently. "Now you just go get yourself ready, and I'll take care of this. Come on, Roz, chin up. You've got to make a good entrance tonight."

The lieutenant governor stood watching his wife as she left the room. He murmured to nobody in particular, "I wish I could believe you." He reached for the phone.

"Will you connect me to room 210 please? . . . Harry, it's me. . . . Can you come right up?"

He stood thinking a few more minutes, then lifted the phone again. "I want to place a long-distance call to Capital City. Yes, I'll hold." He fiddled with some papers nervously. "Hello, Bob. Hamilton Alcott . . . I want you to try to run something down for me, tonight yet, if you can. A fellow named Ben DiVacco was paroled from State Prison a few days ago. Can you find out who his parole officer is? Judge Cranmere may give you the lead. . . . Then call his parole officer to see if he knows where DiVacco is right now. . . . I know it's late to be calling people. . . . Well, if you can't connect tonight, keep trying tomorrow. . . . Well, it's like this, Bob: if he's someplace else, everything's O.K.; but if he's up here in Wauconda Falls, I got troubles. . . . It's a long story that can wait. . . . Yes, I understand. Do what you can, will you, Bob? . . . Thanks. . . . I'll be waiting to hear. . . . Program, reception, the usual, so make it eleven o'clock or later. . . . I'm in Suite 200."

He hung up and sat staring into space. His eyes moved again to the door through which Rosemary had made her exit. Ben . . . I wonder, if I'd known about Ben, would I still have . . . I sure was a greenie.

A buzzer sounded. Hamilton strode to the door. "Who is it?" he called.

"It's me, Harry." Hamilton turned the key and a man entered. Hamilton closed the door quickly and turned the lock.

"Glad you got here so quick," said Hamilton. "Got a problem." Softly Hamilton reviewed the story about the newspaper clipping, the man in the phone booth, omitting only the connection he might have with Rosemary. Harry listened without expression. "I'll go to work on it. Can you describe him?"

"Ben DiVacco's strictly Italian. Dark skin, black hair, little less than medium height—if he's the ex-convict we're talking about. He could make trouble, serious trouble. Who you got to help you?"

"Got two with me—Denny and Blake. I'll get them into circulation. Italian, you say. Not a very big town, not very many

44

strangers, not many Italians." He looked at the lieutenant governor thoughtfully. "I think I'd better chauffeur you tonight and sit someplace close to you during the program. Do you know where you're going to be out there at that convention center?"

"Not exactly. Special section, I believe. Spotlights—the usual, I suppose—a few words of greeting."

"Not a long speech? Can you keep it short?"

"I think so."

"See if you can arrange for you and your wife to sit on the end of a row. Don't let yourself get buried in the middle someplace." Harry patted his shoulder holster. "I'll be real close so nobody can get to you without me seeing him and taking care of him."

"Thanks, Harry. I'll see if I can arrange that. You go on ahead now. We'll be along in a few minutes, as soon as Mrs. Alcott is ready."

After Harry had left, Hamilton put on his coat, adjusted his tie, smoothed his hair. He picked up his notes, and slipped them into his inside coat pocket.

"Ready soon, Roz? We're on in half an hour and our chauffeur's waiting."

8 / Saturday at 7:00 P.M.

Jake Krasuski paused in his chewing. "Did you see him, Magda?"

His wife reached for the margarine, spread some on her bread, gave a shrug. "Yeah, I seen him."

"So did I. Real good." Jake sneered. "I seen our little snotnosed brat. All growed up now, dressed up like a dude, long hair curlin' down around his ears, smilin' and wavin' at them fools crowdin' around."

Magda tilted the catsup bottle over her fried potatoes. "And did you hear them gals screamin'?" Her voice rose to a fake squeal. "Sonny...it's him...it's Sonny Hitchcock. Oh, Sonny." She sniffed. "Buncha dumb broads."

"Bet you they wouldn't have squealed like that if they'd seen him like *we* used to. Dirty-faced, sassy little bastard."

Magda jabbed at her chunk of meat. "Still wettin' his pants when he was six. Gettin' in fights and tearin' his clothes. Always in trouble at school. When I think what I had to put up with—and all for a few lousy dollars." She pointed her fork at her husband. "Remember the time he run away and the cops found him way over in Sparksville? Wish they hadn't . . . wish he'd got lost or that he'd kept runnin'."

Jake picked up a piece of meat with his fingers, took a bite, then looked sideways at his wife. "He seen us, Magda. He knew we was there."

"I know, Jake. He was that close to me, I could have touched him. Looked right at me, never let on he knew me. Walked right on by, smilin' and wavin' at them squealin' kids."

"Damned bastard." Jake chewed viciously. "We took him in when his own mother didn't want nothin' to do with him. Now he's rich and famous and he don't know us from nothin'."

Magda reached for her coffee, stirred in sugar, then paused with spoon in air. "Jake, . . . How rich? How rich do you suppose he is?"

"Plenty. All them fancy clothes. First-class airplane, you notice. One of them manservants to fetch and carry. Yeah, all that's for guys with plenty of cash. And I seen the fancy big ring flashin' on his hand. What kind of a man you think goes around wearin' diamond rings? Rich ones, that's who. That ain't for poor guys. Yeah, he's got plenty of money."

Magda sipped her coffee. Her eyes narrowed. Over the cup she said, "If he's rich, Jake, maybe . . . maybe he would . . ."

"Maybe he'd what? You gettin' an idea, Magda?"

"I was just thinkin' that if he didn't want to let on he knew us. . . . Well, how much would he feel like payin' to keep us quiet?"

Jake stopped chewing. "What do you mean, to keep us quiet?" He gulped, he stared, then slowly a grin twisted his lips. "I get it. Yeah, I wonder how much."

Jake shoved his plate back and stood up. "Come on, Magda. Get yourself fixed up. We're goin' to that program tonight."

"Goin' to . . . oh, changed your mind, have you?" There was a faint smile on Magda's face. "Thought you said you wouldn't be caught dead in all that crowd just to see a fool program."

"Yep, changed my mind. Our little Sonny boy is goin' to be there. I'm kind of lonesome to see him after all these years. He might be

46

disappointed if his old Jake and Magda wasn't there to admire him in all his fancy clothes."

"You better go shave, then, and put on your Sunday suit." Magda piled dishes and rose to carry them to the sink. "I'll just clear off. Won't take *me* long to pick out what I'm goin' to wear." She looked over her shoulder. "Jake, maybe soon I can have two good dresses so that I can choose which one to wear."

Jake guffawed. "Two dresses? A dozen, Magda. Our little Sonny is rich now, and he's goin' to remember his Jake and Magda that took such good care of him when he was growin' up." He reached down and eased off his shoes. "Maybe there'll be some fancy slippers for you too. Won't be havin' to walk to no program. How'd you like to be ridin' up in style, up to the front door, maybe, in a Cadillac or one of them foreign cars?"

"Aw, get dressed," said Magda.

Far up in the balcony they sat, Jake in his Sunday suit, Magda in her cheap dress.

"Where'd all the people come from, Jake?" Magda asked, turning her head from side to side. "Must be everybody that lives in Wauconda Falls is here. Won't be anybody at home tonight."

"Free show, warm night, someplace to go, nothin' better to do," muttered Jake. "Everybody's got to be goin' someplace these days."

"What do you suppose all them seats are for down there?"

"Where do you mean?"

"Down there on the floor." Magda pointed. "See them all roped off?"

"Oh, them. For the big shots probably. Got to have some fat asses, you know. We pay the taxes for this big pile of bricks, and somebody down yonder takes all the credit."

"Must be nice to be a big shot. I'd sure like to sit down close like that instead of way up here." Magda lowered her voice. "Jake, do you think I could have some popcorn?"

"Oh, for Christ's sake, Magda, you and your—"

"Maybe just the dime size, Jake?"

Jake raised the pitch of his voice. "Just the dime size, just a little one. A dime here, a dime there—" He stopped suddenly. "Sure," he said. He smiled. "Sure, why not? Hell, after tonight who's goin' to worry about a stinkin' little dime? You want some popcorn? We'll both have some." He motioned to the popcorn boy. "Hey, fellow, over here. Two of them. The quarter size."

They munched contentedly awhile.

"Jake," said Magda softly, "I think she was there this afternoon."

"She? This afternoon? Who you talkin' about?"

"You know who. *Her.* Suppose she figured to see her boy now that he's famous and rich?"

"My god, Magda. Do you suppose she'd have the nerve?" Jake's face hardened. "The bitch. I just bet she would. Sure, Magda, she'd want to cut in on us."

Magda leaned closer. "I think I seen her. Not sure—it's been such a long time. There was this woman standing off to the side. Had a big umbrella up and one of them floppy hats kind of down over her face. But when he came down off that airplane and along side, she turned to look real hard. Jake, I think it was her."

"Well, damn her if it was," Jake exploded.

"S'hhh, Jake, not so loud." She looked around uneasily. "People are lookin' at us." She grabbed his arm. "Oh, look, Jake, that fellow's comin' over here."

Jake looked up defiantly as an usher made his way toward them. "Lookin' for somebody, fellow?"

"Excuse me," the usher said politely. "Are you Jake Krasuski?"

"What if I am?"

"I have a message for a Jake Krasuski. Is that you?"

"Message? What kind of a message?"

"I was asked to give this to you—if you're Mr. Jake Krasuski."

"Yeah, I'm him. Give it here."

Jake snatched the envelope from the usher's hands, looked at it suspiciously, then glanced around, glaring at the people looking their way.

"Well, go on," said Magda. "Open it."

When Jake made no move, she snatched it from him and ripped the envelope open. She pulled out the paper inside.

"That's funny. No name. Can't tell who it's from."

"Who cares? What's it say? Come on, read it."

Together they read the typed words.

"I saw you at the airport this afternoon. It's been a long time—too long a time. We have some talking to do. I can't see you tonight, you understand. Be at home tomorrow afternoon and I'll come about four o'clock. I know where you live. I ought to."

They looked at each other, then read it again.

"Oh, Jake, he does remember us. He wants to see us. He's comin' to our house."

Jake smiled grimly. "It sure looks like it. He's goin' to walk right into our house all by himself. We won't even have to try to see him tonight."

Just then the lights dimmed and a dazzling spotlight lit up the arena floor. A procession of handsomely gowned women and smartly dressed men advanced across the floor to take their places in the special chairs roped off for them.

"Oh, look, Jake," whispered Magda. "Isn't that—I can't be sure—isn't that her?"

"Her? Who? Where?"

"Down there. Oh, you're too late," she said as the spotlight moved to the center of the floor, leaving the special guests in darkness.

"Wait a minute. He's going to introduce them. Listen."

As the master of ceremonies named the guests of honor and each took a bow, Jake and Magda watched intently

"Guess I was wrong. Didn't see her or hear any name."

"You're just imagining like always. Get an idea in your head—"

He broke off. "Listen Magda. That's *him* they're introducin'. Listen to them yell. That's our boy, Magda."

"Yes, listen to them," said Magda and reached out to grasp Jake's hand.

9 / *Saturday at 7:00 P.M.*

"Sorry I'm late, Marg. Something came up at the college," said Irving Redmond.

"Why, of course. Something's always coming up at the college." Margaret Redmond tried to sound calm and almost succeeded. "I'm

49

not sure if you're married to me or to the college."

"Don't worry," said Irving, giving his wife a quick hug and a kiss. "Not much pleasure in kissing a college or going to bed with it. You've still got the advantage, Marg."

"Silly! A little sweet talk to calm an upset wife," said Margaret, half pleased, half annoyed. "It won't work, especially if you're going to muss my hair with your flattery." She pointed to the table, neatly set. "Hattie kept your dinner warm, so sit down." She rang a bell. "Do you like my dress?"

He swept her with an appreciative glance. "Very nice. But what else? Anything you wear always looks stunning." He nodded to the maid who was bringing in a tray. "Looks awfully good, Hattie. Nice of you to keep it for me. I may be late, but I'll give it the attention it deserves."

"No trouble, Dr. Redmond. I just hope it's still good," said Hattie. "Could I bring you something, Mrs. Redmond?"

"A cup of coffee will be all, Hattie." She sat down opposite her husband. "I didn't take any chances. I ate my dinner in a civilized way. With you I never know." She paused as Hattie set the cup down before her. "Thanks, Hattie. That's all for a little while."

"Glad you liked my dress," Margaret continued. "You probably won't be seeing it the rest of the evening."

Irving paused in his eating. "Oh? Now what do you mean by that?"

"I mean that Mrs. Alcott. I hear she's quite a beauty."

"Well, good for her. And better yet for our lieutenant governor. Having a beautiful wife is a great help, as I ought to know." He took up knife and fork again. "Don't worry, Marg. Even if your Mrs. Alcott is as seductive as Cleopatra, I won't have time to fall under her spell. My attention will be directed to other people, and I'm hoping yours will be too."

"Aha, I think I smell a project in the air. And what little scheme is President Redmond thinking of promoting for the improvement of his college this so-called social evening?"

"Will you pass the jam over here, please? I see Hattie's turned out some of her delicious rolls again." He busied himself with spoon and jam jar.

"Come on, answer the question, Mr. President."

"Well, I hear there's a delegation from the State Arts Council here tonight. A nice hefty grant from the council along with a favorable recommendation to the Commission for Higher Education would help a lot toward getting our fine arts building."

"Why, of *course*. I should have guessed. Our fine arts building. Just what I've always wanted. Any woman would be the envy of all her discerning friends if she could display a nice new fine arts building."

"What?" Dr. Redmond looked annoyed, then he laughed a bit too heartily. "Oh, come off it, Marg. What's wrong with building up our campus? That's what a college president is for and how he makes his reputation. I don't intend to spend the rest of my life out here on the prairie, you know. You and I are intended for bigger and more important things."

"Like what, Irving?"

"Like president of a big university. Not that little poverty-stricken church school out west that was putting out feelers last year. I mean Ivy League or big state university." Fork raised high, he leaned forward eagerly. "I haven't told you, but I had a hint that a certain big school in Florida is asking questions."

"A certain big school in Florida. *Now* maybe I'm hearing you. Florida, Arizona, Hawaii, anyplace where it's warm and sunny and it doesn't get to twenty below zero in January and there's more than two weeks of summer."

"I know, Marg. Wauconda Falls isn't worthy of your charms and beauty nor of my ability. But you'll have to admit it's been good about helping me make a reputation. College presidents aren't chosen for their brains anymore. The alumni are looking for a man who can raise the money, get the buildings built, wangle grants, and get the budget passed. That's where I shine and where you've been a big help."

"Hooray for me!"

"So get in there and pitch tonight. The three women from the State Arts Council are all yours." He resumed his eating. "And I'll be working on Hamilton Alcott. I hear that Governor Shackleford is on his way out and that Alcott is the fair-haired boy."

"So the women are all mine, are they?" Margaret sighed. "Probably three old bags. Couldn't you let me work on the handsome lieutenant governor while you charm the old ladies? Come to think of it, are you sure it isn't the charming Mrs. Alcott that suggested this arrangement to you?"

"Aha, she's jealous." He tossed down his napkin, pushed back his

51

chair, and beckoned. "Come here." He folded his arms around his wife and gave her an ardent kiss. "That, Mrs. Redmond, is for your jealousy!"

"Well, if you put it that way," said Margaret with mock demureness, "how can I refuse? All right, I'll bedazzle the old witches while you work your spell on the lieutenant governor. Only, any remarks made to Mrs. Alcott must be strictly business."

"Strictly business, eh? Here's my word for it." He pulled her close again.

"All right, I'll take that as surety for your bond—for now." She gave him a gentle push. "Now you'd better get dressed. Your clothes are all laid out for you. As for me, I'd better tone down my makeup. Mustn't make my beauty too obvious. Older women don't like the contrast to be too great."

Halfway up the stairs, Irving turned to call down to his wife. "Who are the old gals, anyway? Know anything about them?"

"Just a minute and I'll look. That Anderton fellow sent out the list a few days ago. It's here someplace. Oh, yes, here it is. There's a Marjorie Yates, a Carolyn Warren, and a Phoebe Sears."

"Did you say Phoebe Sears?" asked Irving.

"That's right. I can hardly believe it myself, but it's really Phoebe. I didn't know they named anybody that anymore."

Irving Redmond was down the stairs and snatching the paper from his wife's hand. "Phoebe Sears."

"What's the matter, Irving? You look . . . upset."

"Upset? Oh, no." He forced a laugh. "Like you said, what a funny name." He turned. Over his shoulder he said, "Looks like you'll have an interesting evening." He took the stairs two at a time.

Margaret looked at him thoughtfully. "It isn't *that* funny."

In his upstairs den Irving Redmond reached for his phone. "Miss Stevens? Irving Redmond . . . Awfully sorry to bother you at this hour, but I'm trying to remember a name. . . . Who was the student the dean had in my office this afternoon, . . . a discipline problem. . . . Good for you, I knew you'd remember. . . . It isn't as if it were Smith or Jones. . . . Witold . . . Spell his last name slowly. Zacherewicz. These Polish names are pretty complicated. . . . I have it, thanks. . . . Could you possibly tell me how I could call him? . . . Oh, he's the only one in the phone book? Of course, with a name like that. . . . Thanks. Will you give me the number slowly, please? . . .

52

Hope you enjoy the show at the convention center and that your little nephew does well."

He sat thinking, then dialed another number. "Yes, I'd like to speak to Witold if he's there. Thank you.... Witold? This is Dr. Redmond.... Since you were in my office this afternoon I've been thinking.... Are you going to be busy tonight? ... You're going to the convention center? ... Could you plan to be there soon? ... A little more than an hour before show time. Oh, your friend Karyl is driving you.... Well, tell Karyl to park close to the stage entrance just off the parking lot, and I'll meet you at that door.... You remember you said you'd do just about anything to make up for that foolish stunt of yours? ... Well, I've a germ of an idea.... I'll see you there."

As he hung up, his lips puckered into a half grin. "This is crazy," he muttered to himself, "but if it's really Phoebe. Funny thing, the very thing Witold was being disciplined for is what I'm going to suggest as redemption.... Wonder how I can put it." He chuckled. "If I were fifteen years younger, I'd be tempted myself. Not much worse than some of the things we used to cook up."

"What's that?" called his wife. "Are you talking to me?"

"Was I talking? Oh, yes, I was just practicing a few words aloud just in case I have to say something."

10 / *Saturday at 7:10 P.M.*

Harold Anderton arrived at the convention center early. It wasn't that he had anything urgent to do. With nearly five thousand people depending on him to make everything go smoothly, he just had to be sure that everything was under control. The responsibilities of being master of ceremonies for such a large scale pageant were tremendous.

Then, too, there were those important people from Capital City to greet and introduce, plus the mayor and the representatives from the Labor Council and the Businessmen's Association, and the festival directors, so many names to remember. That television star Wayne Hitchcock was a worry. Would he be temperamental or arrogant? You never can tell about these actor fellows, you hear so many stories about them.

As he and his wife drove into the parking lot and pulled in next to a dilapidated old car right by the backstage entrance, he cried, "My list! I forgot the list, Alice."

"List? What list?" his wife asked.

"The lineup list for our entrance. I've got to have it."

"Here it is, Harold," she said quietly. "And I've got your copy of the program and your script too. They were on the hall table."

"Thank God! What if I didn't have it? I couldn't take the time to go back after it. Look at all the cars behind us, must be fifty lined up. Two minutes later and we'd have had to park way down there under the trees at the farthest end."

He flung his door open and strode around to the other side of the car. "Hang on to those for me, will you, Alice?" he said as he helped her out. "I've got a lot of things to see to before I want those lists and cues."

"Of course, Harold."

"Do I look all right?" He turned around for her inspection.

"You look positively handsome." Alice patted Harold's shoulder reassuringly, then she adjusted the handkerchief in his breast pocket.

"Look at all those people streaming into that entrance," said Harold. "I just hope I'm not too late."

"Now, Harold, don't get excited. Those are just the actors coming early. None of your people are likely to be here yet."

They walked to the dressing room entrance. "Evening, O'Malley," Harold Anderton said to the man guarding the door. "Looks like people are getting here early, doesn't it?"

"Good evening, Mr. Anderton, Mrs. Anderton. It's a good sign when people get here in plenty of time. There's an awful lot of folks in this show, over a thousand, I hear."

"Everything's O.K.?"

"So far, just fine. Everybody's had his pass—well, almost everybody. There was a couple of fellows hanging around just now, looked like they might be troublemakers, sort of hippie types. But when I told them they had to have passes to get in this door, they soon got lost."

"You don't think they might have been—they didn't look like they might be some of our special guests, O'Malley?"

"No indeed, Mr. Anderton, no way! These was just a couple of punks. Anyway, aren't your people supposed to come in the special entrance on the other side?"

"Yes, but I thought they might have gotten lost. Some of them are from Capital City—strangers, you know."

"Well, if any of them come here by mistake, I'll take care of them," said O'Malley.

"And you'll direct them to the Green Room?" asked Alice Anderton.

"Oh, sure, you can depend on it."

Alice took her husband's arm. "Of course, we can depend on Mr. O'Malley," she said, and she gave the doorman a smile. "Maybe we'd better get on, let the people behind us get to their places. Just where is that room we're supposed to meet in? I'm new to this building too."

"At the main hallway, turn right, Mrs. Anderton," said O'Malley. "It'll be the last door on your left before you come to the arena entrance. Want me to show you?"

"We'll find it all right. Thanks, Mr. O'Malley."

The Green Room turned out to be green in name only. The walls had been recently whitewashed. The smell of scarcely dried new plaster, plus the dank closeness of an unventilated basement made the place seem more like a tomb than a drawing room where actors could mingle with their admirers.

Some attempts had been made to soften the hard glare of unshaded bulbs reflecting on newly whitewashed walls by placing folding screens here and there. A beige carpet covered part of the gray cement floor and muffled echoing footsteps. A few chairs, an ornamental sofa, and a few small tables tried to give the impression that here was a place for relaxation and conversation.

As the Andertons entered, Alice shivered. "It's positively clammy in here, and it smells like I don't know what. Here Harold, prop open this door, and I'll open the one on the other side. I'll get this electric fan going. Maybe if we blow out some of this stale air—"

"Oh, I haven't got time, Alice," said Harold impatiently. "I've got to see if the chairs are in place and roped off, and there's the microphone to check—" and he was gone.

Alice looked after her disappearing husband, smiled, and

shrugged. She found the outlet, plugged in the cord of the fan and wedged open the doors. From her purse she took out an atomizer and sprayed perfume. With an exclamation, she picked up a long, thin cardboard box. "From the florist, attention Harold Anderton. Just like him not to tell anybody." She opened the box. "Gladioli, good! Red and yellow, these should add some color to this dreadful all white and beige," she said. "Here's a vase on this table. Well, *somebody* must have been told." She made a gesture of annoyance. "No water. Now what?"

Vase in hand, she walked to the nearest door and looked out. "I say, you two," she called. "Could you give me a hand?"

"You mean us?" Two young men came up to the door. One was dark haired and sported a scraggly mustache. "I don't know," he said. "We're supposed to be meeting somebody here."

"I just want you to take this vase and fill it with water. Isn't there a men's room there down the hall? It really shouldn't take you more than a minute."

"Oh, I guess we could do that," said the other youth. He had stringy blond hair and a pimply face. "You carry it, Karyl, and I'll run interference."

"Careful," said Alice. "It's glass and rather heavy."

"Got it," said the dark-haired Karyl. "Lead the way, Witty," he said, and they disappeared down the hallway.

Alice lifted the flowers carefully. "Nice long stems, that's good." She smiled brightly at the two when they returned. "There, that didn't take long. That looks like a good steady table for them over there. Now I'll just put these glads into your vase. Don't they look nice, boys?" Alice stepped back to admire the effect. "Oh, one more thing, as long as the person you're waiting for hasn't arrived yet. Would you lift this punch bowl out of the box for me? It's awfully heavy too."

"Sure," said Witty, and he reached down to lift a large glass bowl onto the table.

"And I need a strong pair of hands to open these bottles. The caps are twisted so tight I can't budge them. Will you, please?" she said as she handed a large bottle to dark-haired Karyl. He grasped it firmly, gave a twist, and off came the lid.

"See there," said Alice, "I just needed a strong muscled young man for that." Karyl smiled and proceeded to twist the lid off the second bottle.

"By the way, just who are you waiting for?" Alice asked.

Witty shuffled his feet a bit uneasily. "I'm supposed to see Dr. Redmond. He asked me to meet him here."

"Dr. Redmond? You mean the president of the junior college?"

"Yeah, that's him."

"Well, you're in the right place. This is where he will be coming sometime soon." As Karyl handed her another jar of liquid, Alice continued to make conversation. "Lucky for me he isn't here yet. I got your very-much-needed services. There are supposed to be several ladies here to do this, but it looks like they're going to be late. It just seems you can't depend on people anymore. Oh, Witty (is that you name?), there are a couple of plastic bags with ice cubes. Would you open them for me? Thanks. Now we'll just ease some cubes into the punch." She smiled at the blond boy. "Tell me, is your name really 'Witty'?"

"Naw, just a nickname," said Karyl. "We call him that because he ain't." He laughed crudely. "Witty, I mean."

"Now, Karyl, if that's your name, I just don't believe—" Alice broke off in the middle of the sentence. "Excuse me, boys. Thanks for the help. If you'd like a sip of punch for your trouble . . ." She moved quickly to the entrance on the far side of the room.

"Good evening," she said, extending her right hand. "You are the Ryans, aren't you? From the Labor Council? I'm Alice Anderton. We're so glad you can represent your organization at our Centennial Celebration tonight."

Beefy was the word that came to Alice's mind as she looked at the Ryans. Mr. Ryan wore a white coat stretched tightly over an ample belly. He had a short thick neck and a florid face with pendant jowls. With a huge paw extended, he moved toward Alice Anderton. "Pleased to meet you, Miz Anderton," said the gravelly voice.

Mrs. Ryan was almost as wide as she was tall, big of bosom, broad of beam, henna of hair. "Likewise," boomed her manlike contralto.

To Alice's relief, her husband bustled in just then. "Hello, Larry. Hello, Rose, glad to see you. Oh, it's going to be *quite* an evening. You should see the crowd already streaming in. Yes, indeed, quite an evening." He turned toward the doorway. "Oh, good, here are the Kubitzes."

Doll-like, thought Alice. The Kubitzes were miniatures. Scarcely five feet two, Tony Kubitz was a trim, smiling, ramrod-stiff little fellow. Close-cropped hair, an eyebrow of a mustache, a sharply tailored blue-and-white-striped jacket pulled tight, knife-edge-creased blue trousers, and trim blue-and-white shoes, this mini-model of male elegance advanced, smiling brightly.

"Good evening," he said, his voice high and reedy. "Happy to be here, Harold, Alice. You know Gini, of course."

Gini's little-girl voice matched her diminutive figure as she acknowledged the introduction. Alice noted with approval the blue-and-white chicness of Mrs. Kubitz. Best clothing store in town, and what a living advertisement, flashed through Alice's mind as she said aloud, "You know the Ryans, don't you?"

The Ryans and the Kubitzes surveyed each other with stony expressions.

"Sure, how are you, Kubitz?" rasped Larry Ryan.

"Glad to see you here," purred Tony Kubitz. The women smiled frostily.

"Well," said Alice Anderton quickly, "with our labor unions and our businessmen represented, we're ready for the evening, aren't we?" She looked from the Ryans to the Kubitzes anxiously. "Won't you have some punch, everybody?" Harold Anderton discreetly disappeared.

She seemed to be relieved to hear the babble of voices in the outer hallway. A man's voice was heard complaining.

"Well, I do hope the orchestra won't play too loud for my actors. Last night they simply covered the speaking voices in the pioneer scene. I might as well not have worked with the lines on that at all. Katzen, did you tell your conductor to watch that tonight?"

A second voice was heard. "Yes, I did. I hope you told your people to project more. After all, there's got to be a limit to how soft we can play if we want the music to be heard and appreciated."

A third voice was complaining. "I certainly hope that schoolroom comes to life tonight, Goody. At the dress rehearsal it was dead, drearily dead. Some of my best lines were lost."

"Don't worry, Dawson," came the sharp reply. "They'll read your lines as competently as they deserve."

Alice Anderton laughed. "Here comes the production staff. Nice friendly little bunch, aren't they?" She raised her voice to call, "Come in, folks. Do all of you know the Ryans and Kubitzes?" She made the introductions quickly, ending with, "And in case you haven't caught on, I'm Alice Anderton, pinch-hitting for my husband. As usual, Harold is somewhere else, checking on microphones and spotlights, I believe, as a good master of ceremonies should. Ah, here he is."

Harold Anderton bustled over officiously. "Hello, everybody. I see you know each other already. I have programs for you so you can keep track of what's going on. Handsome, aren't they?" He bowed to a small, dark woman. "Our convention treasurer took on this extra responsibility."

As the people broke up into little groups, Alice moved quickly to the hall entrance where a striking woman in a gold sheath had entered.

"Why, Mrs. Redmond, good evening. Isn't Dr. Redmond here with you?"

"He's about. You know Irving," she laughed lightly, "even tonight he's got some business to attend to. He's out in the hall having a bit of a conference with somebody."

Alice glanced out through the doorway. "Those are the two nice young men who gave me a helping hand earlier this evening. I do hope they're not in some kind of trouble."

"If they are, Irving will handle it, you can be sure. Meanwhile, I'll wait right here until he's free."

Irving Redmond was heard saying, "There's a little side room over here where we can talk. Come with me."

Margaret Redmond frowned. "I do hope he won't be long. Really, this is very awkward," she sighed. "It would be nice to have a husband at the right time and place."

In the little side room, Irving Redmond spoke softly. "Karyl, we'll start with you. Are you willing to help Witold, here?"

"Of course, Dr. Redmond."

"You have your car?"

"Yes, it's parked right outside the entrance. We got here right away, got the first place."

"You mean that very old—er—model automobile?"

"Yes, that's my old Dodge, Dr. Redmond."

"Well, I wonder if you'll be willing to make a trade. After the program starts, will you drive your Dodge away and put mine in its place? I've got a rented car down there under those trees at the far end. Then at 9:40, Karyl, you be in my car with the motor running. When Witold here comes running out, you drive him away as fast as you can."

59

"Where should I drive him, Doctor?"

"Oh, just down the street, maybe in the alley behind the filling station. Then you two can come back and get Karyl's Dodge again."

Karyl shook his head. "I don't quite get it, Dr. Redmond. But if it will help Witty, I guess I could do that."

"Very good, Karyl. You will be helping your friend here, be sure of that."

When Karyl had left, Dr. Redmond turned to the blond Witold.

"Now, Witold, you know how we feel about that silly—er—demonstration you put on in the auditorium last Wednesday."

Witold hung his head and shuffled his feet.

"You know it was a foolish, daring thing to do. You know I could expel you from school and that that would be the end for you."

"Yes, I understand," mumbled Witold.

"Yet somehow I can't believe that you meant to be really *bad*. I have to suspect that it was just a silly schoolboy prank done by an overgrown little boy who wasn't thinking straight."

"Yes, that was it, Dr. Redmond," said Witold eagerly. "Some of us were talking about how it happened at some other schools. Like I told you, it was a dare. Some of the fellows bet me twenty dollars I wouldn't do it. I guess I . . ." his voice trailed off.

"Yes, some of the fellows. That's always the excuse, isn't it. Never your own fault, somebody else to blame." Witold stood in silence, eyes cast down. "Well, I've decided on a very drastic way for you to make up for this silliness, this schoolboy dare. I've heard you say you'd do anything to square yourself, to put yourself right again."

"Oh, yes, Dr. Redmond, anything."

"I wonder. It may be something you will find too hard to do. A silly schoolboy dare is one thing, a really bold act is something else."

"Just tell me what it is that you want me to do, Dr. Redmond. I'll try it."

"Well, we'll just see." Irving Redmond lowered his voice and spoke into Witold's ear. Witold listened, mouth agape, eyes widening in surprise.

"Here?" he gasped, "tonight? I—oh, I couldn't do that."

"Just as I thought, Witold. You were brave enough on a dare from your so-called friends. For twenty dollars, was it? This is for a lot more than twenty dollars, and now you chicken out."

"But here, Dr. Redmond? All these people? My god—excuse me, sir—that's an awful lot you're asking."

"All right, Witold, we'll forget it. I found out what I want to know about you. Come to my office Monday morning." Irving Redmond started to walk away.

"Your office? You mean . . . gee, I don't know." Witold hesitated. "Would you let me think a minute?"

"Well—all right. I'll come back in a few minutes," Irving walked a few more steps, then turned again. "We could make it easier for you. A mask over your face and your hair pulled back."

"A mask? They wouldn't see my face to recognize me? Well . . . that sounds . . . Please let me think about this."

"You just go ahead and think. I'll be back in about ten minutes. Or better yet, you just come to that doorway when you're ready, and I'll come on out."

Irving Redmond strode down the hall. "Sorry, Marg," he said to his wife. "Thanks for waiting for me. Shall we make our grand entrance now?" He took her arm lightly and they swept into the Green Room.

"Oh, there you are, Dr. Redmond, Mrs. Redmond," called Harold Anderton. "I'm glad you've come. There are some people I want you to meet." Harold guided the Redmonds across the room, talking as he went. "These are the representatives of the State Arts Council. They've come up from Capital City."

"Sounds like your cue, Marg," whispered Irving. "Front and center ready to go."

"This is Mrs. Yates, Mrs. Warren," said Anderton, "and this is Phoebe Sears." A short, spare woman dressed in purple turned abruptly. "Dr. Redmond."

There was a moment of silence as Phoebe Sears looked at Irving Redmond. "Dr. Redmond, did you say?" Her voice was loud and raspy. "Dr. Redmond? Haven't I met you someplace before? Let's see, . . . back in New York State, it seems to me. Only the name doesn't seem quite right. You did say 'Redmond'?"

"Irving Redmond," said Harold Anderton firmly.

"I wonder," said Irving suavely, "if you have me confused with some other person. I'm sure if I'd have met you, I'd remember it." He smiled.

"I don't ever forget a face. And yours is certainly familiar."

A loud scream rang from down the hallway. Everybody froze. From out in the corridor came shouts. "Sonny! It's Sonny!"

"Oh, good heavens," wailed Harold Anderton as he rushed to the

61

door. "It's Wayne Hitchcock and they're mobbing him. They'll tear the clothes off him. Oh, this is terrible."

Everybody moved toward the door. Harold held up hands to stop them. "Thank God, I see some policemen! Yes, they've gotten him away from those—those—teen-agers." Harold looked relieved. "Yes, he's all right now. Here he comes. . . . Oh, Mr. Hitchcock, are you all right? Sorry about—"

The handsome Mr. Hitchcock strode into the room, smiling broadly. "Good evening, everybody." There was the sound of applause. "Well, thank you, folks. I appreciate the welcome." He waved and smiled. "It's been a long time since I left my hometown here. It's good to be back. Why, there's my old dramatic coach, Mr. Goodman. How are you, Mr. Goodman. . . . Do I dare to call you Goody after all these years? And isn't that Mr. Dawson?" Talking and gesturing, he moved across the room, followed by a crowd of admirers.

At the opposite side of the room three figures appeared in the doorway. "It's Mayor McGinty," somebody called. The Andertons hurried to greet them.

"Good evening, Your Honor. How are you, Mrs. McGinty, Mrs. Cline. This is a very important evening, Mr. Mayor," said Harold.

"Oh, what a beautiful dress," said Alice, "such a striking shade. And I love your beads. Amethysts, aren't they?"

"Thank you, Alice, dear," said Maude. "Yes, something special for a very special occasion."

"Could I guess?" asked Mrs. Cohen, who had moved quickly to shake Maude's hand. "Didn't I hear something about a—well, a certain bequest—"

"S'hhh, Judith. Not yet. The announcement comes later," said Maude.

"Aha," said Alice. "Sounds intriguing. I love important secrets."

"You know almost everybody here, Joe," whispered Harold Anderton. "But I'd better introduce you to the ladies from the State Arts Council." With the slightest of glances at Maude's cane he said, "Just stay right here. I'll bring them to you."

He was back in a moment. "This is Marjorie Yates. And this is Carolyn Warren, Mayor and Mrs. McGinty. And this is Phoebe Sears."

A sudden hush fell as all turned to stare. Phoebe Sears and Maude McGinty froze. "Purple," gasped Marg Redmond to her husband. "Good God, they've both got almost the same dress. How awful."

It was the mayor who broke the silence. "Well, well, Mrs. Yates, Mrs. Warren, Miss Sears, how nice of you to take the trouble to honor us on this auspicious occasion. A hundred years to be celebrated and a fine new convention center to be dedicated at the same time. We're proud of both items, and we bid you welcome."

Elsie Cline took Maude's arm and gently maneuvered her toward the punch bowl. Marg Redmond engaged the trio of visitors in an animated conversation. The mayor linked arms with Tony Kubitz and Larry Ryan. The production staff huddled around Sonny Hitchcock. Nobody noticed Irving Redmond as he beckoned at the doorway nor heard him say softly, "She's the one in the purple dress. Can you see her? O.K. Good luck. If you carry it off, you'll be a free, forgiven student again."

Nor did anyone notice as the door on the far side of the room opened and a man entered cautiously. Except that he seemed to be in some type of uniform, something like a chauffeur's outfit, there was nothing distinguishing about him. He looked carefully about the room as if inspecting it, then he moved to Mayor McGinty and said a few words.

Quickly the mayor moved toward the entrance, hand extended, a broad smile on his Irish face. "Welcome. Come in, come in," he called in a loud voice. "Good evening, Mr. Alcott, Mrs. Alcott." All heads turned, all eyes stared. There were soft murmurings. "Wow . . . she's gorgeous. . . . Isn't she lovely? . . . So that's her."

"Ladies and gentlemen, may I present the Honorable Hamilton Alcott, our lieutenant governor, and his lovely wife, Rosemary Alcott."

There was a burst of applause. Hamilton Alcott bowed formally. "Good evening, my friends of Wauconda Falls. Thank you for your invitation to be here. We are honored, Mrs. Alcott and I, to join with you in celebrating this important occasion in your city's history. I hope, your Honor, you will be good enough to introduce us to all of these wonderful people."

Speaking and gesturing excitedly, Irving Redmond was at the lieutenant governor's side with Harold Anderton hovering eagerly nearby. Mrs. Redmond was talking earnestly to the three ladies of the State Arts Council. Sonny Hitchcock, sensing where the center of attention was shifting, had maneuvered himself so he could monopolize Rosemary Alcott as a circle of admirers gathered around the two of them.

Off at the side, Maude McGinty tapped her cane impatiently. "What a disappointment. That awful woman, in my dress. Oh, I could scream."

11 / Sunday at 12:15 A.M.

It was well after midnight before Detective Ross and Officers Conners and Mulvany got back to headquarters.

"God, what a night this turned out to be," said Mike Mulvany.

Barney Ross nodded grimly. "Bad enough to have a murder. But did it have to be the mayor's wife? Did you hear the late news broadcast? 'Streaker strikes, mayor's wife dies!' I can just see the headlines tomorrow morning." Barney sagged wearily into his chair and rested his elbows on the desk.

"It could have been worse, you know. Like the lieutenant governor's wife," said Curt Conners.

"That story Harry Manson was telling us? Yes, that could have happened—if the story is true," said Barney. "That's one of the first things we'll have to check in the morning."

"In the morning?" asked Mike. "What do you think it is now?"

"You're right, Mike," said Barney. "I know it's late. Want to call your wife?" He pointed to the desk phone. He turned to Curt while Mike was dialing. "Glad you're still a bachelor, Red," he said softly. "It's kind of hard on the wives and families." He nodded toward the outer office. "How about seeing if there's some coffee? Sometimes they don't empty out the urn, and if you don't mind it being a little strong, you can heat up what's left."

"We've got a murder," Barney began when Curt and Mike had settled opposite Barney's desk with cups in hand. "Not just an ordinary little murder in a back alley or a barroom brawl but one done right out in the open with five thousand people looking on laughing and cheering. Everybody saw him do it, but who was he? Out of nowhere and back to nowhere.

"How'd he do it? Stabbed with a knife. But where'd he get the knife? He didn't have any clothes on, so there was no place to hide it, yet there it was.

"Who got murdered? Maude McGinty, our mayor's wife, about as unlikely a victim as you could pick—a quiet homebody who's lived here all her life, of good reputation. So what was the motive? Robbery? Nothing was taken. A jealous lover? Ridiculous. Maude McGinty wasn't the kind of woman men would play around with. Revenge? For what? So out of this unlikely mess we've got to find the killer and fast, with His Honor and the city fathers breathing down our necks."

"That's the beauty of it," said Curt. "I mean the crime, not the city fathers. Somebody with a very clever brain figured this out." He had a bright gleam in his eye. "It's all so senseless and impossible. That's the idea."

"That's my boy, Red," said Barney. "You've got something clicking under that carrottop of yours. Keep talking, boy. Explain yourself."

"Well, first of all, the way it was done. Surprise and shock. You break into the middle of a show when everybody's mind is on what's happening down there on the stage. You don't just appear, you come naked. What happens? Everybody's shocked. And when they're shocked, they scream, they laugh, they clap—but they don't think. They cover their eyes or they stare at you know what, and nobody sees anything important. And while they are in shock, you move fast, before anybody can come to enough to stop you."

"And where'd he get the knife?" asked Mike.

"I can think of a couple of ways. You brought the weapon, didn't you, Barney? Been checked for prints so we can handle it?"

Barney nodded and produced a long thin copper blade.

"This isn't really a knife. It's an ornament, probably a letter opener." Curt held it up. "The kind people keep on their desks for looks as well as use. About eight inches long; a flat polished metal handle, maybe half an inch wide; then a long thin blade only about a quarter inch wide tapering to a sharp point. Not much good for cutting and slicing, but with that sharp point, just fine for stabbing."

"Sure, I see that," said Mike. "But where would a naked man carry that?"

"He could carry it in his hand like this." Curt put the flat handle in the palm of his hand, with the blade extending up his inner arm. Bending his fourth and fifth fingers to grasp the blade, he spread his arms wide. "Remember, he did a spread eagle. How many people would notice this blade against my arm, especially if I move fast and when they're sure to be looking at something more exciting than my arm?"

Barney nodded approvingly.

"But I think there's another way, maybe better." Curt pulled from his pocket a circlet of brown cloth with a feather attached. "I found this in the Indians' dressing room along with a loincloth. Our Indian might have dropped them in his hurry to exit. Now notice, Mike, when I slip this over your head the feather sticks up in the air."

"Sure, what's unusual about that? All the Indians did that tonight."

"Well, look at this." Curt removed the band from Mike's head and pointed to the base of the feather. "Notice where the feather is sewed on to the cloth? Well, look at this extra little pocket." He inserted his finger into a little fold of cloth, about half an inch wide and almost two inches deep. "Now let's try again." Curt slipped the handle of the letter opener into the extra pocket, then replaced the circlet on Mike's head. "There's your weapon, streaker, sticking up in the air right behind the feather. So you're absolutely naked, aren't you, Mike. Five thousand people are prepared to swear to it. Yet there it is, ready for you to grab. You remember that Mrs. Yates said the streaker put his hand up to his wig."

"Nice going, Red," said Barney. Mike reached up and pulled out the letter opener and acted as if he were to stab Curt. "Sure works, all right," he said.

"You say you found this and a loin cloth?" asked Barney.

"Haven't had a chance to tell you yet. I tried to catch up with the streaker, you know. I couldn't—too many people got in my way." Curt told how he had been delayed by the band players, of the first stagehand and his mention of a mask.

"Haven't had a chance to figure that one out yet. That Miss Sears said the streaker's eyes were blue. This stagehand says he was wearing a mask. I don't think you can tell the color of a guy's eyes through a mask. Or can you?" Curt shook his head and looked thoughtful.

He resumed. "Saw this second stagehand. He told of seeing this older fellow hanging around the Indians' dressing room—war paint and feathers and all that. Gave me a little to go on. Five feet nine or ten, neither skinny nor fat—that is, if this was the streaker."

Mike Mulvany snorted. "Five feet nine or ten, not fat nor skinny, blue eyes. Must be a couple of thousand fellows like that."

"Yeah, I know, but there's more," said Curt. He told O'Malley's tale of the old Dodge car being replaced by a rented car, of the figure dashing out and being driven away. "If that *was* the streaker, then we've got a well-planned murder. A driver, maybe two, a car waiting for a quick getaway right on schedule. There would have to be more than one fellow in on this, and a careful plan made."

Barney looked up from his note-taking. "An old Dodge, a rented car? There's something to go on." He turned to Mike Mulvany.

"You were on duty there too, Mike. What can you tell me?"

"Well, when the streaker came out, I—well, I couldn't believe what I was seeing. Like Red here says, I froze for a minute. Then when he began coming toward us, I started for him. I—" he hesitated. "I started, but I tripped. Doc Quinlan had put his bag down on the floor. I guess my foot hit it, because I lost my balance and sent the bag sliding. By the time I caught myself, the streaker was bending over Mrs. McGinty. I made for him, but he was too fast. I saw Red taking out after him, so I turned just in time to see Mrs. McGinty's head go down, and she slumped onto the floor.

"I thought at first she fainted from fright or something, so I stretched her out on the floor and motioned for Doc Quinlan to come. I saw the lady that was sitting next to her bent over like she was going to pass out too. Mrs. Quinlan was coming right along with Doc, so I told her to look after the second lady. The mayor was making for his wife; I grabbed his arm because Doc had his stethoscope out. I heard Doc say 'I can't get any pulse nor heartbeat.' Then he motioned to me and said, 'Get an ambulance and clear the way. I think she's been attacked. Got any more policemen around?' So I high-tailed it out into the lobby.

"I found Kottke and Garrison; sent Kottke to phone for an ambulance and extra help, and Garrison to get some assistance with crowd control.

"That took only about five minutes. By the time I got back, most of the VIP's had caught on that something was up. Couple of women were helping Mrs. Quinlan, and some of the men were with the mayor. Doc Quinlan waved me over to him. That's when he flashed the light and I saw the knife sticking out and heard Doc say she was already dead.

"You came along then, Barney. How come you got there so quick?"

"I was already there. My niece's daughter was one of the dancers. When I saw the streaker and Red here going after him and you running around, I knew something was up. I heard my name called so came right on down."

"Good thing you were there, Barney," said Mike.

"Before we go on, Red, you said there were a couple of other things about the streaker. Want to tell us now?" asked Barney.

"You say it isn't enough to know that the streaker is five feet nine or ten and has blue eyes. Will it help to know he's left-handed?" asked Curt.

"Left-handed?" asked Mike. "Now how the hell do you figure that out?"

"By the way the knife was sticking in the body."

"Oh, come on, Red, what're you giving us."

"Well, Mike, you just take the letter opener. Now pretend you're coming at me. You want to hit me just below the breastbone. Aim the point there and act like you're stabbing me."

Mike grabbed the knife and jabbed it at Curt.

"There. Hold it, Mike," said Curt. "Notice it's going into me a little bit from the right, at about a twenty-degree angle."

Barney nodded. "And that's what you were signaling to me? I got it. The blade was slanting in to the *left*. Take it in your left hand, Mike, and try again."

"Sure enough," said Mike, looking at the angle of the blade. "That's a big help. Left-handed guys with blue eyes aren't quite so common, either. Only a couple hundred."

"There's one more thing," said Curt. "You got a good look at him, Mike. Was he cut?"

Mike stared blankly. "Cut?"

"I mean, was he circumcised?"

Mike shrugged his shoulder and extended his hands, palms up. "How should I know? Only, now that you mention it . . . It's possible he wasn't. Yeah, I think I can see . . . I'm not sure, but maybe—"

"Well, I am sure," said Curt. "I'm not cut either. Maybe I'm a little extra conscious about it, but there aren't very many of us these days; that's why I notice."

Mike's laugh was scornful. "So now all we have to do is go around looking for a guy that's not circumcised." He raised his voice and in an affected tone said, "Pardon me, but could I take a look? I want to see if you've been circumcised." He laughed again. "No way, Red, no way."

"O.K.," said Barney Ross, "we've gone as far as we can for now on the streaker. Let's talk about the weapon." He pointed to the letter opener on the desk. "Doc Quinlan says that death was quick, owing to a stab right into the heart."

"In a way," said Curt, "that makes it simpler. No gun, so no ballistics; no poison, so no lab tests; no blows on the head to be analyzed."

"Any fingerprints?" asked Mike.

"None. Doc was careful not to touch the handle until after we got to the morgue and we'd had a chance to dust."

"You know, that's sort of funny," said Curt. "The killer must have had a firm grip, and the handle is perfect for picking up prints. You'd think there'd have been a thumbprint at least." As he spoke, he picked up the letter opener, grabbed the handle firmly, and held the blade directly in front of himself. "Notice how my thumb has got to press down hard? Wonder how it got wiped clean.

"There's one thing, though," he continued. "If this is part of a desk set, we'll find who sells such things. Maybe they can tell us who bought something like this."

"Worth a try," said Barney, making a note.

"Now let's talk about motive," Barney continued. "Why Maude McGinty? Who'd want to get rid of her? Middle-aged, lame, doesn't get out very much, noted for charities and civic projects like a good mayor's wife should be. Never any scandal I ever heard about."

"Still she's a woman," said Curt. "Maybe something long ago."

"Yes, but why such a screwy way to do it? How easy to knock the cane out from under her, a push downstairs, an accident at home. Why all the pizzazz with bright lights, crowd looking on, cars moving on schedule, a couple of guys in on the deal? All for Maude McGinty? Makes no sense."

"Unless," interrupted Curt, "it wasn't supposed to be Maude McGinty but somebody else."

"Oh, yes, back to the story about Mrs. Alcott's first husband, the switch in the seating arrangement?" said Barney.

"What are you talking about?" asked Mike.

"Your beautiful doll, the lieutenant governor's wife, was married before to a small-time crook," said Curt. "He gets nabbed in a heist and is sent to the pen. She divorces him while he's in the clink. Along comes handsome Alcott, and she marries him. Now husband number one is out on parole and feeling sore since his ever-loving wife threw him over."

"It's a made-to-order motive," Curt continued. "The jealous lover two-timed by his woman. Heads straight for where she is, goes at her with a knife, only, in the excitement he gets the wrong dame." He shook his head. "Perfect, except for a couple of things."

"Oh?" asked Barney Ross. "Like what, Red?"

"Just out of jail, yet he gets a team together and works out a fancy job. Husband number one (What was his name, Barney? Oh, yeah, Benito DiVacco) must have been a big shot in the brotherhood to get going so fast."

"Makes sense, Red," said Barney. "What else?"

"Not murder. Any smart operator would see his chance better than that. You know: 'Pay up or I'll sing my song to the newspaper boys! You got plans, Mr. Alcott? What if it comes out your beautiful wife was married to a crook before she married you? How much is it worth to both of us to keep this hush-hush?' Should be good for a steady stream of blackmail." Curt shook his head. "I'm not saying we should wipe this out, in case DiVacco is more hot-tempered than smart, but I don't think we should buy it right away either."

Barney nodded. "Right now, I hope you're right. It's bad enough to have our mayor's wife involved, but if we get people from the state mixed up in this, all hell may break loose. We get in *that* kind of a ball game, one false move and we'd be the ones getting the knife."

Mike Mulvany sighed. "Besides, she's such a gorgeous dish."

"Watch it, Mike," jeered Curt. "Your tongue's hanging out."

"While we're talking about getting a wrong victim," Curt continued, "how about the other women? Maybe one of them was supposed to be the lucky gal. Mike's sex kitten might not have a corner on the shameful past."

"Well, let's see," said Barney, getting out his notes. "There was Mrs. Anderton, Dr. Redmond's wife, and those three dames from Capital City—some kind of committee—all in the front row."

"Not likely Mrs. Anderton," said Mike. "Anybody that'd marry fussy Harold must have been desperate, not the sexy type."

"Now Mrs. Redmond's a different package," said Curt. "She

looks like she's been around. As for the three others, seems to me they're pretty well over the hill for anything like that.

"Miss Sears, a raspy-voiced old maid? No man'd get close to her. More than likely does her murdering with her tongue, doesn't need a knife. Mrs. Warren, a me-too gal, not enough push to think up a murder or make anybody mad at her. Mrs. Yates—well, maybe, if you go back forty years.

"Of course, it doesn't have to be sex and the jealous lover," he continued. "Could be politics or some shady money—hand in the till or under the table. Or maybe somebody who has been smeared by the Sears witch."

"I think," said Barney, "we'll get the chief to use his Capital City connections to do some checking on that. Somebody down there would know. Also if there's any scuttlebutt about our 'glamorous Mrs. Alcott."

"Barney," said Curt, "while we're talking about the broads, how about the men?"

"The men? Oh, you mean our streaker boy got mixed up and was aiming at one of the . . . but that'd have to be Joe McGinty, His Honor himself. Now who'd want to be attacking our mayor, always smiling, always making with the Irish jokes?"

"He's a politician," said Curt. "Sometime he must have made somebody mad, decided the wrong way, something that's been eating somebody for a long time. Which would throw it right back into our own town again."

"Unless it was the lieutenant governor. Remember that switch in places," said Barney Ross.

"Oh, yeah, . . . back in Capital City again."

"Or if it was Harold Anderton they wanted," started Curt.

"Anderton? Who'd want him?" Mike's voice was scornful.

"Or Dr. Redmond. Is he having a feud with anybody?" said Curt thoughtfully. "A guy like him who's on the make doesn't have enemies? He's always sucking around for everybody to be on his side. But could be that somebody's jealous. Could be he might have fired somebody once or kicked a student around that's still carrying a grudge."

"God, what a mess," said Mike. "Suspects all over the place. While you're at it, how about the second row?"

"You mean the local guys and gals? Can't see any of them being involved at the killing level," said Curt. "Music director Katzen,

71

script writer Dawson, dramatic coach Goodman. They're interested in making the show go, not in any hanky-panky. Balkan's for publicity, but not this kind. Mrs. Cohen is treasurer and was sitting way over at the end. Ryan, the labor president. Any labor unrest lately? Mr. and Mrs. Kubitz, they're from the Businessmen's Association, might have had a run-in with His Honor a long time ago."

"Don't forget Dr. Quinlan," said Mike.

"Dr. Quinlan. You know, I wonder about him."

"Another idea cooking, Red?" asked Barney.

"It's funny about his happening to have his little black bag and instruments right there. Not usual for doctors to carry them in to a show. Usually leave the bag in the car." Curt turned to Mike. "Wasn't he the first one to touch Maude McGinty?"

"No, I was," said Mike. "I saw her bend over and start to slide out of her chair, so I grabbed her and eased her down onto the floor."

"Did you see a knife handle sticking out?"

"No, but it was dark and I wasn't looking for anything. I thought she fainted—you know, shock at having that naked guy come right up to her. So I was signaling to Doc Quinlan to come."

"Did you watch Quinlan when we went to work on her?" asked Curt.

"Hell, no, I was getting help for that what's-her-name friend who was starting to faint too."

Barney was looking hard at Curt. "Are you thinking, Red, that maybe Doc Quinlan gave her the knife while she was passed out on the floor?"

"Not for sure, Barney. Just thinking of all the possibilities. In case we find some bad feeling between the mayor and Doc or between the wives."

A heavy silence fell. Barney Ross was looking at his notes. Mike Mulvany was leaning his head on one hand, eyes drooping. Curt Conners was staring into space.

Finally, Barney Ross cleared his throat and shuffled his papers to break the quiet. "It's late, men, and we've got lots to do tomorrow and the next day, too.

"Before we break up, here's some of the items to get right onto first thing."

"What do you mean, 'first thing'?" asked Mike sleepily. "Noon, I hope."

"Noon, hell. Eight o'clock. But neither of you have to be around on this. You've got your regular assignments to take care of."

"Let's hear what's to be done," said Curt.

"O.K., here's my list," said Barney. "Here's what we have to do." He handed Curt a paper on which he had written. Mike read over Curt's shoulder.

Check with the auto-rental agency to learn who rented cars. Check with Harry Manson. What about Mrs. Alcott's first husband?

Find Sheppard, the head usher; Henderson, the fire marshall; O'Malley, the doorkeeper; and maybe those four ushers that helped Mulvany.

Find the two stagehands that Conners talked to, especially the second one.

Who sells desk sets? Who've they sold them to around Wauconda Falls?

Ask chief to get some inquiries going down at Capital City. Most of all, be on the lookout for a youngish man, five feet nine or ten, who's left-handed and uncircumcised [Mike laughed coarsely at this] and oh, yes, probably has blue eyes.

"Let's call it a night and get some sleep," said Barney, stuffing papers into his bag.

Mike stood up. "The old lady's waiting. See you." He left.

"Barney," said Curt slowly, "I'd like to work with you on this. Do you suppose the chief will let me? You know how I like detective work, and there's damn little chance for it around here. And besides . . ."

"Besides what, Red?"

"Besides, I feel pretty foolish about tonight. I should have caught that damned son of a bitch. If I hadn't frozen stiff, if I'd used my head, I'd have run him down. So I've got a special reason for asking."

"Got you, Red. I don't think I'll ask the chief; I'll just tell him."

12 / *Saturday at 11:55 P.M.*

It was nearly midnight when Gordon "Goody" Goodman, teacher of drama at Wauconda Falls High School and coach for the centennial pageant, heard the doorbell ring. He put down his magazine and was getting up from his chair when the door opened and Wayne Hitchcock walked in.

"Sonny! You came." Goody spread his arms wide and moved across the room to envelope the younger man in his embrace. "Let me look at you." Goody put a hand on each of Sonny's shoulders and held him at arm's length. "God, but I'm glad to see you. You look wonderful." He frowned. "But tell me, you big ham, what trick did you use to get in by yourself? I could have sworn that door was locked."

"It was. I used this." Sonny Hitchcock grinned as he held up a key.

"Where did you get that?"

"Why, you gave it to me. Don't you remember? Or is twelve years too long ago for your busy mind to have hung on to such a detail?"

"I can remember, but I can't believe! You've still got that same key? After all this time?"

"Sure thing. It's been a kind of good-luck charm. Whenever things get rough and I feel sort of low, I bring it out and hold it in my hand. I say to myself, 'I can always go back there. Goody will take me in.' And each time I do that, one of my lucky breaks comes along and things get better."

He put the key to his lips. "From the time you gave this little key to a snot-nosed Polack hood, it's been bringing me the lucky breaks. You didn't see Tony Krasuski tonight, you know. You saw Wayne 'Sonny' Hitchcock, glamorous star of television. Some improvement, yes?" He bowed elaborately.

"Some improvement. A real fine performance." Goody nodded approvingly.

"Same old place." Sonny Hitchcock walked around the room. "God, but it looks good. Same picture, I see. Oh, oh, a new stereo. You probably needed that—I sure helped to wear the old one out. H'mmm, there's that old easy chair where I used to read so many of your books. You remember. *Me*, the stupid no-good they couldn't teach to read." He reached out an arm and pulled the older man close to him. "Those were good days for me. Sometimes I think I'd like to tell them all to stick it and come back here to live with you again. This was the first place I ever felt welcome, and you were the first person that ever"—his voice dropped in pitch—"that ever loved me."

Gordon Goodman was listening to Sonny with a half smile on his lips and a look of puzzled wonder in his eyes. Gradually he pulled himself away and moved the young man around in front of him.

"What the hell are you talking about?" He put out one hand to gently tweak an ear. "You been drinking too much? Or are you getting maudlin at coming back home after all these years? Aren't you being hard on your father and mother in all of this first-that-ever-loved business?"

Sonny gave a short, hard laugh. "My 'father and mother'? You mean old man Krasuski and his stupid wife? You must have known they weren't my parents. The only reason I was living with them was that a check came in every month from somebody.

"I could tell when it was the first of the month, you know. They'd give me a bath, cut my hair, feed me a good breakfast for a change, put on the special suit they kept locked up the rest of the month, and we'd all parade off to church, the picture of an ever-loving family. I never did know who was supposed to see this little show—my first starring role." His lip curled. "The rest of the month I was *the little bastard* that ate too much, got his clothes dirty, wet the bed. Just how old do you think I was before I began to catch on?"

"You mean the Krasuskis weren't your real . . ." said Goody. "You were adopted?"

"Not even adopted. It was all for money. They let me use their name, gave me a home, such as it was, all for pay—strictly business—and they were pretty good at making a profit out of it. The less they fed me, the fewer clothes they bought me, the bigger the profit."

His expression softened. "Remember that night? You let me be on the stage crew—strong back, weak mind, I suppose. Ten o'clock, it was snowing hard, nobody showed up to get me. You drove me out there. House locked up tight, not a light showing. My ever-lovin' Krasuskis out and to hell with the poor bastard. So you brought me up here to spend the night."

Gordon Goodman nodded. "Yes. I remember wondering what kind of parents would do that to a kid."

75

"And I didn't want to come here with you." Sonny opped his eyes. "But there wasn't anyplace else to go, and when I got here, it was so—well, soft lights and you turned on some nice music..."

Sonny glanced out of the corner of his eyes at Gordon, then gave a self-conscious laugh. "I remember the awful sinking feeling I got down in my stomach when you told me to take off my clothes, go into the bathroom, and take a shower. I was worried and ashamed."

"Ashamed? Worried? Why?" Then his eyes widened. "Oh, for God's sake, Sonny, you were afraid I was going to ask you to—"

"Let you play around with me?" Sonny laughed softly. "No, I wasn't worried about that. I was ashamed because—" He hesitated, then with a wry expression he continued. "I was ashamed to have you see what dirty ragged underwear and socks I was wearing."

Gordon threw back his head and laughed. After a few minutes, Sonny joined him in the laughter.

"I can laugh at it now," he said, "but it wasn't funny then. People thought I dressed like a hood because I wanted to. I didn't. My stingy caretakers didn't give me anything better to wear. The only decent clothes I had were locked up except for special occasions. I wasn't only the dumb kid who couldn't read and the bad kid that made trouble—I was the dirty kid, too, that nobody wanted to touch. I didn't want to be."

Goody stopped laughing abruptly.

"Well, when I got out of the shower," Sonny continued, "there was a pair of clean pajamas. Did you guess that was the first pajamas I ever wore? And there was a plateful of sandwiches for a guy who hadn't eaten much all day, and a clean bed made up on that sofa over there." He got a faraway look in his eyes. "We sat and listened to that music while I was eating, music I'd never heard before. Then you said, 'There's your bed, my boy. Good night,' and you turned off the music, went into your bedroom, and closed the door. That was the first time I can remember that anybody anywhere was nice to me in all my life—just to be nice, I mean. You never asked anything in return. You didn't even touch me... not *that* night, anyway."

Gordon Goodman's face was a study in shifting emotions. Slowly he walked to his easy chair and sat down.

"The next morning," Sonny continued, "you gave me breakfast and drove me out to my house. The Krasuskis were asleep and didn't even know I was gone all night. Not that they'd have cared. You know, I just absolutely hated to put on my own clothes again that morning. You must have guessed. A few nights later it happened again, and this time there was a pair of new jeans and a pullover sweater—my first present from anybody. That was the time you slipped me this key and said that anytime I needed a place to stay, just use it."

He held the key up high as he said, "Now you know why I think of this key as my lucky piece."

"Well, I'll be damned," muttered Goody Goodman.

"The first lucky break came right away," continued Sonny Hitchcock. "Tommy Tomkins got sick four days before the winter play and you asked me to take his part. Jeez, how you worked me, hour after hour, and Christ, was I scared! Well, I made it, and, angels in heaven, how good that applause sounded in my ears. People were clapping for *me* and some of the stuck-up kids spoke to me like I was somebody instead of dirt under their feet."

Goody was smiling. "Yes, I remember. And I remember you as the comic lead in the spring play and then as the villain in that murder mystery. First time I had anybody that could move from comedy to heavy like that. Yes, Sonny, you turned out to be very, very good."

"And then, bless you," said Sonny, "you got me that scholarship for the dramatic school in Chicago. Oh, boy, but the Krasuskis were mad when they heard they were going to lose their meal ticket. Old Jake almost had apoplexy, and he couldn't do one damn thing about it. That's when I was *sure* they weren't my real parents. He didn't have any adoption papers, not a single, solitary thing to hold me by. I was free of them at last, . . . free, and on my own.

"Off I went to Chicago, riding high and happy, though I didn't have a dime to my name—just a piece of paper for a year's tuition. And you know what?" He leaned toward Goody Goodman and waved the key. "I got this out, and the charm began to work. The registrar handed me a note. I was to go to a nearby bank. There I was handed a checkbook with six hundred dollars already deposited. I was to use it for my room and board."

"Just like that, Sonny?" asked Goody. "Don't try to make me believe this key did that kind of magic. Somebody must have put the money there. Who was it?"

"I wasn't supposed to know," said Sonny. "I figured it was the same person that was paying the Krasuskis all these years." He smiled. "It's an exciting feeling to know there's somebody you belong to—a secret angel. I'd wonder if it was my real father or mother. Or a rich uncle. I don't suppose you'll ever know what that thought means to a kid who's been kicked around all his life. Somebody out there knew who I was and cared enough to give me money."

"Not a very rich uncle," said Goody Goodman. "Six hundred dollars isn't very much—or was that just for the first month?"

"Hell, no, for the whole semester. But after the Krasuskis, I was used to a dreary room and skimpy meals. Besides, I soon found out the second lucky thing."

"The second lucky thing?" asked Goody. "What was that?"

"There's always somebody around who finds a young man attractive. In return for some . . . favors, . . . he's willing to make life easier. In just a couple of days, I noticed that one of my teachers, old Nigel Bellamy, found me to his liking. Would I like to come to his studio for a bit of extra coaching? Maybe I could come up to his apartment for a more quiet session? There were some books there I ought to be reading. If it got late, why not stay the night?"

The older man was looking at Sonny intently.

"He never gave me money or made me feel I was a hustler," Sonny said, defiantly. "But there were presents like a watch, a suit of clothes, tickets to a special play downtown. Always a good dinner and breakfast. And when he saw I was learning how to act, I got a part in a play—at least a walk-on part, a few lines to say.

"The next one was Terry Blake, the movie actor. He was coming back to his old alma mater, where he got his start, to take the lead in a spring play. Lots of publicity, natch; important people to be in the audience, of course; reviews in the Chicago papers—the whole star-treatment bit. I got out my good-luck key. The charm was plenty powerful. The boy who was to play the juvenile lead got sick. I read for the part. Terry Blake liked me, asked them to let me take the role. I thought at first it was for my acting, but I soon got the message that he wanted me for something else, too. And I was willing. What the hell, a famous Hollywood star . . ."

Sonny looked at his former teacher, head high. "And I was good in the part too. I got some good notices. People looked at me with respect.

"The next summer I headed for Hollywood and moved in with Terry Blake. He introduced me around. I learned fast, not just how to act but how to play the angles, who to please, how to make the right contacts. I got a few bit parts, people began to remember my face and voice. Terry Blake wasn't the only one who was willing to give me a break in return for my time.

"The good-luck charm was still working. I landed a juicy part on the old *Crescent Comedy Hour*, and from then on I was in." Sonny's eyes grew brighter. "They began to send for me because I could *act*, not just because . . . well, because I was an attractive young man. My agent got me an audition for *Battleground*, and I got the lead. The show's been running nearly five years now, and it looks like it'll go five more years. And there's sure to be reruns after that, with residuals and my pick of parts besides."

Sonny lifted the key again and waved it. "So you see, Goody, I owe a lot to you."

"To me?"

"Sure to you. You took a little snot-nosed, hoody kid and gave him his first break along with the first bit of love he ever had. God, how I appreciated this apartment of yours. I still do. That's why I've kept this key all these years. Besides bringing me luck, I knew I'd be back to use it again."

"I can't believe it. All this time, Sonny." Then Goodman frowned. "You aren't putting me on, are you, boy? What about that big place you own out in California and your wife and those two kids of yours?"

"Oh, yes, my wife. The glamorous Glenda Graham." Sonny's lip curled. "The perfect wife, the ideal marriage. Glenda and Sonny and their two adorable cherubs. Oh, we're the darlings of the flick magazines, all right. Well, I'll tell you a big fat secret. That bull is strictly press-agent stuff. Sure, I married Glenda and the P.R. boys got plenty of mileage out of the wedding. They even had pictures of the bed we were going to sleep in on our first night. Gloria's nightgown got special pictures, and there was about a column on whether I'd wear pajamas or not."

Gordon Goodman shook his head in wonderment. "But how about the children? You did acquire a couple of kids, didn't you?"

"You know it! A perfect marriage has to have children. My God, the pictures and stories when we got those two brats! I could puke. They're adopted, of course. Glenda wasn't about to have all that bother of having them herself. You know, time off from work and her figure spoiled and messing with wet nurses and babies crying.

"No, Goody, our marriage is strictly business. I've got the perfect wife, the picture-book house, the ideal family—what every shop girl and pimple-faced high school dropout dreams of—and I'm lonely as hell."

"So that's how it is?" said Goody.

"I told you that one of the reasons I came back here was to see this old place and you in it. I can still play that first night scene without dropping a line or missing a cue.

"Just watch me, Coach. You won't catch me in a slip." Sonny thought a moment, then struck a pose. "Look, son, you take off your clothes and go take a shower. I'll find some pajamas for you and fix some sandwiches. You must be hungry. You can sleep there on the couch."

It was Goody's turn to laugh, a bit self-consciously. "So far O.K. Your memory's all right so far." He frowned. "But should we take the time to play out the scene? Won't you be missed? Shouldn't you be someplace?"

"No, I told Dennis he could have the night off, go out on the town. And there wasn't anybody in this stinking town I wanted to be with—except you."

"And who's Dennis?"

"Dennis is my latest. I figured if people were ready to give me a boost up the ladder, there must be another little guy down there who needs a lift too. Dennis's got what it takes, but he needs to know the ropes and make the connections. So he goes with me as 'my man,' fetches and carries, keeps me company. He's as loyal as they come in this cutthroat business, which means he'll stick with me as long as I've got something to give him. He's probably out at Daley's Corners, making out on his own tonight."

"In that case, student Tony Krasuski, you're invited. Be my guest." Goody Goodman bowed deeply. "Along with the sandwiches could you do with a drink? Coffee, tea, too tame? How about beer? Or something stronger? Now that you're old enough, I mean."

"Beer sounds good enough."

Goody only laughed. In a mock peremptory tone, he said, "Off with those clothes, young fellow, and into the shower." A faint smile touched his lips. "I hope you won't be embarrassed, young man, if I find your underwear unbearably dirty and ragged."

Sonny snickered and headed for the shower, tossing coat, shirt, shoes aside as he went. With a feigned girlish titter he half opened the bathroom door and tossed out bright-red bikini-brief undershorts. Goody picked them up, laughed, then turned to go into the bedroom. He reappeared in a few minutes, dressed in a lounging robe and carrying a pair of pajamas. He laid the pajamas on top of the sofa, then busied himself in the kitchen.

When Sonny reappeared, wrapped in a towel, there was a pile of sandwiches and two mugs of beer ready. "Thanks, Mr. Goodman," he said with mock bashfulness. "I haven't had much to eat all day." He fell to eating.

"Sonny," said Goody seriously. "You've forgotten to tell me something."

"What's that, Goody?"

"You said there were two reasons you came back. What was the other one?"

Sonny dropped the fake little-boy pose. "The person who paid the Krasuskis for my keep and arranged for that money in Chicago." He looked at Goody, cocking his head to one side. "I once thought it was you that provided the six hundred dollars. It wasn't though, was it?"

"No, it wasn't. Not that I'd have been unwilling. I just never thought of it."

"I didn't think so. But it couldn't be anybody very rich or it would have been lots more. And they'd have put me up with somebody better than those stingy, stinking Krasuskis."

"Do you know who it was? Had any luck finding out?"

"I found a detective agency out in Los Angeles that specializes in that kind of thing. It took some doing, I guess, because somebody had tried to hide the trail. But it seems things like birth records have to be kept, and they came up with a good lead. It led right back here to Wauconda Falls."

"Care to tell me about it?" asked Goody.

"No, even if you are a trusted old friend. After what happened at the arena tonight, I—" He stopped suddenly, mouth open in mid-sentence.

Goody waited for the rest of the sentence. Then he said, "After what happened tonight?" He stood up suddenly. "What do you mean? My God, Sonny, do you mean the murder?"

"The murder?" Sonny's face was mask-like. "Who said anything about any murder?"

The older man studied his former pupil's face intently. "Sonny, you don't mean . . . you don't know . . . you didn't have anything to do with that—"

"With that stabbing? Of course not. No, Goody, if you remember, I was across the arena, reading my lines. How could I?"

"No, of course not."

"I was referring to something else. Something I'd just as soon not tell anybody else about, not even you."

There was an awkward silence.

"Oh, come on, Goody, relax. Forget what I just said." He put down his empty beer mug and stood up, stretching his bare torso and pulling the towel tight around his hips. "Thanks for feeding this starving Polack kid. Now it's time for bed. Can I help you make up my place here on the couch?"

"On the couch? The glamorous Hollywood star of television, Wayne Hitchcock, spend the night on a couch? By no means. Tonight you sleep in comfort in a bed. *My* bed."

A slow smile spread over Sonny's face. "I'm honored." He held up the pajamas and shook his head, dropping his eyes in mock embarrassment. "These pajamas—well, I'm not as skinny as I used to be. I'm afraid they're too—" He pulled in his waist, almost losing the towel, and held the garment up. "They're just too tight. I was thinking that after you turned out the light, I'd just slip this towel off and sleep in the raw. But if I'm to share your bed . . ."

Goody laughed. "That makes two of us." He dropped his eyes in fake dismay. "That happens to be the only pair in the place right now. So I was planning to go without, too."

They looked at each other and laughed. Then Sonny very slowly unknotted the towel and let it fall. Goody elaborately extended his arms and dropped the robe from his shoulders. He drew Sonny to him and wrapped his arms around his shoulders in a warm embrace.

"Welcome home, Tony Krasuski," he said.

13 / *Sunday at 8:00 A.M.*

Barney got down to headquarters early Sunday morning. He was on the phone when Curt Conners breezed in.

"Hi, Red, glad to see you. Good, you're not in uniform," Barney greeted Curt. "I'm just getting something here." He spoke into the phone. "Yes, anytime in the last two days. No, you don't need to give me the names of your regular patrons. We just want unusual people, that is, people who don't rent your cars every week or so. Yes, I'm ready to take the names." As Barney listened, he uttered an occasional "Yes. . . . Oh? . . . Well, well, . . . that's interesting." He concluded with "Thank you. You've been very helpful. I'll be sending a man for the complete list later today. He'll be in uniform, so you'll know it's legitimate to release your information to him. Thank you again.

"A good start, Red," Barney said. "Listen to the names of people who rented cars yesterday. Phoebe Sears was in, a man from the college for Dr. Redmond, Harold Anderton, plus Esther Quinlan. Then there was somebody named Anthony Jones. And here's a big surprise. On Friday two cars were rented for Wayne Hitchcock by somebody named Dennis Peters."

"Did you say on Friday?" asked Curt. "Dennis Peters, huh? That's the name of the fellow with Wayne Hitchcock. But our television star didn't arrive until Saturday afternoon. You're sure she said Friday?"

"No doubt about it, Red. She said Friday."

"Why two cars? Why on Friday? I'm sure about Dennis being Hitchcock's man. We saw him right by Hitchcock when we broke up that gang of fans before the show at the Convention Center. Could be that he came in a day early to make arrangements. But I still don't see . . ."

"What don't you see?" asked Barney. "You catching on to something?"

"Maybe. Who were those others again? Sears? Oh, yes, one of those gals from Capital City, short, kind of bitchy. Redmond? Wouldn't a college president have a car of his own—two cars? Esther Quinlan? Seems like Doc Quinlan's wife wouldn't have to be renting anything, what with that foreign import she's running around in. Looks like we've got some questions to start on all right, Barney."

"Meanwhile, I've got a call in for Manson, Alcott's chauffeur," said Barney. "Desk clerk said he went out early, in a hurry, maybe something urgent. Also, since Kottke's on duty today, I asked him to look up that head usher, Sheppard, and the fire marshal, Henderson, just in case they might have something to tell us."

Curt nodded. "You never know. Could be they saw someone wandering around instead of watching the show—like a guy five feet nine, left-handed, blue-eyed."

"Oh, sure, maybe forty or fifty like that," Barney laughed. "Chief called me about seven this morning to tell me I was to handle this case. I enjoyed telling him I was already on the way. He's coming down soon, so I'll get him to help us out with a call to Capital City—the Manson angle, you know. And, Red," Barney spoke seriously, "I asked him for you. He started his usual bitching about being shorthanded, didn't see how he could spare you."

"Oh?" Curt looked worried. "What did you say?"

"I just asked him if he'd seen the morning papers or heard the newscasts. He had, all right. Then I reminded him this was the mayor's wife and the whole city council would be on him from now until we find the guy that did it." Barney smiled. "That's all it took. He folded right away. Sure, if I want Conners, or Mulvany, or the janitor, I could have him. So you're in, Officer Conners, whether you like it or not."

Slowly a grin spread over Curt's face. "Whether I like it or not, eh? I think you know the answer to that one."

"No worries about union hours and coffee breaks?"

"Never heard of them. What are they?"

"Won't mind Hickson nosing around or giving us the needle?"

"That little flea? I'll just use my flyswatter."

"Speaking of newspapers, Red, have you seen the headlines today?"

"Have I seen them? Think I'm blind? Hell, I could almost hear them screaming at me. Largest type, couple of inches high: 'Streaker strikes, mayor's wife stabbed to death.' That little pip-squeak sure had a field day. I'm surprised he isn't here right now, asking his damned questions."

"Careful, Red, maybe that's him now," said Barney. "Oh, no, it's Kottke. Come on in, Otto!" he called.

"Hiya, Otto," said Curt. "Hear you've been up since the crack of dawn."

"Of course, all in the line of duty, Red," said Otto Kottke.

"How'd you make out with Sheppard and Henderson?" asked Barney.

"O.K., Barney. Both of them were home. Henderson said he

doesn't remember anybody unusual hanging around—a real quiet night. Except for a few kids having to go potty or wanting popcorn, there was hardly any traffic once the program started. I gave him the description, but he doesn't remember any fellows at all, blue-eyed or brown-eyed. I told him thanks, you'd call him if anything came up, but otherwise to forget it.

"Sheppard said there were a couple of happenings. A gang of kids hanging around gate three, wisecracking and heckling. But these were more like fourteen or fifteen years old. Then there were two fellows that came in after the show started and hung around the lobby instead of going on in. One of the ushers told them they had to sit inside, and when they wouldn't, he called Sheppard. They couldn't make up their minds. Sheppard heard one of them say, 'But we got to be out there at 9:40.' When Sheppard got tough, they left. They weren't really sassy; he almost forgot about them until I gave them your description. 'Yeah,' he said, 'they was *both* about five nine or ten, and one of them was sort of blond, hair stringing down to his shoulders,' and—well, he *thought* he had blue eyes."

"He heard them say 9:40, Otto?" asked Barney. "Out there? Where would that be?"

"Sheppard didn't make any guesses. He just said they disappeared. Probably out in front or in the parking lot, don't you suppose?" said Kottke.

"Did he describe them?" continued Curt. "I mean, more than what we said?"

"No, except he did say they looked like they was too old for high school—more like college kids. Oh, yes, one had a mustache—not the blond one. Both sort of—you know—sloppy—in jeans and old T-shirts."

"Not much to go on there, I'm afraid," said Barney Ross.

"No, except for something that happened this morning," said Kottke.

"This morning? What's that?" asked Barney.

"Well, thought I'd take my old lady and my oldest girl to mass on my way down this morning. You know, there's a six thirty at St. Wen's. Well, I let them out and thought maybe I'd go in with them a little while. The wife's been on me for having to work on Sundays and missing mass, and I'm not due here till seven, so—"

"Yes, yes, Otto," said Curt impatiently, "we're glad to hear about your religious life, but get on with the story."

85

"Well, I heard this fellow let out a yell, something like 'Hey, Witty,' and come tearing across the walk, waving a morning paper and pointing. Hadn't seen the paper yet myself, so I moved over to take a peek, just in time to hear the other fellow say, 'But I didn't do it. I didn't have anything to do with it at all.' Then the first one said, 'If you've got me mixed up in anything,' and his voice got too soft to hear. 'I haven't got you—' said the light-haired one. 'Well, I'm going out to see Redmond, Witty, right now before I find—' Just then he caught sight of my uniform. He stopped talking and headed over to the church parking lot. The blond boy took out after him, talking a hundred words a minute and waving his arms like a windmill. 'But my folks—' he said, looking back. The first hollered, 'Screw your folks, and you too.' "

"You followed them, didn't you?" asked Barney.

"You bet. Nothing to it. First one almost running, second one trying to catch up and jabbering—they forgot all about me. The first one jumped into an old jalopy and gunned the motor. The second boy barely made it, was still grabbing the door and climbing in when they were off. Saw them turn right on Main Street. No muffler, motor like a lawn mower—no trouble knowing where they was. By the time I got into my car and made it round the corner, they was about ten blocks ahead."

"Where did they go?" asked Curt.

"Out toward the college. Pulled up in front of a big brick and stone house. By now it was almost seven o'clock and I was due to check in for duty, so I left them there and headed back. Kind of forgot it till Sheppard told of them two guys in the lobby, and all of a sudden something clicked. One was blond, one was dark with a little mustache, college boys, average height, long hair. Do you think— Can you make anything of it?"

"Maybe," said Curt. "Did you get the address of the house?"

"Yes, wrote it down. Where'd I put that paper? Oh, here it is—4100 College Avenue."

"Hand me the phone book, will you, Barney?" said Curt. "Sure enough, Redmond, 4100 College Avenue. They were calling on our college president." He turned to Kottke again. "Did you say it was a jalopy, Otto? Like what make would you say?"

"I'm not sure. Maybe like one of them old Dodges we had about ten years ago."

Curt looked at Barney. "An old Dodge, five feet nine, blond, Dr.

Redmond had a rented car, O'Malley's story." He grinned. "It begins to add up, doesn't it, Barney?"

There was a commotion in the hallway, and a voice was heard calling, "No, you can't go in there. Detective Ross is in conference."

"Oh, oh, he's here," said Curt. "The press waits for no man and for no closed door."

Kottke looked worried. "Well, if you don't need me anymore, I'll be on my way."

"O.K., Kottke. Wish I could go with you," said Barney. "You might stop at the auto-rental agency on Market Street and pick up a list of names. They know somebody's coming. No hurry, just on your regular rounds. And, Kottke, thanks for this morning."

"Yes, thanks," added Curt. "You were right on target this time."

"Glad to hear it. Be seeing you." Otto Kottke disappeared through a side door.

Barney opened the door to the outer hall. "What's the matter out here? Oh, it's you, Hickson. Come on in."

"Good morning, Detective Ross," was the breezy greeting. "Hi, Conners. Quite a thing, last night. Did you see my write-up in the morning *Bugle*?"

"Yeah, I've seen it." Barney's voice registered boredom.

"Not bad for a hurry-up job, yes?" Hickson rubbed his hands together. "Especially without much help from—well, some people who could have opened up a little more."

"If you mean the police, Hickson, we didn't tell you much because we didn't know very much," said Barney patiently. "In fact, judging from your article, you know more facts than we do."

"For instance?"

"Mrs. McGinty was murdered. *We* don't know that for sure, but looks like *you* do. Might have been an accident, you know, or even a suicide."

"Oh, come off it, Ross. They found the knife sticking in her, didn't they?" Hickson's lip curled. "You trying to say she stuck it into herself or it just got there by accident?"

"I'm not saying anything yet. The doctor said her death was caused by a knife wound. You can quote him on that O.K. But how the knife got there—"

"Oh, bull! The streaker jabbed it into her. Five thousand people saw him do it."

"Did they now? Did anybody really see him do it? If you can find even one who will swear on the Bible, bring him in, Hickson. For that matter, find me somebody who can tell us who the streaker is. Five thousand saw him, you say? Well, somebody out of that five thousand ought to have recognized him."

"There you go, twisting things around, getting yourself off the hook."

"No, we're not twisting anything. I'm reminding you that *we* can't go jumping to conclusions or accusing anybody until we've got proof." Barney lowered his voice. "We've got a few leads, and we'll get some more if people will just leave us alone so we can get to work." He smiled patiently. "As fast as we know something for sure, we'll let you in on it. Right now, all we know is that Maude McGinty died of a knife plunged into her heart."

"Couldn't have been a mistake? You know, wrong victim?"

"Victim? If she *was* a victim, but we don't know she was. You got somebody or something in mind, Hickson?"

"I've heard a couple of rumors, some names mentioned. You wouldn't know whose knife it was, would you?"

"Nobody's claimed it yet."

"Could the streaker have been a jealous lover?"

"I don't know. Who was the streaker? And are you hinting that our mayor's wife is involved in a scandal with a guy that runs around without clothes on? That would make a juicy story, wouldn't it, Hickson? And get your editor in good with the mayor."

"What about the money she was going to leave to the convention center? That deal still on?"

Barney's face was devoid of expression. "Why not?" he asked. "Any reason to think it isn't?"

Curt Conners stood up and crossed to stand beside Barney Ross. "I've got an idea for your next story," he said smiling genially.

"What do you mean?" asked Hickson. "You gonna tell me how to write my copy?"

"Just a suggestion, Hickson." Curt was still smiling ingratiatingly. "You have to have a story. We've got nothing to tell you yet. Now take the streaker, you've got a natural in him. Who is he? Where'd he come from? The boy next door or down the block? Why, a clever guy like you could blow that up into a full spread."

Hickson looked at Curt suspiciously. "Clever guy like me, eh? You filling me full of crap?"

"On a Sunday morning, right after church?" Curt's expression was bland. "Just giving you the best lead we can. You gotta have a story; we're helping you get one."

Barney stood up. "I'll tell you, Hickson, you come back this afternoon. By that time we may have something for you." He took Hickson by the elbow and bent close to his ear. "Let that streaker angle simmer awhile. You'll think of just the right way to handle it."

"O.K., O.K. So long—for now. See you." Hickson made his exit, and Barney closed the door firmly behind him.

"Money for the convention center? I got it, Barney," said Curt. "Don't know what it means, but we'll find out." He sat down. "Thank God he's gone," Curt continued. "I have to hand it to you, Barney, you got more patience than I'd ever have. I'd have given that jerk a kick in the ass and sent him flying."

"No, you wouldn't. His editor would have your job if you did—and real fast. Besides, he might be useful in his stinky way—like that streaker angle you suggest. Thanks for that one, Red. You might develop that some more, in case we have nothing for our friend Hickson this afternoon."

The telephone rang. "Yes?" said Barney. "Oh, put him on. . . . Hello, Manson, glad to hear from you. . . . Yes, we can come over, say in half an hour? . . . What's the room number? 210. . . . See you there."

Barney turned to Curt. "That Manson's already on the stick. Got some news for us. Doesn't want to leave the hotel. Guess he's keeping an eye on our lieutenant governor. Like you said, he's more than a chauffeur." He broke off to exclaim, "Well, hello! Look who's here."

"Mike Mulvany!" shouted Curt. "What the hell are you doing down here so early in the morning?"

"Just thought I'd stop by to see if maybe I—well, if I could maybe lend a hand some way." He smiled sheepishly. "After the way I goofed things last night, stumbling over that case and all, I just thought—"

"Come on in, Mike. There's plenty of jobs for everybody." Barney put an arm around his shoulder. "As for that deal last night, forget it. Could have happened to anybody. We're wondering what the case was doing there anyway."

"Yeah," said Curt. "Funny how he just happened to bring it into the show with him, instead of leaving it in his car."

"You got something for me to be doing?" asked Mike.

"Sure have. How'd you like to work on this?" Barney opened a desk drawer and pulled out a brass letter opener. "It'd sure help if we knew where this came from."

"What is it?" asked Mike. "Oh, yes. This is the knife that did the job last night?"

"Right," said Barney. "Pretty little thing, isn't it? Near as we can guess, it's one of those ornamental letter openers that people have lying around their desks. There can't be more than five or six stores in town that sell these. Brass, you know, sort of expensive, more like something you'd find in that office supply store on Center Street or Fitch's Gift Shop over near the National Bank."

"What do you want me to do?" asked Mike.

"See if any of those places recognize this, carry it in stock. Might take five or six telephone calls and a couple of trips. Stores aren't open on Sunday, but if you can locate the manager at home and show it to him—"

"I got it. Sure, I'll give it a try."

"Good. Just don't let the letter opener out of your possession."

The phone rang.

"Yes?" said Barney. "Oh, he is? Can he see me now? Fine, I'll be right there." He reached for his notes. "Chief's in, wants a report. And that gives us a chance to get him onto the Capital City calls. Maybe he can find out a few things for us down there. Let's see; ... the three old bags—Sears, Warren, Yates—Lieutenant Governor Alcott and especially his wife, a parolee named Di-Vacco. ... Anybody else, Red?"

"Yes, fellow named Manson. You know, just in case he's been feeding us a line, playing us for suckers."

Barney registered surprise. "Good thinking, Red. O.K. Manson's on the list too." He strode toward the door. "Shouldn't take long. Be back soon."

Mike Mulvany slipped into Barney's chair. "Let's see, where's the phone book? Will it bother you if I do some calling from here, Red?"

"Go right ahead, Mike. I haven't got much on my mind right now," said Curt. "Think I'll do a little sketching over here on the side table."

"Sketching? Didn't know you were an artist. Let's see, yellow pages, office supplies. O.K., here goes."

Barney was back in a surprisingly short time. "Chief was in a good mood for a change," he said. "Listened while I told him about the medical report, heard what we were planning, then gave me a little pep talk about how we're on the spot—the mayor and city council and all that. I gave him my list, and when I left he was already reaching for the phone."

"Did you mention me, Barney?" asked Mike.

"Sure did. Told him you came in this morning on your own time. Gave you full credit. Any luck with your calls so far?"

"Some. Two leads up to now. I'm on my way to see if this little toy looks familiar to either of them." He made for the door. "Be seeing you."

"And what might you be doing, Red?"

"Giving Hickson his story—if he'll buy the idea. How's this?" Curt held up a large piece of paper for Barney to see.

WHO IS THE STREAKER?
Is he the boy next door? The kid down the block? You saw him last night, nothing on but a feather and moccasins. Did he look familiar? Did he remind you of somebody you know? If you can identify him, call this number. . . .

"Barney," said Curt hopefully, "Maybe we could even get the paper to offer some kind of reward or make it some kind of contest."

"Well, . . . it sounds a little corny to me," said Barney, "but it might work."

"Oh, it needs Hickson's expert touch, naturally," grinned Curt. "We're just giving him hints, you understand. We wouldn't want him to think we know his job better than he does."

"That's the right angle, Red. He'll probably buy it. If nothing else, it'll keep him off our backs for a while so we can go to work. And speaking of getting to work, we're just about due at the hotel. Mustn't keep Manson waiting. With luck, we may also get a word or two in with the lieutenant governor. Might ask those three dames some questions, too, before they get out of town." He grinned broadly at Curt. "Want to take a minute to comb that curly red mop of yours and straighten your tie? We just might get a chance to talk with the glamorous Mrs. Alcott, too, and she *could* be susceptible to red-headed bachelors."

Curt's cheeks turned pink. "Oh, go to hell," he muttered as he reached for his pocket comb.

14 / *Sunday at 9:15 A.M.*

There was no answer when Barney knocked lightly on the door of room 210.

"That's strange. Manson said he'd be expecting us," he muttered as he knocked more firmly.

At the far end of the hall a door opened and Harry Manson glided out. He closed the door softly behind him and silently moved toward Barney and Curt. It wasn't until he had cautiously unlocked the door to 210, beckoned them to enter, and eased the door shut that he spoke.

"Morning, men. I was in Alcott's room, keeping an eye on things."

"Oh?" said Barney. "What sort of things?"

"Just in case. We don't know where DiVacco is. If he's here in Wauconda Falls, he might decide to pay us a little call."

"What do you mean you don't know where he is?"

"He reported to his parole officer last Thursday on schedule. He isn't due to report again until next week."

"And you think he might have caught a plane or a bus or maybe driven a car to Wauconda Falls?"

"It's possible," said Manson. "He's not supposed to leave Capital City without permission, but that doesn't mean he couldn't have tried it."

"Have you checked the airport and the bus depot?"

"One of our men is taking care of that now. The airport will be easy, but with ten buses leaving Capital City each day and no reservations required, we can't be sure a ticket agent would have noticed him especially. We've got a good description and some good pictures. Somebody might remember."

"Have you got a picture we could look at?" asked Barney.

"Not with me. But I can give you a pretty good description."

"Mind reading it so Conners here can write it down?"

"He's Italian and looks it. Black hair, dark skin, a little on the short side—say about five feet eight. He used to be kind of fat, but prison life slimmed him down to about 140 pounds. He used to be a sharp dresser—flashy clothes, hair slicked back and parted in the middle. His parole officer says he's let his hair grow longer so it covers his ears, and he's shaved off his mustache."

"Any distinguishing marks?" asked Curt Conners.

"You mean like a mole or a scar? No, I don't think so. Oh, yes, he's ambidextrous—can shoot with either hand—or wield a knife."

"Left-handed as well as right," repeated Curt. "What color are his eyes?"

"H'mmm, that's funny. It says here blue. I thought all Italians had brown eyes."

"Blue eyes, . . . left-handed with a knife sometimes." Curt looked at Barney. "About five feet eight, not fat anymore."

Barney nodded. "I'll see that this description gets around. There aren't many Italians in Wauconda Falls. One of our men might spot him, if he's here."

"Tell me, Manson," said Curt, "where's he living and has he got a job?"

"The parole officer says he's living in a room with a family, one that's O.K. He's got a part-time job helping out at the Coliseum, a sort of janitor."

"The Coliseum?" asked Barney Ross. "Isn't that where they have their sports events in Capital City? Like pro basketball and wrestling?"

"That's the place. I think DiVacco helps set up equipment and cleans up after the show's over."

"A stagehand, you mean?" asked Curt.

"Well, maybe. I think just janitor is more like it."

"Manson, would you go over that story about DiVacco and Mrs. Alcott again?" asked Barney. "And Conners may want to take some notes, so go slow."

"It's on the hush-hush side, you understand," said Manson, "but DiVacco was Mrs. Alcott's first husband. She was pretty young when she married him, and it didn't last long. He was running with a gang, got caught in a bank robbery, and was sent up. I don't know all the details, but he was stupid enough to use his gun. Nicked one of the bank people pretty bad. That did it for him, no chance for any plea bargaining. Got thirty years, I think."

"What's he doing out so soon?" asked Curt.

"He played it smart. Behaved himself, a model prisoner, learned a trade—electrician, I think. You know how soft parole boards are nowadays. Thirty years is the sentence, and you're out in ten."

"How about Mrs. Alcott?" asked Curt.

"Oh, she got a divorce. Can't say I blame her. Went out West someplace. Well, she's pretty good at playing the piano, sings a little, and looks like a million dollars, so she got a job in a nightclub. With her looks she did all right, was playing some posh places—big hotels and private clubs, that sort of thing. Alcott fell for her, married her. Now she's the wife of the lieutenant governor and might even be the wife of our next governor, from what I hear."

"Only it's almost midnight and the coach may turn into a pumpkin," said Curt.

"What the hell's he talking about?" asked Manson. "Football coaches and pumpkins?"

"Oh, Conners likes to use a secret code once in a while," said Barney unsmilingly. "What he means is if DiVacco decides to raise hell, Mrs. Alcott's in trouble and so is Mr. Alcott."

"Yeah. A juicy scandal might keep him from being governor. He'd be finished."

"But I don't get it," said Curt. "Why would DiVacco want to kill his ex-wife?"

"He's got a nasty temper, I hear, and he's been in prison a long time. A guy can get to thinking screwy things when he's locked up like that. She was his wife, she two-timed him. She should have been waiting for him at the gates when he got out. Instead she's married some other guy. No dame's going to get away with that."

"But I don't see . . . Why go about it—" Curt started to say, but Barney interrupted him.

"O.K., Red. Let's take it easy. We don't know if DiVacco is here, and if he is, we don't know that he had anything to do with Maude McGinty's death." Barney turned to Manson. "Do you know DiVacco?"

"Well, I've never seen him more than once or twice. I've heard about him from—well, different people. And I been studying his mug shots."

"Where were you last night when the streaker appeared?" asked Curt.

"Me? In the front row, right behind Alcott's chair, keeping an eye open. Alcott was right there, front and center, a sitting duck for anybody who wanted to take a shot at him. I wanted to be handy in case some kook tried something."

"Then you got a good look at the streaker?"

"Well, yes, sort of, except, when he started heading for those chairs, I was moving in close."

"Did you think he looked like DiVacco?" asked Curt.

Harry paused to think awhile. "I'm not sure. Like I said, I was thinking of my job. When the streaker came on and stood there in the spotlight, all I could see was a naked Indian with a feather. Guess I thought it was part of the show."

"A naked man in a family type show?"

"Why not? All these rock musicals and centerfolds these days. I never thought about any family type show. I was worrying about my job."

"So you can't tell us if it could have been DiVacco?" asked Curt.

"Well, now, as I think back, it could have been. Dark skin, not tall. But I couldn't be sure."

"How about his face? Did the mask fool you?"

"Mask? Was he wearing a mask? I didn't see any mask."

"Are you sure? About the mask, I mean. I was wondering about his eyes, if you could see them."

"Oh, what the hell? I wasn't looking at him that close."

"Because," said Curt slowly, "you were looking at something else?"

"At something else?" Manson's eyes narrowed, his soft voice took on a hard edge. "What do you mean? Look, Conners, I'm no fairy. Seeing a guy naked doesn't send me."

"O.K., O.K.," said Barney, "take it easy. We're off the subject. Right now we need to know where DiVacco is. If he's in Capital City like he's supposed to be, we got no problem. If he's in Wauconda Falls—well, let's see what we can find out."

Manson looked at his watch. "Yeah, I better be getting back. A call might have come in, and maybe DiVacco's made a move."

"Do you suppose Alcott would see us?" Barney asked. "There are a few questions he might be able to clear up."

"Oh?" Manson hesitated a minute. "I could ask him. Want me to?"

"Do that, will you? You can call us on the house phone if he says O.K."

Carefully Manson opened the door and looked cautiously up and down the hallway. He sidled along the corridor, knocked quietly on Alcott's door, opened it, and disappeared.

"My God, Red, what made you get in that last crack? Were you trying to make Manson turn on us?"

"I drew blood, didn't I, Barney?"

"Blood? What do you mean, Red?"

"I just asked if he was looking at something else. He didn't look dumb or make a wisecrack. He got mad and started to deny he was a fairy. Who said he was?"

"I see what you mean, but what difference does it make if he is or isn't? He's on *our* team, isn't he?"

"Is he, Barney?" asked Curt.

Barney Ross stared at Curt Conners. "My God, Red, are you thinking—"

Just then the phone rang. Barney lifted it quickly. "Yes? . . . Oh, he'll see us. . . . Good. . . . We'll be right there."

As he replaced the phone, Barney said, "What's going on in that mind of yours now, Red?"

"I got to thinking, maybe we'd better be sure who Manson is. What if he isn't what he tells us he is? How do we know he *was* sitting there in the front row all evening?"

Barney gave a low whistle. "Yeah, an interesting question." He started for the door. "Come on, we better go."

"Just a minute. What was the name of that other fellow who rented a car? Not one of our special guests."

"Jones, I think. Yes, Anthony Jones."

"Anybody seen Mr. Jones, a stranger in town? He might be—"

"I get it. Thanks, Red," said Barney. "But we better not keep the lieutenant governor waiting."

Hamilton Alcott exuded cordiality and charm. "Come in, officers. On the job bright and early, I see. It speaks well for the police department of Wauconda Falls, one of the best in our state, I understand. Detective Ross, isn't it?"

"Thank you, Mr. Alcott," said Barney. "This is Officer Conners."

"Yes, I remember. How are you, Conners?"

"We're sorry to intrude so early in the morning," continued Barney, "but, after last night, you can understand we have some inquiries to make."

"Yes, of course. Won't you sit down?" The lieutenant governor indicated several chairs. "Could I offer you something to drink?"

"Thank you, no—regulations, you know," said Barney, seating himself on a straight chair opposite Alcott. Curt casually moved to a place by the window, where he had a full view of the lieutenant governor's face. Harry Manson took a position by the hall door.

"Oh, yes, regulations." Hamilton Alcott dropped casually into an armchair, leaned back, and crossed his legs comfortably. "Well, that certainly was a shocking episode last night, an unexpected ending to what had been a delightful evening. Tell me, how is Mayor McGinty taking it all?"

"I really can't say. He was remarkably calm last night, but the trip to the morgue was—well, he showed signs of strain. I was glad that Dr. Quinlan went on home with him. I think probably he gave the mayor a sedative, and Mrs. Cline too."

"Mrs. Cline?"

"Mrs. McGinty's companion. A cousin—and rather devoted, I understand. Mrs. McGinty was somewhat crippled, result of polio."

"Oh, yes. I must send condolences to His Honor." Hamilton Alcott smiled. "And now what can I tell you, Officer?"

"First of all, about the streaker. Did you get a good look at him?"

"A good look?" Alcott laughed. "Didn't we all? He gave us a rather complete view, wouldn't you say—spotlight, center stage?"

Barney leaned forward slightly. "Did you recognize him?"

Alcott shot a quick glance at Manson, then lowered his eyes to study his hands. "Recognize him?" Then, looking at Barney directly, he said calmly, "No, I'm sure there was nothing about him that reminded me of anybody I've ever seen before."

"That's both reassuring and disappointing," said Barney, "after your remark last night."

"Last night? Oh, you mean that it could have been Mrs. Alcott or I if we hadn't changed the seating arrangement? The thought hit me all of a sudden."

"I have to ask this question," said Barney, shifting his position

97

slightly. "Is there somebody who would want to attack you or Mrs. Alcott?"

"There are always some crackpots and soreheads around. Even a lieutenant governor makes enemies, and there are those people on the fringe ready to strike out at anybody who represents the Establishment, if you know what I mean." He smiled brightly. "And you have to admit that our streaker would classify as a freak."

"But you can't think of anybody definite, someone in particular?"

Casually Hamilton Alcott reached for a cigarette. As he clicked his lighter, he turned his face so that he was looking directly toward Manson. Cigarette lit, he leaned back.

"Have you any reason, Ross," he asked in a flat, expressionless voice, "to think there might be somebody definite?"

"Let's say that if there is somebody in Wauconda Falls that might be capable of murder, we'd like very much to know who he is."

"Why don't you tell them, Hamilton?" said a feminine voice.

Barney rose and turned. In the cold light of the day, Rosemary Alcott was as breathtakingly beautiful as she had been under artificial light the night before. Dressed in a flowing pink negligee that suggested but didn't explicitly reveal, she posed with one arm resting lightly on the door frame, the other hand, fingers curled, reposing on her hip.

"Good morning, gentlemen," she said in a throaty voice. "I think, Hamilton, these are honest officers of the law who know how to listen and act." She gave Barney a dazzling smile. "Am I right, Officer?"

"Are you sure that it's wise—that you want to, Roz?" asked Alcott.

"Perhaps you don't have to tell us all the details," said Barney coolly. "Our concern right now is with the possibility that we have a murderer in our city. Why or how you might be involved is not important."

"There, you see, Hamilton?" she said, moving gracefully into the room. Flashing a smile at Barney, she asked, "You are...?"

"Barney Ross, Mrs. Alcott."

She extended a hand. "How do you do?" Her eyes turned to Curt. "And this is...?"

"Curt Conners, who is working with me."

She bowed her head slightly. There was the suggestion of a gleam in her eye and a smile on her lips as she noticed the color tingeing

Curt's cheeks. "Mr. Conners," she said softly. "How nice."

She glanced toward the hall door. "Good morning, Harry." She moved toward the divan and seated herself. "Please sit down, all of you."

Alcott continued to stand stiffly behind his chair, Barney resumed his sitting position, Curt found a chair by the telephone stand, and Manson leaned against the hall door.

"Do you want to tell them, Hamilton, or should I?" she asked.

Alcott stood silent, frowning.

"Oh, all right, I'll do it." In a low voice she continued. "As my husband has said, there are sometimes people who feel they have been badly treated, and maybe sometimes they have a reason. I'm afraid when I was younger and less experienced I acted foolishly." Her head drooped slightly, her hands fell into her lap.

"Very effective," thought Barney. "Wonder if she's putting on an act." Out of the corner of his eye he caught the expression on Curt's face. "She's got Curt on her side all right."

Rosemary Alcott continued. "His name is Benito DiVacco. He's got a nasty Italian temper and has been known to carry a grudge to the point of doing something vicious and cruel."

"Even to murder, Mrs. Alcott?" asked Barney.

She shuddered. "Yes, I think even that. He's been in prison because he used a gun—along with other crimes. His crime didn't have anything to do with me—with us directly. We just learned that he's been paroled."

"And you think now that he's out he might come looking for you because of a grudge he's been carrying?"

Rosemary's voice was barely audible. "Yes, it's possible."

"Are you thinking perhaps he might have been the man who appeared at the convention center last night and that he mistook Maude McGinty for you?"

"Oh, it's a terrible thought. I don't know. That poor woman and her family, victims just because of a mistake."

"Not so terrible as if it had been—" interrupted Alcott harshly. He moved quickly to stand beside his wife.

There was a moment of heavy silence. Barney cleared his throat. "Mrs. Alcott, there's a question I'd like very much to ask you, if you feel up to answering it."

"Now really, Ross—" began Hamilton Alcott.

"That's all right, Hamilton." His wife reached up to touch his arm lightly. "What is your question, Mr. Ross?"

"You saw the streaker. Do you think he could have been the man DiVacco?"

"I don't know. I've been thinking about that myself. I'm afraid—" Here she dropped her eyes and twisted her hands. "I'm afraid I didn't see him very well. I—well—I covered my face when I realized he was—"

"I understand," murmured Barney.

"It could have been Ben," she continued. "The glimpse I got . . . well, it could have been. But somehow it seems all wrong. Ben—I mean DiVacco—well, I don't think he'd go at it like that."

"What do you mean, Mrs. Alcott?"

"It seems a little too well planned. Ben wasn't really very smart. He'd be more likely to use a gun in a crowd, or something like that."

"Unless," said Hamilton Alcott, "he knew we had a bodyguard and he tried to get close before without luck. This way he could get at us from the front before he could be stopped."

Curt had risen silently and moved to where he could get a full view of Rosemary Alcott's face. She raised her hands, palms upward, and shrugged. "I just don't know. You may be right, Hamilton, but somehow . . ."

Her voice trailed off, and there was another moment of awkward silence. It was Curt Conners who spoke this time.

"Do you suppose, Manson," he asked, "I could use the house phone in your room? There's a call I'd like to make."

For a fleeting moment Barney looked at Curt, then with a matter-of-fact tone he said, "Do you mind if Manson goes with Conners for a few minutes?"

"Not at all," said Alcott. "Go ahead, Manson."

Manson looked uneasily at the lieutenant governor, then cautiously opened the hall door, stepped out, returned, and motioned Curt to follow him.

When they had gone, Barney said casually, "I take it Manson is more than just a chauffeur?"

"Yes, I think you realize the situation," said Alcott. "He's a very capable man, able to do lots of things besides drive a car, just in case there are other matters that need attention."

"Yes, I see. Has he been with you long?"

"With me? No, he's not our usual man. This trip came up suddenly, you know, when the governor found he couldn't make it.

We'd promised Morrison he could have the week-end off. Manson was available."

"Know much about him? Has he been around long?"

"I really don't know. Several months at least, probably longer. He knows his business all right. Why do you ask?"

"Why, I was wondering if you'd like to have one of our local men assigned to you while you're here. If you'd feel safer with an extra man, you know."

"That's very kind of you, but I don't think it will be necessary. You may not know it, but we have an extra operative or two along. Right now they're scouting around, looking for any sign of DiVacco, I believe."

"Well, in that case—" said Barney.

There was a light knock and the door opened. Curt entered, followed a bit later by Manson. Curt nodded slightly to Barney.

"Now, if you will excuse us," said Barney, "we'll be on our way. You know, Mrs. Alcott, it's quite possible we've no cause to worry about your—our Mr. DiVacco. He may not be here in Wauconda Falls at all."

Rosemary smiled brightly and extended her hand. "Thank you, Mr. Ross. Let's hope you are right. Good-by, Mr. Conners. Perhaps we will meet again soon?" She let her hand linger in Curt's an extra second.

"Good-by, Ross," the lieutenant governor said. "I'm glad you're on this job, and Conners, too. Manson here will get in touch with you if there are any developments." Manson nodded but said nothing.

As they walked to the elevator, Barney said, "Thanks, Red, for the chance to talk to the Alcotts about Manson. You'll be interested to know he isn't their regular man."

"Oh," said Curt. "Which means we can't be dead sure of him, doesn't it?"

"By the way, Red, what was the phone call you cooked up?"

"Called the desk to ask if Anthony Jones is registered here. He isn't. Wonder where he spent last night."

15 / *Sunday at 10:30 A.M.*

In the lobby, Barney Ross stopped at the desk. "Could you tell me the room numbers for Miss Sears, Mrs. Warren, and Mrs. Yates? ... 310, 312, 314? Thank you. Is there a house phone I could use? And oh, yes, is there a place on the third floor where we could all talk together? Parlor 3A? Is it available? Good."

While Barney was busy on the house phone, Curt asked for an outside line and dialed a number.

"All set, Red," said Barney a few minutes later. "Our three ladies will meet us in the parlor on the third floor. Everybody was nice and cooperative except that Sears woman. Wonder why she's so bitchy about everything."

"I just located our Anthony Jones, Barney," said Curt. "Called a couple of places while you were busy. He's in that run-down old Wauconda Falls House, room 14. Pretty crumby place. He's probably there because it's cheap. Do you suppose Chief could have a man take a look at him to see if he matches the description?"

"Sure, why not? Just time to put in a call," answered Barney. "I'd better call from Parlor 3A. Shall we take a look at it?"

Parlor 3A turned out to be a comfortable room just across from the elevator. While Barney made his call, Curt grouped chairs for the coming interview.

Barney had just finished when Mrs. Yates entered, followed immediately by Mrs. Warren, who said, "I do hope I haven't kept you waiting."

Down the hall a door slammed and Phoebe Sears bustled in. "This isn't going to take very long, is it, Officer? The morning service at St. Andrews is at eleven and I don't want to be late."

"We'll try to keep this short," said Barney. "Won't you please sit down?" He gestured to the three chairs.

"Well?" said Phoebe Sears impatiently.

"There are a few questions we are asking everybody who sat in the special section last night," he began.

"What sort of questions?" snapped Miss Sears.

"Did any of you know the victim, Maude McGinty, before yesterday?"

All three ladies assured him that last night in the Green Room was the first time any had met the mayor's wife.

"And if I'd known she was going to wear her purple dress, I certainly would not have worn mine! Inconsiderate of her!" said Miss Sears.

"Now, Phoebe, she didn't do it on purpose. How could she have known your plans?" said Carolyn Warren soothingly.

"Really a compliment to your good taste, my dear," said Marjorie Yates, "that she should have chosen a dress similar to yours."

Phoebe Sears sniffed.

Barney continued. "We are very eager to discover who the streaker is. So far nobody has come forward to identify him. Can any of you help us out?"

"You mean, do *I* know him?" exclaimed Miss Sears. "Certainly not! None of the young men I know would ever stage such a crude exhibition."

"No, indeed," said Mrs. Yates, and Mrs. Warren echoed, "Oh, no."

"I assure you I didn't mean he could possibly be an acquaintance of yours," Barney said quickly. "Let me put it another way. Did you notice anything distinctive about him so you could recognize him if you were to see him again?"

"I've already told you about his blue eyes," said Phoebe Sears.

"And that he had no mask? You're sure about that?" asked Barney.

"And no mask. Definitely no mask!"

"I thought," said Mrs. Warren hesitatingly, "he looked quite athletic."

"Yes," agreed Mrs. Yates, "he moved so swiftly, and when he flexed his arms he seemed quite muscular."

"And a very slim waist too," breathed Mrs. Warren. Seeing the other two women eyeing her sharply, she added, "Oh, dear, I didn't mean I was noticing."

"Of course you were, Carolyn," cut in Phoebe Sears. "We all were. And when he embraced poor Mrs. McGinty he seemed *very* ardent. No wonder she didn't scream with those strong arms about her neck."

"Mrs. McGinty made no sound, no move to avoid him?" asked Barney.

"I'm sure the poor dear was too surprised and shocked," said Marjorie Yates. "I know I was quite paralyzed at the suddenness of is all, and he came nowhere near *me*."

"Oh, he wasn't as quick as all that," contradicted Phoebe Sears. "It seemed to me when he got close he sort of paused and looked us over, sort of like he didn't have the nerve. That's when I noticed those blue eyes. Then he gathered himself together and threw himself at her, hugging her tight and giving her a big kiss." She looked around at Curt scornfully. "I'd have thought one of you policemen would have captured him by that time." She turned back to Carolyn Warren. "And of course she couldn't scream with him covering her mouth with his."

"Really, my dear," gasped Carolyn Warren.

Barney cleared his throat. "Now, ladies, may I repeat my question. Do any of you think you could identify him if you saw him again?"

"Oh, I don't think so," said Marjorie Yates.

"And I couldn't either," echoed Caroline Warren.

"Well, *I* could," said Phoebe Sears firmly. "Even with his clothes on. I never forget a face."

"Excuse me," said Curt, "may I ask a question of these ladies?"

Barney nodded. "Please do. This is Officer Conners, you remember?"

"Suppose we could arrange for you to look at several young men, would you be willing to say if any one of them might be the streaker?"

"With their clothes on, you mean?" said Carolyn Warren.

Without a sign of a smile Curt nodded. "Completely clothed, of course."

"I really don't think I'd be much help," said Marjorie Yates.

"I don't think I would, either," said Carolyn Warren.

"Well, I will," said Phoebe Sears. "If one of them is the streaker, I'll identify him. I never forget a face."

Barney said, "How long will you be staying here in Wauconda Falls?"

"We originally thought we'd take the afternoon plane," said Marjorie Yates, "but since none of us has ever been in your part of the state before, we thought we might stay over until Monday to do a little sight-seeing."

"Yes, I've rented a car," said Phoebe Sears, "so after church we plan to do a little driving about."

"Yes, we thought that would be nice," added Carolyn Warren.

"Besides, we want to talk to Irving Redmond about the new fine arts building he's planning," said Marjorie Yates.

"Yes, that Redmond," said Phoebe Sears. "Tell me, Officer, what do you know about this Redmond fellow?"

"Dr. Redmond?" asked Barney. "He's the president of our junior college."

"Oh, I know that," snapped Phoebe Sears. "I mean what do you *know* about him?"

"Well, folks around here think a lot of him. He's certainly built our college up a lot."

"Well, you may think a lot of him, but I'm not so sure. I've got my doubts."

"Why, Phoebe," said Carolyn Warren, "whatever do you mean?"

"I'm sure I've met your Redmond fellow someplace before. He tried to tell me different last night, but you know I never forget a face. I've been trying to think *where* all night. Seems to me it was some kind of trouble, something to do with money."

"Now, Phoebe." Marjorie Yates's voice was severe. "You mustn't say things like that without cause."

"Without cause? Humph, we'll see." She turned to Barney again. "I won't be leaving this town till I've had a chance to talk to this Redmond."

Barney smiled politely. "In that case, could you be available, say, sometime this evening? Or even tomorrow morning?"

"You just bring on your young men, Officer," said Phoebe Sears. "If any one of them was last night's streaker, I'll know him. I never forget—"

"Yes, of course," said Barney hurriedly. "And now it's getting on toward eleven o'clock. Miss Sears wants to get to church." Barney stood up. "We'd like to thank you ladies for being so kind. I hope you enjoy your drive this afternoon."

The three women rose. As they walked out the door and down the corridor, the harsh voice of Phoebe Sears could be heard. "I tell you, this fellow Redmond . . . I'm just certain there's something about him."

"Quite a woman, that Sears dame, eh?" said Barney.

"What a character," said Curt. "But you know, Barney, if she's right about what she says—"

"About Redmond, you mean?"

"Well, that too, but I was thinking about one or two other things she mentioned."

"Like what?"

"Like...H'mmm...mind if I sort them out a bit, Barney? You've got so much on your mind right now, I wouldn't want to be throwing you any bum steers."

Barney looked hard at Curt, then shook his head. "What's this scheme about lining up some suspects for Sears to look at? We haven't got any suspects."

"Just an idea so far. No harm if it doesn't work out. But Barney, could we have somebody check on airplane schedules, and where did Hitchcock board the plane he came in on yesterday afternoon, and where did he spend Thursday night? Also could we find out how many miles he's put on those rented cars of his?"

"Whoa, take it easy, Red. I see what you're getting at. Wait till we get back to the station, will you?"

"Sure. And can we get hold of the stagehands that worked the show last night? There are some questions I'd like to ask two of them. Also the head usher and the fellows that helped—four of them, I believe there were. And maybe the doorman—what's-his-name—O'Malley?"

Barney shook his head. "Easy. Take it easy, Red. We've got a little talk with Redmond to get in, and sooner or later I've got to pay a call on the mayor, and don't think *that* won't be a hard one to get through." He gathered up his notebooks. "Come on, we'd better get moving."

On their way through the lobby, Barney pointed to the hotel coffee shop sign. "Time to take a break, Red."

"What for? We're just getting a good start," said Curt.

"Well, we'll soon run out of gas if I don't get something to eat. I didn't have time for much breakfast in my hurry to get down to the station." He looked sharply at Curt. "And I'll bet you didn't eat much, either."

"Well, now that you mention it..."

"I thought so. Come on, Red, time to stoke up."

Together they entered the coffee shop and found two stools at the counter.

"Good morning," said a young waitress cheerfully. "What'll you men have?"

"Right now, coffee. Then a couple orders of eggs and bacon and plenty of toast."

"Right away. Coming right up."

Curt pivoted his stool to survey the room. "Not many customers

106

today. Must be the slack hour. Did you bring your newspaper with you? I haven't had a chance to read the details according to Hickson."

"No, I left it on my desk."

"O.K., I'll just get one over there at the cashier's counter."

Curt slid off the stool and strolled over to the far end where the cashier was gossiping with another waitress. As he picked up a paper, he heard the waitress saying, "No kidding, Hilda, he came in big as life and stopped right there, so close I could have reached and touched him."

"Really, Marie? You're sure it was really him?" said the cashier.

"You kidding? I been watchin' him every Sunday night since I was a kid. It was Sonny Hitchcock all right."

Quietly Curt sat down on the nearest counter stool and spread the paper, as if reading it intently.

"And then he spoke to me. Just like that he talked to me."

"What did he say, Marie?" asked the cashier.

"He asked me where the private dining room was. Said somebody'd reserved it for him. I said if he'd just follow me, I'd be glad to show him. And then he smiled at me. Oh, God, Hilda, he's got the cutest smile and the whitest teeth. 'Thanks,' he says, 'lead and I'll follow.' Just like that he said it, and I says, 'Sure, Mr. Hitchcock.' And then guess what, Hilda."

"What, Marie?" asked Hilda breathlessly.

"He says real soft-like, 'No names, please, darling.' Did you get it, Hilda? He called me *darling*. And then he says, 'I don't want people to know I'm here yet' and he slipped me a five dollar bill."

"A five dollar bill? Just for showing him to our private room?" The cashier was incredulous. "You making all this up, Marie?"

"No, honest, Hilda, I'm not making this up. Five dollars for showing him the room *and* not telling anybody."

"Well, if you say so," said Hilda. "Then what?"

"Well, I took him over to that little side dining room. It was kind of dark, so I reached for the light switch. 'No,' he says, 'No lights. I like it dim and quiet like this.' "

"Gee, that was funny," said Hilda.

"No, it wasn't, Hilda," Marie snickered. "There was somebody already there waiting for him. It was a woman."

"A woman? Already there? How'd she get there?"

"How should I know? Probably through that side door, 'cause I

didn't see her come in from the lobby or from the outside entrance."
She snickered again. "Oh, Hilda, do you suppose he was—that they
were—you know—"

"Could be, Marie. Why not? These Hollywood actors, you know."
They both giggled.

"What'd she look like?" asked Hilda.

"I couldn't tell. Like I said, it was real dim, and she had her back
to me, and she was sittin' sort of—well, she was resting her head on
one hand. If she hadn't had one of them kind of floppy summer hats
on, I wouldn't even have known it *was* a woman."

"Then what happened?" asked Hilda.

"Nothin' for a while. He put his hand on my shoulder—right
there he touched me, Hilda—and kind of pushed me out the door.
After a while a young fellow came to the counter and says, 'Three
cups of coffee and some of those cakes. Just put them on a tray and
I'll bring them in myself. Here's the money.' "

"Young fellow? What young fellow was that?" asked Hilda.

"I don't know, I never seen him before. Kind of cute, one of them
sort of a pageboy hair cuts and a real cool smile." Marie sighed. "He
must have got into that room the same way the girl did, by the side
entrance."

"Marie, do you expect me to believe all this? Sure you're not
making all of this up? Sounds like something you might have read."

"No, honest to God, Hilda. That's the way it was and I've got the
five dollar bill to prove it, fastened up on the wall in my bedroom."

"Just my luck," said Hilda. "Friday's my day off and that's when
Sonny Hitchcock comes in for a date with some woman and passes
out five dollar bills for tips." She sighed loudly. "You don't suppose
he might come in again today—" She broke off. "Hey, Marie, better
get over to booth number three. That dame's been there awhile and
is beginning to look pretty mad."

Slowly Curt Conners folded the paper and strolled back to join
Barney.

"Coffee's getting cold, Red," said Barney. "You must have been
memorizing Hickson's story."

"Just doing my job, Barney," Curt answered softly. "If I heard
right, our television star was here Friday afternoon."

"Well, you didn't hear right. He came in on the Saturday noon
plane from Chicago via Capital City. About five hundred people saw
him."

"Maybe so, but one little waitress named Marie has a five dollar bill to prove he was here in this coffee shop Friday, and she says he had a date with a lady right over there in a little private room."

"But that's not possible, Red."

"Maybe no, then again maybe it is. If our little waitress was making all this up, we got no problem. But if she was telling the truth—well, then we got a good one." Curt got a faraway look in his eyes. "He might have ... No, that wouldn't work. ... Or he might have ... But why all the hush-hush and pretending to come in Saturday? A woman?" Curt's voice trailed off.

"O.K., O.K., Red." Barney nudged him in the ribs. "That brain is working, I see. But right now your eggs are getting cold."

"And the young fellow with the pageboy haircut?" Suddenly Curt smiled and stopped. "Oh, all right, Barney, all right. Pass the salt and pepper, will you?"

16 / Sunday at 9:00 A.M.

The Krasuskis went to Mass that Sunday morning. It wasn't that they felt particularly religious; they were absent from church more often than not.

They both had gotten up earlier than usual. After breakfast Magda fussed about the front room quite a while. She swept the threadbare carpet, dusted long-neglected corners, wiped off the fumed oak leather-covered davenport and rocker. Reaching into a seldom opened drawer, she brought out a gaudy pink-and-green table runner, spread it over the long library table. On it she placed a large amber glass vase into which she put a bouquet of artificial flowers: purple lilacs and orange poppies.

Catching the spirit of industrious housekeeping, Jake applied a rake to the patches of grass in the front yard and trimmed the scraggly barberry bushes by the walk. Then he used a broom not only on the front walk but out into the street along the curbing.

"Now get yourself cleaned up, Jake," said Magda. "We're going to 9:30 Mass."

"What's got into you now, Magda?" complained Jake. "On a hot day and company coming?"

"We ain't got nothin' to do from now till this afternoon. Somehow I'm feeling antsy, gotta keep busy."

"What the hell you got to feel antsy about? Ain't nothin' special goin' to happen."

"Huh, you're all worked up too, Jake. You know you are. I been livin' with you long enough to tell." She spoke more softly. "Besides, Jake, maybe a few prayers might help us. Nothin' wrong with gettin' God and the Virgin to be on our side. Might make a couple of thousand dollars difference."

Jake shook his head. "For God's sake, the heat gettin' to you? You sure as hell are talkin' crazy."

"Nothin's wrong with me, and I'm talkin' sense." Magda's voice got shriller. "Now you get yourself cleaned up. We got ten minutes' walk to St. Wen's, and God ain't gonna think much of our prayers if we come late."

Jake turned toward the bedroom. His chin jutted out stubbornly. "But I ain't gonna wear no coat. Too hot. Goin' in my shirt sleeves. And ain't gonna shave again. Shaved last night."

"Shirt sleeves, nothin'. This is Sunday. Won't kill you to wear your coat nor to run that razor over your chin again."

Muttering and complaining, Jake disappeared.

Ten minutes later the Krasuskis stood at their front door. Magda turned to look at the room. "Does it look all right, Jake? See anythin' needs fixin'?"

"Looks all right to me, and them flowers make it real fancy." He laughed scornfully. "Who you showin' off for? He ain't comin' to see our house, he's comin' to see us."

"Oh, so, then what'd you tidy up the yard for?"

"Aw, shut up with your pickin' at me." A crafty smile appeared on Jake's face. "After tonight, who's gonna think about this old house? New furniture, fancy carpets, and a car so we won't have to walk anywhere no more."

Magda's worried look faded. "Hope you're right, Jake." She adjusted her straw hat. "Come on, we don't want to be late. Fifteen minutes, so we kin be early and get in a few extra prayers. I'll ask for the new house, you can pray for that new car."

It was well after noon when the Krasuskis returned home. There had been a lunch in the parish hall, seventy-five cents, with beer

110

extra. In a burst of generosity Jake urged Magda to stay.

"Is it all right to? Think we can afford it, Jake?"

"Sure, of course we can. This is a special day, remember?"

Magda didn't hesitate. "Come on, then, let's sit with the Shinskys. I ain't seen Anna for a long time, not to talk to, anyway."

Mellowed by beer and unaccustomed sociability, Jake even bought into the bingo game. On the fifth round, he won. "See, Magda, this *is* out lucky day," and he waved his winnings at her.

When they got up to leave, Anna Shinsky said, "Why don't you stay longer? We'll give you a ride home if you wait awhile. It's too hot to be walking home today."

"No, we gotta go. We're expecting some company, so we gotta be sure to be home." Magda leaned closer. "Somebody sort of special, you see."

"Come on, Magda," Jake called.

"Coming." Magda turned back to Anna. "Stop in a minute when you come past. We might have some news." She adjusted her hat. "O.K., Jake, I'm coming."

It was a happy-looking Jake and Magda that walked up to their front door.

"Look," said Magda. "What's that package doin' there?"

"Well, I'll be damned. Somebody must have left it while we was gone." Jake picked it up, looked it over, and handed it to his wife.

"Just wrapped in brown paper. No name on it," she said. "Open the door quick and bring it in. Let's see what it is. Maybe there's a name inside it."

Jake fumbled with his key, flung open the door, and headed for the kitchen. "Here, give me," he said, grabbing and tearing at the wrapping paper.

Inside was a tall narrow box, wrapped in tissue paper. Jake made short work of that. "Hey, it's a bottle. Hear it gurgle?" He held it up to Magda's ear, shaking it gently. "And here's a note tied on with a pink ribbon."

"Here, let me have the ribbon," said Magda. She untied it carefully and opened the small white envelope attached.

"What's it say, Magda? Who's it from?"

"Here, read it for yourself." She handed him the card.

Slowly, Jake read aloud. "Today is something special and here's something to help with the celebration. I have sent it on ahead so you can put it on ice to get it properly chilled. If you want a drink before

I get there, go right ahead. Just see that you leave enough for all of us later on."

They looked at each other silently. Magda turned the card over, looked at the envelope. "Ain't no address. Card ain't signed. Wonder why not?"

Jake wrinkled his brow. "Maybe . . . maybe he ordered the bottle downtown and somebody there writ the note. Didn't want nobody to know Sonny Hitchcock was sending anything to us, so he didn't give 'em no name to sign."

Magda nodded. "Sure, that's it, Jake. But what is it? It ain't beer in such a fancy bottle. Do you suppose it's whisky?"

"Naw. Can't you tell? That's got to be wine, and I'll bet that fancy printing is French or Italian. Ain't German or Polish."

"Think we could have some, like it says? Just a little taste?"

"Not yet. Got to be chilled. We got to put it in the icebox till it's cool. Wish we had one of them electric refrigerators. That'll be one of the first things we get."

"That'll be nice." Magda sighed. "You can have your beer real cold, and I kin . . ." her voice trailed off.

"How about some sandwiches while it's coolin'?"

"What, you hungry again, Jake?"

"Hell, yes. I ain't had nothin' but them skimpy hot dogs and chips at church. Seventy-five cents too. What a gyp."

"Well, I've got some sausage. I'll fix up a couple of sandwiches. Won't take long. You go cool off out in the backyard. Might look to see if there's any radishes up yet. Maybe that wine will be cold enough by then and we could have a sample taste."

It was almost three o'clock when the Krasuskis finished their sausage sandwiches. Jake leaned back and belched. "Must of been them radishes."

"Now, Jake?" asked Magda eagerly. "Can we taste it now?"

"Why not?" Jake pushed himself up and walked to the ice chest. "Get some glasses. Maybe some of them small glasses like you get jelly in."

Magda rose, carried a handful of dishes to the sink and reached up for two glasses. She brought down a small plate and a package of cookies with them. "Let's make this a party."

"Wonder how you open this," Jake was mumbling.

"First take off that tin foil around the top. Here, you need a knife?"

"Naw, it's real loose, comes off real easy. And it ain't tin foil, it's *gold*. Now for the cork." Jake examined the stopper. "Funny, it's kind of crumbly, like somebody's been at this before. You been messin'?"

Magda shook her head violently. "No, oh, no."

"Here she comes," grunted Jake. "Careful none of them pieces get inside the bottle. Gee, almost ruined it." He surveyed the crumbling bit of cork. "Guess there's enough left to use again, though." Cautiously he poured out the pale liquid.

"Wait," called Magda. She brought two candles in candlesticks from the cupboard. Carefully she lighted them, then pulled down the window shades to cut off the sun's slanting rays.

"What the hell," exclaimed Jake. "Bright sunny afternoon and you need candles?"

"Wine and soft candlelight, they go together. I read it someplace in one of them ads." Awkwardly, almost shyly, she raised her glass. "Here's to us."

Jake's look softened. "Sure, to us."

They sipped. Jake made a face. "Ugh, can't say I like its taste."

"Wine's supposed to be kind of sour bitter," said Magda. "Here, have a cookie to sweeten it up. And, Jake, later on, when he's here, pretend like you like it real good. Wouldn't want him to think he sent a present we didn't like."

Jake looked at his wife blankly, then smiled sheepishly. "Sure, I got you. I'll pretend like it's my favorite drink." He finished his glass with a quick gulp and took a bite of the cookie. "See how I enjoyed that?" Carefully he put the crumbling cork back into place and opened the icebox door.

"Now I'll just clear off this table and leave the dishes till later," said Magda, draining her glass. "Think I'll get out of this dress and take a little nap. It's awful warm, and my eyes are getting heavy. You sit in the front room by the window and watch so you can call me when you-know-who gets here, in case I sleep too long." As she talked, she picked up plates and glasses and moved them to the sink. Then, unfastening her dress, she walked toward the bedroom.

Jake took off his shirt and shoes and sank into the big chair by the front window and leaned back to keep watch.

It was almost five o'clock when the Shinskys drove by the Krasuskis.

"That's funny," said Anna. "Front door shut tight, shades pulled down. Thought there was goin' to be company."

"Maybe they're not home. Might have gone out," said her husband.

"No, they'd have left the door open to let in some air. Besides, I said I'd stop by. Wait for me while I go see."

She knocked, waited a moment, knocked again, then cautiously opened the front door. She was back at the car in a few seconds.

"Come quick. It smells of gas and every door and window is closed, shades pulled down tight. I'm scared."

Together they rushed back to the house. "Wait here a minute," called Shinsky. He pushed open the door, rushed through to open the back door. Then, handkerchief over his face, he made for the kitchen. He was back immediately. "Yup, gas jets on full force. They're both in there. Wait a minute till it clears a bit and I'll try to pull 'em out. You find a phone across the street someplace and get the cops out here—ambulance—somebody."

"Yeah, but—be careful. See if you can get some windows open first." Anna called as she rushed away.

By the time the ambulance came wailing down the street, windows in the house were open and Jake had been pulled out on to the front porch.

"Afraid you're too late, men," said Mr. Shinsky. "I think he's dead. And she's still in there someplace. I couldn't find her."

They found Magda in the bedroom. The ambulance attendant shook his head. "We'll give it a try, but it looks like they're both gone. What was it, suicide?"

17 / *Sunday at 11:00 A.M.*

"Hi, Barney, the chief wants to see you," called Mac, the dispatcher, as Barney and Curt entered headquarters.

"Thanks, Mack, right away," answered Barney, "as soon as I get rid of a few things here."

"How's it going?" asked Mac.

"Oh, you know, plugging away. Too early to know," said Barney. "Any other calls?"

"No, but Otto Kottke said you'd want to know he picked up a couple of kids heading out of town on route 89, doing fifteen over the speed limit. Said to tell you they were driving an old Dodge jalopy, that you'd understand. Do you?"

"An old Dodge, eh?" said Curt.

"Where are they?" said Barney.

"Inside there. Otto's got them, getting the preliminaries. He can stall them along for you if you say so, till you can come."

"Tell him for me I got a little business with the chief, will you? About ten minutes worth, if all goes well," said Barney.

"Mind if I talk to them, Barney?" asked Curt. "I'd like to soften them up for you if you think it's all right."

"Why, yes, Red, that might be all right. You know what you're after. Only be sure to keep it all legal, especially if they're under eighteen."

Barney stepped into his office. He emerged a few minutes later and hurried down the hall to the chief's quarters. Curt walked past the switchboard and through a door leading to an inner room.

Otto Kottke was writing at a small desk. Before him stood two worried-looking youths. Dressed alike in close-fitting body shirts and bell-bottom jeans, one had stringy shoulder-length blond hair framing a pimply face, the other had dark-brown hair just covering his ears and a scraggly mustache across his upper lip.

"A defective muffler and going 60 in a forty-five-miles-per-hour zone," Kottke was saying. "Where were you headed so fast on a Sunday morning?"

"Oh, nowhere special," said the dark-haired boy. "Just driving."

"Weren't heading out of town for any reason?"

"No, just out for a ride."

"Well, I'll have to keep your driver's license till you get your hearing. It's Sunday, so it won't be today. Let's say ten o'clock tomorrow. Of course, you can't drive anywhere without your license."

"How'll we get home?" asked the blond pimply-faced boy.

"Walking is one way. Or you can call your folks."

"Excuse me, Officer," interrupted Curt. "Mind if I come in?"

"Oh, good morning, Conners. Sure, come on in."

115

The two youths exchanged glances, then looked at him uneasily.
"Couple of speeders, Kottke?" asked Curt.

"Afraid so, and on a Sunday morning with a noisy muffler."

"An old Dodge, maybe?" asked Curt.

"Why, yes, as a matter of fact, that's what Karyl here was driving," said Kottke.

"Then I'd like to ask a few questions if you don't mind." The two boys shifted uneasily. "Just a minute, boys," said Curt, and he turned toward the outer office. "Mac, would you come in here for a minute? I want you to hear something." Curt turned back to the youths. "You understand, fellows, you don't have to answer any questions. Anything you say here may be used against you later. And you have the right to have a lawyer, you know."

The dark-haired Karyl swallowed nervously. "I don't have any lawyer."

"Your parents, then. You can call them on the telephone there if you want to."

Fear showed in both faces. "Do we have to?" asked the blond boy.

"No, but you have the right to have a responsible adult present if you like. Dr. Redmond, perhaps?"

"Dr. Redmond?" stammered Karyl.

The blond boy, with a frightened look in his eyes, asked, "Why would—What would—How come you said Dr. Redmond?"

"I thought, since you are college students, you might find him more understanding than your parents."

"We don't need nobody to know about this. We're both twenty years old," said Karyl defiantly. "I don't see why my folks got to know about this at all."

"I see. Well, you can change your mind if you want to." Curt turned to the dispatcher. "Thanks, Mac. Guess these men know what they're doing."

Mac nodded and left. Curt walked to the desk where Otto Kottke sat and picked up the driver's license. He turned to the dark-haired fellow with the mustache. "I see your name is Karyl Pilchoski. You were driving?"

Karyl nodded.

"And your name is . . ." he said, looking at the pimply-faced blond.

"Witold Zacherewiez." His voice broke slightly.

"I'd like to have you boys tell me about last night," said Curt.

They stared at him, then looked at each other. "Last night?" asked Witold, and again his voice broke slightly.

"Karyl, your Dodge was parked right by the stage entrance to the convention center, wasn't it?"

Karyl's mouth dropped, his eyes opened wider.

"You must have gotten there awfully early to get such a good place. Yet you weren't in the show. Why get there so early?"

Karyl looked at Witold. Witold hung his head as he sagged into a chair. Curt studied the two a moment.

"It was nice of you to drive Witold there, Karyl. But he wasn't in the show either. Why did you want to get out to the convention center so early, Witold?"

Witold looked down at his hands and said nothing.

Curt turned back to Karyl. "After a while you moved your old Dodge away so another car could take its place. Why did you do that?"

Karyl reached out to steady himself and dropped to a sitting position. Again he looked at Witold, and again Witold avoided his gaze.

Curt looked steadily at Karyl. "Why did you do that, Karyl?"

Karyl fidgeted uneasily, still trying to get Witold's eye.

"You know, Karyl, anybody who helps another person is called an accessory. He's just as guilty and can get into just as deep trouble as the fellow he helps."

"Trouble?" Karyl's voice cracked. "Guilty? I haven't done nothin'. Just drove my car around. What's wrong with that?"

"That depends. How was Witold dressed when he came running out and you drove him away, Karyl?"

"Dressed? What do you mean, 'dressed'?"

Curt turned to Witold. "What do I mean by 'dressed,' Witold? What were you wearing when you dashed out of the building last night?"

Witold was staring at Curt. His throat twitched. He swallowed but said nothing.

"Too bad you forgot an important part of your costume, Witold." Curt reached into his pocket and drew out a domino mask. He held it high, then tossed it into Witold's lap.

Witold looked at the mask and cringed back in his chair. "Wh—wh—what's that?" he stammered. "Where did you get that?"

117

"I found it in the hallway where you dropped it. You must have been in an awful hurry to drop such an important part of your clothes. In fact, there wasn't much more than this, was there, Witold? It was about all you were wearing." Curt turned to Karyl. "Wasn't it, Karyl? Did Witold tell you he was going to be coming out without his clothes on? Did you have his pants and shirt in your car, Karyl, waiting for him?"

"He—no—yes—I mean, I don't know what you're talking about."

"I mean, for Witold to be running around naked was against the law, and if you helped him get away with it, you're guilty too."

"Guilty? You mean . . . jail?"

"I mean you're already in trouble for speeding and having a noisy muffler. If you were also helping a fellow make his getaway—a fellow that's been breaking the law—what do you think the judge is going to do? And what will your parents say when they read about it in the paper?"

"In the paper? My parents?" Karyl sniveled and wrinkled his eyes as if he might be going to cry.

"And how about Dr. Redmond out at the college?"

Witold found his voice. "Dr. Redmond? What's he got to do with it?"

"Oh, come on, Witold," said Curt. "You had Karyl drive you out to Redmond's house this morning. Now use your head. Do you think Dr. Redmond's going to stand up in front of a judge and ask him to pardon you for what you did? I think you know better."

It was Karyl who lost control. "Oh, for Christ's sake, Witty, why don't you tell him?"

"Shut up, Karyl."

"Sure, shut up. Who's in here for speeding? Whose old man's going to beat the hell out of him for getting his name in the papers? Me, that's who. And why? 'Cause my pal asks me to do him a little favor, a little driving last night. Come on, Witty, get me off the hook. Tell them why I got you there early last night."

Karyl was standing up now, feet wide apart and fists jammed on his hips, a scowl on his face. "Tell them whose idea this was, will you? Get me out of this, Witty, get me out of this, I tell you."

Witold stared defiantly up at Karyl, then he cast a quick glance toward Curt, glared at Karyl again, shifted his eyes toward Otto Kottke. His glance wavered, his body sagged. "O.K. It wasn't Karyl's idea. It was just that he had his car and I needed a ride." He sneaked another look at Curt. "I was supposed to streak. I had to get there early to get my instructions, so I talked Karyl into driving me up there. Well, he got us a place real close to the door like he was supposed to. Only, I guess his heap of junk looked pretty shaky, so he was supposed to take it away while I drove another car into its place. Then when I came running out, he was supposed to get us away from there before anybody could catch me."

Witold stood up. "That's all Karyl did. I swear to God he didn't have nothing to do with my streaking."

Curt Conners stood motionless and silent. Witold took at step closer. "Honest, that's the truth. Karyl didn't have nothing to do with it. You got to believe me."

"And this morning?" asked Curt coldly. "Whose idea was it to get out of town?"

"That was my fault too. We were going to go up the river to where my uncle's got a cabin. I told my folks we was going to camp out for a few days."

"Getting out of town, eh? What were you afraid of?"

Witold's face turned pasty white. "I read about that old lady getting killed. Jeez—I didn't want to get mixed up in no killing. I only thought we'd better get the hell out of town as fast as we could." He looked from Curt to Kottke and back again. "Don't you see? The paper said she was stabbed. Well, come on, can't you understand? I didn't want to get nailed for that."

"And now you are, aren't you, Witold?" asked Curt grimly. "You were the streaker and a couple thousand people saw you."

"But that's just it. I wasn't the streaker. I never did streak."

Curt's head jerked up and his cheeks flushed. "Watch it, kid. Don't you lie to me. What do you mean you weren't the streaker?"

Witold stepped back in fear. "Honest to God, I'm not lying. I didn't streak. I didn't even get all my clothes off." He turned to Karyl. "Tell them, will you? I had my jeans on when I came out. You saw me. Tell them, Karyl. Lots of guys run around with only their jeans on in the summer."

Karyl nodded. "Sure, lots of guys."

"Wait a minute," said Curt. "Let's take this slow. You didn't streak? What do you think we all saw if it wasn't a streaker? Come on, Witold, no lying now. Who was it we saw?"

"I don't know his name. I never saw him before. You see," he said, looking toward Karyl for reassurance, "I hadn't got my nerve up to really do it. I was in the hall. All of the sudden this door opened and out came this Indian. You know, a feather in his hair, moccasins, and one of them squares of cloth hanging down in front. All of a sudden he pulled the string and tossed the cloth to me. 'Here, kid, you keep this for me,' he said, and then he ran like hell into the auditorium. I could hear the audience yelling and whistling and screaming."

"What did this Indian look like? Tall, short, skinny, fat, what, Witold?"

"Heck, I don't know. All I remember was how relieved I was. Somebody else was doing the streaking, and I wouldn't have to. So I cut across the back way to the exit. I pulled on my jeans and tossed off the mask that I was going to wear so people wouldn't recognize me."

"Anybody see you?"

"I don't think so. . . . Oh, yes, I guess I did pass a guy in coveralls, one of the janitors. I remember now, he looked at me kind of funny. No wonder."

"Then what happened?" asked Curt.

"Nothing. Karyl was waiting. He drove me away till we got where he'd left his old pile of junk. We parked and moved over to the Dodge and went on home." Witold sank back as if relieved. "That's all."

"Not quite," said Curt. "You've left out some important details."

"Oh," said Witold.

"You said you were supposed to streak. Who said you were supposed to?"

"Why—er—why, nobody."

"Oh, sure, Witold. You just got the idea, all by yourself. Same as you just decided to have Karyl take you out to visit Dr. Redmond this morning."

Witold and Karyl looked at each other. Curt glanced swiftly at Otto Kottke with the slightest trace of a smile. It was Karyl who spoke first.

"Aw, come on, Witty, might as well tell him the whole story. He knows most of it already anyway."

Witold shrugged. "Well, you see, last Thursday in the locker room out at school we got to talking about streaking and what they were doing in some of the other schools. I guess I shot off my big mouth too much like usual, because a couple guys dared me to streak. I told them nothing doing at first, but they raised twenty dollars and told me it was mine if I'd streak across the stage at an assembly. Well, I needed the money, so I took the dare."

"Twenty dollars, eh? Was it worth it?"

"Hell, no. I got hauled into the dean's office and then right up to the president himself. Old Redmond let me sweat things out a couple of days. Then yesterday he called me, told me he wanted to see me out at the mushroom—I mean the convention center. He give me a choice. One was if I was so keen on streaking and showing myself off, I could just streak at the performance. Otherwise he would probably suspend me and I couldn't graduate next week."

Curt looked at Otto Kottke, then at Witold. Disbelief showed in his face. "Witold, are you telling me that Dr. Redmond *told* you to streak?"

"Not really. He said I could take my choice." Witold stepped closer to Curt Conners. "You don't believe me, you can ask him. Go ahead, ask him."

"Right now I'm letting you tell me your story. Sounds fishy to me, Witold. Take it easy and tell me the truth."

"Well, that's just like he said it. And I was to run over to a woman in the front row, she'd be wearing a purple dress—he even had me take a peek at her from the hall so I'd be sure who she was. And I was to sit in her lap."

"Wow!" exclaimed Curt Conners. "That beats everything you've said so far. Your story gets wilder and wilder. Go on. I can hardly wait for the rest of it."

"There isn't any more. You already heard the rest."

Curt stared at him steadily in silence. Witold stared back, then slowly shifted his eyes to Karyl, to Otto Kottke, back to Curt Conners. "You don't believe me? Honest, it's true. I'm not making this up."

"Um-h'mmm. It's all true, is it?" Curt held his face muscles set as he turned toward Karyl. "How about it, Karyl? Got anything to add to or change in your friend's story?"

Karyl shrugged and dropped his eyes.

"O.K. then, for now. I'll just turn you back to Officer Kottke," said Curt. "You've got a speeding charge to answer for. If you know what's good for you, you'll stay real close to home, no funny ideas about going anyplace. Meanwhile, Witold, we'll check on your story. And if you've made anything up, you'll be in trouble—in deep trouble."

Curt turned abruptly and strode from the room. He heard Kottke saying, "Tomorrow at ten o'clock. Like you heard, better not be going anyplace between now and then."

Curt had hardly gotten to Barney Ross's office when Otto Kottke was there saying, "Nice going, Red. Didn't know you had it in you."

"Found out a lot, didn't we, Otto?"

"Come on, now, how much of that did you know already, and how much was bluff?"

Curt laughed. "Thanks to you, Otto, it wasn't hard. You gave us the stuff to start with this morning. I just told them what you'd already told us, acted like I knew what I was talking about. They were just a couple of dumb scared kids. Did you see Karyl's look when I talked about his old man hearing about it?"

"What do you think, Red? Do you believe his story about that other streaker?"

"You know, Otto, I sort of think I do. Witty was too shook up about then to be making anything up—unless he was so scared he would make up just about anything." Curt shook his head. "It'd be a lot easier for us if he was lying. I thought we'd found the streaker, now maybe we've got to keep looking, and right now who knows where to look?"

"Well, like you say, he might have been so shook up he made up the first thing that came to his mind."

"Otto, does that kid look like the kind of a guy that would carry a knife and stick it into a woman he didn't even know?"

"Yeah, I see what you mean," said Kottke. "He sure as hell don't seem the type. How about that Redmond story?"

"Oh, yes, Redmond!" Curt got a faraway look in his eyes. "You know, Otto, I'm looking forward to a session with our college president. It should be real interesting."

18 / *Sunday at 11:30 A.M.*

"Things are moving," said Barney. "Never saw the chief so cooperative." He dropped his voice to a whisper. "He must be scared."

"Mayor McGinty, maybe?" asked Curt.

Otto Kottke winked broadly and said, "Makes a difference whose wife gets killed around here."

Barney tossed his notes on the desk and lowered himself into his chair. "Here's what's happened so far. He's got Mike Mulvany watching room 14 at Wauconda Falls House to see if this Anthony Jones might fit the description. We're in luck about the stagehands and ushers at the convention center. There's a band concert at three this afternoon, so they'll all be on duty." He turned to Otto Kottke. "Chief says it'd be easiest if *you* stopped by the airline office, since you're in the squad car anyway. See if they can find out where Hitchcock boarded the plane he came in on yesterday and if he might have stopped over there the night before. O.K. by you, Otto?"

"By me? Oh, sure. There's a cute chick at the ticket counter it'll be a pleasure to talk to. It might even take fifteen minutes, with luck."

"Sorry, Red, about the rented cars. They're still out, so nobody can check mileage till they come in." Barney picked up his notes and continued. "Now about those calls to Capital City. Probation officer said DiVacco checked with him on schedule last Wednesday, isn't due again till next Wednesday. He'll try to get DiVacco's sponsor family to see if they know where he is.

"Also, Manson's legit. Been with the security force over half a year. Not one of their top men, but he's been out on a few jobs like this before, enough to show he's capable. He was with the Chicago force first, then moved to Denver before he came to our state. Had good references from both places."

"Not one of their top men, you say?" asked Curt.

"They usually send old-timers on out-of-town jobs, especially for VIP's like the governor or one of the supreme court justices. Lieutenant governors don't rate top men, I'm guessing."

"Chicago, you say, Barney? Wasn't DiVacco originally out of Chicago?"

Barney looked startled. "H'mmm, . . . I see what you're thinking,

123

Red. I suppose it's just barely possible."

"Anyway, that makes another guy for the Sears broad to look at in our lineup."

"Our lineup? Oh, yeah, that. Wait a minute, what do you mean another guy?"

Curt told of the interview with Witold and Karyl, calling on Otto for corroboration.

Barney smiled with satisfaction. "So we've got our streaker, have we?"

"I don't think so, Barney. Probably not."

"Come on now, Red, what's with this 'probably not.' You're not buying that wild tale about Redmond, are you? Or about there being another streaker?"

"I haven't exactly. Only that kid didn't look like the kind that would stick a knife in anybody. Crazy enough to streak, sure, but a killer, no. I just can't see it. Can you, Otto?"

Otto Kottke shook his head. "Ain't likely, Barney."

Barney's face showed his disappointment. "Too bad. It'd sure be a big help if we could say we found the streaker." He stood up. "Well, there's one thing we can check on. I think we're due for a call on Irving Redmond, our college president."

He turned to Otto. "Thanks for help this morning. Now do you mind heading out for that airline ticket office?"

"Mind? Hell, no. I'm on my way."

"And so are we, Red," said Barney. "We've got a lot of balls flying in the air right now. Hope we can keep track of them all. Think we can?"

"Yeah, sure," laughed Curt. "This is better than pounding a beat any day, anytime."

It was just twelve o'clock when Barney and Curt drove out of the parking lot at headquarters. "Looks like we're just in time to let Redmond get home from church, in case he goes," said Barney.

As they headed up the hill from downtown, the houses became larger, the lawns more spacious. One of the largest and most imposing of all was 4100 College Avenue.

"Well," said Barney. "looks like college presidents are doing all right these days."

"Hold it," called Curt. "Turn into this driveway a minute."

In an instant, Barney's foot was on the brake pedal and his hand jerked the wheel. "Now what?" he asked.

"Glad we've got an unmarked car. Look."

From the Redmond driveway came a modest-looking automobile with a man driving. Next came a long, low expensive model driven by a woman. The two cars headed back toward town.

"The rented car, Barney," said Curt. "Looks like Redmond's returning the last night getaway job. Might as well drive down to the next street and pull around the corner and wait till our bird comes back to the nest. No, wait! Speaking of rented cars, how about going on down to the hotel garage? There's time, and I'm kind of curious about those two vehicles that Sonny Hitchcock still has out. A little look at the mileage registered might be interesting."

Barney headed back toward town and pulled up in front of the hotel garage. "Looks kind of quiet. Sunday drivers must not be out yet. Hi, there, Pete," called Barney. "How are things today?"

The attendant sauntered over to the car. "Oh, hi, Barney. Just fine. Can't complain, now that summer's finally here. What brings you down here today?"

"Just thought we'd like to look around a bit. You know Curt Conners here?"

Pete nodded. "Hi."

"Sonny Hitchcock been by yet to take out that job he rented?"

"You mean the TV star? Naw, haven't seen him since he came in about eleven o'clock. Nor that fellow with him, neither."

"Came in about eleven, eh?" asked Curt. "He must've gotten up early."

"Oh, no," laughed Pete. "I mean that's when he got in. He's been out on the town, haven't seen his car here since early yesterday evening. And Zeke's report (that's the night man) doesn't show he's been in or out since." He leaned closer. "They say these show people know how to live it up. Wonder where he spent the night."

"Out all night, eh? How about his man, that Peters fellow?" asked Curt.

"Well, our night record shows he came in about eleven o'clock, and went right out again at eleven-thirty, and *he* didn't come in again till about fifteen minutes ago."

"Mind if we look at the cars a bit?"

"Naw, go right ahead."

Curt checked the gas gauges, the numerals on the speedometer registering trip mileage, looked under the seats, in the glove compartments, behind the sun visors. Except for a scrap of paper clipped to a sunshade, he found nothing unusual. He was about to toss the scrap when he noticed 305 NORIV written faintly. Slipping it into his pocket, he waved to Barney, who nodded.

"Well, thanks, Pete. Hope we didn't cause you any trouble."

"None at all, anytime," said Pete. "Be seeing you."

The two were about to drive off when Pete signaled them to stop. Pete leaned close to Barney. "Don't look now, Barney, but that's the guy. You know, Sonny Hitchcock's man. Looks like he's in a rush, too."

Pete hurried back to his booth. "Hello, Mr. Peters. Want me to bring your car out for you?" Dennis Peters shook his head. "O.K., Mr. Peters. Here are your keys. Have a nice drive."

Barney waited until Dennis Peters had driven off in the direction of the center of town.

"Took the blue one, I see," said Curt. "Barney, does this mean anything to you? 305 NORIV. Found it on a scrap of paper in that blue car Peters just drove away."

"Can't say that it does, offhand," Barney said as he pulled the car from the curb and headed up the hill again. "Combination to something, maybe? Or a drugstore patent medicine formula?"

"Let's see," said Curt, "305 -N-or-four? 305 nor ivy?" He shook his head.

"Well, whatever it is, skip it." They were approaching Redmond's house. "Looks like our folks are back home by now. And you must have been right. There's one car less in the driveway this time."

It was Mrs. Redmond who answered the doorbell.

"Sorry to disturb you, Mrs. Redmond," said Barney politely. "I'm Officer Ross and this is Officer Conners."

"Yes, I remember from last night. Oh, that dreadful episode. I've just been reading the story in the paper. How could such a thing happen right here in Wauconda Falls, and to somebody like Maude McGinty?" She paused. "Oh, of course. That's why you've come, isn't it?"

"Well, yes, Mrs. Redmond. We've a few questions we're asking everybody that was in that special section last night."

"Won't you come in? We've just come from church, so this is a good time." She led them across a large entrance hall to a small, elegantly furnished reception room. "Please sit down. I'll call my husband."

"Some house," murmured Barney appreciatively when she had gone. "Wonder who's paying for all this. Taxpayers, do you think?"

Footsteps were heard across the hall, and Irving Redmond appeared, smiling genially. "Good afternoon. Glad to see you. How are things going?"

Barney shrugged. "A bit slowly, I'm afraid."

"Oh? Could I offer you a drink to bolster your spirits?" When Barney shook his head, he said, "Of course, regulations, policemen on duty. Coffee, then, or at least a Coke?"

"Thank you," said Curt from near the window. "Coffee would be fine."

Barney threw a surprised glance toward Curt, then echoed, "Yes, thanks, I believe I would like some too."

Irving Redmond stepped out into the hall and called, "Margaret, is there coffee?" And her voice answered, "Yes. I'll have Hattie bring some right in."

"Cigarette? Cigar?" continued Redmond cordially. "No? Mind if I smoke my pipe?" He went through an elaborate ritual of selecting, filling, tamping, lighting, and puffing. "Ah, here you are, Hattie. Just set the tray over there." Carefully he put down his pipe and lifted the silver pot on the tray. "Cream or sugar, Ross, Conners?"

"Sugar, please," said Curt. "Two lumps."

"Righto," said Redmond cheerfully, picking up the tiny silver tongs. "Here you are, Conners. Wouldn't you prefer to sit right here in this comfortable chair, rather than way over by the window? No? Well, as you like." He turned to Barney. "Here you are."

Redmond settled himself in his chair, crossed his knees, picked up his pipe, and said comfortably, "Now, gentlemen. What can I tell you?"

"We have some questions we are asking everybody," began Barney. "First of all, did you get a good look at the streaker last night?"

"Well, yes, I suppose I really did. Oh, of course I did. He certainly made himself very visible to us."

"And did you recognize him?"

Redmond reached for his lighter, drew a few puffs on his pipe. "Can't seem to keep this thing drawing today," he muttered. Then with an air of thoughtfulness he said, "I really can't say. Now that I think about it, I'm not so sure I really got a good look. More like a blur, I'd say. You know, Indian feathers, hair in braids, the shock at seeing his—er—genitals exposed, and then a mask makes it awfully hard to recognize a face."

"A mask?" asked Barney. "What kind of a mask?"

"One of those eye-piece things, dominoes, I think they're called."

"He was wearing a domino mask, then. Was there anything else? A distinguishing mark, something about the way he moved, anything like that?"

"No, I don't think so."

"Could it have been one of your students?"

Again Redmond paused. "One of our college boys? Why, I don't know. I suppose it's possible, but why our college especially?"

Barney put down his cup and looked directly at Redmond. "Tell me, do you know a young man named Witold Zacherewiez?"

Redmond's pipe went out again, so he carefully went through the motions of relighting it. "Witold Zacherewiez? Yes, . . . it has a familiar sound. . . . Certainly an unusual name . . . Polish, I should think."

"Wasn't he in your office just last week?"

"In my office?" Redmond smiled patiently. "Quite possibly. I see lots of students in the course of a week, and faculty, too."

"But not many are guilty of streaking, would you say?"

Redmond froze for a few seconds, then smiled broadly. "Oh, I see. You know about that? We had thought we wouldn't let reports about that silly incident get out. Some things are better kept quiet, you know, strictly within our college walls."

Barney shrugged. "I understand your point of view. May I ask what punishment you gave Witold?"

"Punishment? Well, really, Ross, I'm surprised. Wouldn't you say our methods of handling our discipline problems are strictly for *us* to know about, and nobody else?"

"Ordinarily, yes, Dr. Redmond. But in view of last night's streaking, wouldn't you say that maybe this time it has moved into our territory?"

"Into your territory?" Redmond stiffened and leaned forward. "Oh, I see. You are implying that our Witold was doing a repeat on a grander scale last night?"

"It's quite possible, you know," Barney's tone became grimmer. "I'll ask you again, what punishment did you give Witold?"

Irving Redmond sat stiffly silent.

128

"Dr. Redmond, you had two callers early this morning. One was Karyl Pilchoski; the other was our Witold Zacherewiez. Why did they come calling so very early on a Sunday morning?"

"Now, really, Ross, you're going too far again. Students calling on me? That's hardly a concern of the police."

"Again I say, in view of last night, it *has* become the concern of the police. Dr. Redmond, did you encourage young Witold to streak again last night?"

Redmond stood up, glaring angrily. "Did I *what*? I certainly see no justification for a question like that."

Curt interrupted quietly. "Perhaps Dr. Redmond would let me read from my notes." He produced a paper from his pocket, held it up so the light of the window fell on it, and read. " 'Dr. Redmond gave me my choice. He said I should not graduate, but if I wanted to do something to prove I was really sorry, I could repeat my performance Saturday night in the convention center.' "

"What are you reading there?"

"Just what Witold told us this morning down at headquarters."

"This morning? You've had him in for questioning?"

"Well, you see, Witold and Karyl had some bad luck this morning. Somebody had encouraged them to get out of town for a few days, and they were heading up the river. But they were going sixty in a forty-five-miles-per-hour speed zone, and so one of our traffic detail brought them in. One thing led to another, and pretty soon Witold and Karyl were telling us about his streaking business."

"Oh, I see." Redmond sat down again. Suddenly he flashed a smile. "I guess I'd better admit my stupid mistake. You see, Witold was in, yes, he had streaked. He was very stubborn about admitting he'd done anything wrong. I mentioned the usual penalties, like loss of credits, working out a fine by campus labor, even threatening him with not being allowed to graduate with his class. He just wouldn't admit that streaking was wrong, that it deserved any punishment. Finally, I'm afraid"—here Redmond looked down as if ashamed— "I lost my temper, something that doesn't happen often. So I said if Witold was so set on streaking and thought it was a fine thing to do, he could just do a repeat performance Saturday night. I thought for a minute it was going to work, because he did stop and think awhile. Then he surprised me by saying he just might do that. Frankly, gentlemen, I didn't know what to say then. I'd given him a choice and he said he was going to take it. Should I back down? Well, I

129

procrastinated, let it slide, took care of other things, and all of a sudden it was Saturday night."

"So Witold was the streaker last night?" asked Curt. "Did you recognize him?"

"Why, of course! Who else would I think it might be?"

"Yes, who else? There's one thing that still puzzles us, Dr. Redmond. Why did he think he had to sit on the lap of a lady in a purple dress? Was that part of his choice of punishments too?"

"Purple dress?" Redmond's voice faltered. "I'm not sure . . . I know . . . what you mean."

"I think you do," said Barney Ross. "Better tell us, Redmond."

There was a heavy silence. Far in the distance a door slammed and voices murmured softly. Redmond said nothing, and the two policemen sat silently watching him.

Barney cleared his throat lightly. "Perhaps the name Phoebe Sears will encourage you, refresh your memory? She was wearing a purple dress last night."

An expression of pain appeared on Redmond's face. "Phoebe Sears! That name again!" He sat motionless as if making a hard decision. "Gentlemen," he said softly, "I see I must tell you something I've told very few people, not even my wife. You are men of law and order, you will appreciate my confidence and not betray it?"

"I can't promise that. I must warn you that anything you say can be used against you," said Barney. "But I can assure you, off the record, that only if it becomes necessary to protect an innocent party."

"It was when I was a senior in college. I went to a small college in upstate New York, mostly because my folks were poor and it was close to our home. I worked my way through, and sometimes I didn't have very much to go on. Well, I got the job managing the college book store, selling supplies and textbooks, you know. One time I needed some ready cash real quick. I borrowed some money from the till, expecting to put it back two days later when I was due to get paid. It seemed so easy at the time, and I was a kid fighting hard to keep going till I got my degree. Bad luck! Somebody decided to balance accounts, and I was in trouble.

"Well, I told my story, had my paycheck in my hands, ready to replace the cash. Everybody was ready to forgive and forget—some were even real sorry for me—but there was this one old gal on the board who wouldn't give in. You've guessed it, her name was Phoebe Sears."

"We've met Miss Sears," said Barney. "I think I know what you mean."

"Well, I graduated all right, got a job, and have been making out ever since. Just my luck, this Sears woman moves out here, gets on the State Arts Council (she always was a pusher), and now here she turns up. So I panicked, I thought like a college kid again."

"You panicked? What did you do?"

"I got the idea that if she could be embarrassed, really shaken up, she might forget about me. I just had an hour before I was to meet her, so I got hold of Witty and gave him the instructions. Stupid, childish, asinine—call it what you will, but I could just see ten years of climbing up the ladder wiped out completely once that Sears dame started on my reputation."

"Are you telling me the straight story now, Redmond?" asked Barney. "Have you left anything out?"

"No, as God is my witness, I have not."

"You didn't tell Witold to carry a knife?"

"A knife?" A look of bewilderment was followed by a look of terror. "Oh, my God, a knife? You think I told Witty to use a knife? Oh, dear God, no, never."

"We haven't said we think so. And we don't think Witold is the kind of fellow who would, even if you or anybody else told him to."

"But then . . . what . . . "

"But then," said Barney intensely, "if it comes out that Witold was the streaker and five thousand people say they saw him sit in Maude McGinty's lap and we found a dagger sticking in Maude McGinty—well, what do *you* think?"

"They'll say he killed her!" Redmond's voice rose in pitch. "What can I *do*? I can't let Witold get accused of something like that. Tell me what to *do*, will you?" He sat down suddenly.

"I'm sorry, Dr. Redmond," Barney answered. "That is something I can't tell you. Right now if I were you, I'd pray for a miracle, like finding a different streaker or figuring out some way that knife got into the mayor's wife if the streaker didn't put it there. I wish I could repay your hospitality with something more comforting, but right now, we're fresh out of comfort." Barney was standing by now. "We'll say good-by, Dr. Redmond. You can be sure we'll be in touch with you, and we hope, if you think of anything, you will call us."

Irving Redmond barely looked up from where he sat, hunched in his chair.

"Good-by, Dr. Redmond," said Curt. Together they walked to the front door.

"Just a minute," said Curt, pausing outside the open front door. From inside the house came the sound of footsteps across polished floor, and a high feminine voice saying, "Well, Irving, dear, let's hear you talk yourself out of *this* one."

"You know, Barney," said Curt, "I almost feel sorry for the guy, except I feel sorrier for Witty. Barney, we just can't let that poor Witty get mangled."

Barney nodded. "I know. I feel the same way. But we'll have to take it like it comes, Red. That's the way it is."

As they were walking to the car, Barney gave Curt a shrewd look. "I appreciate your pulling that report from out of your pocket. Now suppose you tell me where you got it."

Curt grinned. "Oh, that? That was the back of a cleaner's bill. Glad Witty wasn't there to check up on me. I don't think I read it just the way he said it."

"God, what a bluff!" snorted Barney.

As they were pulling out from the curb, Barney remarked out of the side of his mouth, "Since when do you take two lumps of sugar in your coffee?"

"Why, since today. You noticed Redmond did the pouring and passing with his right hand, didn't you?"

"Yes, I did. Oh, come on, you aren't thinking that Redmond himself could have been—"

"Well, not really." Curt laughed. "But I'm just keeping in practice. One of these times I'm going to catch a southpaw, and if he's got blue eyes—" He paused, then leaned close to Barney's ear. "There's one other test to use too, but I haven't figured out how to apply it easily."

"Oh, what one is that, Red?"

"Well, you can check on the color of his eyes and hand him something to see if he's left-handed. You can estimate his height and weight. All of these you can do without his even knowing you're doing it, but how do you go about seeing if he's been circumcised without him knowing you're doing it?"

19 / *Sunday at 1:30 P.M.*

It was after one o'clock when Barney and Curt left the Redmonds and started back for headquarters.

"Lots of people yet to talk to," said Curt. "Maybe we'd better do some organizing."

"What do you have in mind, Red?" asked Barney.

"The band concert is at three o'clock out at the convention center. Once the program has started, the ushers and stagehands won't be busy. And maybe our local people are going to the program so we could talk to them about the same time."

"Makes sense, should work," said Barney. "It's not far from here, so we'll just spin out there to see what we can set up."

In spite of the early hour, a few people were already parking their cars and heading for the main entrance. O'Malley's door saw a steady stream of uniformed, instrument-carrying performers filing in.

"Hi, O'Malley," said Barney. "Got you working already, I see."

"Yep, these are busy days. How's it going with you two? Any news about the you-know-what last night?" asked O'Malley.

"We're just plugging away. You know how it is. Too early to say we've got anything."

"Then I take it you're not here to listen to the band concert today."

"Afraid not." Barney shrugged. "Got no time for pretty music."

"Back to visit the scene of the crime, like they say in them detective stories, eh?"

"Well, not exactly." Barney shook his head. "Maybe you can tell us, O'Malley. Do you suppose there's a corner somewhere where we can talk to some people quietly?"

"I think so. We only got a band today, not a thousand like last night. The band are all gathering in that big back room, so you can just about take your pick of any other place you like. How about that same room you was in last night? But you'll have to check with Flanagan."

"Flanagan? Who's he?"

"He's the boss of the janitors out here. Big bald-headed Irishman, just a fringe of red hair. Used to be as good-looking as Conners here, with a real Irish-red mop, but, well," O'Malley gave a mock sigh, "you know how old age changes us. You'll probably find Flanagan right on the main floor of the arena, seeing that things are set up."

"Thanks," said Barney. "And, O'Malley, after the program starts, maybe a few words with you? We'd like to go over what you saw last night."

"Sure, why not? Once the cars are all parked I'll have time." O'Malley lowered his voice to a mock whisper. "How about it, Barney, should I be looking for an old Dodge to drive up again? Or check the back rooms for a streaker?"

Barney smiled and winked. "You never know. Keep your eyes open for both of them. Be seeing you."

The two detectives found Flanagan right away. Sure, they could see the whole building crew after three o'clock, except maybe the two working the lights. They might have to be up in the balcony. But they were on the lights last night too, so prob'bly wouldn't have anything to say worth hearing anyway. A room? Why not the Green Room? It'd be real handy, and with the doors closed, the music wouldn't be too loud.

Sheppard, the head usher, was in the lobby. Yes, the same ushers were on duty this afternoon as last night. No, no reason why they couldn't be available for a short talk, once the crowd was in place, just so they wouldn't be away very long. Yes, he remembered the four who helped last night. He'd send them down about 3:15 or so.

"Looks like we're all set, Red," said Barney as they headed back to the parking lot. "Let's get on down to headquarters."

"Maybe Mac could call our people," said Curt. "You know, the local folks sitting in the special section. If they're going to be at the band concert anyway, maybe they could come down to the Green Room at intermission."

Barney maneuvered the car out of the parking lot.

"Know which ones they are, Red?" He swerved to avoid two teenagers who darted across in front of him. "Damn fool kids," he muttered.

"The Andertons, the Kubitzes, and the Ryans, first of all," said Curt. "Then the Balkans (he was the promotion guy), and the fellow Dawson, who wrote the play, and his wife, and Mrs. Cohen, the treasurer. Let's see, there was that Goodman fellow, and Mr. and Mrs. Katzen. How am I doing?"

"Almost perfect, Red," Barney said in admiration, heading the car downtown. "You forgot one family—Dr. and Mrs. Quinlan."

134

"Not really, Barney. I sort of thought we'd talk to the Quinlans separately, if you don't mind."

"Oh?" Barney looked slightly puzzled, then smiled. "I get it, the doctor's case Mike stumbled over."

Curt nodded. "That and a couple of other things. Hey, slow down, Barney." Curt pointed to a garage on the corner. "There's the car rental agency. Let me out. I'll just take a minute."

Barney pulled up to the curb and Curt hopped out. He was back almost at once. "Got what I wanted, Barney. Now let's see." He pulled a paper from his pocket. "Um-h'mmm, here's something interesting. One of the cars put on over three hundred miles according to the check-out mileage and what I saw this morning. Now how could that be? Where could Hitchcock have been to put on that many miles between Friday and Sunday?"

"Good question, Red, but no time to answer it now." Barney pulled into the station parking lot. "Pile out, Red."

Together they strode into the side entrance. "Any news, Mac?" Barney called to the man working the switchboard.

"A little, Barney. Mulvany's in your office. Kottke left a message on your desk. Chief said to stop in when you've got a minute."

"Thanks, Mac. I've got a little job for you if you've got time. How are things?"

"Real quiet. Sunday afternoon slump. All the actions's out at the center, and band concerts don't usually give trouble. What have you got for me?"

"A list of people to call to invite them to a little party. I'll have it for you in a few minutes."

"Delighted to be your social secretary. What sort of a party? Am I invited?" Mac grinned.

"If you'd like to come. Don't think it's going to be the high point of the social season though." Barney turned toward his office. "I'll have the list of the lucky guests in a few minutes."

Mile Mulvany was waiting for them. "Hi, Barney, hi, Red. Got a couple of things for you."

"Good," said Barney, sliding into his chair. "Let's hear them."

"First, I connected with two stores on that desk knife. The man at Fitch's Gift Shop recognized it. Part of a set—a fancy pair of scissors and this letter opener to match, all in a leather holder. He remembered selling six sets just before Christmas. Cleaned him out, so he had to reorder, and then nobody's bought any since." Mike

Mulvany smiled. "Guess who bought those six sets. Doc Quinlan."

"Doc Quinlan, eh?" said Curt, whistling softly. "Well, what do you know. Let's hope Doc remembers who he gave them all to, that is, if he gave all six sets away."

"And the other thing, Mike?" asked Barney.

"The fellow down at the Wauconda Falls House stayed pretty close to his room. Didn't show till about twelve-thirty. Then he sort of sneaked out and across the street to Larry's Diner. Headed for the counter stool farthest back from the door and bent down low over the menu." Mike laughed. "All the same I got a couple of good looks at him. He could be the guy you're looking for, Barney. Doesn't match exactly, but he's close."

Barney and Curt exchanged glances. "One more guy for my line-up," said Curt, "if we can get him there."

"Wait, there's more," said Mike. "Somehow I got to feeling hungry, so I ambled in and on toward the back, sat down next to him. I kidded the waitress a bit, just to soften things up. Teased her about being out at the Mushroom in the Meadow and was she thrilled to see the streaker. You know, got her to giggling. I noticed our guy was beginning to listen, so I said out of the corner of my mouth. 'Look at her blush. What do you think, fellow, was she embarrassed or do you think she was kind of pleased?' He sort of smiled. 'What did *you* think of it?' I said, turning right to him. 'And how do you like our new convention center?' He said he didn't know anything about it, didn't know what I was talking about, so I acted surprised, played up the streaker bit, and what did he think of a town that had such things going on? He said somthing about not knowing much about streakers. So I went on about not only do we have streakers, but this one stuck a knife in one of the women in the audience. *That* got him. 'You mean he killed her?' he asked. 'Sure, ain't you seen none of the morning papers or heard the radio?' I said. He just shook his head and got up like he was going to leave.

"I reminded him he hadn't finished his dessert, but he said he just remembered he had to catch a plane. I told him to relax, he was too late for the one o'clock flight, and there wouldn't be another one out of here till eight-thirty tonight. So he sits down again but clams up, won't say a word, eats real fast, pays his check, and hightails it back to his room."

"Hey, Mike, that's all right," said Barney. "Handled it just fine. He didn't suspect you were a cop?"

"Don't think so. I'm not in uniform, and I don't usually hang out at Larry's Diner. Pretty lousy food there."

"Looks like our guy doesn't like to be around where there's a murder," mused Curt. "And looks like he'll be here till almost eight o'clock, in case we want to get in touch with him. Do you think he was putting on an act about not knowing anything about the killing, Mike?"

"I don't know. He seemed awful shook up, but like you say, he might have been playing it real cool. Want me to go back and keep an eye on him, Barney?"

"Maybe. What do you think Red?" said Barney.

"Might be better to leave him alone. He's got six hours. If he really is DiVacco, he may get an idea and start something. If not, well, there's time later this afternoon." He looked thoughtful. "Barney, can you think of any excuse to get him in here for questioning?"

"Not right off. We can't nab a guy and pull him in, just like that." He picked up a paper and let out a whistle. "Hey, listen to this. Kottke says here that Wayne Hitchcock boarded the plane at Milltown on Saturday morning. He must have spent the night there, too, since there's nothing in or out of there after about ten o'clock the night before."

"Milltown!" Curt exclaimed. "That's halfway between Capital City and here. Must be about 130 miles, wouldn't you say? Two times 130 is 260 miles. It fits, Barney!"

"Fits, Red? What do you mean?"

"Don't you see? He leaves here Friday night with Peters, drives to Milltown, checks into a motel, Peters drives back here with the car. Saturday Peters gets out to our airport and makes like they both came in together. No trick for a Hollywood actor."

"Um-h'mmm, yes, it's possible, Red, it's possible."

"But I don't see why. What was Hitchcock in here on Friday for? Why all the hush-hush and making like he wasn't? And who was the woman he was meeting?"

"Hey, Barney," yelled Mac from the doorway. "Where's that list of names? If you want action, you better give it to me right now."

"Right, Mac. Here they are." Barney produced his seating chart from the night before. "I've checked the names of the people we want. They're all local, so numbers should be in the phone book."

"What am I supposed to say?" asked Mac.

"First tell them you're calling for me so they know it's legit. Then ask if they're going to be at the band concert at the center today. If they are, would they mind coming down to the Green Room at the intermission for just a few minutes. The Green Room is where we gathered last night, in case they ask."

"Got you, Barney." Mack made an exaggerated bow. "Secretary Mack at your service. Hope your party is a huge success." Mack disappeared.

Barney headed for the door. "Better see what the chief wants. If he's in his office on a Sunday afternoon, it's got to be important. And I'm not going to keep him waiting."

After Barney had left, Mike winked at Curt and grinned. "Barney's moving pretty fast, isn't he?"

"Sure is. You can see why. Chief owes his job to the mayor. Mayor's wife is killed. Mayor wants action from Chief. Chief wants action from Barney. And Hickson, the reporter, wants action from everybody. So I guess it's up to all of us to swing into action. Only, it's hard to act when you don't know where to start."

"Can I help, Red?"

"You already have, a lot. Nice work this morning. Especially since this is your day off."

"What the hell? I want to." Mike shook his head. "That sure was a stupid stunt last night, stumbling over Doc Quinlan's bag. I should have nailed the streaker right then and there."

"You and me both, Mike. I messed it up pretty bad myself." Curt lowered his voice. "Mike, can you think of any way we could bring that guy from the Wauconda Falls House down here?"

Mike's brow wrinkled in thought. "There'd have to be a charge, and so far he hasn't done anything."

"I know, I know. But I'm wondering. Could we get him to do something, or maybe could we *say* he's under suspicion?"

"Like what, Red?"

"That's what I'm trying to figure out. Was he sitting close to you at that lunch counter?"

"Yeah, but he didn't do anything, didn't touch me or say anything."

Curt spoke more slowly. "But suppose, Mike, you went to pay and your billfold was missing—money, driver's license, you know."

"I think I'm catching on. I should maybe go to his room and accuse him of picking my pocket?"

"H'mmm. No, not quite. If he's really DiVacco, he's a tough one. No, you'd have to have a warrant, and you wouldn't dare go alone. Maybe . . . maybe Kottke—he's still cruising in the squad car. You'd be a private citizen, Mr. Michael, mad as hell. Kottke asks for his identification—like a driver's license. If he's got one and it's Anthony Jones, well, maybe that's all. But if he can't produce one, well, you bring him in for questioning. By that time you'd catch on if he's scared or uneasy or trying to hide something."

"So we get him down to the station, then what?" asked Mike.

"Yeah. Then what?" Curt was silent a few minutes. He reached for the phone book, looked up a number, lifted the phone to his ear. "Give me an outside line, will you, Mac?" He dialed. "Hello, will you connect me with suite 201? . . . Hello, oh, it's you, Manson. Conners here. Suppose I could talk to the lieutenant governor? . . . Hello, Mr. Alcott, Officer Conners speaking. I'm glad you're still in town. We think we've located DiVacco. . . . No, not for sure, this fellow's using another name. . . . We're wondering if we bring him in to the station, could you identify him? . . . Oh, I see, you don't know him personally. . . . Well, would Mrs. Alcott be willing? . . . Yes, I understand that, but maybe she could see him from out in the hall. . . . Well, it would have to be a little while yet, of course, since he's still at large. . . . He'd be well guarded, and you'd have Manson with you, wouldn't you? . . . Yes, I know it's a touchy matter, but wouldn't *you* feel easier if you knew if DiVacco is here or not? . . . And did I hear you say you've got a couple of men besides Manson? By all means, have them on hand too."

20 / Sunday at 2:00 P.M.

Barney returned from the chief's office looking grim. "Chief says he wants me to pay a call on Mayor McGinty. If we go right now we can stop there on the way out to the Mushroom in the Meadow. Ready, Red?"

"Sure, Barney."

Barney turned to Mike. "Thanks again, Mike."

139

Curt added, "Good luck this afternoon."

As Barney and Curt walked out into the parking lot, Barney continued. "Can't say I want to make this call. Never have been good at saying words of condolence. But the chief says 'do it.' "

"I know, Barney." Curt's voice was sympathetic. "I'm glad *you* have to do the talking, and I get to listen. You never know, the mayor just might drop a clue that could help us."

As they drove out into the street, Curt asked, "What did the chief have to tell you, Barney? Any new developments?"

"A few, but we'll have to wait to hear them. We've arrived."

"Already? Why, you've only gone about three blocks."

"Of course. The mayor lives downtown. Look at the house, Red. Turn of the century, twelve to fifteen rooms, an attic as big as that whole apartment you live in, and a front porch you could hold a dance on. When that house was built, this was probably way out on the edge of town, the showplace of the village."

"Some difference between Redmond's house and this one. Wouldn't you think the mayor could be more up-to-date?"

"Politics, Red, politics. Redmond's on the make, got to impress people with his ability and success, the latest thing and all that. Joe McGinty's a man of the people, just plain folks, none of this stuck-up fancy stuff. He's living right down among the Irish and near the Polacks. They're the ones who vote for him."

"You know, Barney, maybe he's better off too. This is ten times the house that Redmond's is. Look at all that wood—cost a fortune nowadays. McGinty's father must have been in the money to build all that."

"Come to think of it, Red, he wasn't. The mayor's fond of telling everybody how he's a self-made man, just a poor little Irish mick that came up the hard way."

"Then how come all this?"

"His wife's, I think. Maude McGinty's grandfather came out here when land was almost free. Sat tight on a couple hundred acres, then sold them off for lots when Goodleighs brought in the poor Irish. Played it close, saved every dime, and ended up—well, not as rich as the Goodleighs up there on the heights, but able to afford this place. So Maude inherited the house; Joe married Maude, and—oh, hell, here I am stalling, telling you all this when I should be going up those steps, walking across that big porch, and ringing the doorbell. Like I said, I'm not eager for this little job."

"Well, come on then, Barney. *I'll* go up those steps and *I'll* ring the doorbell," said Curt. "But I won't do the talking, just the looking and listening."

The doorbell was answered by a pleasant-faced, generously built older woman who looked as if she would be more at home wielding a mop and broom then greeting callers. "Yes?" she asked.

"Is the mayor in?" asked Barney.

She looked shocked. "The mayor? Oh, yes, of course he's home, but I don't think he wants to see anybody. Haven't you heard about last night?"

"Yes, that is why we are here. We're from the police department."

"Police? Oh." She recoiled slightly. "Well, I don't know. That's different. If you'll come in, I'll go see." She opened the door and led Barney and Curt into a front parlor. "Just you wait here and I'll go find out."

There was an oppressive silence. The two men looked at each other uneasily. Barney crossed to examine a handsome marble fireplace in detail. Curt picked up a magazine, laid it down, studied a picture, and crossed to look at an antique mahogany desk. Suddenly he gave an exclamation. Barney turned to see him holding a pair of scissors. He was about to ask Curt what he had found when a soft feminine voice said, "Excuse me, gentlemen. Can I help you?"

The men turned toward the doorway leading to the entrance hall. There stood a woman, rather hesitant in manner.

"We were hoping that we might speak with Mayor McGinty," said Barney.

She fumbled at a brooch at her collar. "Oh, I'm afraid . . . well, you must understand, . . . the mayor is badly shaken. . . . The dreadful shock of last night . . ." she paused uncertainly.

"Yes, we understand. I am Detective Ross and this is Officer Conners."

"Oh," she drew her breath in softly. "Police? Does that mean that you've come to . . ." she paused, her eyes moving from Barney to Curt and back again.

"We've come to assure His Honor that we are doing everything possible to catch the person who . . . was the cause of last night's tragedy."

"To catch the person?" Again her hand fumbled with the brooch. Then she forced a smile. "How kind, and how reassuring. I'll be happy to convey that message to the mayor."

141

"You are Miss Cline, I believe?" asked Barney.

"*Mrs.* Cline. Mrs. Elsie Cline. I am Maude McGinty's cousin."

"You live here, I believe?"

"Yes, for some time now, ever since my husband died in Chicago. Maude needed a companion—her lameness, you know—so I came here. I have appreciated living in this fine old house and having some family. And I think I have been some use to Maude, driving the car, helping her about, running errands, keeping her company."

"Perhaps, Mrs. Cline, you could tell us something about your cousin?" Barney asked.

"About Maude?" Her voice trembled slightly. "Well, I'll try."

"Did Mrs. McGinty have any enemies?"

"Enemies?" Elsie Cline looked shocked. "Dear me, no. She lived here very quietly, her lameness, you know. Some church work, some community projects, and charity. She tried to do her share socially. That is, I mean, the mayor is a very important man, so there were certain obligations—dinners and receptions, you know. That's when she needed me, and I tried to repay her for her hospitality by being some help to her. But enemies?" She shook her head.

"Do you think her being the mayor's wife might have had anything to do with . . . with what happened?"

Elsie Cline's eyes widened and she drew in her breath sharply. "Why, whatever do you mean?"

"I was thinking," said Barney, "that perhaps somebody has it in for the mayor and this was one way to get at him. Only the weapon missed its mark and got the wrong person."

"Somebody hated Joe? Why, no, Mr. Ross." Her soft voice took on a sharpness. "Everybody likes Joe. He's a fine man, admired by everybody, and very popular."

"Of course. I couldn't agree with you more. Only there's often some offbeat character or some crank who thinks he's been picked on and who broods on it until he goes off his base."

"You mean it was *Joe* that somebody was trying to attack? Some crazy person meant the knife for *him*?" She sat down suddenly. "Why, how very clever of you." She managed a faint smile. "Of course, it was a crazy person who got Maude by mistake." She stiffened suddenly and put her hand to her throat again. "But does that mean there may be another attack?"

"Just a possibility, Mrs. Cline. We have to explore all sorts of

142

possibilities." He smiled encouragingly. "Don't worry. We'll have the mayor under surveillance from now on. If the knife was meant for him, we'll see that nobody gets close enough for a repeat performance."

A heavy masculine voice boomed from the hallway. "A repeat performance of what?" Mayor McGinty stood there, his usual smile replaced by a scowl. "What are you men telling Elsie?"

"Please don't be upset, Joe," said Elsie Cline. "These officers were just suggesting that maybe . . . that you were . . ." She stopped helplessly. "Oh, will you tell him please, Officer?"

"Yes." The mayor stepped into the room and pointed a finger at Barney. "*You* tell me, Ross."

"We were suggesting as a possibility that it may have been you that the—er—attack was meant for," said Barney.

"Me?" His mouth opened in amazement. "You think they were after me? Now whose idea was that?"

"It *is* a possibility, Joe," pleaded Elsie. "It would be an explanation, you know."

He looked at her, then at Barney. "Yes, I see what you mean. It *would* be an explanation."

Barney spoke. "Somebody who is carrying a grudge. Somebody who thinks you've done him a dirty trick."

"A dirty trick? Me?" Joe McGinty was indignant.

"I said 'thinks,' Your Honor. Somebody with a twisted mind."

"And it's your idea, Ross, that poor Maude . . . my wife . . ."

"I'm sorry," said Barney quickly. "We didn't mean to trouble you at a time like this. Officer Conners and I came to express our condolences and assure you that we are going to do our best to discover who did this terrible thing."

"Thank you," Joe McGinty said.

"And I can promise you on behalf of the chief that, until the murderer is caught, you'll be kept under surveillance. There won't be a second attack as far as you are concerned."

"Thank you for that too." He moved over to take Barney by the arm and glanced over to where Curt was standing. "And now I know you're busy, men." He gently urged Barney toward the front door. "You might tell me, how are things coming with your investigation?"

"Oh, we are making progress, but it's early yet, and there are so many people yet to talk to."

"Yes, I can understand that. I hope you will keep me informed."
He steered Barney through the door and looked back to see that Curt was following.

"One thing, Ross, before you go." He lowered his voice. "This idea of yours. I find it hard to believe. I really think this whole thing was an accident, and that that young fellow—well, in the excitement he slipped."

Barney nodded but said nothing.

"What I'm trying to say is poor Maude is gone, there's no bringing her back. I wouldn't want some young fellow to have his life ruined just because of—well—because of an accident."

"I see. Very magnanimous," murmured Barney.

"Of course, you have to carry on your investigation. But if it should turn out that you don't find the streaker, I as mayor won't hold it against your record."

Barney's face was impassively polite. "Thank you, Your Honor. I appreciate that assurance."

Joe McGinty stuck out his hand. "Good-by, Ross. Good-by, Conners. Do keep me informed."

Barney was very thoughtful as he walked to the car. As he climbed in behind the wheel, he said out of the corner of his mouth, "I never expected that, Curt. I thought, with that Irish temper, McGinty would be screaming for action."

"Yes, pretty forgiving spirit, I'd say," agreed Curt, slamming his door. As they drove off, he turned to look at the mayor, who was still in the doorway watching them. "But if he thinks I'm going to ease up, he's mistaken. We got too many suspects that could have done it, including one streaker too many. I take it, Barney, you aren't too serious about there being some nut out after His Honor."

"Just a possibility, Red. We've got to consider all possibilities, you know."

"That's what I'm trying to do, and that's my trouble."

"What do you mean, Red?"

"There's just too damn many possibilities."

21 / *Sunday at 3:00 P.M.*

The band concert was just about to start when Barney and Curt pulled up at the Mushroom in the Meadow.

"Everything under control, O'Malley?" called Barney to the doorkeeper.

"All O.K. Last band player just went down the hall. You should hear the music in about two minutes." O'Malley smiled complacently. "Nobody back here at all. Every dressing room's empty, rest rooms cleared, even the broom closet inspected."

"Sounds good, O'Malley. Guess we can go right into the Green Room?" asked Barney.

"You sure can. You've got the place to yourselves."

"While we're here," said Curt, "would you go over the description of last night again? Barney here hasn't heard it."

O'Malley reviewed the story of the old Dodge car at the entrance and the replacement by a more modern car. He explained why he had left his post to straighten out a parking problem, and how as he was returning he saw a figure dash out and drive away in that second car. It was from a distance that he saw this, and it all happened so fast he couldn't say much more than that.

Had O'Malley seen or heard anything later that might seem important, like somebody else leaving later or loitering? Well, he'd told Curt Conners about the two young fellows hanging around earlier in the evening and how he'd shooed them around to the front entrance. And there had been a couple of stagehands going about their business. Nothing else. Of course, he was keeping an extra careful eye open this afternoon just in case, but so far nothing had turned up.

The two went on down the narrow side hall and into the main passageway. Curt opened a few doors as they moved along, found nothing. The Green Room was as they had left it the night before. From the arena not far away came the faint sounds of band music.

Sheppard, the man in charge of ushers, entered with four teenagers in tow. "Hello, Ross, here are the four ushers who were in the lobby last night. I don't mind telling you they came through pretty well. Got the crowd ushered out real efficient-like, before anybody could catch on that there was an emergency." He turned to the boys. "This is Detective Barney Ross, fellows, and over there is Officer Conners."

The four ushers nodded self-consciously.

"Glad to meet you, men," said Barney. "Thanks for the super job you did last night."

There were more nods plus a blur of murmured responses. The usher with his hair hanging down to his shoulders added, "We didn't even know about the murder ourselves till the building was all clear and Mr. Sheppard told us."

"Good thing, too," said Barney. "If word had gotten out, everybody would have been crowding in to see."

Sheppard glanced at his watch. "You want to ask these fellows some questions?"

"Yes, I do. Were all four of you where you could see when the streaker came out onto the floor?"

At the word *streaker* there was a slight titter as they looked at each other quickly. "Yes, we all saw him. We were there all right."

"Will you tell me what you saw?" asked Barney. "I mean, where did he come from? What did he look like? What did he do?"

They looked at each other, then at Barney, at Curt. Several started to speak, then stopped. Barney smiled. "I see. Better be one at a time. You." He pointed to the boy with shoulder-length hair. "What's your name?"

"Hal. I'm Hal Mulholland."

"Well, suppose you start, Hal."

"It was all of a sudden, while a dance was going on. He comes streakin' out of that runway over at the right and through the dancers. Then when he was right in front, he did a jumping jack—that's when you swing your hands up over your head and spread your feet wide. In the spotlight you could see he didn't have any clothes on, and his prick—" Hal paused. There was a coarse laugh from one of the other boys and Hal's cheeks turned pink.

Barney looked severely at the other three. "What's with the giggles? This isn't kid stuff, you know. Go ahead, Hal. You're doing fine."

"Well, like I said, there he was, all bare." Hal glanced quickly at the other three. "He bowed, and when the girls saw his—what he was showing—they began to scream, and even some of the fellows let out a bunch of whistles. By that time he was running right toward us, sat down in a lady's lap. That's when the screaming got real loud.

146

Before any of us could move, he was up on his feet and streaking through the dancers to that exit on the left."

"How about it, the rest of you?" asked Barney. "Did Hal tell it like it was?" There was a murmur of assent.

Curt spoke up. "You say the streaker sat on her lap? Is that all he did, Hal?"

Hal thought a moment. "No. He put his arms around her neck and leaned toward her like he was going to kiss her." Again there was a titter from behind, and again Barney gave them a stern look.

"If he put his arms around her neck, Hal, could you see his hands?" continued Curt.

"Why—er—yes. Sure, both of them."

"Did he have anything in either hand?"

"No, he didn't." Hal's eyes lighted up. "I see what you mean. If he didn't have anything in his hands, how could he stick a knife in her?"

Curt nodded, then looked at the other three. "Is Hal right? Any of you see his hands and did he have anything in either hand?"

"Yeah, I could see. . . . Empty, . . . no knife or anything else."

Hal's voice was high-pitched with excitement. "But he could have jabbed it real quick, and *then* hugged her." He looked at Curt eagerly. "Look, I could show you."

"Go ahead," said Curt. "Here," he said, pointing to one of the boys, "you sit over in this chair. Oh, come on, this isn't kid stuff, and Hal's not going to hurt you. That's it. Now, just sit there like you're watching a show. Ready, Hal? O.K., show us. Start with that jumping jack."

Hal leaped into the air and landed, hands aloft, feet wide. Then he made a dash for his fellow usher, put a hand to his chest, then sat on his lap, hands around his neck.

"Yes, Hal, that would work," said Curt. "But one question. He'd have had to be holding a knife in his hand as he ran, wouldn't he? No pockets, remember."

"Oh." Hal stood up with a sheepish grin on his face. His companion hooted derisively. "Yeah, I forgot. He didn't have any knife when he did that spread eagle."

Curt looked at the usher still sitting on the chair. "Let's see if you can help us out, since you're pretty good at laughing. Are you sure the streaker was absolutely naked? He wasn't wearing *anything*?" The boy looked blank. "Like on his head, maybe?"

"Oh, you mean that feather. Yeah. But that can't count," said the boy indignantly. "You can't stab anybody with a feather."

"Suppose we try again, Hal. This time after you bring your hands down, reach behind that feather quick-like, pretend there's a knife there."

"How?" asked Hal. "Like this?" He repeated his jump, and as he brought his arms down, one hand touched the top of his head lightly. "But now what?"

"Bend over," ordered Curt. "Hold your hand close to your chest as you run. O.K., here he comes."

Hal ran toward the boy on the chair. He pressed his hand to the victim's chest quickly, then jumped onto his lap and clasped his arms around his neck.

"How about it, Hal? Fellows? You two over there, especially," Curt said. "Possible?"

"Yeah, I think so. Looks O.K. to me," murmured the others.

"Only..." said Hal and paused.

"Well, Hal, only what?" asked Curt.

"He didn't run that way. I think he had his hands to his sides, swinging wild." He hesitated, his eyes clouded. "That's the way I remember it. But I'm not real sure."

The others shook their heads. "Hal's right." "No, he's wrong. The guy was bent over." "No, he swung his arms. "No, he didn't. He was hunched over, sort of." "No, he had his head up."

"Well, if you can't agree, fellows, try this one. What color were his eyes?" asked Curt.

Four boys stared blankly. "Eyes?" "Color?" "Jeez, I don't know."

"Was it because he was wearing a mask?"

"A mask?" exclaimed Hal. "There wasn't any mask. At least, I didn't see any." The others echoed his answer. "Naw, he wasn't." "No mask." "Hal's right." "I didn't see none."

"Are you sure?" insisted Barney, who had been standing quietly aside.

"Oh, yes, I remember." Hal's voice broke with excitement. "When he did that jumping jack, he was smiling, white teeth in the light, mouth wide open, and his eyes—well, they sort of crinkled, half closed, like. Wait a minute. I can still see...the light shining...yeah, I think they were blue."

Curt looked at Barney, a smile touching the corners of his mouth. Then very sternly he continued, "Anything else you can tell us?"

"Like what?"

"Like how tall, fat, skinny, hair color?"

"Hair was black. Two braids hanging down." "He was kind of tall, but maybe the feather— No, come to think of it, not real tall, more like Hal here. How tall are you, Hal?" "Five eight, but I'm still growing." "Not real fat, either. More like well built." "Good muscles—*not* like Hal here." An adolescent guffaw.

"All right, fellows," said Barney, squelching them with a look. He noticed Sheppard looking at his watch again. "Maybe we'd better stop for now. You've been a great help, and our thanks to you, Mr. Sheppard. Hope it hasn't caused any problems while they've been gone."

"Excuse me," said Curt. "If Hal could wait just a minute? No longer than that, I promise."

Sheppard nodded and left, followed by three ushers.

"Hal," said Curt, "could you come down to headquarters after the show this afternoon? We may have a few suspects there, and you could be a great help in picking out the real streaker if he's one of them."

"You mean like a witness at a trial?" asked Hal.

"No, not quite. Just to look and identify, give us a sign if you see anybody that just *might* be the streaker."

"A secret signal? Like in those stories on TV? Sure, I'd like that."

Curt smiled. "Now, Hal, don't be getting any fancy ideas in your head. Just a look and maybe a signal. And no danger."

"Maybe like a detective's assistant? Sure. And I wouldn't be afraid even if there was danger."

"Just a minute," interrupted Barney. "How old are you? Maybe we'd better check with your folks."

"I was eighteen last week, so I'm of age. And my folks won't mind, anyway." He smiled eagerly. "Oh, come on, Mr. Ross, I'd like to help. I've always thought I'd like to be a detective."

"O.K. You know where headquarters are?" said Barney.

"And don't expect anything real exciting, Hal," added Curt. "Detective work isn't like you see in the movies or on television. Really pretty dull."

"Oh, yeah?" asked Hal. "Well, I'll be there. Be seeing you."

It was only a few minutes until Flanagan entered. "I've got the work crew. Do you want to see them now?"

Barney nodded. "Sure, bring them right in."

149

Flanagan opened the door into the hall again. "O.K., men."

Eight men filed in, all dressed alike in jumperlike overalls. "This is Detective Ross, men. He'd like to ask you a few questions about last night."

The men nodded stolidly.

"All of you were here? Anybody missing?" Barney began.

Heads turned, shoulders shrugged. "No, that's all of them," said Flanagan.

"How many of you saw the streaker?" was the next question. Everybody relaxed at the word *streaker*. There were sly smiles, a head was tossed, two men laughed, there was a wink and a snicker.

"I guess they all did," said Flanagan.

"I mean well enough to describe him," said Barney.

An awkward silence was broken when one man spoke up. "I guess Bill and me did. We was pushing a dolly down the hall, we was almost at the end of the hall when all of a sudden we heard a door open and somebody said, 'Here, catch. Hold this for me.' We turned to look and there was this Indian fellow tearing down the hall. Bill here yells, 'My God, he's naked' and then 'Hey, you, come back here. You can't go out there like that.' By that time he was through the runway into the arena and we could hear the crowd screaming and laughing. I remember saying, 'Come on, Bill' and we high-tailed it after him to see what was going on."

"And what did you see?"

"Got there in time to see him streaking toward the other exit. He sure must have moved fast. Then I saw a red-headed cop going after him." He stopped and looked at Curt Conners. "Hey, that was you wasn't it? Did you catch him?"

"No," said Curt, "he was going too fast and some people got in my way. But tell me, how'd you know he was an Indian?"

"I could see a feather stuck in his hair, and the hair was black, and he had moccasins on his feet."

"Would you recognize him if you saw him again?" asked Barney.

"Naw. We never saw his face. Pretty hard to tell one ass from another." There was coarse laughter.

Curt was looking at the others. He pointed to one stagehand. "How about you? Aren't you the one that I talked to last night?"

"Yeah. I been thinking ever since." He shook his head. "I don't think I could recognize him either. He streaked by me so fast I didn't get a chance to look at him real good. Had my hands full of stuff, some of it breakable, and when I got it set down careful and turned, he was gone. Out the door, most likely. Then you come along and I told you everything I could."

Curt turned to Flanagan. "Where's the other one?"

"Other one?" echoed Flanagan. "What other one?"

"There was another fellow. Came out of the men's room. He must have been one of your men because he was wearing coveralls just like these fellows."

Flanagan shook his head. "No, these are all that were working last night. Right, fellows? Anybody missing?"

Heads shook, eyes looked blank.

"He couldn't have been one of my men," said Flanagan. "Sure he was wearing the same kind of suit?"

"Yes, I think so. Got any of these stagehand uniforms hanging someplace around here?" asked Curt.

"Yeah, in the supply room at the next to last door. None missing though."

Barney spoke up. "Thanks, Flanagan. Guess we've heard what your men had to say. Anybody think of anything else that could help us?" There was silence. "Then thanks, men, thanks, Flanagan."

After they had gone, Curt looked at Barney and said, "Want to take a short walk with me? I'd like to look in that storeroom."

It turned out to be a dark little place smelling of soap and wax and paint. Along one wall there were hanging three or four of the coveralls like those used by the stagehands. As Curt lifted one off the hook, something fell to the floor. Barney reached down and held it up for inspection. "What about this, Curt?"

Curt looked and nodded. "Um-h'mmm. He was wearing a cap just like that one, a big bill in front. Want to give me a good swift kick? I noticed he kept pulling it down over his eyes, but I didn't catch on why." He gave a short, dry laugh. "He didn't want me to get a good look at his face. I've been asking everybody else what color his eyes were. Hell, I don't know myself, and I was standing right next to him, talking to him. Two things are certain: I'm a lousy detective, and that streaker guy is a mighty cool operator."

151

22 / *Sunday at 3:30 P.M.*

Mrs. Cohen was the first to arrive during the intermission. She was full of enthusiasm. "What a great crowd. The concession stands are doing a terrific business. We may make a profit on this whole affair yet." Then, as if realizing what the presence of two policemen meant, she continued more quietly, "I was afraid that after last night people might not be in the mood to enjoy this afternoon concert."

"Mrs. Cohen," said Barney Ross, "we can be very brief. As you think about last night, can you add anything to what has been said that might be helpful?"

"No, not really. I was sitting on the far end, you remember, so I couldn't see very well. In fact, it was some time before I realized that poor Maude McGinty had been"—she shuddered—"murdered. And I'm afraid the first thought that flashed through my mind was to wonder if we would still get the donation she promised us."

"Donation, Mrs. Cohen?" asked Barney. "I'm not sure that I've heard very much about that."

"Oh? Why, Maude had promised to give us enough money to finish that recital hall."

"I don't understand. What about the recital hall?"

"You see, we ran out of money. The recital hall is built, but we don't have the funds to decorate and furnish it. When Maude heard about that, she said she'd like to give us the money needed if we would name the hall in memory to her father."

Curt spoke up. "But that would take a lot of money, wouldn't it?"

"Oh, yes. Maude said she could donate three hundred thousand dollars."

"Did I hear you right, Mrs. Cohen?" asked Barney. "Three hundred thousand? That's hard to believe. Did Maude McGinty have that kind of money?"

"She talked as if she did. She was even thinking of announcing the bequest last night, but then she decided she would do it today."

Harold Anderton bustled in, followed by his wife. "I got your message, Ross. Came as soon as I could. Oh, dear, I do hope nothing serious has happened."

"Nothing as drastic as last night," said Barney.

"I was hoping you were going to tell us you've identified the streaker. To think that murderer would do such a brazen, bare-faced—" He stopped with an expression of dismay. "I mean such an utterly bold thing. I can't think of anybody in this town capable of such a shocking thing—and on this special occasion too."

"We haven't found the streaker yet," said Barney. "Let's say we've got some good leads. Tell me, Anderton, Mrs. Anderton, as you think back, can you recall anything about him that would help us?"

"I'd say," said Mrs. Anderton, "he's young and athletic. He had such a slim, compact figure, and a good set of muscles."

"Really, Alice," exploded Harold Anderton, "think what you're saying. You shouldn't have been looking at him . . . that way."

Mrs. Anderton gazed at her husband and smiled. "But I was looking at him that way. He had a beautiful body."

"Oh, my God," gasped Harold Anderton.

He was about to say more when the voice of Larry Ryan boomed out. "You want to see us, Ross? I hope you're going to tell us you've caught the streaker."

Barney shook his head. "Not yet."

"Well what the hell you been doing? I'd have thought you'd have nabbed him by now."

"Yes," said Rose Ryan. "If you'd have been doing your job, you'd have captured him right then and there. What were your men doing to let him get away? All this time gone by and you're still looking for him?"

Barney smiled patiently. "It's not twenty-four hours yet. We're not dealing with a silly prankster but a very clever murderer. We don't arrest people or even charge them until we've got mighty strong evidence."

"Evidence, hell," roared Ryan. "He was an Indian, a naked Indian. All you got to do is round up the Indians here in town and —"

"Talking big again, Ryan?" It was the high reedy voice of Tony Kubitz that broke in. "Think you're talking to your union boys down at Labor headquarters? Look, Officer Ross here doesn't come around telling me how to run my clothing business. He doesn't tell you how to be a plumber. Why don't you let the detective here run *his* business his own way?" Kubitz pulled himself up, puffed out his chest and bristled his mustache up at Ryan. Very gently Gini Kubitz moved closer to her husband and said something softly. He looked at her, glared again up at the hulking figure of Ryan, adjusted the handkerchief in his breast pocket, then turned and strutted to one side.

"Why, you little sawed-off squirt," muttered Ryan.

Barney interrupted suavely. "Your idea is good, Mr. Ryan, except for one or two details." Barney motioned to a group that had just arrived. "Tell me, you directors, how many Indians were there last night?"

It was Dawson, the author of the pageant, who answered. "Lots of them. I wrote two scenes featuring Indians. How many exactly would you say there were, Goody? You had to coach them."

"Let's see, six rows, four in a row, that makes twenty-four," answered Gordon Goodman. "Yes, twenty-four were dancers. Then I suppose twelve more older folks in the other Indian scene. Why not ask your wife? She helped with the makeup." He turned to Mrs. Dawson. "How many do you think?"

"You're right about helping with the makeup. Look." Mrs. Dawson held up her hands for inspection. "Still brown under the fingernails from all that body paint. How many? Let's see. We ordered three dozen wigs, used all but two."

Curt spoke up. "Could any of your Indians have been the streaker?"

Gordon Goodman laughed scornfully. "Unthinkable. The boys in the war dance were all junior high kids; the oldest was maybe fifteen. We ushered them all up into the stands as soon as they were dressed, so they could see the show."

"All of them, Mr. Goodman?" asked Curt.

"All of them. Supervised. No chance for any running around and getting in the way."

"How about the adults?" asked Barney.

Mr. Dawson answered. "The four braves were that quartet from the St. Wenceslaus male chorus. They had to change their makeup and costume so they could sing in the Gay Nineties episode. It just wouldn't have been possible for any of them."

Gordon Goodman added, with a sly look, "There were six women. You'll have to agree none of them could qualify as the streaker." He uttered a sound somewhere between a laugh and a snicker.

Tony Kubitz looked over at Larry Ryan and burst out laughing. His wife quickly put out a restraining hand. Both the Ryans glared around as more titters spread through the room.

Curt stepped closer to Mrs. Dawson. "Did you say two of the wigs?" he asked.

"Yes, I think so. No, I'm real sure there were two we didn't need. Yes, I can still see them on that property table."

"Were they still there after the show was over?" asked Curt.

"Why, . . . I don't know. We came back here after the show, you remember; it got late, so I didn't look to see. They must still be there, . . . I mean—oh, my goodness, I hope nobody's got in there to mess with them. Excuse me." She hurried out the door and down the hall.

"Look here," said Gordon Goodman. "If you're thinking any of our boys could have been the streaker, forget it." He looked directly at Mr. Ryan. "Absolutely none of *my* actors."

"Yes," said Mr. Dawson, "don't go blaming anything on *my* cast."

Mrs. Dawson was back, slightly out of breath. "They're still there, one on the stand, the other down at the end of the table."

"Was everything else there that should have been?" asked Curt.

"You mean the other costumes? Oh, our people were very good about putting everything in place before they left. I had everything in the proper boxes within half an hour after the last kid was out of the shower and in his street clothes."

"Everything? How about a loincloth? All the headbands?"

"Funny you should mention those two things. There was only one headband and one loincloth unaccounted for." She looked apologetically at her husband. "They're such small items. We shouldn't blame anybody if one of those is missing."

Barney interrupted. "I believe we're all here except Dr. and Mrs. Quinlan, and Doc's on a case. I'm going to ask you once more to think back over last night's events. Is there anything you remember that might be worth telling us? Or even something that doesn't seem important."

Nobody spoke.

"Did any of you recognize the streaker?"

Heads shook.

"Let me put that another way. As you think back, did he resemble in any way anybody you know? I mean, his size, the way he moved, anything."

There was a slight stir. Barney flashed a look at Gordon Goodman. "Yes, Mr. Goodman. You are thinking of something?"

155

Mr. Goodman looked abashed. "Why—er—nothing, really, really nothing at all."

"Oh, go on, Goody," said Mr. Dawson. "You're thinking about that bow. Tell him what you told me."

Barney looked at Mr. Goodman and waited.

"Just a thought, a detail. After he hit the spotlight, center stage, he bowed. It was a dancer's bow. I mean, like a professional dancer would bow. You've seen them take a curtain call. A deep bend, one hand swings back, the other out and over the head into a pose. Not like an Indian at all."

"Did you say 'out and over the head'?" asked Curt.

"Why, yes," answered Mr. Goodman, "like this," and he illustrated.

"Thank you," said Curt.

Mrs. Balkan spoke up next. "Maybe you should tell them your remark to me, dear," she said, looking at her husband.

"Oh, that," Mr. Balkan said. "I'm not really sure. You know, when he came running toward us, I thought he sort of stopped just before he got to the first row, and his eyes swung from side to side. For a minute I thought he was looking right at me, over there near the end next to Mrs. Cohen, then it seemed to me he was looking at the ladies in front of us. Then he looked back at the center where Mrs. McGinty was sitting, and over at the end again, then he sort of leaped forward and into Maude's lap. Do you make anything of that, Officer?"

"Maybe like he couldn't make up his mind which lady he was going to attack?" asked Curt.

"Yes, I think so," said Mr. Balkan. "Why, yes, that's it, like he wasn't sure. But it all happened so fast, maybe it was just an idea. You said 'anything at all.' "

"And I thank you," said Curt. "Yes, I thank you very much."

"I have one more question," said Barney Ross. "Did any of you actually see a knife in the streaker's hand?"

Nobody spoke.

"Mr. and Mrs. Katzen, you were next to the Dawsons and directly behind the Redmonds, according to my sketch. You would have been in a good position to see if there was a knife in the streaker's hand."

The Katzens looked at each other and shook their heads.

"Could you see his hands at all?" asked Barney.

"His hands?" asked Mr. Katzen. "Oh, sure, his arms were around Mrs. McGinty's neck, but only for a second. The mayor started to reach out like he was going to grab hold of the streaker, so he jumped right up and dashed away." He looked at his wife, then at Barney. "Well, I think that's the way it was, I'm not sure."

"I saw it that way too," said Mrs. Katzen, nodding her head. "The mayor started to move and the streaker was gone, just like that. Then I heard that Mrs. Cline give a sort of cry, and she reached out toward Maude McGinty, like she was trying to hold her up, only Maude started to sag down onto the floor. Then Dr. Quinlan came rushing up and laid Maude out and bent over her, and I couldn't see any more." She looked at her husband, then at Barney Ross. "That's the way I remember it, only it happened so fast I'm not real sure either. But I *am* certain I did not see a knife in that streaker's hands when he put his arms around Maude's neck."

"Mrs. Dawson, Mr. Dawson?" asked Barney. "Do you have anything to add?" The Dawsons shook their heads. "Mr. and Mrs. Balkan, Mr. Goodman?" There was no answer. "Then I'd like to thank you for your time. And may I add that the pageant was excellent. You people who worked so hard to stage it deserve the highest compliments. And from what Mrs. Cohen says, it will also be a financial success. Congratulations to you all."

As they were leaving, Mr. Kubitz crossed over to Barney Ross. He stretched to his full height, threw out his chest, cast a haughty look toward the Ryans, and said, "You are doing just fine, Officer. No matter what some people say, you know your business." He turned, extended an arm to his wife, and with a last look at the Ryans, strutted from the room.

Larry Ryan, very red in the face, said, "Come on, Rose," and strode to the door. He turned, started to open his mouth, then thought better of it.

"Well?" said his wife, "aren't you going to say something? You going to let that little jerk show you up?" Larry Ryan's face was almost purple as he shouted, "Come on, I said," grabbing his wife's elbow and shoving her out the door. There was a loud bang as Mr. Ryan slammed the door behind him.

"Dear me," exclaimed Harold Anderton, "I didn't know there was so much feeling between those two."

Alice Anderton started to laugh. "Love that Mr. Kubitz. Little, but oh, my. I'll bet it's been a long time since anybody stood up to our pompous plumber like that. What a bantam rooster!"

"Really, Alice," said Harold Anderton. "This is hardly the time or place. And you know you and I should never take sides."

"Yes, Harold," Alice said with a mock sigh, her lips still twitching with suppressed laughter. "I know. But sometimes I wish—oh, taking sides is so much more fun." She started to laugh again. "Especially when David fells Goliath."

"I think we'd better leave now, Mr. Ross. That is, if you've finished with us." Harold Anderton wiped his brow. "I'm at your service if you need me, you know."

"Yes, thank you," said Barney. "I appreciate that. If we need you, we'll be in touch." There was a hint of a smile as he looked at Alice Anderton. "Thanks to you too."

After the room had cleared, Barney looked at Curt. "Whew. I could do with a drink right now."

Curt didn't answer. He was gazing into space. He groped for a chair, turned it backward, and sat down, straddling the seat, his elbows leaning on the back.

"Hey, Red, you can come out now. Everybody's gone. Wake up, Red."

"Barney," he said in a voice coming from far off. "Do you think we could have some time to think? It's all sort of close and beginning to take shape. A trained dancer . . . He could have had a knife, but nobody saw one. . . . three hundred thousand dollars . . . The Indian wig was there afterward, but the loincloth wasn't. . . . He arrived on Saturday, but he was here Friday. . . . A purple dress . . . He says his name is Jones. . . . Scissors but no knife . . . The doctor laid her out. . . . Harry Manson was in Chicago. . . . Damn it all to hell, Barney, it's almost all there. Pieces fit over here, pieces fit over there, but none of them go together! If I could just have some time to think, but it's all coming so fast."

"Time to think and to eat, too," said Barney. "We've been going along without time out for a decent meal except for that little pickup at the hotel. Come on, Red, we've got a good dinner coming. How about a nice steak, medium rare?"

23 / *Sunday at 4:15 P.M.*

"Hey, Red, the waitress wants to know if you want more coffee." Barney was smiling broadly. "Come on, get with it."

"What? Oh, yes, maybe a half cup." Curt sighed contentedly. "You know, I sure appreciated that steak." He looked up at the waitress. "Tell the chef, will you?"

"Oh, yes. Yes, I will." The girl smiled eagerly. "Will there be anything else?"

Barney looked at her, at Curt, then said with a wink, "Not right now. This is a working day for us. But this bachelor with the red hair might be interested at a later time."

"Well, sure," she said to Barney, but she looked at Curt invitingly. "Except Wednesday. That's my day off."

"I'll make a note of it—for Red here especially." Barney winked again.

"Hey, lay off, will you?" muttered Curt, his cheeks slightly pink.

"Why, Red, is that sunburn or are you blushing? I can hardly see your freckles." Barney's smile was malicious as he leaned forward to whisper. "Guess I'll have to ask you again. Are you still a virgin?"

"Oh, go to the devil." Curt's face was a bright pink up to his forehead. He stirred his coffee vigorously, eyes down.

Barney heaved a deep sigh and looked at the disappearing waitress. "Got to do something about that." He enjoyed Curt's embarrassment awhile, then suddenly he became serious. "Better be moving on. Lots to do yet."

Curt nodded. "I'm ready. Barney, could we drive by Dr. Quinlan's? There are a couple of questions I'd like to get an answer to."

Barney looked at his watch. "Well, all right. There's just time."

Mrs. Quinlan answered the door. "Oh, hello. It's Officer Ross and Officer Conners, isn't it? Come in." She opened the door cordially. "Doctor is just back from a call. Give him a few minutes to freshen up."

She led them to a comfortably furnished living room. "Won't you sit down? Can I get you anything? A drink, maybe?"

"Thank you, no." Barney held up his hand. "Regulations, you know."

"Oh, then this isn't a social call?"

"Not exactly. We've come to ask the doctor about last night."

"Of course. Is it in order for me to ask how you are coming along? Found the streaker yet? Any suspects?"

"Well, let's just say it's early yet. Lots of leads to follow up and lots of details to check on. As for the streaker—well, not quite yet."

Barney seated himself in a straight chair opposite the divan Mrs. Quinlan occupied. Out of the corner of his eye he noticed that Curt had unobtrusively moved to the side of the room.

"Speaking of the streaker, maybe we could ask you the same questions we've been asking everybody else."

"Why, I suppose so. What sort of questions?"

"First of all, did you get a good look at the streaker?"

Mrs. Quinlan laughed heartily. "*That* I did. He wasn't exactly a modest violet, was he?"

"Recognize him?"

"Recognize him? *That* I did not. I can't include him in my list of friends or acquaintances."

"Let me put it this way. Was there anything about his movements or manner that was distinctive, that reminded you of anybody or that might help you recognize him if you saw him again?"

Mrs. Quinlan thought a moment. "No, . . . I don't think so. I really supposed at first that this was a part of the pageant, tasteless and out of place. Then when he rushed over toward us and attacked Maude, I was more worried about her, my husband, the mayor, and that poor Cline woman. *She* took it awfully hard." She was silent a moment, then continued. "I was glad I could give her that amethyst necklace, but I thought afterward that I should have removed Maude's rings, too."

"Amethyst necklace? What about an amethyst necklace?"

"Why, Maude was wearing this beautiful necklace, quite expensive, I think. Mr. Conners here should remember. He took it off poor Maude. Although poor Elsie Cline was so shaken she could hardly speak, she was making sure it got back to Mayor McGinty. That's why I wonder about the rings. He'll be wanting them, I'm sure, and you never know with all those people about. . . . Well, you understand."

"Why, yes, we'll check on them. The mayor's not apt to think of valuables until later."

Curt interrupted. "May I ask a question? This pair of scissors here on the table. Aren't brass scissors a bit unusual? Part of a set?"

"Let me see," Mrs. Quinlan said. "Why, yes, it is. There's a letter opener to match, and a leather case to keep them in. I'm sure the opener's around here someplace. But it's so useful, it wanders all over the house. As a matter of fact, we ordered several sets and gave them as presents last Christmas. . . . You know, gifts for people who have everything." She looked at Curt and frowned. "Why do you ask?"

"I thought I saw a pair of scissors just like it before, today. It seemed a coincidence, so I thought I'd ask. Who were some of these people who received these gifts?"

Mrs. Quinlan looked a bit uneasy.

"Why, I don't really remember. Several of our doctor colleagues, and the president of the chamber of commerce—that's Harold Anderton—and—"

"And Mayor McGinty?" asked Curt.

Mrs. Quinlan looked even more uneasy. "Let's see, I'm not sure. Maybe—"

"Maybe what?" boomed a voice. "What aren't you sure of?"

"Oh, here you are," exclaimed Mrs. Quinlan. "I didn't hear you come down. These officers are waiting to talk to you. We were just chatting until you came. Officer Conners here was admiring our desk set."

"Oh?" Dr. Quinlan looked at Curt intently, then he smiled broadly. "Well, I'm here now, and sorry you had to wait. What can I do for you?"

"Can you tell us more about Maude McGinty? You were the one who discovered that she was dead," said Barney.

"Yes, I was. Believe me, nobody was more amazed than I. I thought, of course, that she had fainted—shock, you know. When I couldn't feel any pulse, I used my flashlight and discovered she'd been stabbed. I—well, I simply couldn't believe it. I still don't see how or why it was done."

"Death was almost instantaneous then?"

"Within a few minutes. The knife went right into the heart."

"Isn't that unusual? I mean, only somebody with a very good aim and a knowledge of just where to strike could find the vital spot so accurately."

"Well, not necessarily. It could have been just a lucky—if that's the word—accident."

"I see, a lucky accident," Barney said, impassively.

161

Curt spoke up. "It was lucky that you were there and that you had your bag with you, wasn't it?"

"Lucky? Yes, I suppose so." Dr. Quinlan shrugged his shoulders. "I'd come directly from the hospital. My wife was there already, so rather than driving my own car and finding a parking place, I asked one of the orderlies to drive me over. Of course, I couldn't leave my bag in his car, so I just brought it in with me." He made a wry face. "Unfortunately one of your men stumbled over it in the dark and sent it flying, so it took me a few precious minutes to get hold of it. Not that it would have made much difference. I couldn't have saved poor Maude, anyway."

"She died instantly, you say?"

"Well, almost. Very soon at least."

Barney resumed his questions. "Dr. Quinlan, you've been in practice in Wauconda Falls quite a few years. Can you think of any reason anybody would want to do away with Maude McGinty?"

"I've been trying to think along those very lines. You know, I really can't. Maude's always been rather retiring. She felt quite self-conscious about her lameness, you know." He looked earnestly at Barney. "I'm sure that knife was meant for somebody else. You remember that remark of the lieutenant governor's, don't you? If I were you, I'd concentrate on that."

Barney nodded. "We are investigating that angle very thoroughly. Thank you for the suggestion."

"And now how about a cold drink?" asked Dr. Quinlan.

"They've already refused me, dear," said his wife. "It seems there are regulations."

"I see." Dr. Quinlan extended his hand. "In that case, we'll just have to ask you back again when you are off duty." He adroitly moved Barney toward the door. "If I can be of any help, do call on me again. And I hope you'll keep me informed."

"We will, Doctor," said Barney affably. "Coming, Conners?"

As they walked toward the car, Curt glanced back to where the Quinlans were watching them. Softly he said, "Did you get the idea we were getting the bum's rush? Wonder if we were getting on some touchy subjects."

"Could be, Red. Could be."

"A pair of scissors but no knife to match. Wonder what would have happened if we'd ask Mrs. Quinlan to look for it and show it to us."

Barney slid under the wheel, then looked steadily at Curt. "You aren't suggesting—"

"Gotta play all the angles. We have the doctor's word for it that she died instantly, nobody else's. Could *you* find a person's heart in the dark, or would you need a flashlight?"

24 / Sunday at 4:30 P.M.

Curt Conners was unusually quiet in the car. Barney looked at him curiously out of the corner of his eye but said nothing until they were pulling into the parking lot. As he switched off the motor, he said, "You've got that faraway look in your eyes, Red, and you haven't said a word since we left Doc Quinlan's. What are you figuring out?"

"I was just supposing," Curt said slowly, "well, maybe we've been thinking about this all wrong."

"All wrong? What do you mean?"

"I mean—?" Curt stopped at the sound of a siren. "Listen. Isn't that the ambulance? Wonder what could be up on a quiet June afternoon?"

"Never mind the ambulance," Barney said, heading for the side entrance. "You were about to say something."

"Nothin' yet, Barney," answered Curt. "Just a crazy idea for a minute. Let me think about this by myself awhile."

As they stepped inside the back entrance hallway, they saw Mac waving to them vigorously.

"What's up Mac?" asked Barney.

"Am I glad to see you two! Where the hell you been?" He beckoned them closer. "First of all, that reporter fellow, what's-his-name, has been bugging me for the last hour. He's just crying to see you. Lucky break for you he heard the ambulance siren just now and took off, but he'll be back for his story."

"Aw, hell," Barney exploded. "*Him* I don't need to see right now."

"And there's a little party going on in there." Mac pointed a thumb toward the door leading to the inner room. "Kottke and Mulvany have got somebody in there for questioning. We've just called Judge Neuhaus to come so they can make a formal charge. Mike said for you to take a look. Something about a man named DiVacco."

"Oh, my God!" Curt exclaimed. "Give me an outside line, will you? I'll use Barney's phone." He dashed into Barney's room and closed the door.

"What the devil's going on?" asked Barney. Mac merely looked blank.

Curt was back almost at once. "Alcott's on his way with his wife and Harry Manson. I'll fill in details later, Barney, but Mrs. Alcott's willing to identify DiVacco—if he is DiVacco."

"Hi, Mr. Conners. Remember me?" said an adolescent voice from back in the corner.

"Sorry, Red, I forgot about Junior here," said Mac. "He's been waiting for you. Says you're expecting him."

"Oh, hi, Hal," said Curt. "Look, we're not ready for you yet. Can you come back later?"

"Sure, but why can't I just sit here and watch? I got nothing to do for awhile."

Curt looked questioningly at Barney. Barney shook his head. "I don't know about that, Hal. Things are pretty busy around here. You might—"

Barney stopped. The entrance door had opened and three people entered. Curt was down the hall to meet them before they'd taken more than two steps. "Hello, Mr. Alcott, Mrs. Alcott. Hi, Manson. We've got our man here for questioning. Come with me."

Curt motioned them to a place opposite the door leading to the inner room. "You remember Detective Ross?" Barney nodded to them. "Now if you'll just stand here," Curt continued. "I'll get that door open so you can get a good look. If it's DiVacco, Mrs. Alcott, give Detective Ross the nod, will you?"

"Now just a minute," said the lieutenant governor. "If there's any danger, we'll stop right here."

"Oh, you needn't come in. He doesn't even have to know you're here," Curt reassured Alcott. "All we want is a sign from Mrs. Alcott that this is our man, and we'll go on from there."

"Don't worry about me," said Rosemary Alcott. "I'm not afraid. If it is Ben, I'll feel a lot better knowing for sure where he is."

"All the same," said the lieutenant governor, "Harry better be ready for anything." Harry Manson said nothing but simply moved his right hand inside his coat.

Curt strode to the door, and opened it wide. The people in the hall got a glimpse of Officer Kottke's back; then as he moved aside, they could see two men seated on straight chairs facing the door.

A voice, querulous and high-pitched was heard. "Are you the judge? I got a complaint to make. I've been brought in here by these two on some stupid charge. I'm a stranger in town, minding my own business, and these two—"

"It's my billfold," broke in a second voice. "I sat next to him in the lunchroom and after he left my billfold was gone."

"So what?" said the first voice. "I don't know anything about your damn billfold. You got no right—"

"Why, hello, Ben." Harry Manson was standing in the doorway. "Remember me?"

There was an instant of silence, then the first voice was heard again. "And who might you be? My name's Jones, Anthony Jones to my friends—and you're not one of them. I don't know you and you don't know me."

"Sure you do, Ben. Chicago, Ben," said Manson. "It wasn't that long ago." Manson moved into the room, closer to the complainer. "I couldn't forget that dark curly hair and that handsome face."

"I tell you you've got me mixed up with somebody else. My name's Anthony Jones, and I ain't done nothing."

"Of course, you can prove it," said Barney Ross. "You got a driver's license or a social security card?"

"Sure I have, only not on me right now. If you'll just let me go back to my room—" DiVacco made for the door. At the sight of Rosemary Alcott he froze. In that split second, Curt Conners slammed the door shut.

"Going somewhere, DiVacco?" Curt asked.

"What's the matter, Ben?" jeered Manson. "See somebody you know?"

"Shut up, Manson," DiVacco snarled.

"Manson, eh? Still say you're Anthony Jones?" asked Barney.

The man stood glowering sullenly. There was a sudden movement, a flash of metal, and DiVacco was crouching with his back to the door, knife in outstretched hand. "Get away from me, Manson, and you, too, Copper."

"Drop that knife," yelled Barney.

"You ain't keeping me here. Oh, no. I'm leaving. Anybody try to stop me—" He flourished the blade.

"Don't be a fool, Ben," said Manson, taking a tentative step toward him.

DiVacco turned to stop him. "Keep back, I said!" There was the flash of an upswept arm, a sudden cry, the thud of flesh on flesh, and DiVacco went sprawling, Curt and Harry on top of him. Mulvany's foot came down hard on DiVacco's hand. There was a yelp of pain, and the knife went spinning across the room. Kottke bent down and handcuffs were snapped.

"You can get up now," Barney ordered.

"Still the fool, Ben," said Manson. "Quick on the draw but no brains in your head. Anybody but you'd know better than to try a stunt like that."

DiVacco stood sullenly silent.

"Mighty quick with that knife," said Curt. "Was that the way you did it last night?"

There was a flicker of response in DiVacco's eyes. "Last night? What are you talking about?"

"The streaker who murdered the mayor's wife last night. Up till now, nobody would tell us who the streaker was. Looks like you just let us know."

"Me? What the hell you trying to say? You ain't pinning that on me. I didn't stab nobody, and I don't run around without my clothes on."

"Who said it was a stabbing?"

For just an instant DiVacco caught his breath. "Read it in the papers. And you said it just now."

"Where were you last night?" asked Curt.

"Minding my own business."

"Well, we'll have plenty of time to find out," said Barney Ross. "As soon as Judge Neuhaus comes in, we're booking you for carrying a knife and threatening a police officer with it. That will do for a while, till we find out about your whereabouts last night."

"There's a probation officer down in Capital City," said Harry Manson, "that will want to know you're here too, Ben."

A look of hatred flashed across DiVacco's face.

"I think you'd better search all the way down to the bare skin,

Kottke," said Barney. "He just might have one more of those little blades hidden. Conners, maybe you'd like to stay to observe?"

Barney exited and motioned the Alcott's to his office. "Sorry you were put in that bad moment, Mrs. Alcott," he apologized. "But it wasn't until he saw you that he cracked. He's DiVacco, all right, and we're holding him until Capital City gets the word and transfers him down there."

"What about the future?" asked Hamilton Alcott. "The man's dangerous. Someday he'll get out again and then what?"

"I don't think he'll be getting out," said Barney. "He's broken his parole, so he's going right back in to finish his term. You may not have heard the commotion, but he pulled a knife, threatened to use it, and resisted arrest. We can throw the book at him for that. If it turns out that he was the streaker, we'll get him for murder."

"The streaker?" Rosemary Alcott asked. "Ben was the streaker?"

"Maybe. He proved today that he can handle a knife, and he's mighty quick in his actions."

"But why Maude McGinty?"

"Could have been a mistake. The spotlights were bright, he couldn't see well. He thought the Alcotts would be sitting right there in the center. You were supposed to be there, you know."

"Then it could have been—" Hamilton Alcott started to say.

"But it wasn't," interrupted Barney. "No, I don't think you have to worry. He won't be getting out to bother you, not either of you."

"And the publicity? Will we have to testify? That would mean reporters and news articles," said Hamilton Alcott.

"Oh, I see what you mean," said Barney. "No, you won't have to appear. You weren't involved in what happened back there just now nor with his breaking probation. No, you can be kept out of this."

"Well, that's a relief," said the lieutenant governor. "I don't know how to express my very deep appreciation, Officer Ross."

"And my thanks to you, too, Mr. Ross, and to that other officer, the one with the red hair. I'll be eternally grateful." Rosemary Alcott turned to her husband. "And now, would you take me back to the room? All of a sudden I feel tired."

"Of course, my dear. I think I'll tell Manson we'll be staying the night. We can leave early in the morning."

At the door, they stopped. Down the passageway stood a hand-cuffed figure surrounded by several policemen. Rosemary turned to bury her head on her husband's shoulder. She shivered.

Barney motioned to Manson. "That was mighty fast work in there. How'd you do it?"

"An upward cut to the wrist, a leg across the back of his knees. A trick I learned the hard way long ago. And DiVacco was a sitting duck for it. He's really a dumb guy."

"How come you call him dumb?" asked Curt.

"Well, first place, what's he come up here for? He might know he'd get caught for breaking probation. And if he wanted to get even with Mrs. Alcott—well, why not take care of it right in Capital City? Unless—"

Curt looked at him, waiting for him to continue. "Unless—what?"

"Unless he was hired for that job last night? Sounds like a fancier setup than he could ever figure out himself. He might have been offered a hefty wad of money—and he needs money."

"I see what you mean," said Curt. "But if he was the streaker, and somebody hired him, who would it be? And why the mayor's wife—unless he got the wrong one."

Manson looked at him and smiled. "Well, just remember, Di-Vacco wasn't aiming for the mayor's wife. I'll be moving along. Got some chauffeuring to do."

"Right. Be seeing you. We might get in touch with you tonight, in case we get some more news."

Barney was coming down the hall with an older-looking man. Curt caught bits of the conversation. "Got a big one for you, Judge. . . . Out on parole, . . . carrying a knife. . . . Drew it on us when we tried to arrest him." The two went into the inner room and closed the door behind them.

"Now, Red, give," hissed Mac.

"Yes, Mr. Conners," came an adolescent voice from a back corner. "What was going on?"

"Who's that?" said Curt. "Oh, Hal, I forgot you. You been there all the time?"

"I saw some of it and heard the rest. Who was he? Was he a real dangerous criminal?"

"Hal, listen to me," said Curt, seizing him by the shoulder. "What you saw in there you're not to talk about it to anybody, see?"

"Cripes," gulped Hal. "Secret stuff, eh? Well, if you say so."

"See that you don't." Curt released his grip. "The man has been in prison. Why he came here is none of your business, but he's out on parole. Now he's being booked and will be going back to prison." He looked sternly at Hal. "Now, do you think you recognized who else was here?"

"I think so. Wasn't that the lieutenant governor and his wife?"

"If it was, you forget it. You never saw them, understand?" He gripped Hal's shoulder again. "You never saw them."

"Why, sure, Mr. Conners." He rubbed his shoulder when Curt let go. Then Hal's eyes widened and he grinned. "Do you suppose I'd ever be able to handle a guy like him?"

Curt and Mac exchanged amused glances. Then with a straight face Curt answered, "I don't know, Hal. Maybe if you really want to."

"Psst," hissed Mac. "Don't look now, but your favorite friend is coming."

"Oh, cripes," groaned Curt. "Hal, get back out of sight." Then Curt flashed a dazzling grin. "Why, hello, Hickson. We were wondering where you were. I expected you to be here all along."

"Oh, yeah? Like hell you were," Hickson replied. "I been around all afternoon looking for you." He smirked. "Got an extra story out of it. Followed that ambulance. Couple committed suicide. Turned on the gas."

"Suicide? Gas?" Curt exploded. "You know about that, Mac?"

"Sure, got the call for the ambulance about half an hour ago. Called the squad car. Schwartz is on this afternoon. He acknowledged. He should be in with his report any minute now."

"Pretty slow, wouldn't you say?" gloated Hickson. "I already been and got my story, and you guys are just finding out about it."

"Hold it," called Mac, "here's the call now." He spoke into the mouthpiece. "Yeah, Schwartz. . . . Yeah. . . . What's that address again? 305 North River? . . . Name Krasuski? . . . Both of them, eh?" Mac looked over his shoulder at Curt Conners. "Yeah, I'll tell him. Shouldn't be long." He swiveled around so his back was to Hickson. "Schwartz thinks Barney Ross and you should go out there. There are a couple of details, he says. You get that address?"

"Yes. 305 North River." Curt stared thoughtfully at the slip of paper Mac handed him. Then without a trace of expression he said, "Get word to Barney in there, will you?"

"In where?" asked Hickson suspiciously. "Something going on in there?"

"Yeah. A routine job," Curt said casually. "Some guy booked for violating his parole. We're holding him to send him back to Capital City." He pretended to smile. "Might be worth a couple of lines. You can pick up the report anytime." Curt smiled more ingratiatingly. "Now if you'll give me a few minutes of your valuable time, come on over and look at something I've got for you, like I promised." He headed for Barney's office, motioning for Hickson to follow him. "You remember, I asked if you would put out a call for your readers to help. Just see if this will give you an idea." Curt urged Hickson into the room. "You'll know how to build it up into a big spread." The door closed while Curt was still talking.

Mac had just turned to look at Hal, sitting back in his corner, when the door to the inner room was flung open and Judge Neuhaus appeared.

Barney Ross extended his hand to the magistrate. "Thanks for coming down, Judge," said Barney. "It really was an emergency, you know. He was giving us a pretty bad time for a few minutes."

"Yes, I got the idea. Glad he's behind bars," said the magistrate. "Has this anything to do with—well, with what happened last night?"

"Very possibly."

"In that case, I'm even more happy I could be some help. That was a terrible thing," Judge Neuhaus said. "I hope you can find the murderer very soon."

"Thank you, Judge. We're working hard and making a little progress."

"Good. I'll be ready if you need me again. Good-by," said Judge Neuhaus, and walked down the hall toward the parking lot.

"Barney," called Mac, "A message for you. A double suicide out on North River Street. Schwartz thinks you better take a look."

"Just what I *don't* need," exploded Barney Ross. "What the hell do *I* have to go out there for?"

"I don't know, but when I passed the word to Red Conners, he said I should tell you right away. You see, our reporter friend Hickson was here, ears bent to catch anything he could. Red just gave me one of his—well, you know, one of them steady looks."

"Hickson here? I don't see him."

"Red's got him in your office. Something about showing him some plan." Mac winked. "I kind of got the idea he wanted to get

Hickson out of the way."

The door to Barney's office opened slowly and Curt's voice was heard. "I'm sure you'll know just how to handle this. You can see how you'll be helping us out. Somebody's sure to come forward. When that happens, we've got the streaker and you've got your story—before anyone else, of course."

"Well, O.K., I guess," said Hickson. "It'll take a little work, you understand. You cops just don't know how to put good copy together." Hickson smirked. "But if the press can solve your crime for you detectives, why, we're only to glad to oblige." He looked at Barney Ross. "How about a progress report? How you coming? Any new developments?"

"Sure, lots of them," Barney said. "But nothing for publication."

"I thought not," Hickson sneered. "Twenty hours gone by, and nothing to show." He looked at Curt, then back to Barney. "Oh, yes, what about that little story Conners here was telling me about?"

"He means DiVacco, Barney," said Curt quickly. "He wanted to know what was going on in there. Does this cover it? Ben DiVacco was just paroled in Capital City, good behavior. He was supposed to stay in Capital City, but he was recognized up here today. When apprehended, he was found to be carrying a weapon, which is illegal for a felon. So we're holding him here until he can be returned to Capital City. Did I tell it right, Barney?"

Barney nodded. "Right. You might give Officer Kottke credit for bringing him in."

"What was he in for in the first place?" asked Hickson.

"I think it was a bank robbery ten years ago." Barney smiled his most friendly smile. "You will mention Kottke?"

"Oh, sure, sure. Always glad to give you guys plenty of good publicity—when you deserve it." Hickson stuffed his notebook in his pocket. "I hate to leave you, but I've got a couple of stories to file. Don't feel too bad about my going. I'll be back." With that he turned and swaggered down the hall.

"Oh, sure, anytime," called Barney after him. "Don't let us keep you."

After he disappeared, Barney mopped his brow. "Devil take all reporters, . . . and Hickson first of all," he muttered. He turned to Curt. "Now, Red, what about this double suicide? Haven't we got enough to do without *that*?"

171

"Did Mac here give you the *dope*? Couple named Krasuski? Name mean anything to you?" Barney shook his head. "The address is 305 North River?"

"So?" asked Barney.

Curt fished in his pockets and brought out a scrap of paper. "Remember this? I found it in one of Sonny Hitchcock's rented cars this morning. It says 305 NORIV. The Krasuskis live at 305—"

"OK, OK, I got you. Come on, let's go."

25 / *Sunday at 5:00 P.M.*

They saw the police car parked in front of the house, and Officer Schwartz standing on the curb, surrounded by a small group of curious onlookers. As Barney pulled up, the group fell back and Schwartz came over to Barney's side of the car.

"Got your message, Schwartz," said Barney. "What was this? Suicide?"

"Could be, but there are a couple of things that look funny. Thought you ought to come on out here to see."

"What kind of things?"

"Maybe I'd better tell you inside." Schwartz motioned toward the house. "Got the place pretty well aired out, so it should be safe enough."

As Barney and Curt got out, Schwartz beckoned toward two of the people standing nearby. "This is Mr. and Mrs. Shinsky. They found the bodies."

"You found the bodies, eh?" asked Barney. "Want to show me where the bodies were—in the house I mean."

As the five of them walked toward the front porch, Shinsky began to explain. "We come by on our way home from church. Noticed the door was closed and the shades all pulled down. Thought that was funny, so Anna here went up to see if anybody was home."

"Yeah," said Anna Shinsky. "Magda told us to stop by. She said she might have some good news for us."

"Oh?" asked Barney. "What kind of news?"

"She didn't say. But she said they had to hurry home from church because there was somebody coming to visit them."

"Did she say who?" asked Barney.

"No, she acted kind of funny, like it was a big secret or something?"

"So what happened?"

"Well, I knocked and nobody answered. So I opened the door." She looked apologetic. "No, I wasn't trying to be nosy. Magda asked me to come by."

"Sure, I understand," said Barney.

"Well, then I smelled the gas. So I ran back to get Steve here."

Steve Shinsky took up the story. "Minute I smelled that gas, I knew something was wrong. I opened the door wide and ran through real fast, holding my breath, to open the back door. Came back and yelled for Anna to get on the phone and call the ambulance."

"Very good. That was quick thinking," said Barney.

Mr. Shinsky drew himself up proudly. "I remembered from a TV show. I put a handkerchief over my nose and found the kitchen. Gas burners was wide open. Turned them off and ran back out. On the way I seen Jake stretched out on the floor. Got me some fresh air, then went back in and pulled him outside by his feet. He sure looked like a goner. I could tell."

"And then the ambulance came," said Anna Shinsky, "and they found Magda lying in the bedroom. They pulled her out, too, and started working on both of them, but nothing happened. Guess we was too late."

"And I opened all the windows I could," said Steve Shinsky. "Ambulance took Jake and Magda away, and this cop drove up in his squad car."

"See anybody around while all this was happening?" asked Barney.

"No, nobody at all," said Steve.

"Who were they, Schwartz?" asked Barney.

Schwartz looked at his notebook. "Name of Krasuski. Jake and Magda Krasuski. Lived here a long time, just the two of them. He works at Goodleigh's, day laborer."

"When did you last see the Krasuskis, Mr. Shinsky?" asked Barney. "Alive, I mean."

"At church, St. Wenceslaus. They stayed after Mass for the lunch and played a little bingo. Anyway, Jake did."

173

"And Magda and I talked," said Anna Shinksy. "That's when she told me about expecting company. She must have been, too, because she's got out her fancy table runner and her vase of flowers."

"Did either of them seem worried about anything?"

"Hell, no—excuse me, I mean no," said Steve. "Jake was all happy at winning something at bingo."

"And Magda talked like usual," added his wife.

"Just a minute before we go in," said Curt. "Mind if I ask these folks over there something, Barney?"

Barney nodded. "No, go ahead."

"Any of you folks happen to see anybody going into the house here this afternoon?" Curt asked the little group still standing near the curb.

Heads shook. "I was watchin' the ball game on TV." "We just come back from a picnic." "I was takin' a nap." "I took the kids to the park." One woman heard a car drive up, but she was out in back so didn't pay it any mind. One of the children thought she saw something parked in the alley in back of the house, but she wasn't sure. No, she didn't remember what kind of a car. One boy did see a car drive up about eleven o'clock. A fellow got out, knocked; no answer, so he left a package inside the screen door and drove away.

"Sunday afternoon in June all right," muttered Curt to Barney as he rejoined him on the porch. "Middle of town, broad daylight, and nobody sees a thing. Our visitor knew what folks do on a Sunday afternoon around here."

"Let's go on in," said Barney.

Steve Shinsky showed them where Jake had been lying, the kitchen and the gas stove, the bedroom where they found Magda.

"Is that all there is?" asked Barney.

"Well, there's a bathroom off the kitchen." Steve opened a door. "Pretty small, not much room in here."

"What's behind this door?" asked Curt. "Oh, I see, there's an upstairs," he said, looking at a steep narrow stairway. "What's up there?"

"I never been," said Anna, "but there must be a bedroom. A long time ago Magda had a kid living with them, not their own. I guess kind of an orphan they got paid to keep and raise. Then when we first knew them, Magda and Jake slept upstairs, and the bedroom here was kind of an extra sitting room. But the stairs got sort of much for Magda, and there wasn't no bathroom upstairs, I guess, so lately they've just lived in these three rooms."

Curt climbed the stairs, looking about carefully.

There was a small bedroom looking out over the street, sparsely furnished, neat enough but with a visible layer of dust on the dresser and a film over the mirror. The heat under the low slanting walls was stifling, and only with the greatest force could Curt get the single window open. There was no screen. "Nobody's been up here for a long time," he said thoughtfully.

At the back of the house, opening off the same small landing, there was a storeroom, equally hot, equally dusty, with a confusion of cast-off bits of furniture, cardboard boxes, and old trunks.

"Nobody's been up there for a long time," said Curt to Barney when he returned downstairs. "He'd have died in the heat and left his mark in the dust if our visitor was hiding up there." He turned to Steve Shinsky. "Is there a basement?"

"Yeah, but you got to go outside to get to it. Magda was trying to get Jake to put in an inside stairway so they could get a furnace and a laundry room, but Jake never got around to it. They still had a stove in the front room there all winter."

"And Magda was still cooking on an old kitchen range till two years ago—coal and wood, you know," added Anna. "I remember when she finally talked Jake into getting her that gas stove." Anna shook her head. "Poor Magda, messing with coal buckets in the winter and carrying ice in the summer."

"Were the Krasuskis poor, then?" asked Barney.

"Jake always talked like they was," Steve said disgustedly, "but I don't think they was. Not *that* poor, anyway. He was just a stingy old Polack, squeezed every nickel he could."

"Yeah," Anna broke in. "Magda's cousin said she told her once they had a bunch of savings bonds in the bank, but Jake wouldn't buy her a refrigerator, the old icebox was good enough. Yeah, Jake was a stingy one all right, and sometimes kind of mean, too." She stopped and crossed herself. "We shouldn't be talking about the dead like this."

While the Shinskys were talking, Curt was moving about the kitchen. He opened the icebox door, looked in at the meager contents. He was about to close the door again but he stopped. He reached in and pulled out a bit of gold foil. He studied it carefully, then put it on the kitchen table. As he did so, he noticed some small crumbs, picked them up and rolled them between his thumb and forefinger before putting them down by the gold foil.

He looked at the dishes in the sink and lifted each item, examining it carefully. Then he looked about, as if trying to find something in particular. He opened the cupboard door and inspected each shelf. When he got to the topmost shelf, he reached up and took down three glasses, using a handkerchief as he handled each. He held each glass up to the light, smiled with satisfaction, and put one back on the top shelf. The other two he carefully put on the table by the foil.

He looked over at Anna Shinsky. "I've been listening to what you've been saying. What was that about the Krasuskis having a boy live with them?"

Anna shrugged her shoulders slightly. "Can't tell you much. Magda only mentioned him once or twice and never seemed to want to talk about it. I kind of think he didn't turn out so good. You know, one of them bad boys that makes trouble."

"You don't know what his name was or what became of him?" asked Curt.

"No, I don't. Seems to me he was with them quite a while—maybe till he got up to high school."

Curt nodded. "Thanks, Mrs. Shinsky."

Barney added, "Could I have your address and telephone number? You've been a great help, and I don't think there's much more we'll be wanting, but just in case, we'd like to know how to call you."

When the Shinskys had gone, Curt got busy opening drawers, looking under furniture. He picked up a dress thrown carelessly over the bed, shook it out, reached into the pocket, and pulled out a length of pink ribbon, which he studied carefully, then placed on the kitchen table.

"Let's have a look in the cellar," he said to Barney. As they went out the back door, Curt stopped to look into a trash barrel. He snapped his fingers in disappointment, as if he had expected to find something.

They rounded the corner of the house. "My God," laughed Barney, "an old-fashioned outside cellar door. I didn't know there was one left anywhere." Seeing Curt's questioning look, he explained, "When I was a real little kid, we went to visit out in the country. My cousin and I used to slide down one. This was before they had slides for children in the park. You see, in the old days before furnaces and central heat and laundry rooms and indoor plumbing, you went into the cellar from the outside. It was just a hole dug under the house, dirt floor, and you kept milk cool in the summer and vegetables stored in the winter. Then people got water pipes and a furnace, so they finished their cellar off and put in an inside stairway—unless they were poor."

"Well, let's see what's down here," said Curt. A quick survey revealed nothing but old household castoffs. "Somebody might have hidden down here, but it doesn't seem likely."

Back in the kitchen, Barney asked, "Looking for something special, Red?"

"I think I am," Curt answered Barney. "Suppose the Krasuskis didn't decide to turn on the gas themselves, but somebody from outside wanted to do them in. They wouldn't just lay themselves down for him, especially in separate rooms. They'd put up a struggle, there'd be some screaming, and even in this quiet part of town somebody would have heard it."

"I follow you so far, Red," said Barney.

"Look at that gold foil and those bits of cork. What kind of bottle do they suggest? Hardly beer, maybe whiskey, more likely wine. But no bottle has been found so far. All the glasses on that top shelf were turned over and dusty except two right side up and shiny clean. But dishes were still in the sink, so how come the glasses were washed? Looks like somebody was being careful to remove a bottle and clean up some glasses. Especially with a package delivered for the Krasuskis to find when they got back from church—probably wrapped in pink ribbon, unless Magda went out around with pink ribbon in her pocket all the time."

"Makes sense, Red," said Barney.

"But who? And why? Careful planning, like it was necessary to get rid of both of them, two old Polish people, poor nobodies." He shook his head. "Fingerprints, might be some on the glasses, on the gas-burner levers. Can we check that, Barney? You know, before we buy this, maybe we'd better be sure there wasn't any attack—you know, bashed on the head, choked, or tied up and gagged."

Barney reached for the phone, dialed a number, spoke briefly. "Just talked to the morgue. No signs of violent marks of constraint of any kind," he said. "With luck we'll hear about any drugs or sleeping potions in the stomach maybe in a couple of hours."

"That helps," said Curt, "but what follows? There was that paper in Hitchcock's car. Is our TV star mixed up some way? If he is, what's the connection between Maude McGinty and these two poor old people? Hitchcock couldn't have stabbed the mayor's wife—no way at all from across the arena. Anyway, what reason?"

Curt sank into a chair, propped his elbows on the table, and rested his face on his fists. "Like I said, Barney, you get little sections to fit together by themselves, but they don't match any other sections."

He sat quietly thinking while Barney found a paper bag and put ribbon, gold foil, cork fragments, and glasses wrapped in a bit of newspaper into it.

"Hickson!" exclaimed Curt suddenly. "Maybe *that* would work."

"Who did you say?" asked Barney. "What's that damned flea got to do with this, Red?"

"Barney, what was the name of the fellow who coached the pageant—that older fellow?"

"You must mean Goodman, the fellow they called 'Goody.' "

"Yes, that's the one. He wouldn't know my voice, would be?"

Barney answered thoughtfully. "I don't think so. You never said much when we were questioning all those people."

Curt grinned. "Barney, I'm going to do a little playacting myself." He reached for the phone book, then dialed a number. "Hello, Mr. Goodman? . . . I'm Hickson, the reporter for the paper doing a little feature story on Sonny Hitchcock. Am I right that you had him as a student when he was here in high school? . . . Oh, he got his first acting experience under you, did he? . . . Uh-huh. . . . Well, I want to put *that* into the write-up. I don't suppose many people know that *you* started his career. . . . You won't mind if I build that up a bit?"

Curt looked at Barney and winked as he listened to a long harangue.

"Why, yes, Mr. Goodman, that's what I wanted to know. I *knew* I should call you. . . . Oh, yes, one more thing. 'Sonny Hitchcock' is a stage name, isn't it? Did you help him choose it? . . . No? Well, what *was* his name when he was going to school here—I should know it, but somehow I haven't got it on the tip of my tongue. . . . Wait a minute, would you spell that? K—r—a—s—u—s—k—i." Curt looked at Barney and made a sweeping gesture of triumph, then in a very matter-of-fact tone he spoke into the phone. "Yes, I've got it. I may call you back for more detials if I find I need them, if you don't mind. Thank you very much, Mr. Goodman."

Curt let out a long whistle as he replaced the phone, and banged both hands onto the table. "Hallelujah! Did you hear that? It fits, Barney, it fits."

"It sure does," exulted Barney. "So the Krasuskis had a son, and he used to live right here, eh?" He slapped Curt on the back. "A clever trick, Red."

"But," said Curt, "what next? Did Hitchcock come out here to *kill* his parents—or foster parents? It seems more likely he'd be out giving them money and setting them up for something to live in better than this dump." Suddenly he hit the table with his fist. "Of course! The woman!"

"The woman?" asked Barney. "What woman?"

"Down at the hotel dining room? Sure, that could explain things. Sneaked in a day early to visit dear old mom before things got too thick—But no." He banged his fist again, this time in disgust, and stood up. "Oh, hell, it only makes it worse. He wouldn't come out the next day and kill his dear old mom." He paced up and down. "I think, Barney, we're ready for another session. Suppose we get Hitchcock and that what's-his-name-fellow of his, Peters, and our two little college boys, along with Redmond, all in one room. Oh, yes, Manson ought to be there and that I-never-forget-a-face witch, Phoebe Sears."

"Got in mind what you want to do?" asked Barney.

"I think we're getting awfully close—close enough to put on a little pressure." He laughed. "I'm looking forward to seeing Redmond's face when he meets Witty and Karyl. While you break the news of the Krasuskis' suicide to Hitchcock, I want to be where I can watch how he takes it." His laugh froze, and he put a hand to his forehead. "Oh, my God, I forgot about the evening news broadcast. What time is it, Barney?"

"Almost six o'clock."

"What if he hears it over the radio? The Krasuski suicide will probably get top billing."

"Don't see how we can stop it."

"Wait a minute!" exclaimed Curt. "What's on out at the Mushroom in the Meadow tonight?"

"There's a community church service at seven—one of these all-churches-united deals. Then a square dance demonstration at eight. Remember that hassle about dancing on Sunday? So the big dance was cancelled, but nobody objects to square dancing. Figure that one out."

179

"Not me," Curt said. "Too much to figure out as it is. How about the Green Room again? It worked this afternoon, so it should work again tonight."

"Sure you know what you want to do, Red?" asked Barney.

"Pretty well. We can get it worked out on the way there." Curt reached for a phone book. "Right now we'd better get our bunch together."

Curt dialed a number. "Will you connect me with Mr. Hitchcock's room, please?" He drummed his fingers on the telephone for what seemed a long time. "Mr. Hitchcock? Oh, it's Mr. Peters. This is Officer Conners calling for Detective Ross. Would Mr. Hitchcock be able to come to the convention center for a few minutes this evening? There are some new developments, and a few points he could clear up. . . . Oh, no, not right now."

As Curt listened, a broad smile spread over his face. "Why, of course, we wouldn't want to interfere with *that*, how about seven-fifteen? Yes, I'll hold while you check." Curt covered the mouthpiece and whispered loudly to Barney, "We're O.K. A *Battleground* rerun is on from six to seven and the star of the show has to watch it." He removed his hand from the mouthpiece. "Dinner with Mr. Goodman at eight? Oh, we wouldn't keep you long enough to interfere with that." Curt waited quietly awhile. "Mr. Hitchcock says this will work out? Good. We'll count on seeing both of you at about seven-fifteen in the Green Room."

"Did you say Goodman?" asked Barney. "Wayne Hitchcock's having a cozy little dinner with him tonight?"

"That's what his man said. Anything special about that, Barney?"

"Maybe, maybe not. I'm just trying to remember." Barney spoke slowly. "There was some kind of deal about Goodman a few years ago. The man never married, lived alone. Story was he would invite some of his older boys to stay with him overnight. There was some kind of showdown; he denied it; nobody stepped up with evidence of anything wrong."

"And you think Hitchcock might have been one of Goodman's nightly companions?" asked Curt.

Barney shrugged. "Could be. Not that it seems to have any bearing on this deal right now."

"Maybe not, but you never can tell," said Curt thoughtfully. "I'm not throwing away any pieces in this jigsaw puzzle. Maybe we'll invite Mr. Goodman too, so he can meet his dinner companions."

Curt passed the phone book to Barney. "You'll be wanting to call Redmond and those two students of his, Karyl and Witty. And I'll not mind a bit not having to talk to Phoebe Sears or Manson." He stood up. "I'll just take a look once more to be sure I haven't missed anything."

Barney got busy on the phone, and Curt made the rounds, closing doors and windows, peering into cupboards and under furniture. He was just about to pick up the paper bag when Barney called, "Good luck, Red. We're batting a thousand. Redmond's on the program, so he was already planning to be there. Karyl's folks are going to the church service, so he and Witty can ride with them. Phoebe Sears will be delighted to come." He made a face. "Said she was looking forward to it. Manson's making arrangements for somebody to keep an eye on the Alcotts."

"Barney," said Curt, "can we go by the station to drop this off?" He held up the sack. "I've got a young usher named Hal down there, wouldn't want him to wait much longer. Besides, I've got a little scheme working. Maybe we can use a high school boy to find out something for us that we cops can't."

"Oh? Careful, Red." Barney shook his head. "If there's any danger or chance for trouble—well, you know."

"I know, I know. Let me think it out before I tell it to you. Anyway, we can't let him sit down at the station all evening. Besides . . ."

"Besides what, Red?"

"The machine needs a little attention, a drain and fill." When Barney looked blank, Curt laughed. "I've just about used up that steak we had. And a chance to sit in solitude—"

Barney guffawed. "Thought you were superman. Come on, let's go."

On the front porch, Curt stopped suddenly. "Barney, who would know what to put into a bottle of wine so it would put two people sound asleep?"

"Why, I suppose just about anybody. No, . . . it would have to be somebody who knew about sedatives and—" he looked sharply at Curt—"would have the stuff right handy, ready to use on a Sunday morning. Red, are you thinking of a doctor?"

"A doctor? Well, he'd be in a position, wouldn't he?"

"Doctor Quinlan?"

"Well, let's say a doctor who had a letter opener missing from his

181

desk set and who carried a little black bag with all kinds of emergency items—including maybe a sedative or two."

26 / *Sunday at 5:30 P.M.*

Andy, the swing-shift dispatcher, was at the switchboard when Barney and Curt came into headquarters. "Hi, men," he called out. "Barney, the chief wants you to call him when you can. He left here about an hour ago, says you should call him at his home."

"O.K., Andy, will do." said Barney.

"Barney," said Curt, "when you talk to him, see if he'll O.K. a call to Los Angeles. It's still afternoon out there, so somebody ought to be able to help us out. See if they've got anything on Wayne Hitchcock and, just in case, on Dennis Peters."

"You aren't thinking that Hitchcock might be—"

"Just tidying up any loose ends I can see hanging out," said Curt.

Andy continued. "Also, Doc called from the morgue. There were traces of—oh, hell, I'll let him tell you the fancy name. Anyway, a couple of sleeping pills mixed with alcohol, I think, was the idea. Make sense to you, Barney?"

Barney nodded. "Thanks, Andy, it does."

"And, Red," Andy said turning toward Curt, "you've got a young fan waiting for you. And you can take him out of here anytime you want to—like drown him, maybe? Ears open to hear everything, eyes and fingers poking into all kinds of places, and questions, questions, my God, the questions!"

"Sorry about that, Andy," Curt struck a pose. "You can understand my attraction for the young fellow, I know."

Andy thumbed his nose.

"And I'll take him off your hands. But you got to give me a couple of minutes first."

"Two'll be too many," Andy grunted, then he turned to Barney again. "And that reporter fellow Hickson called, said to remind you he'll come by about nine o'clock for that story you promised him."

"That's all I need," groaned Barney. "Sure as hell I'd like to have a couple of sleeping pills to put into *his* alcohol." He turned toward his office. "O.K., Andy, and thanks. I'll think of something, though I swear to God I don't know what." At the door to his office he called back. "Get the chief on the phone and hitch him on to my line, will you?"

Andy nodded and waved. Curt peered into the inner room behind the switchboard. "Hey, Hal, pssst," he hissed, "get away from that desk."

"Oh, hi, Mr. Conners. You're back?" came a high-pitched adolescent voice. "I was just looking at—"

"I see, I see. Well, just stop looking," Curt warned. "Sorry to keep you here so long."

"Oh, that's all right, Mr. Conners. It wasn't so long. I've had plenty to look at and listen to."

Curt's lips twitched as he caught sight of Andy's expression at that remark. "Yes, so I've heard, Hal. But what about your folks, aren't they going to be worrying about you?"

"Naw. They were going out to my grandpa's after the band concert and then back to the square dance tonight."

"Well, how about supper, Hal? Aren't you getting hungry? A growing boy like you, you know."

"I can get by on a couple of hamburgers and a milk shake."

"Now, come on, Hal, we have to do better than that for you," said Curt. "If you're willing to do a little job for us, I'll stake you to a real dinner."

Hal's eyes sparkled. "You mean it? About the job, I mean? Sure. I'm willing." He patted his pocket. "And you don't have to buy me any dinner. I've got enough money."

"Oh, ho," teased Curt, "don't want to be seen eating with a couple of cops, eh? Folks might think you were in trouble, eh?"

Hal's eyes widened in dismay. "Oh, no, I don't mean that at all, Mr. Conners. I'd be proud to eat with you."

Curt stuck out his hand. "Shake, it's a deal. You'll be my guest. Now if you'll just stay here quietly for about ten minutes"—Curt turned so he wouldn't see the expression on Andy's face—"we'll be heading for that restaurant."

"But what about the job? Aren't you going to tell me what I have to do?"

"At dinner, Hal, at dinner," he called over his shoulder as he headed for Barney's office.

"You bastard," muttered Andy as Curt passed the switchboard.

Barney looked up as he entered, covered the mouthpiece of the telephone with his hand. "I've got Los Angeles on the line. They're checking. Chief's a little antsy again, wants to know what we're doing. Between him and that damned Hickson ... Well, I calmed him down, asked him about making this call, and told him he'd have a report tonight."

Curt nodded. "Now I'm going to use your little boys' room to sit down awhile and do some quiet thinking at the same time. And have you got a spare razor, Barney? Even us redheads have to shave off our beautiful golden fuzz once in a while."

When Curt emerged about ten minutes later, Barney was frowning. "Los Angeles ran into a snag. Something about the name, the right man being off duty. They promised to call back later, so I'll have the call transferred to the convention center." Then he smiled quizzically. "Now tell me about your usher spy."

Curt talked earnestly for a few minutes. Barney shook his head. "I don't know, Red. It sounds like you might be putting the kid into a mighty shaky position, mighty shaky."

"I've thought of that," said Curt. "How about Manson helping out? Even if he's still on our list, we can use him as a safety precaution by having him close by." He raised his shoulders and spread his hands. "How else we going to find out if anybody's been cut?"

"Yeah, I see the problem all right. But an eighteen-year-old kid, Red, and using Manson when we aren't sure ... Well, let's get Hal in here and see how he reacts. And Red, this time I'm letting *you* do the talking."

Curt opened the hall door. "Hey, Hal, will you come in here?"

Hal walked in eagerly. "So you'd like to be a detective, Hal?" Curt began.

"Yeah, I sure would, Mr. Conners."

"How old are you, Hal?"

"I thought I already told you. I was eighteen last week. Just made it before graduation."

"Well, Hal, there is a little job that needs to be done. None of us cops can do it because everybody knows we're policemen. But just a young fellow like you, hanging around—well, it might work."

"You mean *I'd* be the fellow. Jeez."

"You might be, if you're willing. I should tell you this is a kookie

184

type of job. I don't mean there's any danger, but you might not want to try it when you hear what it is."

Hal looked puzzled. "No danger, you say? Why wouldn't I want to do it?" He looked crestfallen. "I know, you think I *can't* do it, I'm not smart enough or something."

"No, Hal, that's not it. It's—well, let me tell you what we want. If you feel like it's not something you'd be willing to do, well—"

"Try me, Mr. Conners."

Curt thought a minute, then began, "Hal, we're looking for a certain man. We have reason to think he's about five feet nine or ten, not skinny but not fat, just in between. He has blue eyes. We think he's left-handed. And Hal"—here Curt paused to look directly into Hal's eyes as if waiting for a negative reaction—"he isn't circumcised."

Hal blinked. A faint blush reddened his cheeks. He swallowed hard.

"Do you know what that means, Hal?"

"Yeah, I think so. . . . Yeah, sure I do. It means like Sam Scolfield."

"Sam Scolfield? Do I know him?"

"He's one of my friends. Some of us asked him once why he was—you know—different. He told us his old man belongs to some special church and they don't believe in—cutting—you know."

"You've looked at Sam then, so you could tell if somebody was like him?"

"Sure, I've seen Sam plenty of times, ever since eighth grade. If I could get a—you know—get a good look. But how would I do that to a stranger, Mr. Conners?"

"That's the job, Hal. We're going to have a meeting soon. One of the men might be the guy we're looking for. After we've talked awhile, there will be a break, and Officer Ross or I or somebody will say, 'Coffee, men?' Maybe some of them will take the opportunity to wander down your way. That's where you would come in."

"I don't get it."

"You have a fine crop of nice long hair, Hal, down to your shoulders. You must have to work hard to keep it so nice looking. Suppose you're down there in the men's room, standing by the mirror, working away with your comb. If you get the right angle and look just right, do you suppose you could tell if any of the men are—"

185

"Like Sam?" Hal interrupted. "Why, sure. I could try, anyway. But how—"

"How'll you let me know who the right guy is?" Curt smiled. "Well, maybe you could signal. A clever fellow like you will figure out some way to let us know."

"And that's all there is to this job?" Hal's face broke out into a grin. "That should be real easy. Is this what detective work is like? What they call on TV 'putting the finger on a guy'?"

"Well, no, not exactly. And our jobs aren't often like this. Mostly they're a lot duller. But you might say this is a sample of how we have to scheme and plan and maneuver to pick out the little detail that leads us to our man."

"I'm really glad you asked *me*, Mr. Conners. Detective Conners, I mean. I know I can do this little job for you."

"Good," said Curt. "Now, if you'll just wait for us out by the squad car, we'll be out right away."

Both men looked thoughtfully after Hal's departing figure. Curt shook his head. "I hope I'm not letting that kid in for something. He did say he's eighteen, Barney."

"All the same," said Barney, "we'd better be real sure Manson's near, just in case. I wouldn't want this kid tagged for something." He headed for the lavatory door. "What was that about sitting down to think, Red? Don't worry, I won't have to think as long as you did."

Dinner was a welcome break. Hal turned out to be a compulsive talker. He was full of questions and gems of juvenile philosophy. He made slanted observations of the passing scene and critical evaluations of teachers, coaches, city officials, and fellow students.

Curt and Barney sat back and listened, exchanging amused glances as they ate. Occasionally one or the other would interject a leading question to set Hal off on a new tack.

Over dessert, Curt asked casually, "That teacher that coached the pageant, what about him? Judging by what we saw, he knows his business. I suppose he's one of the most popular teachers?"

"You mean Goody—er, I mean Mr. Goodman?" Hal glanced quickly from Barney to Curt. "I didn't mean to sound sassy. Everybody calls him Goody—to his face even. He doesn't mind. Yeah, he's popular, only they say he plays favorites. You know, has his pets. Takes a liking for some guy and that guy's got it made. Goody gives him the best parts, gives him extra coaching, gets him

186

out of classes to run errands or work on scenery. But I guess if Goody doesn't care for you, you got no chance."

"Who's the current favorite, Hal?" asked Curt.

"Fellow named Blair, I'd say, and I guess maybe Frank Russel."

"And what girls?" asked Curt.

"Don't know about any girls. Never heard about any, but I wouldn't know. I'm not one of Goody's bunch."

"Why not, Hal?" asked Barney. "Don't you go in for dramatics?"

"Naw, I'm for wrestling and cross country, mostly." Hal launched into an involved discussion of those two sports.

Barney looked at the clock. "Hate to interrupt. Better be getting on out to the convention center. Wouldn't want to keep our people waiting."

27 / Sunday at 7:00 P.M.

On the drive out, Hal sat quietly in the backseat while Curt and Barney conversed in low tones, planning their campaign. As they drove into the parking lot, Curt turned back to Hal and said, "Got a little errand for you. You know where the concession stand is?"

"Sure. I'm one of their best customers."

"Would you see if they can give you a container of hot coffee, some paper cups, a half dozen Cokes or whatever they have, and some ice cubes? Mr. Ross here will give you the money you need."

Barney flashed Curt a quick look, half dismay, half anger.

"Aw, come on, Barney," Curt wheedled. "Chief ought to allow you *that* much expense money."

Hal took the bill Barney reluctantly pulled out of his pocket and dashed off. Curt looked after him and laughed. "Quite a boy. Do you suppose we were ever like that?"

"Don't remember, it was so long ago," said Barney. "But I hope not. I thought it was girls who chattered."

The Green Room was just as they had left it. To the faint sound of organ music from the nearby arena, Curt arranged chairs in a semicircle, and Barney found a small table. Hal bustled in with a helper, bearing boxes.

"Where should I put them, Mr. Conners?" Hal asked.

"There's a long table over there. How about bringing it over by this electric outlet and spreading everything out on it. Have any trouble?"

"Me? Naw. They all know me there."

Dr. Redmond was first to arrive. "Sorry, Mr. Ross, but I'm due in at the service right now. It will be at least twenty minutes before I can get away." As the organ music swelled louder, he said, "In fact, I'm due there right now. See you soon." As he was leaving, Witty and Karyl came through the door. With a startled look, bordering on panic, Redmond looked at them, then back at Barney Ross, opened his mouth as if to speak, and closed it again. Karyl and Witty looked at each other and grinned foolishly. Ducking their head slightly, they said, "Evening, Dr. Redmond." Dr. Redmond nodded and rushed from the room.

"Hello, Karyl, Witold," was Barney's greeting. Curt added, "Sorry the Cokes aren't very cold, but if you like coffee, it's hot and ready."

Karyl and Witty moved over to the table to watch Hal and his helper. Curt nudged Barney. "Not so bad-looking in their Sunday pants instead of jeans. Somebody's made them comb their hair."

There was a commotion out in the hall, the door was flung open, and Wayne Hitchcock made a dramatic entrance, complete with Dennis Peters as guard of honor.

"Well, good evening. We meet again. How are you all?" He put his arm around Peters' shoulder and pulled him forward. "And did you see our rising young actor? His big scene in *Battleground* tonight was fantastic, simply fantastic. Keep an eye on this boy, folks. He's on his way."

"I didn't know you were an actor, Mr. Peters," said Curt. "Somehow I supposed—"

"Supposed he was just my man Friday," Hitchcock broke in. "Oh, he's been that too. Couldn't have managed without him. But guess I'll just have to be looking for a replacement now. This boy's on his way." He lowered his voice to an exaggerated stage whisper. "I knew he had talent. That's why I took him in tow. He's worked hard, yes, very hard. Started the right way—slow and easy, walk-ons, bit parts. But nothing but feature roles from now on, you just watch and see."

Sonny Hitchcock turned to look at Witty and Karyl looking at him with wondering eyes. "And who've we got here?"

"Let me introduce these two young men," said Curt. "This is Witold Zacherewicz and Karyl Pilchoski. Couple of fans of yours. This is Wayne Hitchcock, boys—as if I had to tell you—and that's Dennis Peters."

Wayne Hitchcock's smile was dazzling. "Well, now, that's nice." He extended his hand and gave each boy a vigorous shake. "Interesting names. Polish, I'll bet." The two nodded. "Wouldn't do for stage names, you know. You'd need something short and catchy."

He caught sight of Goodman just entering. "Why, Goody," he shouted. "You here? I'm surprised—and pleased." He strode over to Goody and wound an affectionate arm around his shoulder. "This is the man that gave me my very first start—for which I'm eternally grateful. But how come you're here, Goody?"

"I invited him," said Barney Ross. "Heard you've got a dinner date, so I suggested he meet you here."

"Mighty thoughtful. I appreciate that," said Hitchcock.

Phoebe Sears made her entrance just then. At sight of her, Hitchcock, Goodman, and Peters got very busy talking to Karyl, Witty, and Hal. Barney moved a bit reluctantly to greet Phoebe Sears while Curt stationed himself where he could watch everybody in the room.

Phoebe Sears was staring boldly at the men gathered about the refreshment table. She moved close to Barney; she gesticulated, she pointed; she spoke vehemently. Suddenly she took Barney firmly by the arm and walked officiously toward the group.

Barney cleared his throat. "Excuse me, Mr. Hitchcock, this is Miss Phoebe Sears. Miss Sears, this is Mr. Hitchcock, noted star of the television show *Battleground*."

Phoebe ignored Sonny's outstretched hand. "Hitchcock, eh? Yes, I think I've heard of you. Television? Can't say I look at it much. An awful lot of trash, a waste of time in my opinion."

Without the slightest loss of composure, Wayne Hitchcock smiled. "You're so right, Miss Sears. I'm constantly fighting with our writers to see that *our* show is factually correct. Each Sunday night has to be a history lesson, I keep insisting. Sometimes I have to fight pretty hard." He smiled blandly. "May I present my fellow actor, Mr. Dennis Peters?"

Phoebe looked Peters up and down as if inspecting a bit of

merchandise. "I hope, Mr. Peters, you don't plan to stay in television long. If you've really got talent, aim for the classical drama." Dennis Peters bowed and said nothing.

Slightly red of face, Barney Ross quickly introduced Karyl and Witold as college students.

"Out at Redmond's college?" Phoebe sniffed. "Pity. Hope you can make it to the state university next year. And why do you boys have to wear your hair so long? It doesn't do a thing for you."

She turned away just in time to see Harry Manson entering. She looked up at Barney, then headed for Manson. As she turned her back, there was a sudden burst of laughter from the group at the table. Phoebe turned to glare at them, then advanced toward Manson. Barney hurried to introduce him.

Manson bowed slightly. Miss Sears surveyed him carefully. "Are you a television actor too, Mr. Manson?" she asked.

"Me? No way," laughed Manson. "I'm only a—"

Barney broke in hurriedly, "Mr. Manson is a sort of assistant to Lieutenant Governor Alcott."

Phoebe Sears managed a frosty smile. "Oh, a politician. That's different." She turned toward the door. "I really must be going, Mr. Ross. I suppose you'd like me to tell you which . . ." Her voice trailed off to a murmur.

Suddenly Barney exclaimed, "Really?" They both turned to look at the group about the table and then at Harry Manson. They talked intently a bit longer. Suddenly Phoebe's voice rose in pitch. "You can be sure, Mr. Ross. I never forget a—" She caught herself and lowered her voice.

Curt, seeing Manson stranded in the middle of the room, walked over to him and extended a hand, saying, "Good evening, Mr. Manson. Glad you could come." For a moment Harry Manson seemed startled at the formality of the greeting.

Turning his back to the others in the room, Curt said softly, "Harry, we'd like your help. We've got a little deal going." He continued to speak softly, edging Manson over to the far side of the room. Suddenly Manson stopped, and with raised eyebrows he exclaimed, "You mean you think Hitchcock—" Curt put a hand out, murmured a few more words. Manson nodded, looked back at the group again, nodded again.

"I can count on you then, Manson?" asked Curt. "And you'll keep an eye on the kid, just in case? And if you catch any bits of conversation . . ." his voice died down.

Just then, Dr. Redmond flung open the door and strode into the room, almost colliding with the departing Phoebe Sears. At sight of her, Redmond stopped abruptly and looked about as if trying to find some way of escape.

"Ah, Redmond." The voice of Phoebe Sears became a more strident rasp. "I've been wanting to see you again."

Redmond's recovery was a lesson in self-control. "Good evening, Miss Sears. I'm delighted to see you."

Phoebe sniffed. "I'm sure you are. I hope you'll be in your office bright and early tomorrow morning. I'm coming out to see you. I'd talk to you tonight, but I don't like to conduct business on Sunday."

"Why, of course, Miss Sears. I don't remember what's on my calendar, but I promise I'll make room for you—and Mrs. Yates and Mrs. Warren, too, if they choose to come."

"We'll be there, Redmond." She turned and made a quick exit. Redmond stood watching her until she was out of sight, then wiped his brow.

"What a bitch," exclaimed Barney Ross. He raised his voice so everybody could hear. "I hope you men won't let Miss Sears's remarks bother you. She's something of a character, you know, but she is really a very capable person."

"Why, not at all," boomed Sonny Hitchcock's voice. "It takes all kinds. People like her keep us on our toes. Why, if we listened only to our admirers, we might get conceited." He laughed heartily.

Dr. Quinlan was the last to arrive. "Sorry I'm late, but I've been with a patient. Hope this won't take too long. I really should get back."

"I understand, Doc," said Barney. "Don't worry, this will be short. Now, gentlemen," he said, raising his voice again, "if you'd care to find chairs, I'd like to take advantage of your cooperation and go over a few matters with you."

As the group moved slowly to the semicircle of seats, Curt strolled casually over to the refreshment table. He pretended to examine the equipment as he murmured something to Hal Mulholland. He nodded his head, and Hal walked to the door leading to the hall.

Glancing toward Curt to see that he was stationed where he could see everybody, Barney began. "First of all, I'd like to give you a piece of news that may or may not have something to do with the unfortunate happening last night. There was a second tragedy this afternoon. An elderly couple was found in their home, gas jets turned on full blast, doors and windows shut tight. I wonder if any of you may have known them. Their name was Krasuski.''

Experienced actor though he was, Wayne Hitchcock could not conceal his shocked reaction. "My God," he exploded. Curt saw the color drain from Hitchcock's face and caught the quick look he darted toward Dennis Peters, followed by a flicker toward Goodman. Then he sat rigidly erect, his eyes fixed straight ahead. "Suicide, my God, how terribie," he breathed.

The effect on Dennis Peters was even more pronounced. "Is it surprise, or is it fear?" Curt wondered as he saw Peters almost jump from his chair. Curt noticed that Peters caught Hitchcock's quick glance and that Peters continued to stare at Hitchcock without blinking. Curt could see the knuckles on Peter's hands white from the tension of his clenched fists.

Goody Goodman's reaction was puzzling. At the name *Krasuski,* he turned to look at Hitchcock; his eyes narrowed and his lips twitched as if he were suppressing a smile. He, too, continued to look fixedly at Hitchcock. Almost as if he's watching an actor in a play, thought Curt.

"Suicide, Mr. Hitchcock?" asked Barney calmly. "Yes, that was our first impression too. But as we questioned neighbors and friends, we could find no reason. The Krasuskis had been at a church lunch and seemed extremely happy. They spoke of expecting a visitor, somebody they wanted very much to see." Barney looked directly at Hitchcock. "In fact, they'd gone to some pains to pretty up their house.''

Barney paused briefly. Nobody spoke, Hitchcock sat immobile, like an actor with no lines and no stage directions to follow. Barney continued.

"Also, a package was delivered to their house earlier in the day, a package wrapped up neatly and tied with a fancy ribbon.''

Curt noticed Peters lowered his eyes suddenly and gazed at his hands. Goody Goodman was still watching Hitchcock, a smile touching the corners of his mouth. The others, as if sensing some hidden purpose in this narrative, had their eyes fixed intently on Barney Ross.

"I wonder, do any of you know the Krasuskis?"

There was a heavy silence, then with no trace of his former exuberance, Hitchcock spoke as if in a stage aside. "I did once, long ago, when I was growing up here. That's why it was quite a shock to hear they are dead. But I haven't seen them or heard about them for years."

"You haven't been in touch with them since you've been back this time?" asked Barney.

"No. I thought maybe I'd go by their place later tonight or sometime tomorrow, just to say hello." He smiled wanly. "But I guess there won't be any reason to now. Suicide . . . I can't believe it."

Barney let his gaze wander casually about the room till he caught Curt's eye. There was the slightest lift of an eyebrow and the suggestion of a shrug of a shoulder.

"Well, enough of that for now," said Barney. "We didn't bring you here to talk of this afternoon's events but about those of last night. I'm referring, of course, to the appearance of the streaker. We are hoping that you can help us find that fellow. In fact," he paused significantly, "we think it is possible that he may be in this room."

Everybody reacted to this with exclamations and startled expressions, but it was Dr. Redmond who had the most violent response. He sat bolt upright, his face flushed, and he looked at Witold with an expression of anger mixed with fear. Witold, catching Redmond's glance, shifted uneasily, looked every place possible, and finally focused his eyes on Barney Ross. Karyl was looking worriedly from Witold to Redmond and back again.

Manson had turned in his chair, his eyes scanning each face rapidly. Curt wondered if Manson caught the second rapid interchange of looks between Hitchcock and Peters and if he noticed Goodman's unwavering study of Hitchcock. Dr. Quinlan had obviously caught Redmond's expression, for he, too, was staring at Witold.

It was Goody Goodman who eased the tension. "Did I hear you right, Mr. Ross? You think one of us may be the streaker?" Almost reluctantly his gaze moved from Hitchcock to Peters, then to the two college boys, to Manson and Dr. Quinlan. "I find that hard to believe." Almost as an afterthought, he caught sight of Hal standing by the exit door. He stiffened noticeably, studied Hal awhile, then looked back at Hitchcock.

"It is possible," said Barney. "We know one person here who has appeared previously in public in the nude."

193

Witty and Karyl ducked their heads to avoid Redmond's angry glare. The faces of Peters and Hitchcock were a study in shifting emotions until, noticing Barney's intense look at Redmond, they turned to look at Redmond and followed his gaze toward the two boys. They looked at each other and smiled.

"And you think," said Goodman, "this—er—individual is the one who appeared before us last night?"

"Not necessarily, but—" The door was flung open. Barney stopped and looked with annoyance at an usher who was approaching him. "What is it?" he asked impatiently.

The usher leaned over to say something softly to him.

"Is that so?" Barney exclaimed. "Well, can't it wait, can't you take the message? Don't you see I've got a meeting going on here?" The usher whispered some more. "Oh, in that case . . . All right, I'll come." Barney raised his voice. "I'm sorry, men, but something has come up. Will you excuse me a few minutes?" He rose to follow the usher, then turned back. "Oh, yes, there's coffee over there, or, if you prefer, some cold drinks. I promise I'll make this as short as possible. Officer Conners will see that you men are taken care of while I'm gone." He hurried out of the room.

Everybody stood up and began to talk. Witty and Karyl went to help themselves to Cokes. Redmond followed and spoke intensely to them, pulling them off to one side. Peters and Hitchcock said a few words to each other, and hurried toward the hall exit, gesturing as they went. Manson looked at Curt Conners, then sauntered out after Hitchcock and Peters. Goodman moved as if to follow, but, noticing Manson, he changed his course and wandered toward the coffee urn. Dr. Quinlan looked about uncertainly and then decided to join Goodman. Curt made his way to the exit, looked down the hallway, then turned back to join Goodman and Quinlan.

"What was Ross getting at, Conners?" asked the doctor. "Does he really mean one of those fellows was the streaker?"

"Yes," asked Goodman, looking at Witty and Karyl intently. "Does he mean one of those two young men talking to Dr. Redmond? You know, now that I look at them, it does seem possible. Maybe if I got a closer view . . ." Cup in hand, he sauntered over toward Witty and Karyl.

As he approached, Redmond stopped talking and turned abruptly away. Goodman made some attempts at conversation, but both boys stood silent, sipping their Cokes.

Redmond came up to where Curt Conners and Dr. Quinlan were standing. "Look here, Conners, what's Ross think he's getting at?"

"Good evening, Dr. Redmond," said Curt mildly. "Do you know Dr. Quinlan?"

Redmond nodded. "Evening, Doctor." He turned back to Curt. "If Ross thinks he's going to pin something—"

Curt interrupted him. "I really don't know what Ross is leading up to, Doctor. He'll be back in a few minutes. Meanwhile, will you have some coffee, or would you prefer something cooler?" Redmond grabbed a paper cup, jabbed some ice into it, and filled the cup with Coke.

"Something cold for me," boomed out the ebullient Hitchcock, who was entering from the hallway. "For lack of something stronger, make it a Coke with lots of ice." He flashed a smile at Redmond. "Evening, Dr. Redmond. Looks like both you and I could do with something to cool us off. I've sort of forgotten about these hot June nights after California." He looked at Dr. Quinlan. "I don't believe I've met this other gentleman."

"This is Dr. Quinlan," said Curt. "Mr. Hitchcock is the famous television personality."

" 'Doctor' did you say? Are you a doctor like Redmond here, or are you a real doctor?" He laughed loudly. "Just a little joke, Redmond. No offense meant. A line from one of my shows."

Redmond forced a smile. Dr. Quinlan laughed politely. "I'm a medical doctor, if that's what you mean."

"In fact, Dr. Quinlan was the man who worked on our Mrs. McGinty last night," said Curt.

Hitchcock turned quickly and grabbed a Coke. Spooning in the ice, he called across to Peters just returning. "Hey, Dennis, come over here and get something cool."

Dennis Peters took a cup and poured himself a drink, then found a seat. Throwing one arm over the back of the chair, he rested his head on his hand. Harry Manson wandered casually over to pour himself a cup of coffee, then he stood near Curt Conners, who was listening to Hitchcock as he told about one of his televisions shows in which there had been a knife murder.

"And you know who *did* the stabbing? It was the doctor himself, the medic who was examining the fellow." Realizing from the expression on Quinlan's face that he'd made an inept remark, Hitchcock clapped the doctor on the back and said, "Not that that could ever happen in real life," and he forced a laugh.

Barney entered briskly. "Sorry, gentlemen. These long distance calls, you know. It really was an urgent matter. Shall we continue? I know several of you have other things scheduled for tonight."

He waited a few minutes until they had found places, then continued. "I'm sure you are wondering why we asked each of you to come here. We have been interviewing everybody who was near that special section of seats last night—anybody who was in a position to get a good look at the streaker. You are the last group we've got together, so I'm asking you the same question we've been asking everybody else. As you think back, is there anything about the streaker that sticks out in your mind about him. I mean, anything about his height, weight, coloring, any distinguishing marks or movements that would help us in making an identification."

Barney waited for a response. Nobody said anything. Barney cleared his throat. "Mr. Hitchcock, let's start with you. As the streaker made his exit, he passed near the stage where you were. Did you get a good look at him?"

"Why no, Mr. Ross," Hitchcock said easily. "I was thinking how I could save the show, keep it from falling apart." He smiled broadly. "If you remember, I thought up a one liner on the spur of the moment that made everybody laugh." He looked about him to see if the others appreciated his cleverness, then he shook his head. "No, I'm real sorry, but I've got nothing to help you out with."

"Mr. Peters?" asked Barney. "If I remember right, you said you were in the stand checking on lighting and sound. Did you get a good-enough glimpse to remember anything about him?"

Dennis Peters shook his head and very softly said, "Sorry, nothing."

"Dr. Redmond, you were sitting next to Mrs. McGinty's companion, so you were very close," said Barney. "As the streaker bent over Mrs. McGinty, did you get a good-enough look to catch anything?"

"Excuse me, but it was the mayor I was sitting next to. Mrs. Cline was on the other side of Mrs. McGinty," said Redmond testily. "I remember because the mayor started to get up, so he quite blocked my view. And as I told you before, I was concerning myself about Mrs. Redmond. The only thing I remember is that he was wearing a mask, and you know about that already."

At the word *mask*, there was an exclamation from the college boys that made everybody turn to look at them. Wayne Hitchcock laughed. "He was wearing a mask? Dennis, doesn't that just sound like a plot from one of our stories? Are you sure about the mask, Redmond?"

Redmond did not answer. He was glaring at Witty.

Barney waited awhile, then looked at Dr. Quinlan. "Have you had time to think back, Doctor, so you can recall anything that might help us?"

"No, as I told you last night, I was more concerned with the people the streaker was attacking. All I can remember is obvious—he was naked, he wore an Indian headdress, he had dark skin, and he moved very fast."

"Mr. Manson? You were in the stands immediately behind the special section and rushed right up. Can you think of anything?"

Harry Manson merely shook his head.

"That leaves you, Witold," said Barney. "Your story was that the streaker passed you in the hallway. Have you anything to add to what you've already told me?"

For some reason, this remark caused quite a stir. Redmond looked puzzled, Hitchcock looked startled, Manson stood up to get a better view of Witty.

It was Goodman who spoke. "Tell me, young fellow, did you see him wearing a mask?"

"I don't think so, but I'm not real sure. I guess I was so surprised to see him naked—I was looking at something else besides his eyes, I mean."

Hitchcock let out a roar of laughter and slapped Peters on the shoulder. "Did you hear that, Dennis? That's a good one." Still laughing, he looked around at the others. "Maybe that's what the rest of us were looking at too, only this young fellow is the only one willing to admit it." He gave Witty an exaggerated stage wink.

Witty's cheeks had turned a noticeable pink; he lowered his eyes and said nothing.

Barney cleared his throat loudly. "I seem to have drawn a blank. In which case I think there is no reason to keep you here any longer." He smiled and stood up. "I want to thank you for coming here at some inconvenience. I hope you understand that this was a necessary part of our routine in attempting to solve this case."

Barney looked at Hal, who had sidled in and was bending over the coffee container. Barney called, "Hal, don't be in a hurry to clear that table. I could sure use a cup of that coffee. Maybe somebody else would like some too."

Dr. Quinlan grabbed his bag, waved, and made for the door. Hitchcock and Peters were close behind him, but they turned to call to Goodman, who was saying something softly to Hal. "Hey, Goody, come on. That dinner is waiting for us."

Dr. Redmond started to follow Barney, then he stopped, as if changing his mind, and headed for the exit. Witty and Karyl remained in their seats, talking softly. Then Witty moved over to where Barney Ross was pouring coffee.

"May I say something, Mr. Ross?" Barney nodded and smiled. Witty spoke hurriedly, pointing toward the disappearing trio of Hitchcock, Peters, and Goodman. Barney said, "Are you sure, Witty?" to which Witty replied, "No, I'm not real sure, but it *could* be."

Barney nodded. "Thanks, Witty. Don't you worry too much about—well, about Dr. Redmond. I think I can help you out there."

"Jeez, Mr. Ross, I sure hope you can." He motioned to Karyl and then turned back. "So long, Mr. Ross, and thanks for everything. I'll be seeing you."

Manson moved over to Curt. "You were right about asking me to hang around. I followed them down the hall, trying to catch what they was saying. They were talking awful fast but pretty soft. All of sudden I heard, 'I didn't know anything about that. Honest, I didn't.' Hitchcock looked around just then, so I got real busy with the cigarette lighter. They talked some more, too soft for me to catch until I heard, 'Eight o'clock. You can make it. I'll pick up the car later.' Then they went into the john."

Curt shook his head. "I don't get it."

"There's more," said Manson. "After they'd gone into the john, I waited outside the door for a bit. Then I eased it open and stood inside, behind that metal thing that keeps people from looking in. Sure enough, I heard Hitchcock saying something about what beautiful hair the kid had, and didn't Peters think he was a good-looking lad and mightn't he do for something on the show. I didn't know how much of a greenie your little guy was, so when Hitchcock said something about his room being number 301, I figured it was time. I reached back and opened the door with lots of noise and walked in looking like I had to go real bad. When they saw me, those two moved away real quick and headed out. I tell you, Conners, if those two aren't a pair of queers on the prowl, my name ain't Harry Manson."

"Yes, that figures. You think Hal was shook up at all?" asked Curt.

"Didn't seem to be. Either you got a real babe in the woods, or he's got what it takes. Do you make anything out of what I picked up out in the hall?"

"Not yet . . . unless—" Curt's face lighted up. "Maybe . . . I think so, Manson. Thanks a lot for your help. I'll be in touch to let you know."

Manson nodded. "Anytime," he said and made for the exit.

Curt was at Barney's side at once. "How soon can we get a warrant, Barney? Fifteen minutes enough time? Maybe by using the phone?"

"That quick? Hell, no, no way. What's up?"

"One of our birds is clearing out. There's an eight o'clock plane for Capital City, and we've just got time to stop him from making it."

"O.K., maybe this will work. I'll have Andy get a squad car out here to take you to the airport while I get down to the station, get the warrant and meet you out there. Trouble is, if I'm delayed, you may have to do some stalling."

Barney started off, then turned back. "While you're waiting, look these over. Notice who Sears put the finger on. Our little high school kid did a good job, too. And that wasn't a fake call when I left a while ago. That was a long distance from L.A. They had trouble finding the information we wanted because the name we gave him is the latest one of several he's used. Two years ago it was Pierre Le Beau, and he was—hang on to your hat for this one—a male go-go dancer in a gay bar. As Le Beau he was booked for lifting the wallet of some old guy that was entertaining him in his hotel room. He drew a fine and a couple of hours in jail. A few other little episodes like that."

"A male go-go dancer. Never heard of that one before." Curt called after Barney, who was hurrying toward the exit. "Tell Andy I'll be at the parking lot door."

He looked at the names on the slip. "Two of them—Harry Manson and Dennis Peters. Manson about five feet eight; Peters

199

only about five feet seven, not quite right, but I don't suppose that's serious since people were sort of guessing about height. And blue eyes, both of them."

"Who you talking to, Mr. Conners?" asked Hal, coming in just then.

"Why, Hal, you still here? Guess I was talking to myself."

"Just finished taking back all the stuff to the concession stand," said Hal. "What were you saying about guessing height?"

"You gave us some valuable information. Thanks for a good job."

"Did I do all right? Jeez, I'm glad. Really, Mr. Conners, it was a pushover. What's more, Mr. Hitchcock said he liked my looks and asked did I ever want to be on television."

"What? What's that you say?"

"Mr. Hitchcock wants to know if I'd like to be in show business. If I would, he thought maybe I could come around to his hotel room tonight."

"Oh, my God," exploded Curt. "What did *you* say?"

"Why, nothing. That other fellow came in just then and he didn't say any more. Why, is something wrong?"

"How old did you say you are, Hal?"

"I've told you, just turned eighteen, Mr. Conners."

"You *must* have been around, Hal. You just can't be that innocent."

"What do you mean?"

"Look, you're no actor. You don't know anything about acting. Nobody's going to put you in any show just because you look nice." Curt looked at Hal and shook his head. "You've never heard that old, ancient, worn-out line about 'Come on up to my room some night'?"

"Sure I have, but that's for girls." Hal's mouth fell open, his eyes got big. "Oh, you mean he wanted *me*? You mean he's a fag, a fairy—"

"Hold it, Hal, don't go throwing names around. You've caught on to what he really wanted and you've helped me find out about him. It all fits into a pattern. But let's not let the whole world know what we've found out."

"You mean this is a clue?"

"I mean, learn all you can, but keep your mouth shut about giving out information." His stern look broke into a relaxed grin. "And I won't tell on you, Hal, that you've been propositioned by a famous

TV star. And you're not going up to talk to Mr. Hitchcock about being a TV star yourself. Now you can help me with a problem."

"What problem is that?"

"We're looking for a fellow about five feet nine, blue eyes, not fat, not skinny, not circumcised, and left-handed. You have found me two guys that fit that description pretty well except for one thing. Harry Manson poured his coffee with his right hand and he held the cup in his right hand. Dennis Peters poured his Coke into a paper cup—you guessed it—with his right hand. Neither of them is left-handed. What do I do now?"

28 / *Sunday at 7:55 P.M.*

The airport was usually a quiet, leisurely place on a Sunday night. This was just a feeder line, two planes a day to Capital City, with stops along the way, and once a day a plane left for far-off Chicago. During the week, business was brisk, but on weekends a single attendant was usually enough to handle ticket sales.

It must have been the Centennial celebration that produced so many travelers, for there was a line formed at the check-in counter, and the man on duty was looking rushed and harried as he tried to accommodate everybody.

The plane was on the runway, ready for passenger boarding when a car drove up with a squeal of brakes and a man hopped out. Rushing up to the ticket window, he called out peremptorily, "I'd like a single, one-way to Capital City."

The agent looked up, nodded, and said, "Just a minute. I'll take care of you as soon as I get these bags checked."

The latecomer drummed nervously on the counter, looked at the clock, peered out at the waiting plane, then said, "I'll make it all right, won't I?"

"Oh, sure," was the patient reply. "They won't leave till everybody's aboard. I'll be with you right away. If you want to bring your baggage over here, I'll weigh it in for you."

"I don't have any baggage, except this hand case that I'll carry with me on the plane."

The ticket agent shrugged. "O.K., sir."

Just as the ticket agent was moving to wait on the latecomer, a second car drove up with an even louder squeal of brakes. There was no mistaking the bright red hair of the man who got out of the car. The nervous traveler turned quickly and bent his head over the counter as if studying something carefully.

"I don't think you'd better buy that ticket," said Curt Conners. "I'm afraid you've got to come with me to headquarters."

"What do you mean? I can't go with you. I'll miss my plane."

"You don't understand. You're under arrest."

The traveler flinched, then drew himself up. "You can't arrest me. I haven't done anything. You got a warrant? What are the charges?"

"Do you want me to call them out right here in front of everybody? Or would you prefer I take care of that outside?"

The traveler looked at the ticket seller staring at him, at the other passengers who were watching and whispering. Outside the entrance stood a policeman in uniform by the car. He wet his lips with his tongue, his eyes darted from side to side as if looking for some way to escape, then he shrugged his shoulders. "O.K. I'll go with you." He picked up his hand case, looked around defiantly at the staring crowd, and with head held high walked proudly to the door.

A second car was just pulling up. An older man got out and approached. "Are you Dennis Peters? I have a warrant here for your arrest."

"What are the charges?" asked Dennis Peters.

"Indecent exposure and disturbance of the peace are the charges right now. I should warn you, anything you say can be used against you."

From inside the airport came a booming voice over the loud-speaker. "Passengers are asked to board the plane for flight 309 to Capital City."

Dennis Peters turned and got into the squad car.

During the ride to the station and all through the routine of being booked, Dennis Peters kept a discreet silence except for a few monosyllabic answers to questions. After bail had been set, he was told that he could make one telephone call, either to his attorney or to a friend.

"I don't know any attorney in this town," he said. "I'd like to call Wayne Hitchcock, but I don't know where he is."

"We'll try to locate him for you," said Barney Ross. "He was going to have dinner with Mr. Goodman. Did he happen to mention any restaurant?"

"I think so. Is there some place called the Cocked Oar? I believe that's what Goody said."

"Cocked Oar?" Barney looked puzzled.

Curt said with a laugh, "Could it be the Coq d'Or? It means the golden cock."

"Is that a restaurant?"

"Yes," said Barney. "We'll have Andy call out there and have Hitchcock paged. Now if we can have your word that you won't try any fancy getaway stuff, you can wait in my office instead of back there in a cell."

"You have my word." Peters smiled ruefully. "I wouldn't know where to go in this town if I did try to make a break."

"This way then, Peters," said Barney, leading him across the hall and into his office. He carefully cleared his desk of all papers, looked about the room, then indicated a chair in the corner. "We'll leave you here, nice and quiet so you can think things over while you're waiting for your friend."

Leaving the door open, Barney and Curt stationed themselves behind the switchboard where they could see Peters but he couldn't see them.

"Think we've got a case, Red?" Barney asked softly. "I mean one that'll hold up in court?"

"We've got a case, and I'm hoping it won't have to stand up in court."

"Now what the hell kind of talk is that, Red?"

"We've got him in as the streaker, with enough witnesses to scare him. He won't know Sears is a birdbrain witch and that Witty is a kid that can be challenged. But I've got three or four things to spring on him and on Hitchcock, too. I think they'll crack."

"Three or four things? Like what?" asked Barney.

"A slip of paper with the Krasuski address on it, the sleeping pills in the wine; they won't know how much we know." Curt lowered his voice further. "And if Hitchcock gets to talking tough, I'll mention Hal and threaten to turn Hickson on to them."

"Wait a minute." Barney looked quizzically at Curt. "What's our high school kid got to do with it? And that bastard Hickson? You lost me on that one."

"Oh, you don't know about that one." Curt thought a moment. "I think I'll keep that to myself awhile. It might backfire, and if you don't know about it, it might be better."

"Watch out, Red. You know how the judge is about browbeating a suspect or denying him his rights."

"Yeah, I know. But maybe we'll have *them* asking *us*."

The outside door was flung open and Wayne Hitchcock stormed in. "What's going on here?" he bellowed. "You got Dennis Peters under arrest? You lost your brains, you cops? I'll have you up for false arrest and have them throw the book at you."

"Oh, good evening, Mr. Hitchcock," said Barney mildly. "Your Mr. Peters was asking for you. Good you could be so prompt."

"Sure he asked for me. Sure I'm prompt. I want him out of here right away. Right now, do you hear?" Hitchcock yelled.

"Of course you do, but maybe you'd better talk to your friend Peters first," said Barney patiently. "He's across the hall if you'll just follow me."

Hitchcock rushed over to embrace Peters. "Dennis, my boy. What the hell are these bullies doing to you? Don't worry, I'll have you out of here in no time, and a couple of cops are going to be sorry they ever tried to pick on you."

"Don't you think you'd better hear the charges first, Mr. Hitchcock?" asked Barney.

"Charges? What charges?"

"Indecent exposure and disturbing the peace, Mr. Hitchcock."

Hitchcock guffawed and nudged Peters in the ribs. "Oh, for God's sake, how ridiculous can you get?"

"Are you suggesting, Mr. Hitchcock, that you didn't know Peters here was the streaker last night?"

"Dennis the streaker? Oh, come off it."

Barney looked bored. "We have two witnesses prepared to testify in court, to identity him under oath."

"Witnesses? Witnesses be damned." Hitchcock's lip curled defiantly. "Name them."

Curt broke in. "Not tonight, Hitchcock. But Peters should remember when I was talking with a stagehand who kept pulling his cap down over his eyes, only he didn't pull it far enough. Know what I'm talking about, Peters?" He turned to look at Dennis Peters.

"Besides, Peters, you have the misfortune never to have been circumcised."

"Wh—wh—what did you say?" stammered Dennis Peters. "What's that got to do with all this?"

"The streaker was definitely *not* circumcised. Right, Peters?"

Hitchcock let out another yell. "Look here, what kind of talk is that?" He turned to Dennis Peters. "You don't have to answer to that. Sounds like a trick to me, and a damn sneaky one at that."

"Oh, Peters has been duly warned that anything he says may be used against him," said Barney Ross calmly. "We're just letting you know what he's in for. You asked us, you know." He turned to Peters. "You realize that we can have a medical doctor verify this, and probably will."

Curt turned to Hitchcock. "You also know, don't you, that Peters has been booked before for indecent exposure?" He turned back to Peters. "Right, Pierre Le Beau?"

Dennis Peters's mouth fell open. "What did you call me?"

"It was out in California, February of last year." Curt walked closer and smiled in mock admiration. "You know, Pierre Le Beau, you're the first male go-go dancer I've ever met face-to-face."

"It's all a damned lie," shouted Hitchcock.

"Court records don't usually lie," said Barney gently.

Hitchcock fumed and turned red in the face. "You're brow-beating this fellow here. Police brutality I call it."

"Why, no, Mr. Hitchcock, we're answering *your* questions. Actually we're being very cooperative and letting you know some of the evidence we have before you hear it in court." Barney smiled patiently. "Now you can't call cooperation like that 'police brutality,' Mr. Hitchcock."

"What's more," added Curt, "you knew all this right along, didn't you? In fact, it was you that persuaded Peters here to put on his little act, wasn't it?"

"I don't have to listen to these—these wild ridiculous charges," Hitchcock spluttered.

"No, you don't. We can stop right here," said Curt. "But how about if this gets out in court? It would make interesting reading for your fans if the newspaper reporters grab onto a little item like that."

Hitchcock looked at Peters. "Tell them it isn't so, Dennis. Tell them I didn't have anything to do with it. You've *got* to tell them."

Barney held up his hand. "Don't tell us anything of the kind, Peters," he said. "Remember anything you say here can be used in court."

Dennis Peters crouched down in his chair, avoiding Hitchcock's eyes.

Curt walked over to Hitchcock. "Just as a newspaper reporter would make headlines if he heard you propositioned a high school kid tonight."

Hitchcock drew back. "What's that you say?" he gasped. "What are you talking about?" he said weakly, sinking into a chair.

"I'm talking about tonight in the convention center in the men's room. You didn't know somebody heard you proposition that kid?"

Hitchcock faked a laugh. "Oh, that. I just asked the boy if he was interested in breaking into television. What's wrong with that?"

"Oh, come on, Hitchcock!" Curt's lip curled. "A man goes up to a boy in a public toilet and asks him to come up to his room?"

Hitchcock looked almost sick. "Why would you want to start a story like that?" He straightened up. "You aren't threatening me, are you?"

"Us, threaten you?" Curt shook his head. "Not us. We're just letting you know that the kid might talk it around, the fellow who heard you might repeat it, and one of our reporters would pick up the story."

"Well can't we stop it right here?"

"Freedom of the press, Mr. Hitchcock," said Barney. "Neither you nor I can stifle that."

"Suppose we get back to the business we were talking about," said Curt Conners. "How come you cooked up that little stunt with Peters in the first place?"

Hitchcock grinned slyly. "I haven't said I did."

"No, of course not," said Curt. "And I don't blame you for staying out of it. Not when we think of the more serious charge that our streaker here may be in for."

Dennis Peters looked startled. "What do you mean? What charge?"

"I think you know," said Curt. "You sat on the lady's lap and a few minutes later we found her with a knife stuck into her heart."

"Oh, my God." Terror was in Peters' eyes. "No, oh, no! No, you aren't going to pin *that* on me. I didn't kill her."

"Didn't you, Peters?" Curt confronted him, eyeball-to-eyeball. "Didn't you? Who else? You rushed right at her. You bent down over her. We all saw you. Five thousand people saw you."

"But I didn't kill her, I tell you. How could I? I wasn't carrying a knife."

"Shut up, you damn fool," yelled Hitchcock.

"Shut up?" Peters shouted back. "Sure, shut up. *You* can talk. You conned me into doing that stupid stunt. *You* said it would be a big laugh. You promised me—"

"Shut up, you big blabbermouth!" Hitchcock lunged at Peters. With a quick maneuver, Curt intercepted the blow and pushed Hitchcock back. "Ha! No way, Hitchcock," he grunted. Hitchcock reeled, caught his balance, and sagged into a chair.

"Dennis, you fool," he muttered.

"Not the only one, Hitchcock," snapped Barney. "We suspected all along you were in on this."

"Me? How so?"

Curt reached into his pocker. "Does 305 North River Street mean anything to you?"

Caught off his guard, Hitchcock recoiled, his eyes wide. He recovered himself, lowered his eyelids, and muttered. "I don't know. Should it?"

"It ought to. You lived there once with a family named Krasuski."

"Maybe I did, maybe I didn't."

"How come we found this address in your car this morning?"

Utter bewilderment showed on Hitchcock's face. "In my car?"

"The one you rented for the weekend."

Hitchcock turned to look at Peters, who drew back further in his chair and looked away. "You say you found this slip of paper this morning? In my rented car?"

"Yes. There was also a package delivered to that address this morning. In the package was a bottle of wine, a present to the Krasuskis. The wine had been doped with a drug. The Krasuskis drank that wine. Now the Krasuskis are dead."

An uneasy silence ensued. Hitchcock was staring at Peters. Peters's head was bowed, his hands twisting nervously in his lap. Curt stood motionless, watching Hitchcock.

It was Peters who broke the silence. He looked up at Curt Conners. "You've got to believe me. I didn't kill that woman. I didn't know the wine was drugged. You've got to believe me, do you hear? You've got to believe me." He looked at Barney Ross. "Ask him, ask Sonny. He can tell you. It wasn't me."

Wayne Hitchcock got up slowly and drew himself up. "I think we'd better get a lawyer. We've got nothing more to say."

29 / Sunday at 8:50 P.M.

Detective Ross and Officer Conners sat looking at each other. Dennis Peters had been locked up for the night, and Wayne Hitchcock was warned not to leave his hotel room until further notice.

"Gad, but I'm tired," Curt sighed. "I could curl up right here and go to sleep."

"Go ahead," said Barney. "You've got a right to if anybody has, Red. As for me, I'd like to sneak out and get a good stiff drink."

"Now that you mention it, I'd like to join you. It's been a day, and it's not through yet."

"Not through yet? What do you mean?" asked Barney.

Just then the telephone shrilled. Barney's look of exasperation brought a smile to Curt's face. "Better answer it, Barney," he jeered. Barney lifted the phone to his ear.

"Yes. Oh, *no*," he groaned. "I'm not here, tell him I just had a heart attack, tell him I just died, tell him—Oh, what the hell, send him in."

He looked at Curt and grimaced. "Guess who! Our favorite disease, our gentleman of the press."

The door opened and Hickson barged in. "Good evening, all. Well, well, what a cozy little twosome sitting here quiet and peaceful. Is this how our men in blue capture the villainous murderer?"

"Oh, hello, Hickson, you here?" asked Barney with a yawn. "Now our evening is complete."

"Nine o'clock, you said. Right on the button, that's me. I take it you're ready to give me my story?" He made a show of getting out notebook and pencil.

208

"Well, as a matter of fact," began Barney, "we have—"

"Almost," broke in Curt.

"We know who the streaker is—" said Barney.

"Almost," said Curt.

Barney looked at Curt with an impassive face. "And we've got the murderer locked up—"

"Almost." Curt's face was as impassive as Barney's.

Hickson looked from one to the other. In exasperation he exploded, "Oh, have you—almost? What's with this 'almost,' you guys?"

"Almost," said Curt, leaning back in his chair, "means we're hot on the track. We've got everything pinned down—almost."

"What kind of answer is that? I can't make up a story out of that 'almost' crap."

"It means, Hickson," said Barney, "we can't name names until we put the handcuffs on and have gotten a confession. Until then we can't let you break the story."

"You bluffing?" asked Hickson, looking suspiciously from one to the other. "That's it." He sneered. "You don't know anything and you're ashamed to admit it."

"Oh?" asked Curt. "Well, here's one 'almost' for you. The streaker is about five feet seven, medium build, has blue eyes, and he hasn't been circumcised."

Hickson dropped his pencil. "You bastard," he snarled. "You know I can't print that last. You giving me the shaft, you two? You making this up?" The corner of Curt's mouth twitched, but he kept his face expressionless.

"Why, Hickson, of course not," said Barney. "That's his description. All we got to do is find a fellow to match." He stood up. "Now that I look at you, I'm beginning to wonder. Um-h'mmm . . . five feet seven, medium, blue eyes. One thing left. You been circumcised?" He took a step toward Hickson.

Involuntarily Hickson stepped back, holding hands clasped in front of him. "Oh, no you don't" he yelled. Noticing the expression on Curt's face, he straightened up. "God damn you. You been pulling my leg, haven't you?"

"Not really, Hickson," said Curt. "Only you made that crack when you came in, so we thought you needed taking down a notch or two." He stood up. "Actually we are getting close, pretty damn close."

209

"You telling me the truth now?" asked Hickson.

"Are we, Barney?" asked Curt, and Barney nodded. "Yes."

Hickson grabbed for his pencil. "Well, then, give—give. Who is he? Where is he?"

"That's just it, Hickson, we can't tell you yet." Curt looked at Barney and continued. "I'll try to explain, but if I say too much, Barney will stop me. If we tip our hand too soon, our bird might catch on and fly away. Understand?"

Hickson shrugged. "I suppose so."

"Oh, come on, Hickson, you know any news release will have to come from the chief. He won't give you that till it's all sewed up, sure to stand up in court."

"And what am I supposed to do for a story?"

"I already gave you a story. Who's the streaker? Will somebody come forward and identify him? Add on all the details of where, when, and why it happened. Build it up, boy! This way you'll have enough to last a couple of days." Curt lowered his voice confidentially. "That's more than we gave the radio and TV boys. You're still ahead. Can't say we aren't cooperating."

"And what *did* you give the TV boys?"

"Nothing more than the bare facts—and don't laugh at that. I'm not trying to be funny. You can catch the ten o'clock evening news broadcast to check."

"Well, O.K., then." Hickson looked sly. "But how about a little off-the-cuff dope?"

Barney raised his hand. "Wait a minute. You mean off the record, not for publication? No news leaks?"

"I promise, and I'm listening."

Curt looked at Barney as he began. "We know who the streaker is, and we know where he is."

"You do? Great!" Hickson's face was aglow. "Who is he? A local boy? Why did he kill the mayor's wife?"

Curt shook his head and smiled. Barney folded his arms and stared off into space.

"Damn you," complained Hickson. "What good is it to tell me that much." He threw down his pencil again.

"That's just it. Murder is a pretty serious charge. As long as our streaker's got that hanging over his head, he's going to play it cagey. We've got to be sure—damned sure."

"But I don't see—if you know who the streaker is—what you're waiting for."

"Sorry, that's all you get for now. You've got to let us do our job our own way," said Barney. "But I can promise you this. When we've got our man, the chief will let you know right away."

Sullenly Hickson picked up his pencil. "All right. But I'll be waiting for that call—and real soon." He strode out of the door, slamming it hard behind him.

"Whew," said Curt, sinking back into his chair.

"Double that for me," said Barney. "And thanks, Red. You handled that damned well." He lifted up the phone. "Andy, is there any coffee left? We could use two cups—yeah, you saw who just left here." He opened a desk drawer and brought out the papers stashed there. He greeted Andy, "Thanks. Put the cups right on the desk, will you?"

"Pretty bad, eh?" asked Andy.

"Yeah, pretty much like always." Barney spooned in sugar and shoved a cup toward Curt. "And maybe you'd better shut the door, Andy. We got talking to do, and you never know who's out there."

"Oh, your little high school friend is gone—and I'm not crying." Andy exited, closing the door behind him.

Barney leaned back. "Something bothering you, Red?" he asked.

"That Peters fellow." Curt shook his head. "I don't believe he's that good an actor."

"Oh? Come again?" said Barney.

"Now Hitchcock, I wouldn't trust him any further than I could spit," said Curt, looking off into space. "But Peters? He's just a little punk that Hitchcock is keeping as a companion for—well, you know what." Curt lowered his eyes so he was looking directly at Barney Ross. "What do you think, Barney? Did he look like the kind of a guy that could commit murder?"

Barney said nothing.

"Do you still have that chart that showed where everybody was sitting last night?"

Barney fumbled among his papers. "Should be right here. Somebody crammed my papers all together. Oh, yes, here it is." He passed a sheet of paper over to Curt.

After he had studied the chart for some time, Curt muttered softly, "There was something somebody said, but who? What?

Damn it if I could only remember. Anderton...his wife...
Redmond...Quinlan..." He looked up. "What was the name of
that woman who handled the money? Oh, yes, Cohen."

"Cohen?" Barney's eyebrows shot up. "What's Judith Cohen got
to do with this? You aren't thinking that *she*—"

"Barney, maybe it's time to play a long shot again. We've just
done some bluffing that worked. Maybe our luck will hold again."

"Anything illegal, Red?" asked Barney cautiously.

"No, but maybe a little dangerous. Still, with both you and me
there, I don't see how anything could happen."

"Hadn't you better tell me?"

"I'm thinking that maybe if we bait the hook, our fish will take a
bite."

"Come on, Red, that doesn't tell me anything."

"What time is it? After nine thirty? The Mushroom in the
Meadow! The square dance should be going strong about now, so it
would be better out there. Not here, no way. And not in somebody's
home. Let me have the phone book, Barney."

Curt leafed through the pages, then lifted the phone. "Give me an
outside line, will you, Andy?" He dialed a number. "Judith Cohen?
This is Officer Curt Conners. Would you mind if Detective Ross and
I came by to explain a little matter to you?...You know, you gave
us some information that has turned out to be—well, significant,
and we'd like to follow up on it....Yes, I know it's late, but it's
pretty urgent. Good, thank you, Mrs. Cohen. We'll be right there."

"Come on, Barney," he said as he dropped the phone into place.
"I'll tell you what I have in mind while we drive out there."

Judith Cohen must have been watching for them, for she opened
the door promptly. "I do hope nothing serious has happened,
Officers. Is there something wrong?"

"No, Mrs. Cohen," said Barney. "There's nothing wrong. We're
getting very close to the person who killed Mrs. McGinty last night."

"You are? Really? Who is it?"

"That's where we'd like your help."

"*Me*? Good heavens, how can I help you?"

"By doing something we policemen can't do. We'd scare our bird
away. But you—well, you're a civilian who could pull it off."

"How exciting! I can't think when I've been so thrilled. What am I
supposed to do?"

"We want you to make three phone calls."

Mrs. Cohen's face fell. "Is *that* all? That doesn't sound like much. Who do I call? What do I say?"

"I've written it out for you," said Curt, handing her a card. "If the person is there, read it. If he isn't, you can leave the message. But each person has to get it about the same time."

"Let me see," said Judith Cohen. She studied the card. "This doesn't make much sense. What am I supposed to have seen?"

"That's part of the bait. You don't tell them. Just say it's something you can't discuss over the phone, that you've got to talk about in person."

"Oh." Judith Cohen looked doubtful, then suddenly she smiled. "You know, I've always wanted to be an actress, but I never got up my nerve to try. Maybe this is my big chance." She laughed. "Mata Hari, here's the cue for your big scene."

"There's one more thing," warned Barney. "There may be a bit of danger in this."

"Danger! Better and better. In what way, Mr. Ross?"

"If this works, you may be meeting a murderer face-to-face. We'll be right there, of course, but you might have a bad minute or two. So if you want to beg off—"

"Beg off? Now? Why, I've never met a murderer before. I wouldn't dream of begging off now." She walked over to the telephone. "O.K., who do I call?"

Curt handed her a bit of paper. Judith Cohen drew her breath in sharply. "Really? You mean it's one of *these*? I can't believe it."

"Surprised, eh? Well, we're not really sure it is them either. But if it isn't—well, it's US sticking our necks out, so it won't come back to you."

Judith Cohen lifted the phone and dialed. "Hello, is Dr. Quinlan there? Oh, he's out on a case? This is Judith Cohen, and I'd like to leave a message, a very important message. Tell him that last night I saw something that's been bothering me all day. So far I haven't said anything to the police, but I feel I should. Before I do that, I'd like to talk it over with Dr. Quinlan in person. . . . Tell him I'm at the convention center in the Green Room for the next hour. . . . No, I can't tell you what it is. . . . No, I don't want to wait until tomorrow, it must be tonight."

She hung up. "Was that all right? Did I sound mysterious enough?"

"You sure did. You're doing just fine," said Curt.

Judith Cohen dialed again. "Is Mayor McGinty there? Oh, he's not? Well, will you be very sure he gets this message?" She repeated the words on the card. "No," she continued. "This is for his ears only. . . . No, I can't tell you. . . . Yes, within the next hour in the Green Room where we met last night."

As she hung up, she looked inquiringly at Curt Conners. He nodded his approval.

The third call was for Harold Anderton, and the message was repeated. "There, that's done," said Judith Cohen. "What happens next?"

"Now," said Curt grimly, "we bait the trap. Let's see who bites."

"Am I the bait, Officer?" asked Judith Cohen with a laugh.

"That you are," said Curt. "And I suggest you wear a coat of some kind. It's a bit chilly this early in June, and besides, it would be an extra bit of protection in case . . ." He didn't finish the sentence but turned to Barney Ross. "Shall we go?"

The sounds of a hillbilly orchestra and the voice of a square-dance caller greeted them as they pulled up to the convention center. "Good," exclaimed Curt. "Plenty of noise, plenty of people around. That should make it seem lifelike enough so our fish won't be suspicious."

The hallway was deserted, the Green Room empty. "Luck's with us," said Curt. He smiled encouragingly at Judith Cohen. "Now you just make yourself comfortable over here. Our caller will be coming in through that door over there. We'll just open this other door on the opposite side enough so we two can hear and see and be ready for . . . whatever comes."

Judith Cohen gave a little shiver. "Sounds exciting. I can hardly wait. But you've forgotten something. What is it I'm supposed to have seen?"

"Oh, yes. Here it is, card number two."

Judith Cohen looked at the words. "Oh, yes. I'd forgotten about that. Why, I won't have to make anything up. I *did* see that." She looked quizzically at Curt Conners. "Is that why you had me call Harold Anderton?"

"Glad you know about it. That will make it more realistic. And one more thing, be sure to talk real loud. That music makes it hard to hear. Maybe we'd better try it."

Curt and Barney walked into the hall, almost closing the door behind them. Curt called out, "Are you ready, Mrs. Cohen?"

"I think so," came the muffled reply.

"Louder, Mrs. Cohen. It will have to be louder."

"Like this?" came the question loud and clear.

"Yes, like that. Perfect," called Barney Ross.

Mrs. Cohen sat quietly waiting, hands in lap. Barney and Curt stood motionless outside the door. "Damn that music," muttered Barney. "Wish it wasn't so loud." Minutes went by. Curt looked at his watch. Barney mopped his brow.

From inside the room came the voice of Mrs. Cohen. "Why, good evening." There was a soft murmur, then again the voice of Mrs. Cohen. "Why, I happen to be waiting for somebody."

Curt stretched his neck, trying to see through the crack in the door, then shook his head in exasperation.

"No, I can't tell you," said the voice of Judith Cohen. "I want to talk this over with—" The murmuring got more insistent, almost loud enough so words could be distinguished. "Oh, very well. If you must know, it's about the amethysts. I saw you take them."

The other voice rang out angrily. "Oh, did you! Well, that's none of your business."

Curt stiffened and looked at Barney. They both poised for action.

"No, you're *not* going to tell! They're mine and you've got no right. I've killed once and I can kill again."

Curt pushed open the door. "No, you don't. Stop right where you are." He was across the room in a flash. "Drop that knife."

There was the slap of arm meeting arm, a sharp cry of pain, the clatter of metal hitting the floor.

"Got it, Barney?" Curt called. He looked down at the figure sprawled out on the floor.

"So you've killed before, have you, Elsie Clinc? Well, not this time. Not ever again."

30 / *Sunday at 9:20 P.M.*

"Are you all right, Mrs. Cohen?" asked Barney.

"Yes, I—I think so," was the breathless answer. "Yes, of course I'm all right."

"*You're* all right," snarled the voice from the floor. "You damned stool pigeon." There followed a stream of lurid profanity.

The three of them, Judith Cohen and the two officers, looked at each other incredulously.

"I don't believe it. That can't be who I think it is," gasped Judith Cohen to the two men.

Curt nodded back. "It is, though." He signaled to Barney. "Got the knife?" Barney held up a murderous-looking kitchen blade. Judith Cohen shuddered and turned away.

The flow of obscenities subsided. "I'd better help you up," said Curt. Without waiting for an answer, he took her by the shoulders and stood her upright.

"Easy, now," coaxed Curt. "Better sit down."

"Yes, let me help you, dear," said Judith Cohen.

"Don't you touch me," was the snarling answer. "You stool pigeon."

"Now, now, relax," said Curt. "Mrs. Cohen was acting under our orders. She had no idea it would be *you*. She was expecting somebody else."

"Oh, who?"

"Why, the mayor. Mrs. Cohen had no intention of talking to you. That call was for Joe McGinty."

Instantaneously the defiant expression changed to one of fear. "You mean you thought it was Joe? No, you leave Joe out of this. He didn't have anything to do with this."

"You say it was your own idea to stab Maude McGinty?"

"Yes, and if I had the chance, I'd do it all over again." Her face hardened into ugliness. "For years I watched him take her abuse. She had a vicious tongue, that one, and many's the time Joe got it full force. Most times he never talked back or got mad. She deserved what she got last night, all right."

"But Elsie, why you?" asked Judith Cohen.

"Me? Because she made life miserable for me, day in, day out." She raised her voice to mimic. "It was 'Elsie run there, get that, do this.' She'd smile to her friends and say, 'Isn't it nice of me to take poor Elsie in? Poor dear Elsie—such a charity case.' Then she'd turn to me and pretend to be so sweet. 'Dear Elsie, so kind, so patient, to put up with this poor crippled woman.' " Her voice dropped to normal pitch. "And Joe would smile at me and tell me how grateful he was."

"Why didn't you pull out?" asked Judith Cohen.

"Like I told you, for Joe's sake, and because of my son."

"Your son? You have a son?"

"Nobody knew, thanks to that bitch Maude. Yes, I've got a son, but I might as well never have had. She saw to that. When my husband died, he left me without a dime. My Gene was a good drummer, one of the best. He had plenty of high-paying jobs, all the big bands wanted him, but he couldn't hang on to money—gambling, mostly. There I was in Chicago with a baby and no money. So I came back here, tried to make a go teaching piano. I failed. Then Maude came with her sweet talk. 'I need a companion, somebody to help me get around. Come live with us.' If I'd known then, I'd never have come. Well, I came, and for a while it was fine."

There was a commotion at the door. Harold Anderton bustled in. "Oh, there you are, Mrs. Cohen. You wanted me to—" He stopped abruptly at the urgent signal from Curt Conners. Moving close to Barney Ross, he whispered, "What's going on?" Barney motioned for him to be quiet.

"Then Maude started her tricks. First it was the baby. He got on her nerves. She knew of a fine family—just for a few months till he got older. I could see him, of course. When I fought that one, she said, 'You know I'm not going to live long. Stay with me and I'll leave half of my money to you. It'll be enough so you can take your boy and never have to work again.' "

Elsie looked up defiantly. "Can you blame me? Sure, I believed her. I hadn't caught on to her yet. So the family took my Wayne, and for a while they'd bring him every Sunday, until that got on Maude's nerves too. We'd meet at church, and I'd see him all dressed up, and I'd think, 'Just a little while longer, Elsie! She'll die soon.' Hah, *her die*? She was going to live forever.

"Then Wayne was in school and somehow the years went by. He used to be in plays and things at the high school, and I'd go to see him." She smiled at Judith Cohen. "He was awfully good, you know.

"Then all of a sudden he was gone. Where? That witch told me *she* was sending him to college, to a drama school in Chicago. I found out where and sent him some money I'd got—none of your business how. And then he disappeared, and I didn't know where.

"And all the time Maude was getting worse. She'd have fainting spells. 'Elsie couldn't leave her, she was near the end!' Hah! All fake! She even showed me her will and how she was going to leave

217

half her money to me—and her jewels, too. Did you know Maude was rich? And Joe would smile at me and say, 'Thanks, Elsie, for putting up with her,' and I knew I couldn't go away and leave him all alone with *her*. While I was there, I could take some of it off his shoulders. Poor Joe."

The flood of words stopped, and she sat smiling. Nobody moved. From far away came the sound of a dance tune, its jangly rhythm providing an incongruous background to the scene.

Finally Judith Cohen coughed gently. "And did you ever find your son?"

Elsie roused herself and laughed a quiet happy little laugh. "Yes, just two days ago. I got a telephone call—me. It was a man. He wanted to see me, it was about my son, could I come down to the hotel. I made an excuse about something, took Maude's car and met him. I almost died. Oh, he's a fine son, a handsome man. And he's got a job, doing all right, something on television."

Elsie Cline's expression changed. "We never looked at television much. It made Maude nervous. All this time if I'd have known, I could have been looking at him, and I never even knew—especially with his fancy stagename. But I'd have recognized him if I'd have seen him, no matter what he called himself. Damn that bitch Maude." And again there was a flood of epithets that made Harold Anderton recoil in horror. Judith Cohen moved over close to her and said, "Easy, Elsie, dear."

"O.K.," said Elsie. "But you don't know how good it feels to let loose with my Chicago language after all these years of 'Yes, Maude' and never talking above a whisper."

"Where's your son now?" asked Judith Cohen.

"Why, he's right here. You saw him last night. And do you know, he didn't even know about me. All these years they'd told him his parents were dead, he was an orphan. He told how those Krasuskis had abused him and neglected him. He always wondered, because he remembered a nice lady that talked to him at church when he was little, and that's why he got somebody to check up and how he knew where I was. And I told him how Maude had lied, made me think he was being well cared for and promised me I'd get my son back again someday." She looked up at Curt Conners defiantly. "You know, if I could have got my hands on her right then, I'd have killed her."

Harold Anderton raised his hand. "Now, now, Elsie, you mustn't talk like that." Barney signaled him to be quiet.

Without any sign that she'd heard anything, she continued. "And you know what my Wayne said then?" She reached up to take Judith's hand. "He said he was rich enough now that he'd go back to California, fix up a nice house, and I could come live with him. Could I stick it out a few more weeks?" She laughed and clasped her hands. "Could I? To get away at last? To have my boy back and a home of my own? Oh, could I!

"So I went back. And when Maude gave me a tongue-lashing for being gone, I didn't even mind. Inside I was laughing at her and thinking how glad I was going to be when I just walked off and left her.

"Then last night when we were getting ready, I heard her tell Joe she wasn't going to leave her money to us at all. She was going to give it all for a memorial so people would remember how kind and generous she was." She looked up, her face contorted. "*Her*, kind and generous, oh, my God!

"Then I saw it all. She'd been leading me on, promising me her money, knowing all the time she wasn't going to do it. And that's when I knew I had to do something, and fast. She was going to announce it that night. I didn't have much time, and I had to stop her from cheating Joe of what was his, and she wasn't going to cheat *me*. I'd earned that money, oh, God, how I'd earned it all those years of abuse. She'd lied to me about my son, she'd humiliated me in front of her friends, she'd used me, and she wasn't going to give me what she promised. That money was mine—and Joe's—and somehow I was going to see that we got it."

Curt said softly, "And so you stabbed her?"

"Yes, I stabbed her. I had a letter opener in my purse, and when I saw that naked fellow coming toward Maude and heard the screaming and yelling, I knew this was my chance. If they'd have seen me do it, I wouldn't have cared, but nobody did. Maude was dead, and I was free, and Joe was free, free, *free*."

"But you're not free, are you, Mrs. Cline? You've killed, you've taken a life," said Curt Conners.

"But she deserved to die. They can't punish me for that, can they? She didn't deserve to keep on living." She looked defiantly around the room, then more quietly asked, "What will they do to me? They won't punish me, will they?"

"We don't know that," said Barney Ross. "We won't be the ones to decide that."

"Could I see my son?" she asked softly.

"Why, yes, of course. You mean Wayne Hitchcock, don't you?"

"I mean Wayne *Cline*. His name is Cline. I believe he does use that name you mentioned but only for stage purposes. And could I see Joe too?"

"Joe? You mean Mayor McGinty?" asked Barney. She nodded.

"But first, Mrs. Cline," said Curt, "you have more to tell us. What about the Krasuskis?"

"Oh, them." Again her face twisted, and obscene words poured out. "I wanted to get back at them, too, for the awful way they'd treated my Wayne. So I found their name and address in Maude's deak and wrote a note saying I'd like to come see them on Sunday. That's all I intended at first. But when I saw them coming into the building Saturday night—their mean, ugly faces—I knew talking wasn't going to be enough to satisfy me. So Sunday morning when that Dennis came down—"

"Dennis? Came down? What do you mean?" asked Curt.

"Well, you see, my Wayne and that nice young man with him had been laughing about some trick they were going to pull at the program, 'something to bring down the house,' they said. He might need a place to hide out, Wayne said. So I remembered that third floor bedroom nobody ever used and said Dennis could hide up there; nobody would ever know he was there. I gave him my key to the back door."

Curt looked at Barney and smiled. His lips formed the words *That explains that.*

"Well, he slept all through the excitement of folks coming and going and all that gooey sympathy for poor old Maude, I guess. He came down about noon Sunday, all smiling, and asked me how I liked his streaking last night. I fed him some breakfast and asked him to deliver a package on his way downtown. I found this bottle of wine, got the cork off, dropped in some of Maude's sleeping tablets, fixed the stopper, and wrote a little note. Dennis went off with it, still laughing and joking."

"And did Dennis turn on the gas?" asked Curt.

"Dennis? Oh, no. He didn't know anything about this. When things got quiet, people stopped coming, and Joe was trying to rest. I got Maude's car and drove out, parked around the corner, and slipped into their house by the back door."

"And you found them there?" asked Curt.

"Yes, there they were, all stretched out. I wanted to slap their faces, but I was afraid that would wake them up. So I shut the windows and doors, cleaned up the bottle and glasses, turned on the gas, and left. I made sure nobody saw me, and got home before Joe could even miss me."

"Just like that, eh?" asked Curt.

"Yes, that's the trouble. They didn't get to suffer. They should have known it was me, and why I was doing it, to pay them back for what they did to my Wayne."

Barney stepped forward. "I'm afraid, Mrs. Cline, you'll have to come with me."

"Oh, please, not yet. I want to see Joe first!"

"Why, of course. I think he's coming right now."

Mayor McGinty's voice was heard. "You left a message for me, Mrs. Cohen? What did you—" He stopped, his face a study in bewilderment as he looked about the room. "What's going on? What's the matter, Elsie?"

"Oh, Joe, I'm so glad you've come." Elsie moved toward him, sobbing. "They've found out!"

"Found out? Found out what?"

"About Maude. That you're free of her, that I'm free of her, that now you and I can—"

"We can what? What makes you say I'm free? What are you trying to say, Elsie?"

"That now you and I are free to live without Maude. And I'm the one who fixed it."

Joe McGinty's expression changed slowly from one of bewilderment to horror. "You mean it was *you* . . . that did it? You're the one who—"

"Yes, Joe. I did it for you and for me."

Joe McGinty back away. "You mean *you* killed her? Oh, my God." He stared at Elsie Cline, then suddenly he turned and ran from the room.

"Joe, come back here," wailed Elsie Cline. She wavered, then turned slowly. "He's gone, isn't he. He won't come back, will he?" She looked at Judith Cohen. "Please, my purse, I feel faint. I'd better sit down." She drooped into a chair and fumbled in her purse. There was a quick movement of hand to mouth, she looked up with a smile on her face, then suddenly her body sagged, and she fell to the floor.

221

"Oh, dear God," whispered Judith Cohen as she knelt down beside her.

A voice from the hall door called, "I believe you sent for me, Mrs. Cohen. What is it you want?"

It was Barney who answered. "I'm afraid you have come too late, Dr. Quinlan. I think you will find that she is already dead."

31 / Monday at 8:30 A.M.

Mac, the switchboard operator, had never seen things so busy at police headquarters. People were in and out, the board was alive with telephone calls, squad cars were on the radio every other minute, and somehow the night shift had picked up two characters to occupy the cells over Sunday night.

Most unheard of, the chief came in early—eight o'clock on the button—and on a Monday, at that. What's more, he was smiling and tossing off good-mornings all over the place. He'd hardly made it into his office when he called out to know if Barney Ross and Curt Conners were in yet. When he heard they weren't, instead of blowing his stack, he mildly said, "That's O.K. They deserve a little extra sleep. Just let me know when they arrive." Mac wondered if he had heard him right.

When Ross and Conners finally did come in, Mac looked at the clock significantly as he said, "Well, good morning, you two. You notice what time it is?"

Barney gazed at Curt with an innocent smile and said blandly "Yes, it's almost eight thirty. Why'd you ask?"

"Chief's been waiting for you since eight o'clock," snapped Mac.

"Oh?" asked Curt. "Guess we'd better go see what he wants."

"I suppose so," said Barney with elaborate indifference. "After I've checked into my office."

Mac's voice was sharp. "He said right away."

"Oh?" was Barney's only remark as he headed across the hall.

"Hey, Red," hissed Mac, "will you tell me what the hell's going on?"

"You mean you haven't heard?" asked Curt. "Haven't you got a radio at your house? It's been all over the news broadcasts."

"Didn't get time to listen," said Mac, looking sheepish. "Took my wife square dancing last night, got home late, and overslept. Had to rustle up my own breakfast and drive like hell to make it here on time. Luck was with me. Chief didn't catch *me* coming in late." He stood up and leaned toward Curt Conners. "What happened? Come on, tell me what's been going on."

"Why, sure, Mac. Only here comes Barney, and like you said, the chief wants us right now. It'll have to wait."

"Damn you, Red, at least tell me who those two guys are we got locked up back there."

"Oh, those two. Well, one won't be here long. He's going to be traveling in style to Capital City with a special car and chauffeur and armed escort."

"You mean we've got a biggie? Jeez! Who is he?"

"Later, Mac, later. Remember, the chief's waiting." Curt moved closer to Mack's ear and in a mock whisper said, "The other's *the streaker*." He turned to Barney. "Ready? Let's go." He turned back to Mac. "Better announce us to the chief."

"Bastard," Mac snarled as he reached back for the phone. Then with a crisp tone he announced, "Ross and Conners are here. Shall I send them right in?" With a thumb he signaled to the two to proceed down the hall.

The door was flung open and the chief's voice boomed out, "Come in, men, come in. That was a mighty fine piece of work yesterday." The door slammed shut again.

"My God, I can't believe it," Mac uttered to himself. "Somebody's hit the jackpot." He craned his neck toward the rear of the building. "The streaker, did he say? Well, let's have a look."

He stood up and started down the hallway when he heard a male voice call out, "I say there, is Officer Ross in?" and a throaty female voice followed with, "Or that officer with the gorgeous red hair? What's his name? Conners?"

Mac turned quickly. A tall distinguished-looking man and a stunningly beautiful woman were coming toward him with a man in chauffeur's livery serving as honor guard.

My God, it's the lieutenant governor, Mac thought. And that must be his wife. Gad, but she's a looker. He strode toward them. "I'm sorry, Mr. Alcott, but Mr. Ross is busy in the chief's office right now. I'll let him know you're here. Would you like to step into his office?" Mac ushered the Alcotts in, found chairs, and headed back for the switchboard.

The chauffeur moved over to say, "Ross and Conners, they going to be in there long? I've got to get the lieutenant governor back to Capital City by noon."

"Can't say," answered Mac. "But I'm about to tell the chief who's waiting out here."

"Maybe you'd better not. I don't think Alcott wants to talk with anybody but Ross and Conners. Sort of private, I think."

"I don't know about that. The chief might want to meet the lieutenant governor," said Mac.

Just then the door to the chief's office opened and his voice was heard. "Like I said, when you get the details taken care of, take the rest of the day off. I'll see that the commissioners get a full report, Ross. And Conners, we won't forget your part in all this."

Mac moved as if he wanted to say something, but Manson put out his hand to stop him. The chief shook hands with Ross and Conners and slowly closed the door.

"Hello, Manson, glad to see *you*" said Curt, and Barney added, "Thanks for your help yesterday, Manson. Couldn't have swung it without you."

"All in the day's work," said Manson. "I think you'll find somebody waiting for you in there." He nodded toward Barney's office.

"Alcott?" asked Barney.

"Mrs. Alcott?" asked Curt. In their hurry they brushed right by Mac. There was a flurry of greetings and handshakes.

Mac heard Hamilton Alcott say, "I don't know how to thank you two men for the way you handled DiVacco."

And the voice of Rosemary Alcott echoed, "My thanks too. You were wonderful, especially you, Mr. Conners."

"Tell me, is everything under control?" asked Hamilton Alcott.

"Yes," said Barney. "You don't have anything to worry about. DiVacco will be put away for a good long time. He broke his parole, drew a weapon on an officer of the law and resisted arrest. I'll predict he'll serve his full thirty years and maybe a few more."

"And our little story won't be getting out?" asked Alcott.

"Nobody here is going to say anything. You can be sure of that."

"I've been thinking, Hamilton," said Rosemary Alcott, "maybe

224

it's time to break the news anyway. Now, if I can just get the right angle for our gossip Penny Perry, there'll be a special item in her column about the poor struggling concert pianist that had to do some nightclub playing to get the money for her lessons. I think we can get just the right slant so it'll win some sympathy. Then if somebody tries to use the story later on, it will be old stuff."

Hamilton Alcott chuckled. "That's my Roz. Yes, I get the idea. You're just the one to carry it off, too."

Harry Manson nudged Mac in the ribs. "You can put your ears back into place now, and if you're wise you'll forget everything you just heard. You've just observed the team of Alcott and Alcott back in operation."

Manson straightened to attention as Hamilton Alcott appeared with Barney, followed by Rosemary Alcott with her hand resting lightly on Curt's arm.

"So you've found the streaker," Alcott was saying, "and solved the murder too. My compliments. Tell me, did you ever think your talents might be wasted here in this little corner of the world?"

"Wasted? Oh, no, I don't think so," said Barney. "I'm too old and settled to think of moving. Now young Conners there—well, that's a different story. Just getting started, not married, free to move."

"You're not married, Mr. Conners?" said Rosemary Alcott. "H'mmm, maybe your opportunities *are* a bit limited. You need more scope for your talents."

"Will you look at our redhead blush!" whispered Mac to Harry Manson.

"Can you blame him?" murmured Manson. He turned to follow the Alcotts down the hall. "Be seeing you. It's been fun."

The buzzer called Mac back to the switchboard. Watching the group saying their last farewells at the exit, he lifted the headset to his ear. "Police headquarters. Oh, yes. . . . Good morning, Coroner. Do you want to wait a minute? . . . Sure, I'll give them the message. . . . I'll ask him to call you back if there's any problem." He put down the headphones and glanced at the clock. He turned to switch on a radio. "This is your midmorning news," said the voice of the radio announcer. "Three murders have been solved by a suicide, and the identity of the streaker who interrupted the Centennial pageant has been discovered." Mack listened intently for about five minutes.

"So that's how it is," he murmured. "No wonder everything's roses with the chief today." The switchboard buzzer sounded. He turned down the radio and picked up his headset. "Police headquarters.... Oh, good morning, Your Honor.... Yes, the chief's in. Would you like to have me connect you with him?... No, nobody's with him right now.... You're coming right down?... I'll tell them.... Ross and Conners? Yes, they're both here.... Very good, Your Honor."

Mac looked up at Curt and Barney, who were just returning from the parking lot exit. "Can I persuade you two heroes to wait a minute? I've got some messages." Mac made a connection and spoke into the phone. "The mayor just called. He wants to see you, said he'd be down in about ten minutes.... Yes, I'll show him right in."

As Mac broke the connection, he said to Barney and Curt, "Guess you heard that. The mayor's coming *down here*. Wants to talk to the chief and to you two as well." He made a mock bow. "Guess who's important around here today! Also, the coroner called. He wants you two available for three inquests. Did you get that? *Three*. Tuesday morning for Maude McGinty, Wednesday for the Krasuskis, and Thursday for somebody named Elsie Cline. Who's she? The streaker get her, too?" Mac lowered his voice. "And were you kidding, Red, when you said we had the streaker back there?"

"Well, I'll tell you, Mac, it's a long story," answered Curt. "When we come up for air, we'll give you a blow-by-blow description."

"Can you at least tell me who the biggie is back there in the cooler?"

Barney's tone was confidential. "That's hush-hush stuff, Mac, but I'll give you a hint. He knew the lieutenant governor was going to be here, and he had a knife on him and a nice prison record. We got him in time."

Mac whistled. "Oh, so that's what all that was about just now."

Barney glanced at Curt quickly, then said impassively, "Well, you might say that. You won't be finding much about it in the papers. Some things are better kept quiet, if you know what I mean, Mac."

"What do you take me for, Barney?" was Mac's indignant reply. Then he burst into a broad smile. "Guess you guys have some congratulations coming. Boy, I can't wait to hear all about it."

"Thanks, Mac. We were plenty lucky and had lots of good help."

Barney glanced toward the parking lot entrance. "Better tell the chief the mayor's here."

Mayor Joseph McGinty looked like a broken man. He walked heavily with sagging shoulders. There were pouches under his eyes and deep lines about his mouth. His skin looked waxy. Barney Ross advanced to meet him. "Good morning, Your Honor. May I express my deep sympathy?"

"Thanks, Ross," was the dull response. "This has been a terrible experience. If I had realized . . . if I had suspected . . . I could have prevented it from happening. But I want you to know I appreciate the excellent work you did in finding the person who"—here his voice broke slightly—"killed my wife."

"Thanks, Your Honor. You really mustn't blame yourself," murmured Barney sympathetically. "I assure you none of us knew it was going to turn out this way. Perhaps you'd like to speak to the chief? He's expecting you." He gently guided the mayor toward the chief's office and nodded for Curt to follow.

Mac shook his head as he watched the three disappear. "Poor guy," he muttered, then he reached for his headset as the switch-board buzzer sounded. "Police headquarters. . . . Yes, Mr. Hitch-cock. . . . No, the judge hasn't come in yet, but I see he's got a hearing set for ten o'clock. . . . Well, I can't say for sure, but I should think if you and your lawyer want to come in, he'd be able to talk to you by ten-thirty."

From down the side hall he heard the mayor's voice. "Yes, the endowment of the little auditorium is still in, only it won't be the Ezra Medille Recital Hall but the Maude Medille McGinty Recital Hall. That's what Maude wanted, and that's what she's going to get. We'll have it announced at the funeral services." The voices died away for a while, then the mayor's voice became audible again. "And as mayor I'm going to see that these two men get an award for their work in this case. Will you let me know a good time and place?"

A few minutes later the mayor emerged accompanied by the chief. Good-bys were said, and the chief walked slowly down toward the exit with Joe McGinty.

Mac looked at Barney and Curt with a sly grin on his face. "Tell me, heroes, can I touch you?"

"Oh, go to hell!" snapped Curt.

227

"Why, Red, you're blushing," jeered Mac. "Your face is as red as your hair."

"Stow it, Mac," Barney growled. "That's Judge Neuhaus coming here with the chief. Better look busy." He turned to say a respectful "Good morning, Judge," then he began to edge toward his office, signaling Curt to follow him. The chief nodded to the judge and retired to his rooms.

"Oh, Judge Neuhaus," said Mac. "There was a call from Wayne Hitchcock. He and his lawyer want to talk to you. I suggested they come in about ten-thirty, after you finish this hearing. Is that all right?"

"Did you say Wayne Hitchcock? The television actor?" asked the judge. "Now what could he be wanting?"

"I really don't know, Judge," said Mac. "I can call him back if you don't want him then."

"Maybe I can help," interrupted Barney, who had turned in his doorway to listen. "I think he wants to ask for an early hearing in his case."

"You mean he's on my docket?" The judge sounded incredulous. "What's he done?"

"It's about the streaking out at the convention center Saturday night. Indecent exposure and creating a public disturbance are the charges on the warrant."

"Wayne Hitchcock? Indecent exposure? I can't believe it."

"Hey, Red," whispered Mac. "I thought you said the streaker was back there in the cooler." Curt signaled him to be quiet.

"Oh, not Hitchcock personally," said Barney, "He's just taking a strong interest in the case. Somebody he knows and—well, likes very much."

"Oh, I see," said Judge Neuhaus. "If he thinks his reputation is going to influence me ... h'mmm. Yes, Mac, this little traffic case I'm here for now is going to be very long. The great Mr. Hitchcock can cool his heels like anybody else. Let him come on down, and I'll see him—when I am ready to." He looked about. "By the way, it's almost ten o'clock. Where's the fellow I'm supposed to be trying?"

"Coming right in now, Judge," said Barney, pointing toward the entrance.

"Give me a few minutes, and you can send him on in," Judge Neuhaus said, and he disappeared in the hearing room behind the reception desk.

"Hello, Karyl," said Barney Ross. "Is this your father?"

The older man with Karyl spoke in a thick, harsh voice. "Yeah, I'm the father of this no-good boy. He's got to have a car, like a fool. Yeah, he's got to go driving too fast, like a fool. He makes too much noise, like a fool. So now *I* got to take time off from work to get him out of trouble." Karyl's father looked at Barney uneasily. "What do they do with speeders, Mr. Cop?"

"That's what you're going to find out from the judge, Mr. Pilchoski." Barney turned to the other two. "Hello, Witty. Nice of you to come along with your friend. And is this your father?"

"Yeah, I'm his father."

"Has Witty here told you his part in all this, Mr. Zacherewiez?"

"I know that if Karyl was doing wrong, Witty was doing it too. So I came along with him." He looked at Witty suspiciously. "What's he mean, your part? You done something bad you ain't told me about yet?"

Witty swallowed hard, looked at Barney, then looked back at his father. He was just about to speak when the door opened and a clerk called out. "Karyl Pilchoski? The judge is ready for you now!"

"Guess I'll go in too," said Curt. "This might be interesting." He leaned over Mac as he passed and said, "Witty was a streaker too."

Mac swiveled his chair around to watch Curt as he moved into the hearing room. "I must be going nuts," he muttered. "The streaker's down there in the cooler. No, the streaker's here with Judge Neuhaus. No, the streaker's—Aw, to hell with it. I give up." The buzzer sounded and he shouted into the phone, "Police Department. . . . No, ma'am, we don't handle garbage complaints. You want the sanitation department." He took off his headset and rubbed his temples. "We got enough garbage here as it is."

32 / *Monday at 10:30 A.M.*

From the parking lot came the sound of strident voices, then a robust masculine voice. "Bless you, kids, I love you all. Now you just let me say good-by to my good friends in here and I'll be out again before you know it. Just you don't go 'way."

Down the hall strode a dashing figure accompanied by an older man. "Hello, Officer. We're looking for the judge."

Mac stood up quickly. "Why, you're Sonny Hitchcock, aren't you?"

"That's right. How'd you guess? You one of my fans?"

"Sure. I'd know you anywhere. I never miss your show on television."

There was a flash of the famous Hitchcock smile. "Well, good for you, it's always nice to meet up with a loyal admirer on a Monday morning. Now we'd appreciate it if you'd show us where to find the judge."

"I'm sorry. Judge Neuhaus is in court." Mac walked over to Barney's door. "If you'd like to wait in here, it shouldn't be more than a few minutes."

"Why, thanks. We would like a little peace and quiet. Those kids out there, they're swell, but you know how these younguns can get overexcited. Is it O.K. to smoke?"

"Why sure, Mr. Hitchcock, just make yourself comfortable."

Mac stood admiring the television star, then backed out and closed the door. "Wait'll I tell the kids at home. Hitchcock here in the flesh. Wonder if I could get his autograph."

The door to the judge's hearing room opened. A chastened-looking Karyl appeared, followed by his father, who was saying, "Fifty dollars. Guess *that'll* learn you. And don't think you're going to hook me for it. Down to the shop with me tomorrow. You're going to work your tail off till you pay me back every cent. One good thing, no driving for a month. Wish he'd made it for a year."

"So," said Witty's father. "You bring disgrace on us, do you?" Witty winced as his father grabbed him and turned him toward Curt. "What do you think of this boy of mine, Mr. Policeman? Takes off his clothes and shows himself bare naked for everybody to see. This is what I raised him for?"

"But, Pa, it was on a dare—for twenty dollars," whined Witty.

"Shut up. Twenty dollars. To prove that you're a boy? No wonder, with that long hair making people think you're a girl. So you like to be naked, huh? Yeah, well we'll start with your head. To the barber till we're down to the bare scalp." He shook Witty hard. "You like to let down your pants and show your bare ass, huh? Yeah one *more* time you get to do that, just for me, only I ain't gonna just look at it.

230

I've got a leather strap. You won't be showing it to nobody when I get through. Blisters don't look so pretty."

Barney watched the four of them going down the hall. "Poor Witty," he said.

"I got one big regret," said Curt. "I wish Witty's old man would give Redmond the treatment instead of that scared little guy. Just once I'd like to see old Redmond get what he deserves."

Mac interrupted. "Hey, Barney, you got company waiting for you." He pointed toward Barney's office. "Hitchcock's in there with another fellow."

"Aha," Barney gloated. "Just the man I want to see. Come on, Red."

They found Wayne Hitchcock nervously pacing about. "Oh, hello, you're Ross, aren't you? Meet my lawyer, Dale Croxton. And let's see—Conners, wasn't it?"

The men nodded briefly, and Croxton spoke. "We're waiting to see the judge. We're asking for an early hearing for Dennis Peters."

"So I understand," said Barney. "I'm afraid it will be a few minutes. If you don't mind, I'd like to say something to Mr. Hitchcock while you're waiting."

"Now just a minute," said Croxton. "Mr. Hitchcock isn't on trial."

"Aren't you, Hitchcock?" Barney's voice was cold. "I think maybe you are."

"Me?" said Hitchcock. "What do you mean?"

"You were the one who engineered Peters' little exhibition, you know. And then there was the incident with the high school kid."

"Don't respond to that," Croxton warned. "Be careful what you say."

Curt spoke up. "Maybe you'd like to tell us who the woman was you met in the hotel last Friday."

"I don't see that that's any of your business," Hitchcock snarled.

"Don't be too sure. She told us an interesting story last night."

"Last night? What about last night?"

"I mean she told us who you were, about the Krasuskis, how you came here a day early to see her, and how you cooked up that little deal about the streaker."

"Now look, Conners, she didn't have anything to do with the streaker." Wayne Hitchcock was almost shouting now. "Don't try to get her mixed up with that. That was strictly—"

"Careful, Hitchcock," warned Croxton.

Hitchcock waved his lawyer away. "You can ask her if you don't believe me."

"You know that's not possible," said Curt.

"Not possible? How do you figure that?"

"You haven't heard?" asked Barney.

"Heard? Heard what?"

"Didn't you hear it on the news broadcast? She's dead."

The color drained from Hitchcock's face. He swayed unsteadily, then slowly sank into a chair. Curt moved quickly to keep him from collapsing entirely. In a high, thin voice Hitchcock quavered, "Dead? No, I didn't know. How did she die?"

"By her own hand, and quickly. Digitalis, I think," said Curt.

The silence that followed was oppressive. Three men stood motionless, looking at the pitiful figure sagging with head bowed. They heard a sob, then a whisper. "She was my mother, you know. I never knew her till last Friday, and now I've lost her again."

Barney looked at the lawyer. "I have a suggestion for you, Mr. Croxton. Ask for your early hearing. Your client is Dennis Peters. He is charged with indecent exposure and disturbing the peace, not the most serious charges in the book. If he pleads guilty, he'll probably get a stiff fine, which Mr. Hitchcock here can pay, and if he's lucky, a suspended sentence—on condition he gets out of town and doesn't come back. There are reasons why we don't want either Hitchcock or Peters around here ever again. I can be specific if you want me to be, but I think Hitchcock would rather not have me tell the whole story." Barney looked down at the pitiful figure. "I don't understand his kind very well, but I know he'd better not stay around this town very long. From what I've heard, he's had a rough enough time of it, so maybe we can go easy on him. I sure don't have any stomach to press charges against him. Maybe—well, maybe you understand, Mr. Croxton?"

The lawyer was pondering. "I think I'm getting the whole story, Officer. I can read between the lines. You never know, do you?" He stood up. "If you don't mind, maybe you'd take me to meet Dennis Peters. I think I can put it to him straight without any trouble." Barney nodded and the two left the room. When they had gone, Curt looked thoughtfully at Hitchcock a long time, then rose and softly closed the door behind him.

A half-hour later found the two detectives alone in Barney's office.

Curt Conners put down his coffee cup, lifted his feet up on the table, stretched out, and rested his head on the back of his chair. He yawned. "Everybody gone, Barney?"

"All gone, Red. Case all wrapped up and closed. Mind if I say something nice for a change?"

"I'd rather you'd take me home. I'm so dog tired I could go to sleep right here. All I want is my little old bed and about twenty-four hours of shut-eye."

"Not yet, you golden-haired genius. You know damn well who figured this all out—and left me far behind." He smiled affectionately at Curt. "Thanks for not letting the chief know how *far* I was behind. And now, Red, it's time for you to give."

"Oh?" asked Curt. "Just what am I supposed to give?"

"Come on, you know what I'm talking about. When did you begin to suspect who really did that stabbing job?"

Curt grinned self-consciously. "Oh, that! For a long time I just took it for granted it was the streaker, though for a while I wasn't sure which streaker it was. Even after all that jazz about was he masked or not, and was he left-handed, and where *were* his hands, I still didn't catch on."

"So what made you start thinking it might not be?"

"Not till after DiVacco began to get eliminated. He was the real killer type, so he was tops on my list. But when the Krasuskis were killed, that knocked him out. He might go after the woman who threw him over or he might be doing a little job for somebody else on the lieutenant governor, but why would he want to work on the Krasuskis? Besides, why would he go through all that flimflam of streaking? He was the shot-in-a-dark-alley type—unless somebody else figured out that 'Indian-with-the-knife' routine. He sure didn't have the brains to work out anything that complicated. And then when you engineered that little 'strip-down-to-the-bare-skin' search of him, I got the chance to see that he couldn't have been the one."

Barney interrupted. "I was thinking somebody hired him to get Alcott himself."

"Me, too, for a while, especially with that changing of seats," said Curt. "But when I got the connection between Peters and the

Krasuskis, things made more sense. A male go-go dancer, used to showing off his equipment to the customers, a guy on the make in show business, willing to do almost anything to break into the big time. He and Hitchcock playing up to our high school boy. Hitchcock the hometown boy who knew the Krasuskis, knew the McGintys—it all began to fit. Only would Peters go as far as murder? That's what threw me. He didn't seem to have the guts for it any more than little Witty did."

"What makes you think a fag can't be a killer?"

"Nothing. Some fags, that is. But not *that* pretty little lover boy. I tried coming at the whole thing from a different angle. What if it wasn't our little fairy dancer? Who, then? I thought of the people who could have done it. Doc Quinlan? Perfectly possible. He had a chance when he laid her out, he owned that kind of a knife. The mayor himself? He was sitting next to his wife, and he had one of those letter openers too. Harold Anderton? He'd received one of those little pretties as a gift, and he was all over the place. But what motive? Who could tell? An old grudge, a feud from way back? Something to do with that endowment? And then Dr. Redmond gave me a new lead."

"Redmond? What the hell are you talking about? What did Redmond say?"

"It was a little remark I almost missed. He said Mayor McGinty was sitting next to him."

"So?"

"Try something, Barney. Sit here next to me, on my left side. Now make like you've got a knife. Reach out to jab it into me."

Barney sat down and went through the motions.

"Not very easy, was it, Barney? You had to twist and half stand up, something most anybody would notice. And Redmond had noticed him stand up but didn't see him do any stabbing. Now try it from the other side."

Barney moved to Curt's right and tried again.

"Much easier this time. A quick jab across your body while it looks like you're bending over me to protect me from something. And notice, Barney, the angle the knife has to go in."

A light of comprehension gleamed in Barney's eye. "That's why it looked like a left-handed stroke. The streaker coming at her straight on would have had to be left-handed. But somebody sitting next to

Maude McGinty would have come in from the right side."

"And who was sitting on her right side?"

"Yeah, yeah, I get it."

"But how to find out for sure, Barney? That's where the bluff had to come in. Our killer couldn't be *sure* nobody saw the stabbing. Any suspicion that somebody did, and there'd have to be some action. That's why the telephone call. When Judith Cohen said she saw something and she wanted to talk about it with somebody, can't you see the killer beginning to worry? Cohen said she hadn't told the cops yet, so there was still time for the guilty one to shut her up. We were careful to get a definite time and place where Judith Cohen would be all alone, and that's all the bait we needed."

"Were you surprised when you saw who it was?" asked Barney. "I was."

"Well, yes, I guess I was," admitted Curt. "It could have been one of about six, and there were several others that were higher on my list. There were five knives to choose from, you remember. Anyway, it worked." He yawned ostentatiously.

"O.K., I get the hint, Red. Come on, I'll drive you home."